I0772220

THE SERPENT EMERGES

MAEGWEN SALLEY-MASSIE

An imprint of Green Ferns Publishing House

Library of Congress Cataloging-in-Publication Data
Salley-Massie, Maegwen
The Serpent Emerges/ Maegwen Salley-Massie
542 pages.

Summary: "The Elysians embark on their quest to free their people and break Shunal's curse, only to encounter evils they've never seen before. Avondelle faces a new darkness, while also developing a school of magic." – Provided by publisher.

979-8-9870525-5-6 ISBN (paperback), 979-8-9870525-6-3ISBN (hardback),
Subjects: High Fantasy—Fiction. Love—Fiction. Adventure—Fiction.

Printed in the United States of America

To those who struggle to know their worth: may this book convince you that you are loved and adored more than you will ever truly realize. You matter!

TABLE OF CONTENTS

PRONUNCIATIONS

Adalina (ad-ah-Leen-ah) Roedellen

Adma (Ad-ma)

Adomin (a-Doe-Min)

Aellizzabelle (Ale-Lizz-a-Bell) aka Lizz

Ajorn (Ae-Jorn)

Anadelvia (an-ah-del-vee-ah)

Ashur (A-sh-ur)

Atticos (a-t-e-coe-ss)

Audayia (Aw-Day-ee-ah)

Barm (B-arm)

Bip (b-ip)

Brandle (Bran-Dill)

Brehan (Bree-Hon)

Brenna (Bren-nah)

Caelimont (Cae-li-mon-t)

Char (Ch-Ar)

Corentine (Coer-en-teen)

Cruz (Cr-ooz)

Dag (Da-g)

Doebromir (Doe-broe-meer)

Drystan (Drih-stan)

Ebbalee (Eb-bah-Lee)

Edvard (Ed-var-d)

Elmond (el-mon-d)

Ezen (Ee-Zen)

Favien (Fae-Vee-in)

Finn (Fin)

Gorm (G-or-m)

Graegory (Grae-gor-ree)

Graelynd (GRAY-Lind)

Herb (H-erb)

Herbmando (H-erb-man-doe)

Hueweyn (Hui-When)

Jace (Jay-ss)

Jadelyn (Jae-d-lyn)

Jashun (Ja-Shoo-n) Kafur

Jdru (Droo)

Jem (Gem)

Kailani (Ka-Lan-ee)

Kaiana (Ka-ana)

Karis (Care-Ris)

Kazimir (Kaz-e-Meer)

Keawev (Key-Wev)

Lezlin (Lez-Lin)

Lulana (Loo-La-nah)

Madilina (Ma-di-lee-nah) Oslac

Maekel (May-Kel)

Malum (Mal-um)

Marin (Mar-Rin)

Mauor (Ma-oo-r)

Max (Max) Oslac

Menry (Men-Ree)

Mimby (Mim-bee)

Miola (My-O-La)

Nanceline (Nan-see-leen)

Nawrooshall (Naw-Roo-Sholl)

Nijeel (Nie-Jeel)

Norella (Nor-ell-lah)

Novaly (Noe-va-lee)

Pinx (Pin-X)
Pyry (Peer-Ree)
Quinley (Quin-Lee)
Raquel (Rah-Kell)
Rav (R-av)
Revalyn (Re-va-lyn)
Rielen (Ry-Len)
Rivers (Ri-ver-s)
Royce (Roy-SS)
Ryker (r-EYE-ker)
Ryland (rEYE-Land)
Saemelina (Sae-me-lee-na)
Saemeon (Say-Me-on)
Sakul (Sa-Kool)
Saven (Say-Vin)
Sealyn (SEE-LIN)

Shaenna (Shae-na)
Siany (SEE-On-EE)
Skarpin (Scar-pin)
Sorcha (Sore-Shah)
Stawyer (Staw-yer)
Stev (St-ev)
Sune (Soon)
Temm (Tem)
Tilmond (Til-mond)
Tintallina (Tin-Ta-lee-na)
Toven (Toe-Vin)
Trit (Tr-it)
Tybalt (Ti-Balt)
Vaelinthia (Vael-in-th-ia)
Wullen (Wu-Lin)
Zuri (Z-ur-ee)

A note to the reader…
While reading, you will see an * appear in front of the name of a creature when it's first mentioned. This * lets you know that more details about this creature are available in the Library of Creatures, found at the back of the book.
I did not want to interrupt your reading of the story with too many descriptions, so if you want to know about the creatures you meet, flip to the back as you come across an *.
Enjoy.

The Cursed Seven Kingdoms

Melting Water Seas

The Gelida Seas

Dragon Cove

Sacharro Lagoon

Havas

Dichimus Channel

Glatania

Stoftland

Ara Channel

Pax Island

Shunal

Golden Lake

Golden Lake

The Southlantium Seas

Korpam

Hostile Channel

Golden Lake

Elysium

Ien Nove

Emerald Lagoon

The Marygger Seas

The Snaer Seas

Elysian News

The Latest News and Gossip

Issue #2

Let the Gossip Begin!
First Elysian Newspaper

Greetings, my fellow Elysians. I'm Lady Adalina, but you can call me Lina. I'm here to bring you all the latest gossip and juicy news that the palace doesn't want you to know. Think I'm bluffing? Let's begin.

Lady Zuri is now the Ambassador for Elysium, stationed at her home kingdom in Len Nove, but that's not the juicy deets. She left poor Lord Rav an ultimatum: "Move there, or we're over!"

Painted above: Me, Lady Adalina

From Len Nove, Lord Finn decided not to stay in his home kingdom because he apparently has a special blonde in Avondelle. Speaking of blondes, Lord Ashur, would you please give Lady Lulana a chance?

Think I'm done? Not at all! Lord Aerrick moved his family to Hill Chimes because he blames the royal family for the death of his wife, Lady Raquel, whereas most of the kingdom blames King Jace.

Lord Max and Lady Madilina are constantly seen fighting over the baby dragons that Queen Sealyn has decided to keep alive. Madilina is tasked with training the two very different dragons. Max is obviously not comfortable with this.

Several witnesses say they have seen Lord Sakul frequenting the pub *Liquid Courage* more than usual. Can he pull himself together before the quest?

Lady Brenna weeps night and day over the capture of Lord Jashun, but is she really remaining faithful? Perhaps one should be careful when entering *Mimby's Morsels* late at night.

And lastly, fashion advice from several ladies, Lady Novaly—you're not royal, so stop wearing flower crowns. ~Lady Adalina Roedellen (Lina)

CHAPTER 1
A ROYAL DEATH

The dark ship creaked and swayed—the sounds of captivity. The smell was once grotesquely intolerable, but they were used to it now. Two months at sea will do that to weary prisoners. The wooden room was filled with moldy hay, broken barrels, and a giant iron prison cell, the current home of the captive Elysians.

After Doebromir returned to the group from his dose of fresh air, they tallied the numbers again. The Stoltland captain allowed each Elysian prisoner two hours of fresh, desperately needed air weekly. While the Elysians stretched their legs on the deck, they counted guards and slaves. From ravenous storms to egotistical sword fights, the Stoltland count was going down. Good news for the green-eyed prisoners.

Sorcha stretched her arm behind the cage and pulled out the scrap parchment she had found on her first walkabout.

With her grunt echoing in their damp chambers, the familiar shadow in the corner stirred. They were no longer scared of the red-eye creature but embraced the odd characteristics of the *Rana frog.

She kept the parchment wedged between two loose boards, hidden well from their captives' black eyes. Sorcha's usual round, ebony cheeks were now sharper from the lack of nourishment. Doebromir snatched the parchment from Sorcha's bony fingers and began to write down his numbers before he forgot. They had gathered small bits of half-burned wood from the main deck's fires for writing. Fighting through dehydration, Doebromir's bald brow wrinkled as his mind calculated his tallies. He had also lost considerable weight, and his thick, reddish-brown beard was now inches past his chin. He was not the clean-shaven stud he used to be. Now, he was beaten and starving but not broken.

He blinked and smiled. "I think we could do this." Doebromir held up the parchment proudly for his friends to see. "Those screams we heard last night definitely meant they lost way more men than expected."

Jashun shivered at the thought of the screams they heard through the night. Some sounds echoed over the waters like they weren't sounds but actual forces swaying amongst the salty waves. Then came the blistering screams of the men.

The Elysians had held onto each other all night, fearing what would come for them, but nothing ever came down to their holding room.

"I don't understand what happened last night. What were those sounds?" Jashun asked, sweat forming across his cinnamon-colored brow. The heat of the day was settling in on the ship, bringing with it hot humidity.

"I tried to see but couldn't tell," Doebromir said. "They kept me in one area at the back of the ship this time. The men's faces looked defeated and scared. I did see slaves scrubbing blood off the deck before they shoved me away, but also, the deck looked like it was scattered with round pieces of glass."

"Glass?" Sorcha's eyebrows creased with confusion. "From the lanterns? Well, no, that wouldn't be right because you said round. Lanterns smashing would create jagged pieces of glass. Are you sure?"

Doebromir nodded, forming a circle with his hands. "The reflective properties looked odd too like the glass was tinted green."

"You sure you weren't just seasick again?" Jashun jeered and nudged Doebromir's arm. The Stoltlanders might have taken his freedom, but he was steadfast in making sure they did not steal his humor. How else were their minds to survive?

Doebromir's chapped lips cracked a goofy smile. "Well played, but no need for the Rana frog's services. I've found my sea legs, my friend."

Jashun scratched his black hair aggressively, which, after he was done, made him look like a black cockatoo. Jashun had a more petite frame than the other three men in the cage but was exotically handsome, even malnourished. "Then what could it have been? Doebromir, you say we can do this—this being taking over the ship—but we can't if we have no idea what is killing soldiers at night."

A huff sounded from the opposite side of the cage. The curly, red-haired Sune was lying on his back with his knees bent and hands over his forehead. He cleared his throat. "A sea legend."

The group looked at Sune with surprise in their eyes. Sune hadn't spoken much in the past few days, so his adding to the conversation stunned them. They had each gone through several days of s. Coping with being a Stoltland prisoner had worn each one down, and Sune had been there to help pick each one up, but now, he needed his time to process.

"Say again, Sune," Doebromir said.

Sune propped up on his elbows. His green eyes connected with Sorcha's, and she felt her cheeks go hot.

"I said, a sea legend."

With his burly black beard and chapped ivory skin, Ezen folded his arms and leaned his head against the metal bars. "Elaborate, Sune. We're not in the mood for guessing games." Ezen's foul mood had not helped their situation. He missed his family, and hope dwindled in his eyes. His fingers missed the feel of soil, and his heart ached to breathe in the forests of Avondelle. He was overwhelmingly homesick.

Sune sat up and crossed his legs. "There are several sea legends. They were my favorite books to read as a child. I became obsessed, especially with the book *Mer Clans & Their Secrets.*"

Jashun snorted. "Are you *really* about to tell us that Mer Clans are attacking this ship? C'mon, Sune. Those are make-believe children's tales." He shook his head in disbelief, holding up his hand toward Sune.

Doebromir smacked Jashun's arm. "Wait, do you remember the Pirate Captain saying that even the sea creatures know about Queen Sealyn?"

Jashun stiffened. He remembered the Pirate Captain better than any of them. He repeatedly replayed that night-- how he told the pirate about King Jace, the grey-eyed outcast—now Elysium's king. He hated that Sune still felt he was a traitor to his kingdom. He tried to forgive himself since being a prisoner sure felt like penance, but he couldn't. Jashun nodded to Doebromir and dropped his green eyes and propped his head on his hands.

"Exactly, Doebromir," Sune said. "Mer Clans have their own governments and laws. From Mer-People to *Mer-Maras, they govern the sea creatures. I believe they exist, and from the seamen's studies and stories, everything adds up to their existence being real."

"But what does round, tinted, green glass have to do with Mer Clans?" Sorcha asked, scratching her arm and trying to ignore the sensation tingling through her at Sune's passionate words. Sorcha was wise beyond her years. She kept her mind sharp daily just in case they would need her intelligence to escape.

"Excellent question, my lady," Sune winked at Sorcha. She smiled and looked down. Jashun didn't like what he was seeing between them. He felt loyalty to his friend Sakul, who, for all he knew, was still madly in love with Sorcha—if he made it out of Len Nove alive. Sune continued, "From what the books said, mermaid tails are made of enchanted sea glass. When sailors look down and see a mermaid in the water, the mermaids can angle their tails to look like whatever they want. They can appear to have legs or a dress. Some mermaids are so powerful that their 'scales' can reflect the desires of a sailor's heart. You hear rumors that a mermaid's song lures sailors to their deaths, but mermaids don't sing."

"Then where does that rumor come from?" Jashun asked incredulously. He was sick of hearing childhood tales.

"The sirens sing, and the Mer-Maras create music."

This sent a jolt down Jashun's spine. He remembered the sounds he heard last night. It sounded like an entire group of musicians playing a melody that begged their bones to join the sea. Could that have been from Mer-Maras? He didn't even know what a Mer-Mara was. "What exactly is a Mer-Mara?" Jashun asked while folding his arms with a smug expression.

"According to the books' drawings, a Mer-Mara has the same tail as a mermaid, but the body looks like a seahorse, and its snout is shaped like a horn. They usually hunt with mermaids, which is most likely why people confuse the stories."

Sorcha blinked in disbelief. "I had no idea."

"You're not believing this load, are you, Sorcha?" Jashun sneered. "Let's say this is all real. That means we have no hope of taking over this ship!"

"Why do you say that?" Doebromir stood and folded his arms, daring Jashun to ruin all hope.

Jashun stood, too. He didn't like someone looking down on him. "Because, you big troll, what keeps the Mer Clans from attacking us if we take over the ship? We are much fewer in number than the Stoltlanders."

This piqued Ezen's attention; after all, he was an excellent tracker and knew how creatures thought. Ezen lifted his head from the bars, strands of black falling over his eyes. "Maybe we hide down here. You all have pointed out that they haven't entered this room, so perhaps they are limited with their time on land?"

"Ezen makes a good point," Doebromir said, anticipation filling his words. "We could slightly alter our plan. Kill the guard who comes down, then slowly take out one by one. We spread across the deck in the shadows and take out the rest. We can do this."

"And we hide down here during the night," added Ezen. Doebromir pointed at Ezen and nodded. Ezen, Sealyn's cousin, felt his spirits lift, knowing he was helping his fellow Elysians. He wanted to contribute, but for weeks, loneliness and despair had made a home in his mind. This was a chance for him to redeem his lack of response and give aid to their freedom.

Sorcha rubbed her temples. "So, we're really doing this? As in, the next guard who comes down here to take one of us up is our target?" The Elysian green eyes looked around at each other, nodding. "Well then, it's my turn for exercises. I want to be ready."

The Elysians made sure to keep each other in shape and vital for anything they may face. Even through fatigue, they pushed each other to run in place, jump from squatting, complete pushups, and master pull-ups from the overhead bars. There was only enough room for one person to exercise at a time, so they quietly cheered each other to do more daily. This was not easy, especially with the lack of food provided, but they persevered through their tribulations. They leaned on one another's encouragement. Unique bonds formed in their captivity.

The afternoon hours were setting in, and the Elysians knew a guard would be down soon. Everyone was on edge. This was their only shot. With a quick creek, the door hatch flew open, and a Stoltland soldier dressed in black came stomping down the worn wooden stairs. Scurrying was heard from the Rana frog in the dark corner. "All right, I think it's the queen's blood's turn to smell fresh air." With legs shaking, Ezen stood and readied himself. He felt his nerves tumbling in his stomach. He needed this plan to work. He needed to be home with his family.

The lock clicked. An icy chill went down Sorcha's spine. This was it. No turning back. She held her breath. The Stoltlander opened the rusty cage door and motioned for Ezen to walk forward. He had to be careful because the soldier had his sword drawn, like always. Ezen's ivory brow began to sweat as he eyed the tip of the black sword. One false move and that blade would be inside him. He didn't want to die. He wanted to be back safe, helping his father grow crops for their people.

Ezen looked into the black eyes of the man whose death they had moments ago plotted. He swallowed. Could he do this? Could he take a life? He wasn't a killer. His mouth was instantly dry, and his hand began to shake.

Ezen stepped around the soldier, and as the soldier turned to lock the door, Ezen threw himself against him. Sune grabbed the arm with the sword and held it tight, his knuckles turning white. They only had seconds to pull this off. It had to be now. Doebromir quickly stabbed the soldier in the neck with one of the sharp pieces of firewood. The soldier dropped his grip on the sword. It banged against the bars. Ezen instinctively picked up the black weapon.

Wobbling, the Stoltlander dropped to his knees, both hands holding the lodged piece of wood in his neck, crimson trickling between his fingers. He began choking on his blood. Doebromir stepped through the unlocked door and took the sword from Ezen, then sliced the soldier's neck. He gave him a merciful death; one Doebromir didn't think he deserved.

The Elysians stood around the body in shock at what they just accomplished. The first part of their plan had worked, but now they had to press on. Sorcha's heart pounded. She watched in horror as the blood pool kept expanding. "How are we going to hide the blood?"

A disgusting idea came to Doebromir. "We hide the body behind the stack of hay over there. The hay will stop the blood from flowing for a time."

"And the blood in front of the cage that *clearly* reveals what we did?" Jashun asked.

"Just follow what I just said."

The group worked in unison, hiding the body behind the hay, then stared wide-eyed at the blood pool along with the trail to the hidden corpse. Doebromir leaned over the pool and allowed his mind and body to feel the boat's swaying. The too-familiar nauseating feeling enveloped him. Then he lost his sea legs and vomited all over the blood. The red eyes of the dark corner glowed with excitement. The giant frog hopped over and lapped up the vomit and blood. Luckily for them, the saliva and massive tongue of the frog managed to clean the floor within seconds.

Sorcha faced the wooden wall and braced both hands against it. "I think I'm going to be sick," she said.

"Aim for the blood droplets that lead toward the hay if you are," Doebromir said, half being serious and half trying to break the tension.

An hour had gone by when they heard footsteps coming down the stairs. They had practiced and rehearsed this scene a hundred times. Their acting had to be perfect. The tension in their cage mounted.

"Where's Smitters?" the soldier grumbled.

"Who?" Doebromir asked.

"Smitters. He came down here an hour ago to fetch one of you's."

"Sorry, soldier. No one came down here. We thought you might have forgotten about us." Doebromir prayed to Creator that his acting was convincing.

The soldier glared at Doebromir. "Hmm. Smitters is known to sneak to the barrel room instead. I better take one of you up before the captain thinks we're not doing our jobs."

Sune's hand tightened around the hilt of the black sword under the straw of their cage. The sound of the jingling keys was their signal. The soldier stepped closer to the door. He smelled of fish and sweat. Sorcha took a deep breath and prayed.

The keys rattled.

From his standing position, Doebromir shoved the door hard, knocking the bars into the nose of the Stoltlander. Sune sprang from his hunched-over position and stabbed their enemy in the belly. He reveled in the surprise on the Stoltlander's face. They dragged his body behind the hay, but not before the Stoltlander saw Smitters' lifeless body, then he too succumbed to death's knocking.

"Doebromir, do you puke again?" Jashun asked almost apologetically.

"No. The blood doesn't matter now. The sun has dropped low enough to provide light still but also plenty of shadows for us to sneak around in."

They passed around the daggers found on each dead soldier until they had enough weapons to become shadow killers. Jashun grabbed the black hood from the freshly killed soldier and slid it on. He hoped he could slightly pass for a Stoltlander. They slowly crept up the stairs. The hatch was still open. Warm sea breeze caressed their cheeks.

Ezen went out first, as he was initially supposed to, and acted like his hands were tied behind his back. He took a left and followed the directions Doebromir had given earlier, then went to the back of the ship. He passed by a basket of fish. The aroma made him remember the first time his father, Prince Toven, taught him to fish. Tears stung his eyes, threatening to break free. He shook his head, finding his focus.

Jashun was next, since he had the black hood on. They hoped that would be enough for people to see and not raise suspicions. Jashun felt his body trembling. He let Ezen continue to the back and dropped behind four barrels, waiting for their attack signal. Sune inched his head out but quickly dropped it. "Two sailors almost saw me." Again, he edged his head out and saw the same sailors had their backs to him. Most sailors were overloaded with work and did not notice the prisoners' location. Sune crawled out of the opening to the right, kept his stomach to the ground, and found cover behind a strapped-down load of crates and nets.

Exhaling, Sorcha crouched low on the top step and waited patiently for her moment. Three. Two. One. She sprang towards the other side of the back of the ship. They had to take the back first, then go down to the front. Doebromir was ready to make his exit, but the captain's door opened with force. The captain and four guards stepped out with him. The captain tilted his head at the open hatch, then motioned for the guards to investigate.

Sorcha's heart pounded. They were about to find Doebromir exposed. She heard a different bird call than originally planned. Sune made the sound for an attack rather than shadow hunting. Doebromir sprung forward with the black sword. It collided with one of the guard's swords. Their plan had failed. Now, they had no choice but to fight for their lives because prison-breaking on a Stoltland ship had an enormous consequence: death.

Sune grabbed the netting and tossed it at the four guards, entangling them. He yanked it hard, sending them all to the ground. He scrambled back to his feet and lunged forward, plunging his dagger into the heart of one of the guards while Doebromir stabbed another. Sune saw the other two fighting the net, so he rolled over and stabbed another. Crimson splattered the deck and net, providing a slippery surface for the escape plan.

The captain charged for Doebromir, but Sorcha threw her knife, landing it into the shoulder blade of the captain. He turned to face her, which cost him his life. Doebromir swung his sword, sending the captain's head overboard. His headless body dropped to the ground, twitching. The other tangled soldier screamed for help, alerting the other soldiers on board.

Trying for the tangled soldier, Doebromir slipped on the captain's blood, but Sune crawled through the tangled mess of dead bodies and blood to reach the fourth guard. A quick slice to the throat, and he was gone. Doebromir, Sune, and Sorcha stood in fear at the number of soldiers coming for them. They were completely outmatched. How had they miscalculated so badly?

Three soldiers charged, but Jashun and Ezen stepped in to defend. Clearly, Jashun had military training, and Ezen did not, yet he tried. Ezen wanted to go home badly. He missed his family so much that he could taste freedom. He was ready to be by the cozy fire in the palace's Garden Library, listening to one of King Father Ryker's many stories. He felt his muscles burning. He was no match to the sword skills on board this ship.

Jashun out-maneuvered two of the soldiers, but the third had Ezen up against the ship's railing. Doebromir and Sune went to help, but five other soldiers came for them. Sune stopped and backed up in front of Sorcha, ready to fight by her side. Doebromir and Jashun fought back-to-back, fending off one black sword after another. More soldiers joined the fight.

The Elysians were losing, and they knew it. Ezen let out a blistering scream. The soldier had sliced his side and now had his sword at Ezen's throat. All Ezen could think was, "I don't want to die. I don't want to die. Not like this. Not on some boat in the middle of nowhere. I want my family!"

Sorcha saw what was happening and yelled out. "Stop! He's royal blood. You can't!" The fighting stopped, and everyone faced the soldier and Ezen. Sorcha again begged. "He's Queen Sealyn's cousin. He cannot be killed. The rules of war clearly state…"

Then, the air went still. Silence landed all around them as they watched the Stoltlander's blade slide across Ezen's neck. The red-hot liquid flowed like a mountain waterfall. Royal blood had been spilled. Sorcha cupped her neck, hiding her silver scar, and screamed, or at least she thought she did. She remembered that burning feeling across her own neck. She dropped her sword. Jashun tried to run to Ezen, but the soldiers grabbed him. Other soldiers stepped in front of Doebromir and Sune, holding the tips of their swords at their hearts. The Elysians had no choice but to surrender.

As the final bright pinks and oranges of the sun faded below the sea, the soldier who killed Ezen stepped in front of the prisoners. They were all covered in blood splatters and breathing heavily. Tears fell from their eyes. The murderer glared. "Since you killed our captain, I am now captain of this ship. You will pay the fee for trying to escape."

Sorcha sniffed. "But you just killed one of us. Isn't that penalty enough?"

"No, you stupid woman!"

Sune tried to take a step forward, but the sword at his heart pressed forward, keeping him at bay.

The new captain looked out across the ocean, with the sky darkening. "It's almost nightfall, and the sea creatures will be back. This time, we will give them payment to stay away." He looked back at the prisoners. "Baldy will be a good ship slave along with the red-headed, pretty face lad." He stood in front of Sorcha and stroked her blood-spattered, ebony cheek. "This goddess will stay in her cage and be the leash for Baldy and Pretty Face. They each care for her but in different ways." He gave an evil grin, showing yellow teeth, and grabbed Jashun's arm.

Finally, the ocean went completely black, and the air turned cool. They could hear waves bash against the ship. Light spread across the deck from swaying lanterns, cascading sinister shadows. Jashun's eyes watered. He didn't know why the captain dragged him to the ship's edge. Jashun looked down in the dark waters and thought he saw figures under the waves; then he heard music. It was like a song made for his heart. He didn't feel scared anymore. Was this magic? Was this a trick?

The captain yelled. "They're back!" He pulled his hidden dagger from his belt and stabbed Jashun in the side, then pushed him backward. Jashun fell to the crashing waves with a crimson splash. He could barely hear his friends screaming his name as he settled in for the caress of death. The music made him almost welcome it, but he felt a tug and took a deep breath. He was being dragged into the depths of the ocean. Dark blue was all he could see.

He felt the salty sting at his wound. He looked down and noticed blood twirling around his injury like smoke from a pipe. It was only a matter of time before sea creatures would begin to feed on him. This amount of blood could probably be detected from miles away.

Jashun blinked with burning eyes and saw the most stunning woman he'd ever seen before him. Was his injury making him hallucinate? He could tell she was beautiful even with his blurry vision in dark water. She had electric pink hair, matching eyes, and plump pink lips. If this was his death, he accepted her as the last image he would ever see.

She leaned over his lips and gently grazed them with hers. Next, she coated his lips in what looked like seaweed. She blew on top of the seaweed, which expanded into a large bubble that held air around his head. Was she helping him? She placed something cold, which looked like glass, over his wound. Was that one of her scales Sune talked about? Was she healing him? Weren't mermaids their enemy? He felt her tug and the water's current. They were moving at blazing speeds. Where was she taking him? Probably to her lair to eat him. His heartbeat sped.

Jashun had lost all sense of time and was exhausted. Finally, after what felt like endless hours, the creature stopped. She pushed him above the surface. Jashun pulled the seaweed off and inhaled the fresh air. He treaded water, trying to figure out where she was, only to see her head slowly rise. She was even more gorgeous than he imagined. Sparkles glistened across her face like a mask at one of their masquerade balls.

She giggled. "Have you never seen a mermaid before, sailor?" Her voice sounded like a melody.

Jashun fumbled through his words as he tasted the salt water. "My apologies, my lady. No, I've never seen such beauty nor spoken to anyone of the sea."

Her cheeks blushed. "You aren't like any sailor I've encountered. I must tell you, though. In this sea territory, green eyes are protected. Your Queen Sealyn freed the horned whales from the Stoltland ships in these very waters, so because of that, we honor her, which means you are in no danger from me."

Jashun felt relief rush over him. "Wait. The horned whales were released in the harbor of Port Rowin. Does that mean we're close to Elysium's harbor?"

The pink-headed mermaid smiled. "You're smart, too."

"Too? "What else am I?"

"Very handsome." She moved her body closer to his. Her face was inches away. Water dripped from her nose and down her cheeks. She reached out and held his body, giving him the support he needed to stop treading water.

Jashun didn't know if it was the length of time it had been since a woman had her arms around him or the sheer passion he felt for her, but he gave in to every urge radiating from his core. With her sea strength balancing them among the waves, he cupped her smooth ivory cheeks and passionately kissed her. She was hungrily tasting him back. He tangled his hands in her wet, pink hair, and his body was begging for more and more. He wrapped his leg around her, then felt her tail, and stopped.

Tail? How was he? His mind raced with, "That's right. She has a tail." He had almost forgotten she was a mermaid. She gazed dreamily into his eyes. He felt all the sensations come back. Who cares? A mermaid just saved his life, and he was going to kiss her until she was done with him.

She giggled again. "Perhaps civilities should be exchanged?" she whispered in his ear.

Jashun shivered and stuttered. "What do you mean?"

"My name is Kailani of Mer Clan Kaimana." She gently kissed Jashun's lips.

"Oh, um. Well, I'm Jashun of… um… clan… um… palace military?" he said with a question.

"Why do you question yourself?" She kissed his neck.

"Because I don't carry much weight in my kingdom. I mean, I am one of Queen Sealyn's Vinurs of the Court, which is the highest honor a citizen can hope for, and I am a lord, but I don't hold any big title in the army."

Suddenly, Jashun felt them sinking. "Lord Jashun, you should not doubt yourself." Jashun gasped for air and sank below the water. He felt Kailani's legs wrap around him. Legs? She passionately kissed him more, then just as quick as he felt her legs, they were gone, and the tail was back. Did he imagine that? She pulled him back to the surface.

"All things are possible, Lord Jashun."

Jashun wiped his face. "You can be both?"

"That is a conversation for another time, my lord. I need to get you to shore. You lost a lot of blood."

He felt her arm slide around his waist. She gave one last fervent kiss, then sped forward. Jashun closed his eyes for the journey. Within minutes, he felt pebbles underneath him. He felt around with his hands. He was partly on land. He lifted himself up and looked around, dripping with seawater. This was the landing where local fishermen would leave their boats near Port Rowin. He whirled around and looked out far toward the ocean, and there he saw his mystical creature, Kailani, waving. He waved back, and she dove under the water. He feared he would never see her again.

Elysian News

Issue #3

The Latest News and Gossip

Painted above: the late Lord Drystan

Drystan: Victim or Villain?
Lady Pyry pays the price

Greetings, my fellow Elysians. It's me again with all the juicy details about our beloved kingdom. Today's main issue is discussing whether Drystan really had to die the way he did or whether our new king killed him in cold blood.

You may be thinking, "Lina, Drystan was a traitor to our kingdom." Yes, my dear friend, he was, but the question we must ask ourselves is: did he surrender? Elysians always honor surrender. We have merciful hearts, but a Stoltlander? We all know mercy is not of them. Their hearts are as black as their eyes.

As Lady Pyry nears her and her father's trial, I ask that we, as a kingdom, launch a full investigation into what really happened in Lord Drystan's death. Could Lady Pyry's actions have been vengeance for murder? Could her father have been in pain over his son-in-law's non-merciful killing?

If we don't ask the hard questions, then it's easy to get away with the big wrongdoings.

~Lady Adalina Roedellen (Lina)

Princess Siany Spotlight	**Lord Sakul's Brokenheart**	**Summer Drink Votes are in**
The juiciest gossip	*A personal interview*	*Your favorite drink*
How is the princess coping with not being queen anymore?	What he wishes he could tell Lady Sorcha and what he plans to do.	Find out what drink made the #1 spot and which drinks made the top 5.
Interview with Lady Novaly	Sorcha's family is no longer accepting flowers	Full recipes included from Bartender Barm
Page 2	Page 4	Page 6

CHAPTER 2
REUNITED

Dripping wet, Jashun trudged forward in the gloom of his friends still being imprisoned. His stomach growled, and the sun's heat beat down on him. He needed nourishment to survive. He had only been to Port Rowin a couple of times, and each time, he had gorged himself on the steamy, spiced seafood. His body ached for just crumbs.

Malnourished and with sore muscles, Jashun forced his legs to take each step. His head was spinning. He had swallowed too much sea water, feeling the dehydration draining his mind's sharpness. He needed to find help for his friends, but Jashun was exhausted and wanted a full night's sleep in a proper bed. He couldn't believe the last time he slept in his bed was the night before the great disappearance.

He paused and braced himself against a wall that was covered in white seashells. While he took a short break, he drank in the scenery. Port Rowin's waters were turquoise and lined with tall palm trees. The sunshine warmed his face, and he smelled all the blossoms of the summer flowers. Summer!

Summer meant that he had been away almost a year. Did anyone miss him? What happened to Queen Sealyn and the Len Novian quest? Did they survive? If so, were they looking for him and his friends? He walked on and climbed up a tall staircase made of seashells. At the top, two tropical Elysian trees hung over the entrance to the port city. Their branches spread wide, and long, flowy, vinelike branches full of tiny yellow flowers that gave off a sweet scent hung across the entry. Jashun spread the vines like a curtain and peered through to Port Rowin's vibrant and bustling city.

He could see the tall masts of ships at port far across the city's buildings. The streets were made of crushed seashells and melted limestone. Lush palm trees, banana trees, and orange trees lined the streets, making sure no one went hungry. The stone shops were painted bright green, with vines of purple and blue fireflowers hung throughout the city. Something was happening. Today, the city was decorated with green and gold flags. Flower wreaths were hung on every shop and house door. Jashun heard music playing on every corner.

Did he forget a specific holiday? He was so tired and hungry that his mind couldn't process history or the present very well. He did like thinking about his immediate past. That pink-headed mermaid would haunt and dazzle his dreams forever. Kailani. How he would say her name every night. He was thoroughly enjoying his memory when he bumped into someone, and not just any someone, a lady.

"Yuck! Watch where you're going, you filthy sea mongrel!" Lady Adalina spat.

"Adalina?!"

Adalina gasped. "Jashun?" Her hand went over her mouth. "Jashun, is that really you?"

"It's me, Adalina! It's really me!" Tears fell from Jashun's green eyes down his sweaty, cinnamon-colored cheeks.

Adalina went to embrace Jashun but then realized he was soaking wet and reeked. "Jashun, hurry. Come inside." She grabbed his arm and rushed inside the shop, *Nice Tails.* "Cantaezia. Can you please come out here?" A small, petite older woman peered from the back of the luxury clothing shop. "Ah, there you are. Look, my friend, Lord Jashun, has just returned from a voyage and needs several outfits. Tell your assistant to go two shops over to Sir Westington for two baskets of his shrimp and potatoes. While she's out there, grab a few oranges and a pitcher of lemon juice from Maggie's." Cantaezia nodded.

Jashun shook his head. "I'm ever so grateful. I can't even think about anything else other than food. Wait, hang on. Adalina, how do you know so much about Port Rowin?"

"I honestly can't believe that's your first question for me," Adalina chuckled. "But before questions and answers, let's get you in Cantaezia's personal bath. She won't mind. She owes me for bringing her all the new business because of my latest publication about her clothing shop."

"Publication?"

"We have so much to catch up on, Jashun, but I'm not bathing you, so hurry up and clean yourself. I'll have Cantaezia lay out a few choices for you. Will I need to have clothes ready for the rest of your group? I can't wait to see Sorcha. I've missed her!"

"What?" Jashun felt the sea water churning in his stomach. His mind was foggy.

"The rest of your group, Jashun. Doebromir, Sune, Ezen, and *Sorcha*. You know—The ones all taken prisoner with you. They're here, right?"

Jashun dropped his head. He felt all his emotions rising, and then what he had been trying to block out suddenly hit him like a bolt of lightning. He replayed Ezen's neck being sliced and Sorcha shouting. He felt the pain of the sword in his side. He saw the upside-down view of the ship as he fell to the sea. He had been rescued, not the others. Would Elysium see that as abandonment? Abandoning your comrades was treason. He decided he would stay quiet until he was with people he knew he could trust. Adalina was a friend, but she liked to gossip. "I can't talk about it now, Adalina."

She saw the tears in his eyes. "It's fine, Jashun. Just take your bath, and we'll have food ready for you. Once you're done, I'll take you to Majesty Manor."

"Majesty Manor? That's only for royals."

"Yes, silly. I know that. Queen Sealyn is there."

"She's alive?!"

"Of course," Adalina paused. "Oh yes, you haven't heard. She's here for the trial."

"Who's trial?"

"Lady Pyry, Drystan's wife. Now, before I say more, go take that bath because I really can't stand the smell any longer."

Feeling refreshed from his bath and drinking half the pitcher of lemon juice, Jashun paced himself with the basket of the best-smelling and tasting food. They sat at a small wooden table outside the shop. He was glad he ran into Adalina. After all, she was the one who knew all the news. Jashun exhaled, trying to keep nausea away from eating so fast.

"Jashun, are you all right?"

He cleared his throat. "I'm fine. Please continue. You were saying about your printing business."

"Ah, yes. Well, after everyone returned from Len Nove and the fires subsided from the dragon war…" Jashun coughed on a piece of potato, hearing the term dragon. Adalina eyed him, not liking the interruption. "Anyways, we needed a way to tell Elysium what had happened. I volunteered to aid with this project. I worked closely with Madam Bip, who, by the way, is a Luxen and can manipulate plants, but I don't have time to get into all that yet." Adalina took a sip of her lemon juice in the tall, slender glass. "Madam Bip managed to grow this magical black flower that produces enchanted ink. The black ink has silver sparkles in it, too. I absolutely love it. The magic part is that the ink bleeds through the parchment, and on whatever parchment is below it, the ink makes a copy of what I wrote. It stops making copies once the ink touches stone or wood. I'm able to make hundreds of copies a day!"

"Good for you, Adalina, but I need you to speak more of the dragon war. What happened?" Jashun's heart pounded. He was in shock over an actual dragon war. What would that have even looked like? How much destruction would those creatures have caused, and who survived—more importantly, who didn't?

"I hate speaking about it. They're calling it the Saddest Day in Elysium's History, the Battle of the Dragons. It was bad enough that they slaughtered and burned so many of our warriors, forests, and homes, but then Corentine, that evil witch, targeted the NexGen field. Jashun, the last dragon wiped out an entire generation of *Nichts," Adalina sniffed and dabbed her almond-shaped green eyes with her pink handkerchief. She tucked a small strand of black hair behind her ear.

Jashun shook his head and pounded his fist on the table. "What? An entire generation of Nichts?" Jashun cursed and kept shaking his head. His blood boiled for vengeance. He fixed his eyes on Adalina and spoke with a heavy, serious tone, "How will Elysium recover?"

"Surprisingly, the kingdom rallied behind the royal family, even with Jace—I mean King Jace, beside Queen

Sealyn," Adalina struggled having a Stoltlander as their king when Stoltland was their enemy kingdom that kept destroying the ones they loved.

"Why do you say, 'even with Jace'?"

Adalina's almond-shaped eyes darted around the bright street. "There's a slight bit of unrest in Elysium." She shifted in her chair. "Some feel that all this horror brought in the past two years is because Sealyn chose Jace as her husband. He was already an outcast and unfit to be in society because of his grey eyes—"

"Adalina! I'm shocked. Just because he doesn't know who his father is, and his parents aren't from the same kingdoms, doesn't mean he's a freak of nature."

"Some feel his kind is an abomination."

"And are you included in that some?"

Adalina leaned in. "Look, I know you and Jace were close, but there's just talk, and sometimes that talk makes sense. If he weren't king here, then Queen Corentine of Stoltland would have no interest in attacking Elysium."

"Not true! She wants all seven kingdoms, and last I checked, that included Elysium, so get your facts straight, Adalina, before someone thinks you're spreading treason."

Adalina held her hands up. "Easy, Jashun. We're just talking. You know, kind of like when us ladies helped you get rid of a certain condemning letter from Corentine that ended up with Tybalt's death."

Jashun dropped his green eyes. He hated himself. How could he have gotten into all this trouble? He knew the moment he saw Sealyn, he would tell her everything. Well, maybe not everything, like the on-fire session he had in the waters, but he would tell her about their escape attempt and Ezen. "Listen, Adalina. I'm not saying I'm a perfect citizen. I've made plenty of mistakes in the past, but I do know bad-mouthing Jace isn't good."

"Fine. Understood," Adalina said with gritted teeth. "Regardless, we need to get you to the Majesty Manor."

"Why is Lady Pyry on trial? Is it because they think she knew about Drystan's betrayal?"

Adalina blinked. "I keep forgetting how much you missed. No, she and her father are responsible for the kidnapping or, as some say, the great disappearance."

"What? No way."

"Yes, way. The investigator even found direct correspondence between Pyry and Queen Corentine." Adalina ate a slice of orange. "The trial has been going on for the past three days. It's all anyone can talk about. Her father is trying to take the blame, so the death penalty lands on him."

"Death penalty?"

"Yes, of course. Lord Temm died in Lady Zuri's shop, remember, and on the quest to Len Nove, Lord Stawyer died. His death wouldn't have happened if you all had had the proper army. Then, there's the question of Lady Rivers' death."

Jashun froze. Stawyer was dead. He was a war hero, and he had forgotten about Rivers. How could he have gone through so much that he had forgotten about that terrifying *Arkootha bear digging its claws into Rivers? For many nights, he heard her screams in his dreams. He felt nauseous thinking about the cave collapsing on top of Rivers' body, creating a forever tomb, a monument to a valiant warrior. Jashun's face fell into his hands, trying to hold back tears.

"Jashun," Adalina gently grabbed one of his hands and held it. "You know what happened to her, don't you?" He nodded. "Please," Adalina choked on her words. "Please tell me what happened to my friend."

He wanted to spare Adalina the gory details of Rivers' death, but he felt she should be honored and glorified. "She fought with bravery and gallantly, but she sustained too many wounds, which cost her life. Let us leave it there for now."

"Yoohoo, Adalina, darling," Lady Jadelyn cooed. She breezily strolled next to the small wooden table, wearing a shimmering gold dress with long golden sleeves. Jashun thought the long sleeves were an odd choice since it was warm outside. "Adalina, I've been waiting for you. You were supposed to meet me and the girls for tea at *A Taste of Teas*. What happened?" She looked at Jashun and smiled. "Ah, I see. Found a gorgeous snack, did you?"

Adalina blushed. "Stop that, Jadelyn. No, this is Lord Jashun. He was part of the prisoners on board—"

"The Abbadon ship. Stoltland's ship," Jadelyn gasped. "You escaped! Many happy returns, my lord. Are you well?"

Jashun realized this was the first time since being back that anyone asked about his welfare. He blinked. "Yes, my lady. I'm much better now with freedom and a full belly. You are?"

Jadelyn giggled. "My apologies. I'm Lady Jadelyn from Shunal. I replaced my sister on the Council of Lands for Queen Sealyn."

Jashun knew she was from Shunal. Her bright yellow eyes gave that away. He wondered why she had to replace her sister but decided he really didn't care. He wanted to get to the Majesty Manor quickly. Normally, he would have been distracted by Jadelyn's natural beauty with her long blonde hair and pink lips, but he had kissed a mermaid—all other women were spoiled now.

"I'm Lord Jashun, at your service, but ladies, do you mind taking me to Majesty Manor? I really need to speak with Queen Sealyn."

Once Jashun stood, Jadelyn locked arms with him. Adalina threw her red skirt back with annoyance and glared. "Easy, Jadelyn. Jashun is already taken."

How could Adalina know about his mermaid? Jashun cleared his throat. "What do you mean, Adalina?"

Adalina folded her arms over her sleeveless green top and, with a huff, said, "Jashun, I know it's been a while, but you and Brenna were planning on marrying. I'd say that's taken."

Jashun's mouth dropped open. He had forgotten all about Brenna.

Jadelyn laughed. "Ha! Well, I'm no love expert, but I'd say Lady Brenna is in for a delightful, disappointing reunion."

Jashun's head was spinning. Did Brenna really wait all this time for him? How could he share the news that he wasn't interested now? Could he break her heart and her daughter's heart? What a mess he was in.

CHAPTER 3
ONE SOUR PICKLE

The royal family was finishing their tea in the central drawing room of Majesty Manor. The walls were dark green with golden tapestries depicting sea battles with large ships. A white fireplace was lit with candles of different sizes. Sealyn paced in front of the fireplace while her parents and grandparents sat on two grey couches, facing each other. Princess Siany, Sealyn's sister, and Lady Novaly sat quietly in the corner reading books. Siany wore her hair pinned up with a small emerald crown. Her freckled skin was flushed from anxiety.

The tiny Nicht door at the top right of the massive wooden door opened, and a speed Nicht zipped quickly to Sealyn. Novaly jerked her head up, sending her pink and purple flower crown backward. Her red hair was in several braids that made one big side braid twisted together with tiny pink flowers. She nudged Siany and motioned toward Sealyn.

Jace, wearing a dark green shirt, hovered next to his wife. Sealyn opened the scroll she received and read with relief. "She's agreed and will be here momentarily." The room erupted in cheers and clapping. Jace kissed Sealyn's forehead and hugged her. Composing herself, Sealyn spoke quickly, "Come. Let us go to the throne room to receive our guests."

The royal family hurried out the door to the small throne room. Each royal manor in Elysium had a smaller version of the capital's throne room. Jace held Sealyn's hand, signaling her to let the others go ahead.

"Jace, what is it?"

Jace cupped Sealyn's olive-skinned cheek and stared into her emerald eyes. "Remember, love, having them join us, especially her, not only takes the pressure off you, but it shows your character since they're willing to become allies."

"You're right," Sealyn sighed. "But this is the part of the job that I don't like."

Jace slid his fingers down her sheer, sparkling sleeves. They were tinted emerald and matched her form-fitted gown that flowed at the knees. Sealyn was gorgeous, but he loved her perseverance and determination more. She was strong, but he could tell something plagued her. "Sea, if you need to talk about anything else, I'm here. You can lean on me to help with all things."

Sealyn suddenly felt heavy, like her arms were made of stone. Her head spun, and she felt tired. She had an urge to postpone the trial for years and just drift away on a boat. Facing the large mirror on the fireplace mantel, she caught a glimpse of blue glowing from her eyes. She stepped back, realizing Len Nove's curse was trying to take over. How could she do this alone? Could she channel the mammoth king from this distance? Or could she truly rely on Jace, as he said?

"Push me out the door, Jace."

"What? I'm not pushing you."

"Jace, right now, I need to be forced out that door. Make sure this trial happens no matter what I say or do."

Jace's tan face formed a perplexed expression. "Sealyn, you're confusing and scaring me."

Sealyn wanted to tell him. She begged her mouth to say the words "I need help," but they wouldn't come. In her frustration, she swung her hand against the fireplace, and a large crack formed up the stones. Jace inhaled sharply. Sealyn's eyes bulged. The mammoth strength given to her from breaking Len Nove's curse was still taking some getting used to. She shook her head. "I'm sorry. I didn't mean to."

Jace stepped closer and wrapped her hands in his. He smiled, hoping it would calm her. "My queen, we must go. You're needed in the throne room, and I'm not taking no for an answer, so you can either use those deliciously sculpted legs of yours and walk on your own, or I will scoop you up in my arms and take you myself."

A rush of relief and energy washed over Sealyn. It worked. Accountability was the counter to Len Nove's curse. She jerked her head back to the mirror and saw her emerald eyes again. She looked down at the flames of the candles in the fireplace, and immediately, her mind transported her back to her nightmare. Her eyes looked out over a vast battlefield. She stood at the top of a hill, scared at how many dead bodies were scattered around her. Fires streaked across the ground. She could feel pain, but not only physical—an emotional, spiritual pain. She's lost someone precious, but she doesn't know who. In the final part of the nightmare, she looks up into the flaming eyes of a man, but she doesn't know who he is.

Jace kissed Sealyn's hand. "Everything okay, Sealyn?"

She nodded her head, willing her mind to stay focused on Jace. She smiled at him. "I will do your command, my king. Although, being scooped into your muscular arms does sound appealing. How about we continue that tonight?"

Jace locked arms with his bride and whispered in her ear, "Only if you say please."

Knocking on Majesty Manor's door, Jashun felt nervous. How would he be received, especially once he tells the stories about Rivers and Ezen? The green door trimmed in gold opened to the butler. "Good day, sir. May I present Lady Adalina of Queen Sealyn's Vinurs of the Court and Lady Jadelyn of the Council of Lands, and I'm Lord Jashun—" The butler's mouth gaped, and he ushered them inside quickly.

The receiving entry was large, with walls made of seashells and an emerald jeweled chandelier hanging over a large driftwood table. Several Nichts sped past carrying scrolls. Green velvet couches sat at each wall for visitors to wait, with driftwood coffee tables in front of them. He noticed two lords sitting on a couch, which Jashun didn't expect.

Before him were Lord Char and Lord Sakul, drinking vividly orange drinks with a platter of kiwi, cheeses, and sour apples in front of them. Char wore his usual green tunic and had his brown hair pulled back tightly, with the sides of his head shaved. Sakul wore his palace attire of green and gold, which made his ebony skin shine.

Jashun ran to them. "Char! Sakul!"

Char stopped mid-sip and squinted his green eyes. "Sakul, how many drinks have we had?"

"Only two. We just started."

"That's not nearly enough for me to start seeing ghosts, right?"

"Clearly, you babbling lizard." Sakul sipped his drink, trying to mask his excitement at seeing his long-lost friend.

"So, I'm not drunk, and I see Jashun. Does that mean he's really standing in front of us?"

Jashun laughed. "Yes, you idiots!"

Char and Sakul laughed and jumped up, embracing Jashun with a big squeeze.

Char jostled Jashun's hair. "Well, how in all Creation are you?"

"Better now that I'm here."

"Sorcha! Where's Sorcha? Is she here?" Sakul burst out.

"I'm sorry, my friend. She didn't escape. She, along with the others, are still on board the ship." Sakul dropped his head and plopped back down on the couch, chugging his half-full goblet. He rubbed his bald head in pained frustration.

Jashun turned quickly to Char. If there was one person who could help with his lady issues, it was Char, Sealyn's best friend and cousin. "Char, you must help me."

"Me?" Char eyed one of the female servants walking by. He would have to remember that one for another time.

"Yes, you. I figured Brenna had moved on, but according to Adalina, she remained faithful to me while I was away."

"Faithful?" Char looked at Sakul and laughed. "Well, faithful is one word for it, and what? You don't want to be with her anymore?"

"Well, no, but how can I tell her that after she waited? I can't break her heart and her child. Ugh. I feel terrible."

"She's not your child, Jashun."

"I know that, but maybe she got attached. I don't know. I've been gone for a long time. She could have forgotten about me."

"Like you forgot about Brenna," Char smiled an evil grin.

"Char! Seriously. What am I going to do?"

"Just be honest, my escapey friend."

Jashun blushed. "I can't do that."

Char gasped. "You met someone else? But how? When? Tell me it was your jailer, and you seduced her."

"No, but the *she* is pure perfection, and it doesn't matter because I'll never see her again, but we had a steamy good time. It just goes to show that my feelings for Brenna weren't strong enough. I barely thought about her on the quest, whereas Sakul over there has obviously never stopped thinking about Sorcha," Jashun leaned in and whispered. "There's news on that front, too, about someone else trying to win Sorcha's heart."

Char blinked and downed his goblet of orange drink. "The amount of drama you just spilled in five minutes is overwhelming."

"Oh, that's just the romantic news. I have so much more to tell Sealyn."

"Obviously, that is more pressing than everything else," Char poured himself another glass full. The butler finally handed Jashun a gold goblet, which Char immediately filled. "You're going to need this, my friend. Orange juice and bubbly wine. The best summer drink for lady issues. All the ladies of the court are in the throne room. All, Jashun. All."

"You're joking."

"I never joke about women, Jashun," Char winked. "But I will warn you: Sealyn has special guests in there as well, and I know you have your heart set on someone, so let's be clear: once you set those green eyes on the princess inside, know that she's mine—or at least, I want her. You obviously met Jadelyn, and you can see how gorgeous that gem is, but I think this minx is mesmerizing and even better-looking than Jadelyn! Just get ready."

Jashun didn't care. His heart wanted Kailani, and he was determined to find her once more. Adalina and Jadelyn returned to Jashun after sneaking into the kitchens. They motioned for all of them to follow. The three men downed their drinks and filled their goblets once again. They walked down the long hallway with pictures of past monarchs hung on the walls and stopped at the wide golden doors. This was it. Jashun felt his heart pounding. He took another large gulp, hoping it would calm his nerves and help him find his words.

"What are you doing, Jashun?" Adalina hissed. Jashun looked confused. She grumbled. "You can't take drinks inside."

The three exchanged glances and, again, chugged the contents. Jashun immediately regretted his decision. He felt dizzy. It had been some time since his last alcoholic beverage.

The doors opened, and his eyes fell on a sea of people. They were all dressed in their best summer clothes. He saw Sealyn seated on the throne next to Jace. His heart ached, knowing he might have betrayed his king and friend.

Sealyn saw Jashun and gasped. She jumped up, running to her lost friend. The crowd of people parted for the queen. They both fell into an embrace that made Jashun's eyes slip tears of joy and pain. Sealyn leaned back and grabbed his shoulders. "Jashun, we've been so worried about you. I just heard of your return, so we are most eager to hear your news, but first, come with me. You will also be an honored guest. The trial starts in twenty minutes, so we must hurry."

Sealyn escorted Jashun to the end of the throne room, where her Vinurs of the Court were seated to her left and special guests were to her right. Jashun felt his mouth go dry when he saw Brenna. Brenna let out a squeak. She slowly started walking toward him. She wasn't sure if she was allowed to or not, but hoped once she was close enough, Sealyn wouldn't mind the interruption.

Motioning to her right, Sealyn guided Jashun's attention to the special guests seated across from her Vinurs. "Allow me to introduce you to my special guests. This is Princess Kailani of Mer Clan Kaiana, along with her honored court." Jashun's mouth fell open, and he began to sweat. Char nudged Jashun and winked.

Kailani smiled flirtatiously and stood. She stood! She was in human form! Jashun looked to his left and saw Brenna walking closer. His head jerked back to Kailani, who was now also walking nearer. He began breathing fast. Char noticed the change in Jashun's respiration.

Sealyn continued introductions. "Princess Kailani, allow me to introduce Lord Jashun. He was imprisoned on a Stoltland ship and managed to escape. He's a true warrior."

Kailani stepped even closer. "Escaped all by himself? My, my. He is a treat." Her pink eyes glistened with her sparkling skin.

Jashun's brown skin went a shade paler, and his cheeks turned red. Brenna was a couple of feet away, whispering Jashun's name, trying to get his attention. Jashun turned his head to Brenna. She smiled and mouthed, "I missed you." He snapped his head back to Kailani, who was now inches from him. He could smell her intoxicating aroma that smelled like lilacs and seawater, and her pink hair was long and styled perfectly. He wanted to run his fingers through her hair.

Sealyn chuckled. "We don't know all the details of the escape yet, so I can't confirm if he managed all alone or not."

Sealyn's eyes narrowed at Jashun, who looked like he had swallowed hot peppers.

Everything finally clicked with Char. He stepped back, observing the back-and-forth looks Jashun was making from Brenna to Kailani, the rapid breathing and increased sweating, and the closeness Kailani showed toward Jashun. Char laughed out loud. "Isn't this the sourest pickle you've ever tasted?!"

Everyone looked confused at Char's outburst. Sealyn tilted her head. "Char, I believe you've had a few too many."

"Truuuth, dearestest cousin. Perhaps our esteemished hero can help me to the back corner?" Char sputtered through his words while Kailani giggled.

Char grabbed Jashun without hearing permission from Sealyn. They jogged to the back corner, where all three sat down on the golden chairs. Sakul unfolded a wrapped piece of cheese and began snacking. His mouth full, he asked, "Can someone explain what happened?"

"Allow me," Char said with a smirk. "It seems like our boy here was rescued by our fair mermaid over there and had a 'steamy good time' in the ocean with her, and Brenna didn't know the relationship was over."

"I agree with Char then—that's one sour pickle, Jashun."

Elysian News

The Latest News and Gossip

Issue #4

Who is the Mer Clan Princess?

Can they be trusted?

Greetings, my fellow Elysians. It's me with your favorite juicy details about our beloved kingdom. I must focus on the dazzling Mer Clan Princess, Kailani, who stole everyone's breath.

Painted above: Princess Kailani

I was able to ask her a few personal questions just for you all.

What is your favorite color? "Pink."

Where do you live? "In the royal palace of the Kaiana Clan. The city is called Keawev."

Do you like our Elysian food? "It needs more salt."

How can you breathe underwater and on land? "Enchanted molecular structure given by Creator at the beginning."

Can you share a juicy secret? "I just had the best kiss of my life."

Last one, can we trust your people? "That is in the hands of your queen."

There you have it, Elysians. Our queen decides our fate of peace or war with the Mer Clans. What do you think will happen?
~Lady Adalina Roedellen (Lina)

Princess Siany Spotlight	**Jashun: A Hero's Return**	**Jam Pies: Best Recipes**
The juiciest gossip	*A tribute*	*Baker Nicht spills*
Princess Siany was spotted giving dirty glares to the queen.	I was his first encounter back.	Become as good as Baker Nicht with her secrets.
Interview with Witness	I share my full experience	Who from the royal family loves strawberry?
Page 3	Page 4	Page 7

CHAPTER 4
A LONG CHAPTER

After hours of hearing both from the angry prosecution and the emotionless defendants, Queen Sealyn deferred her decision to her outside choice, Princess Kailani. She watched as her former friend's eyes filled with tears. Sealyn knew Pyry had been depending on their friendship to be the deciding factor for her outcome. Now, she lost all power over the punishment. Pyry looked frail, and her thin brown hair was in tangles, yet she still held her head high like a lady.

Kailani stood in front of Pyry and her father, her deep blue gown spilling over the stone floor. "I have discussed this matter among my court, and we have come to a unanimous decision. A kingdom can only flourish with loyal citizens. You," she pointed at Pyry. "Jeopardized your entire population, and for what? Vengeance for a traitor? Your husband was sick with your curse. You should have stood up to him and cast him to Reformation Rock so he could have received the help he needed, but you were too prideful. You blamed Queen Sealyn for your troubles. You blame everyone else but yourself."

Jashun shivered at Kailani's force, and he liked it. He wasn't sure Pyry needed another scolding after being imprisoned for three months, though; he knew what it felt like to be caged. He suddenly felt the waves knocking against the ship. He closed his eyes and felt the nausea coming. Char hiccupped, causing Jashun's memory terror to fade. Jashun said a silent prayer for his trapped comrades.

Kailani turned her focus on Pyry's father, a frail, old man. "Yet, when a child makes a mistake, especially one this grand, one can't help but turn to the parents' tutelage. You claim full responsibility, and while the prosecution says it should be Pyry completely at fault, I disagree."

Gasps were heard around the room. Did this mean she would let Pyry go free? Sealyn shifted uncomfortably on her throne, knuckles whitening from gripping the throne's arm. She was ready for this to be over. She was tired of talking about her friend's betrayal. She wanted to move on—especially because she wanted to hear Jashun's story.

"You had a choice to carry out Pyry's plan or not. Without your small army, none of the poisonings and kidnappings would have happened. If you had said no, then all Pyry would have done was sulk in her banishment, still living a life of luxury. Here is my conviction," Kailani walked in a circle for dramatic effect. She paused when she saw Jashun and winked. She turned back and faced them. "Lady Pyry, you will be banished to Reformation Rock and be evaluated every year by Faith Commissioner Herb. When he deems you are reformed, then you will work in a shop, mending clothes in hopes you will learn how to mend your relationships with others."

The crowded room clapped and cheered. Faith Commissioner Herb nodded to Sealyn. He let his brown-skinned expression give Sealyn reassurance that he would provide her friend with guidance and growth in hopes that one day she would return with forgiveness in her heart. Pyry glowered at Sealyn, then at Kailani.

Kailani turned her attention to Pyry's father, who had fury written in his green eyes. "You will drink the same poison forced on Lord Temm, and no help will be given. As it was written long ago, 'The code we live and die by is how we treat others.'"

Pyry screamed out, "No!" Pyry's mother began to wail, and the guilty daughter lunged into her father's chest, crying. Betrayal stings, and jealousy murders relationships.

Kailani, pleased with her verdict, sat back in her seat. Char leaned over to Jashun and whispered, "Your woman doesn't play around. She will make a strong ally."

"Ally?" questioned Jashun. "I thought the Mer Clans were enemies to Elysium, which was another reason I was so shocked to see her here."

"Yes, but why else do you think she was chosen? Sealyn wants to make allies with the Mer Clans. They've kept to themselves since King Perdon, but Sealyn has her reasons for this," Char leaned back in his chair. "You know my cousin—she always has a backup plan."

"But a backup to what?"

Char's eyes glazed over, remembering the charging Arkootha bear. "That's forever the question."

Sealyn waited until the guards escorted the prisoners out, then excused everyone from the throne room. Her sister, Siany, was first to her side. Siany knew hearing that verdict was difficult for Sealyn. Pyry and Sealyn had been inseparable for years, but jealousy over Sealyn's rise in rank and her growing beauty pulled threads loose from their friendship. Pyry also never forgave Sealyn for being Drystan's first choice over her, but Sealyn never wanted Drystan. He funneled that rage into trying to kill Jace, only to meet his own death.

Siany placed her hand on her sister's shoulder. "Sealyn, are you well?"

Sealyn smooshed her lips together like she always did when trying to hold back tears. "Maybe not today, but ask me again tomorrow." Sealyn walked over to the Mer-people. They rose and bowed. "Thank you for joining us today and for choosing the verdict on my behalf."

"The honor is mine, majesty," Kailani said with a crooked smile.

"I hope you all will stay for refreshment," Sealyn pointed toward the servants, bringing trays of sparkling gold liquid. "I will have to excuse myself to debrief Lord Jashun."

"May I join you?" Kailani's pink eyes dazzled with mischief.

Sealyn hesitated. She wasn't naïve and saw the tension between Jashun and Kailani. The stakes were high between Elysium and the Mer Clans. Should she risk it? "Are you sure, princess? It could be boring."

"I want to know all that happens on our seas. Shouldn't we share this information if we are to be allies?"

Sealyn recognized the bait but decided to take it anyway and nodded. "Father, please escort Mer Clan Kaiana to Cove Rock Lighthouse so they can participate in Lord Jashun's debriefing."

King Father Ryker stilled. Cove Rock Lighthouse had a secret, a significant and limited-to-who-knew secret. "Queen Sealyn, just to clarify, you said Cove Rock Lighthouse?"

"Correct."

Ryker heard his daughter's tone. She had a hidden agenda. He would have to trust her judgment. He extended his arm to the princess, and together, their parties left the throne room and climbed into their royal carriages.

Jace offered his arm to Sealyn. She looked into his swirling grey eyes. "I will forever accept your arm, Just Jace, but first, I have a feeling we need to save Jashun." They turned to look behind the thrones in the back corner. They saw Brenna, Lulana, Adalina, and Jadelyn speed-walking toward the three lords.

"That doesn't look good," Jace remarked.

Brenna was the first to speak. "Jashun! I've been so worried about you. I'm so excited you've returned. I feel so overjoyed!"

Jashun's face turned red, and he felt nauseated again. He peeled himself from his chair and embraced her. "It's good to see you too, Lady Brenna." Char and Sakul sat huddled together, watching the scene unfold with big, goofy grins across their faces.

"Well, aren't you going to kiss your beloved, Jashun?" Adalina said with a bitter tone. Jadelyn covered her mouth, tittering.

Brenna looked confused and hurt by Jashun's hesitation and stumbling of words. "Jashun? It's been almost a year. Do you not want to kiss me? Did you even miss me? Are you repulsed? How can you not care?"

Jashun began to sweat. Char jumped up and threw his arm around Jashun's shoulders. "Easy, Brenna. The chap probably forgot how to kiss. He just needs the right liquid courage," Char slipped a small bottle into Jashun's hands.

Sealyn approached. "Lord Jashun, I need you to come with me, and anyone you've disclosed information about your time away to needs to come as well. We are already preparing for a rescue mission, so your story is vital to the success of our mission."

Jashun nodded. "I've only spoken details to Char and Sakul." The last thing Jashun wanted was Adalina tagging along with them, judging him the entire journey.

"Very well," Sealyn said. "And Jashun, I know it's been a while, but remember, never take advice from Char."

Char gasped and fell back dramatically, acting like he was hit with an arrow. "Says the woman who told us to charge an Arkootha bear, then had us sealed up in an ice tunnel staring at frozen mammoths."

"And yet, you're still alive," Sealyn jeered.

They walked away from the ladies. Jashun looked back only to have his heart shatter. He saw Brenna sobbing into Lulana's large chest. Stroking her back, Adalina whispered comforting insults about Jashun, and Jadelyn stood cross-armed, smiling at Jashun. His head was spinning. He looked forward, took a long sip of Char's small bottle, and coughed. What an extraordinary day he had had.

Once Sealyn's caravan of carriages arrived at Cove Rock Lighthouse, they all exited with confusion. None of them, including Jace and Char, had ever been to Cove Rock Lighthouse. It seemed unremarkable and run down. Its top had broken windows and faded green paint. The rest of the lighthouse was off-white. Storms had had their way with this structure, so why did Sealyn want to come here? Char looked disgusted.

"Sealyn, no offense, but you should speak with the diplomat of Seanove to fix up this junky, old lighthouse. I feel like I'm going to catch a disease if I walk in there."

Sealyn sighed. "Oh, Char. You have such little faith."

Sealyn walked to the broken stone bridge. Char reluctantly followed. He looked across the massive crashing waves below. How were they supposed to get across a broken bridge to a junky lighthouse? Had Sealyn lost her mind? He heard Sealyn whisper an ancient language as she touched one of the broken stone railings, then she stepped closer and vanished.

"Sealyn!" Jace yelled.

But all the group heard was Sealyn's laugh. "Care to trust your queen today? Step through."

They followed one by one, and to their surprise, they saw the most miraculous fortress built around a perfect lighthouse. They carefully stepped onto the arched stone bridge that was only wide enough for two people to walk side by side.

Jace slid his fingers into Sealyn's. "Love, this is incredible. How? How is this possible?"

"A lot of the records are lost, so there are conflicting theories, but most agree that an ancient enchantress cloaked this section of Port Rowin from any harm. The theories conflict on when she lived and died."

When they crossed the bridge, they were welcomed to another small community. The soldiers here had to live and remain in this section with their families. Schools, shops, hospitals, farms, and homes all existed inside the cloaked barrier. The streets were paved with jade stones, and all the buildings were white marble. The fortress had an outer layer of seashells mixed with limestone onto the massive stones.

"This place is beautiful," Jace marveled. "I could see myself staying here for extended periods of time."

"Without your wife?" Sealyn jokingly questioned.

"Never without her."

Char made a vomiting sound. "If you two are done, I'd like to get this over with. I'm missing the best part of the trial celebrations."

The group continued into the great hall of Cove Rock Lighthouse. This marble building housed the royals and had a small receiving throne room and a large dining hall. Jashun felt himself growing nervous. He would have to relive every painful, scary moment he encountered since he left Sealyn's presence all those many months ago. Should he tell them about the Pirate Captain? What if he saved that information for a private audience with Sealyn and Jace? He wasn't sure what was going to come out of his mouth.

A large seafood combination of shrimp, giant crab legs, clams, mussels, potatoes, and corn with delicious spices was organized down the center of the long marble table, with cups of seaweed at each person's place. Sakul's green eyes bulged. He normally would be singing high praises of the food, but his heart felt low. He felt guilty for wishing Sorcha had escaped, not Jashun. He was happy Jashun was safe, but he deeply missed the one girl he dreamed about.

Once the group had a few minutes of eating the scrumptious food, Sealyn felt it was right to begin the debriefing. She was tired of waiting for answers. During the trial, she felt her anxiety grow, willing it to be over so she could hear Jashun's story. Inspector Caelimont sat to her left. He had helped tremendously with discovering Lady Pyry's betrayal, so Sealyn thought it best for him to listen to Jashun's story. Caelimont was a tall, slender man with hair starting to thin, and he wore tiny spectacles.

Sealyn leaned close to him. "Are you ready for this?"

"Yes, Your Majesty."

"Watch his eyes and other mannerisms. We can't miss anything."

"Absolutely, Your Majesty."

Sealyn clapped her hands and gained the table's attention. She looked at Jashun, who sat opposite her at the table's far end. Caelimont rose from his seat and walked to a wall position near Jashun. He wanted to have the best view in the room. He leaned back on the cool marble and began his silent interrogation.

"As a reminder," Sealyn began. "This is a debriefing, which means please refrain from any emotional outbursts during the recanting. Allow Jashun proper time to tell each part. If you are confused and feel the question will aid our kingdom in some way, then yes, feel free to ask your question, but do not disrupt. We will escort you out if anyone takes this debriefing down an emotional path." Sealyn stared into Sakul's green eyes. Her eyes told him he needed to control his emotions about Sorcha.

Char swallowed his wine and folded his arms. This retelling would not be easy. Would Jashun leave anything out? Could he be trusted? How was he the only one to escape?

"Please, Jashun, begin," Sealyn said.

Jashun squirmed and felt his mouth go dry. He looked to his left at Char and then turned his head to the right at the beautiful mermaid goddess. How was he supposed to find the strength to do this? He noticed the way the inspector was glaring at him. Did he suspect foul play? Why did Sealyn invite him here? Did she not trust him?

Jashun cleared his throat. "Thank you, Queen Sealyn. My story is not of valor or bravery. It's of pain and death. None of this news brings me any pleasure." Jashun continued with as many details as he could. His telling of Rivers' death brought tears to several eyes. Jace shivered at the mention of the frozen army of the catacombs. Len Nove's queen, holding a spear to his neck, was seared into his memory.

Sealyn's eyes narrowed when Jashun spoke about the Pirate Captain. She looked at Caelimont, who lifted his eyebrow at her. She knew something was off about this part of Jashun's story, but whether it was a "good off" or "bad off," she didn't know yet. She also noted that Jashun couldn't make eye contact with her when he spoke about the Pirate Captain. She saw his glances at Jace, looking down and up. His breathing was rapid, too.

Sakul started crying when Jashun told how they were captured and imprisoned on the Stoltland ship. Something bothered him about how Sune kept "being there" for Sorcha. He had to be careful of jealousy.

Jashun saw how eager the royal family was to hear about Ezen. He wiped his face nervously, pausing mid-sentence, and tried to regain the courage he needed to finish the story. He saw how scared everyone was for him to continue. He didn't know if he could, then he felt the gentle touch of Kailani's hand on his. Jashun looked deep into her bright pink eyes. She was giving him her strength, so he continued forward.

Sealyn stood with such force her chair flew backward and crashed. "What did you just say to me?"

Jashun's mouth opened and closed like a fish breathing for water.

Jace stood beside Sealyn and wrapped his arm around her as tears flowed from the royal family. "Jashun," Sealyn spoke hoarsely. "Are you really telling me that you've been here this entire time with the information that my cousin is dead, and you said nothing?"

Queen Mother Graelynd escorted Princess Siany and Lady Novaly outside. They couldn't take hearing anymore. Prince Royce and Prince Adomin looked at King Father Ryker. Prince Adomin mouthed, "How do we tell our brother about his son?" Ryker just shook his head.

Lord Favien swallowed. He knew interjecting himself into royal family matters was dangerous, but he scratched his brown beard and readied himself. "Queen Sealyn, forgive me if this is insensitive, but I don't think Jashun has had a moment even to tell anyone about this news. He's been through a lot." Favien paused and lifted his hands when he saw Sealyn's scowl. "I mean, we all have been through a lot, so I think emotions are high."

Although not blood-related to Ezen, Char was also a cousin to Sealyn, so he thought his voice could help. "I must agree with Lord Favien, dear cousin. Jashun needs to finish his story, and then we can be done with the debriefing."

Sealyn didn't want to finish the debriefing. What was the point? Her cousin was dead, exactly how Queen Corentine wanted. Rivers was dead, precisely what Corentine wanted. Temm and Stawyer dead; again, just how Corentine wanted. And then, all the NexGen Nichts dead; specifically, how Corentine designed. She was tired of Corentine winning. Stoltland had to pay.

Jace blinked and noticed the room had a faint green haze. This couldn't be right. Elysium's curse was broken. Why would the haze return? He quickly looked at Sealyn's eyes. They were glowing green. She was being tempted, but by what?

He grazed her ear with his lips and whispered, "My love, come back to me. There's no need to go down this path."

Sealyn's spine shivered at the warm breath from her love. She looked at Jace, confused, then noticed the haze. Was she struggling with envy? Over what? She paused and settled her mind, forcing the haze to dissipate. She would face what occurred later, but Jashun had to finish the debriefing for now.

"Finish, Jashun."

Jashun lowered his head. As he spoke, he felt the phantom pain of the stab to his side and the taste of the salty sea. He glanced at Kailani, wondering if he should tell their story. She tilted her head, warning him not to. He forced himself to lie. Eyes gazing up, Jashun spoke his final words of the story. "I found some driftwood and luckily ended up in a fast current taking me to Port Rowin, where I ran into Adalina, and she gave me food and clothes."

Sealyn frowned. "Lucky you. Thank you, Jashun." She took her seat. "That will conclude the debriefing. Everyone except Lord Jashun, Inspector Caelimont, King Jace, and Princess Kailani will remain behind."

Even King Father Ryker looked stunned. As he was leaving, he bent down and whispered to Sealyn, "Is everything all right?"

"It will be. I need you to take care of our grieving family right now."

Once the doors closed, an awkward silence fell across the room. Kailani looked at Jashun, then to Sealyn. "Queen Sealyn, why have I been asked to stay behind?"

"Because you and Jashun obviously have more to share and perhaps needed privacy to do so. Jashun should be dead from that stab." Caelimont nodded in agreeance.

Kailani's cheeks turned pink behind her sparkles. "Good observation. I was the one who rescued Jashun. I also healed his wound with one of my scales."

Jace huffed. "I knew that stab was a fatal one. Jashun, why didn't you tell us?"

"I honestly didn't know if Kailani, or I mean Princess Kailani, needed that story out. I didn't even know who she was. A story like that might ruin her reputation."

"Reputation?" Sealyn questioned.

Kailani snickered. "Yes, Jashun's a good kisser."

"What? Don't say that!" Jashun protested. "You weren't supposed to tell."

Jace sucked his teeth. "So, you rescue and save him, and then what; have a make-out session in the water, then toss him ashore?"

"Something like that," Kailani cooed.

"It was basically--exactly like that," Jashun said.

Sealyn gripped her fork so tight that it broke into pieces. "I don't care what dalliances either of you have had in the sea. What I do care about is information being withheld. A debriefing is about honesty."

"But I only withheld that to protect Kailani."

"And the withheld information during your encounter with the Pirate Captain, who were you protecting then?" Caelimont questioned sternly.

Jashun froze, and his body went cold. How did he know that? He stuttered, not knowing what to say next. He would have no choice but to tell the truth in front of Kailani if he wanted to remain free. He cleared his throat. "I was hoping to gain time alone with Jace, King Jace, to discuss the matter."

"Spit. It. Out, Jashun," Sealyn ordered.

He dropped his head in submission. "He wanted information he didn't know about the Elysian throne. Doebromir tried the tactic of telling him of your new reign, Queen Sealyn, but he already knew that. He said, 'Everyone knows about Sealyn, the third-generation bloodline, taking the throne. Even the deepest sea creatures speak about this,' which prompted his men to advance to kill us." Jashun's voice started cracking. "So, I did the only thing I could think to save us. I told him about King Jace."

"What about me?"

"I told him that we had a new king--a new king from Stoltland, but it wasn't until I told him that you were Queen Corentine's illegitimate son that he dropped his weapon."

Kailani laughed a brattish laugh. "Looks like your choice of mate keeps being a problem for you, Sealyn."

"Bite your tongue, fish. Never speak that way about our king, my husband, again, or you'll find yourself rotting in a dungeon or on a troll's plate."

Kailani smiled and nodded. She wasn't offended. She found herself liking Sealyn more and more. Her tenacity just might be what her clan has been waiting for.

Caelimont scribbled a note and slid it to Sealyn. She read it and nodded to the investigator. "I'm going to ask everyone except Jashun to leave. Please join the others for drinks in the main hall. I'm sure my family has already left for the palace.

Jace closed the door with a final glance at Sealyn, then at Jashun. Sealyn stood and then took the seat next to Jashun. "You're leaving out one final piece of the story."

Tears filled Jashun's eyes. He finally understood why Sune was so irritated with him.

"Tell me how the conversation concluded with the Pirate Captain."

Jashun wiped his nose and let the tears fall. He was finally ready to accept his part in betraying Jace. "The captain walked past but stopped and asked, 'The grey-eyed child, correct?'"

Sealyn shook her head. "And you said yes."

Jashun coughed out, "Yes, Your Majesty," in a rush of tears.

Sealyn leaned back in her chair and folded her arms. She closed her eyes and said, "I wonder what game he's playing?"

Jashun was stunned at the lack of formality Sealyn spoke after he just confessed to betraying the king. "What?" Jashun asked.

"What you don't know is that the Pirate Captain sent word via my cousin, Will, that he wants to help us rescue our prisoners. He knows the route and knows where they're being taken. He only requests that I bring King Jace with me to meet him."

"Why would he request that?"

"Why indeed, my friend."

"Friend?"

"Yes, Jashun. After all that has happened, you are still my friend. You are still Jace's friend. I understand why you didn't tell us about making waves with Kailani." She smirked and paused for her pun to sink in. "And I understand why you preferred a private audience to tell me the rest of the story. I know the Pirate Captain's reputation, so your words did save your crew, but a dangerous man knows scandalous details about our king, and for some reason, that caught his attention."

"Whatever you need me to do, Sealyn, I'll do."

"Glad to hear you say that." Sealyn stood and walked to the window, gazing out to the emerald sea. "I think I have the perfect quest for you, but it must be entirely secret."

With his joints still aching, Jashun quickly knelt before Sealyn, trying to show how important making up for his betrayal meant to him. "Name it."

Sealyn slightly nodded with a hint of a smile. What Jashun didn't know was that Sealyn had this mission planned all along; she didn't know who would be the one for the task, though. "Did you know that the curses did *not* affect any of the sea creatures?"

Jashun was baffled. "How is that possible?"

Sealyn shrugged. "No one knows, but I bet your pretty new girlfriend does."

"She's not my…"

"I'm teasing, Jashun, but it seems that she has taken to you. Please stand," She motioned for him to look out the window. "You see that rickety shack over there? The one on the massive rock with the large waves pounding below it?"

"I do."

"I'll be blunt with you. There's sea magic there."

"Sea magic?"

"Yes, their people call it Abyss magic. Nothing can penetrate it. That shack is thousands of years old, and no storm or beast has been able to destroy it. I need that magic."

"Why can't you just ask for it?" The room felt off, and Jashun could sense words not spoken by Sealyn. She was hiding something.

Sealyn folded her arms against her sparkling green dress and shook her head. "It doesn't work that way with the Mer Clans. They orchestrate hand for a hand, tooth for a tooth deals. They will want something major in return. I want you to find out what they would demand from me to strike that deal."

"How am I ever going to find out something like that?"

"Pillow talk?" Sealyn laughed. "Sorry, I know that was lame."

Jashun chuckled lightly. "Sea, I'm speaking as your old friend. I'm truly sorry about Ezen and, well, just everything."

Sealyn dropped her head. She felt like she was twelve years old again, meeting Jashun for the first time. Her father introduced her to Jashun as a new pupil to Commander Elmond's young-generation soldier program. Sealyn remembered how clumsy Jashun was. She took pity on him as others giggled about his poor footwork, but Jashun had a sense of humor that immediately Sealyn liked. She vowed to protect and befriend him.

Now, she looked at her friend, who needed another chance—again. Because of their history, she would give that to him. Sealyn wanted to move forward and begin her other mission.

"I understand, Jashun," she hugged him. "We need grace and trust in this life; I believe this is how we will be victorious in our quests."

CHAPTER 5
SISTER VS SISTER

Princess Siany sat cozy in her sitting chambers, reviewing several scrolls. Her brown hair was braided to one side with a green ribbon. Siany had been doing extra sword training, which was showing through her defined muscular arms. Her two tabby cats, Sid and Tid, curled around her feet, hoping for scratches. Today was not going well for Siany. Her no longer being queen was eating at her. She enjoyed ruling over Avondelle, but not for power. She felt a true purpose, a calling. During her time as queen, she was able to do more for her people than ever. Now, her sister was back in charge.

She crumbled a scroll and threw it across the room, disturbing her cats. She didn't want to feel this way, but she didn't want to become irrelevant either. Where would she find her place? What kind of influence could she have? Could she control these feelings of jealousy, or would they overpower her Elysian blood?

Novaly burst through Siany's door with a crystal vase filled with orange tulips. "Oh, Princess Siany," Novaly sang. "I bring you the most glorious flowers from an admirer." Novaly had her bright red hair in two braids, always adorned with the season's flowers, as well as a seasonal flower crown.

"You know, everyone else knocks before entering," Siany said, folding her arms in her sleeveless brown dress. "All except you. I wonder why that is."

Novaly gently set the tulips on a table and stepped back to gush over them. "Well, I suppose if I did knock, then you wouldn't know it was me."

"I'm guessing I would after you announced yourself," Siany tried not to laugh.

"Oh, right, but this way is so much more fun! Did you see? Look how beautiful these tulips are. They came with a note, too." Novaly shook the scroll, which bore the Hill Chimes seal.

"Ugh. Give me that." Siany snatched the note, pretending to be annoyed, but she was anything but. She liked Novaly's energy and loved how interested she was in her life. Novaly was a true friend to her.

Siany carefully opened the seal and read the letter.

My Dearest Princess Siany,

I hope this letter finds you in good spirits, but if not, I hope it can lift them. I am writing to you not only to say that I haven't stopped thinking about you since the Trundatta ball but also because we are coming to Avondelle! I believe all diplomats are coming, and I would be most appreciative if you would do me the honor of having a private dinner with me in your gardens.

We should be arriving by the end of the week through the new Elysian internal Tor. It will be my first time traveling through, so as you can imagine, I'm very excited and nervous. Your cheery Madam Bip has been here all week, showing us how to use it.

Please do give my request careful consideration. I hope to see you soon.

Affectionately,

Lord Saemeon Berg, Second Diplomat of Hill Chimes

Novaly let out a squeal. "A private dinner with Lord Saemeon! How excited are you, Siany?"

Siany blinked. "I think I'm more shocked than excited."

"Why?"

"He said all diplomats are coming."

"So?"

"This makes it a business trip, not a romantic gesture. I'm an add-on."

Pouting, Novaly crossed her arms and sat in the velvet chair across from Siany. "Why are you spoiling this?"

"I'm not spoiling anything. It's my job to be very aware of everything going on in my kingdom."

"Your kingdom? Siany, you're not queen anymore. You don't have those responsibilities now."

Siany stood with force. "Excellent, Novaly. I'm glad you see that I have nothing to do, and protecting our people doesn't fall under my title."

Novaly hesitated. She didn't realize Siany had been hurting from stepping down, and she needed to tread lightly around this subject. She offered a sweet smile. "No, majesty," she bowed her head. "I meant you get to enjoy your time without the queen's burdens."

"Like what?"

"Liiiiike," Novaly stood, grabbed Siany's hands, and twirled her around. "Dancing with a lord and diplomat under the stars."

Siany laughed. Maybe there was an upside to not being queen, but she still felt a pull to find a place in this kingdom to do more than before. And she knew the right people to discuss these thoughts.

"By the way, Siany, what did Saemeon mean about an internal Tor?"

The two stopped twirling, trying to balance from the spinning room. "Oh, did I not tell you?" Novaly shook her head, irritated. "My apologies. Madam Bip has been studying the kingdom Tors, and she conjured a similar spell but not quite the same."

"Not the same, how?"

"She said that the old magic used to create the kingdom Tors had to add another element because they survived the curses. Remember seeing the Stoltland-Elysium Tor? That massive tree survived dragon fire. The kingdom Tors can also reach larger distances, obviously. Our Tors are only within Elysium's borders and limited in number for now."

"Is that how you and your family returned from Port Rowin so fast? It took our group days to return."

Siany nodded. "Exactly. Port Rowin's Tor is located at the protected lighthouse village."

"Could we go?"

"Right now?" Siany asked.

"Why not?"

"Because I've only had a few days here from our time in Port Rowin, and my family is in the middle of planning my cousin's memorial. You have noticed my brown dress?" Elysians wore brown for mourning. It was the one color that all classes, high and low, could afford since death takes all.

Novaly bowed her head. "Siany, I'm so sorry. Please accept my apology. With all the Saemeon excitement, I didn't even ask how you and your family are coping."

"It's fine. We're fine. Everything's fine," Siany said, feeling tears prick her green eyes and a lump form in her throat. "I-I just…" As she dropped to the floor, tears spilled down her freckled cheeks, and she covered her face with her hands. Novaly stooped quickly and wrapped her arms around her friend.

A knock sounded at the door, and with Novaly's permission to enter, Queen Mother Graelynd swept across the floor and gracefully knelt beside her grieving daughter, wishing she could take her pain away. "Siany, darling, I came to tell you that your sister's caravan has returned. Sealyn is asking for you," She wiped her daughter's wet cheeks. "Now, tell me how I can help these tears of yours."

Siany shook her head. "Everything is rotten, mother. I have no position here anymore. I'm nothing to my kingdom, and our cousin is dead."

"My brave daughter, you have more value than you'll ever know. Just because you do not possess the reining crown does not mean you are less. The world knows you can rule furiously. You were the one to fight against Corentine and her dragons. You saved Avondelle from being destroyed. Your worth does not come from position. It comes from your heart. Tell me, what does your heart desire?"

Siany wiped her nose and stared into her mother's green eyes. "The children."

"I thought so. What about them?" Graelynd smiled.

"We need to do more for them."

Graelynd stood, helping lift her daughter up, while Novaly clung to Siany's arm. "I think you will find what your queen wants to discuss with you most intriguing."

"Why would *she* need to discuss anything with me?"

Graelynd gasped. "Siany! You sound bitter and, and…I dare not say it. Careful of your words. They give away what truly resides in your heart." Graelynd motioned for the door. "Now, go. Do not keep her waiting any longer."

Sealyn had already changed into her brown mourning outfit: a fitted corset top and pants with a detachable skirt. She was pouring over maps and documents from scouts in the war room with her War Council and high-ranking military officers. Hints of another battle loomed in the air. King Father Ryker was standing aside with Prince Royce and Prince Adomin finalizing the memorial details while Favien argued with Jem over where the next skirmish would take place.

"Why are you even here, Jem? You're not on the War Council!" Favien yelled.

Jem's red eyes flared, and he slammed his fist down on the stone table. "I'm here at the queen's request. I'm on your side, Favien."

"Easy, gentlemen," Jace tried to calm the tension. "We need to hear all possibilities and work together as a unit."

The doors swung open, and Siany walked in unannounced. "Well, sister. You called for me, and I'm here." The room went silent. Even King Father Ryker did not address Sealyn so informally in front of others. Sealyn leaned back from the table and bit her lip. She had to resist the temptation to reprimand her sister in front of the council.

"Council members, will you kindly leave us? I need a private word with Princess Siany."

Ryker walked to Siany, leaned in, and whispered, "You need to watch your tone. This behavior is unacceptable." He continued out the door, pained that his daughters were potentially at odds with one another.

After the last person left, Siany whirled around and faced her sister. "I'm waiting, Sealyn. What do you so urgently need to speak with me about when our cousin is dead?"

Sealyn reached for the crystal pitcher filled with the sparkling purple liquid of PurFizz and poured her another glass. She was going to need all the energy this drink could give.

Siany noticed the PurFizz. Was Madam Bip here? Had she already returned from Hill Chimes?

Sealyn swallowed. "Listen, Siany. I know right now we all are grieving, and when we're in pain, sometimes we can speak out of hurt instead of smarts."

"Is that your poetic way of saying I'm stupid?"

"Seriously, Siany? What is your problem?"

Siany clapped. "There she is--my younger sister."

"That's what you want? A little sister-big sister fight?"

Siany stomped to the round, stone table. "No! I want to matter!" She pointed at the maps and documents spread across the table. "I want to be a part of what's happening. I need purpose, and *your* returning took that from me."

Sealyn slightly nodded, trying to calm the rage forming inside her. "I see. Well, I apologize that my survival has gotten in the way of your reign, but…" Sealyn rose from her seated position and began walking toward Siany. "May I remind you that it was you who turned down the crown when it was first offered to you by our parents? You were the one who didn't want the burden, so you tossed it to me. I picked up the load. The people needed someone with the guts to do what is needed." Sealyn stood nose to nose with her sister. "Now, would you and your ego be so kind as to allow me the privilege of telling you what I called you in here for in the first place?"

Siany smiled and curtsied. "No, majesty. My ego and I have other things to do with our time, like planning our cousin's memorial. I bid you good day." Siany turned and walked out, not closing the door.

Jace immediately came back into the war room. "That must not have gone well?"

"No, it didn't."

"Did you at least get to tell her about your idea?"

"No. The crazy thing just walked out before I could," Sealyn said, throwing her hands in the air. "She's lost."

"But your idea can help her find her way."

Sealyn massaged her temples. "I know that, but she doesn't want to hear anything from me." She froze, then clapped her hands. "I know exactly who she will listen to, though, and I'm sure those two are up for plotting."

"Sealyn," Jace folded his muscular arms. "What are you scheming?"

"Scheming? Don't you trust me, Just Jace?" She shot a flirtatious smile at her husband, who melted.

Elysian News

The Latest News and Gossip

Issue #6

Royal Grands: What they do now.

A Tribute

Greetings, my fellow Elysians. It's me, your favorite little gossip, here to spill all the juicy details about our beloved Grand Royals. Today, I will share all the responsibilities a Grand Queen and Grand Lady have.

Painted above: Grand Queen Karis and Lady Ebbalee

According to an inside-the-palace source, Grand Queen Karis and Lady Ebbalee have breakfast almost every morning with Queen Sealyn. Queen Sealyn likes to hear their opinions on certain matters. Do you think this is right?

Grand Queen Karis helps run a food collection for those who have fallen on hard times. Her son, Prince Toven, also serves on this charity. She selflessly donates her time to sewing clothes for the needy and sponsors a family per year in need.

Lady Ebbalee hosts a charity gathering for the elderly that includes painting classes. She also volunteers at the new hospital with her son, Lord Menry.

During their times of rest, they are usually found in either the music room, listening to the harpist while reading, or on good weather days, sitting on the benches in the gardens.

It needs to be said that these were also the first women of their ages to channel power. Apparently, their Tethered Luxen magic isn't very strong, but that's most likely due to age, says a close family source.

We must give credit. These royal women work hard and deserve recognition for their efforts.
~Lady Adalina Roedellen (Lina)

Princess Siany Spotlight	**Lord Char's Ale Tour**	**Potions and Madam Bip**
The juiciest gossip	*Includes map details*	*New Potion*
A loud argument between Queen Sealyn and Princess Siany	It's finally back! The ale tour that was missed the past 2 years.	Want to grow snow? Madam Bip says she found the way.
Can they recover?	Char says no to Queen's quest.	Full recipe included
Page 2	Page 4	Page 6

CHAPTER 6
FIRST HEADMISTRESS

The gold-plated carriage bounced over rocks and holes along the shaded dirt trail. The trees were still green, and purple and yellow wildflowers bloomed alongside the road. Relaxing aromas of the forests filled their noses as they approached a large, grey-stoned entrance with a golden gate. Two phoenix statues sat atop on either side. White fireflower vines draped over the stone walls, helping illuminate a ratty, old sign.

Princess Siany was still sleepy and couldn't believe she had agreed to go on an early morning carriage ride with her grandparents, Grand Queen Karis and Lady Ebbalee. Once the carriage stopped, she leaned her head out and squinted at the faded sign. "Bracken Castle. What castle is this?"

"For all the lands' sakes. What are they teaching royals these days?" Lady Ebbalee jeered.

"Grandma…"

Grand Queen Karis chuckled. "This castle is very old. It dates back even before the Second Chance. The royals used it as a… well…um," Karis stuttered through her words, finding it hard to explain.

"Oh, Karis, don't worry about Siany's delicacy," Ebbalee said. "My dear, they used this castle as a living graveyard."

"A what?!"

"Like I said, a living graveyard. I don't think I could have said it any more clearly."

"Ebbalee, I don't think she questioned you because she didn't hear your words," Karis grabbed Siany's hand and patted it. "She's merely in shock and can't comprehend the definition."

"Oh, well, why didn't you just ask that then?"

Siany's head was spinning. She desperately needed breakfast to deal with these two, but also to understand what living graveyards meant. And why did her grandmothers bring her here?

Karis shook her head, white curls bouncing slightly. "Let me explain," Karis cleared her throat. "Before the Second Chance occurred, magic flowed freely and powerfully. There were those who liked to experiment with land magic and sea magic."

"Wait. I remember something about sea magic. It has a specific name, but I can't think of it."

Ebbalee laughed. "Abyss, darling girl. Honestly, I thought you were the smart one between you and Sealyn."

"Ebbalee! If Sealyn was here…"

"She would laugh and say something smart back, and you know it."

Siany sighed and dreamed of eggs and toast. "Can we please focus?"

The sound of scraping metal caught their attention. Siany stuck her head out and saw the driver pulling the gates open. Were they really going to visit this creepy castle? Were the dead still there? She swallowed hard. Her mouth felt dry, and then they were moving forward. Her stomach dropped. "I need to know what we're doing here."

Karis smiled kindly. "Well, let me continue. Certain elders experimented with the land and sea magic enough that they were able to create a space where you would never die." Siany's mouth fell open. "It was a place where if you emerge on the verge of death, then your loved ones could decide to take you to the castle instead of passing on to the afterlife."

Ebbalee folded her arms and huffed. "But it soon became a place to send the frail and past their prime. If you were too old and weak to fight or take care of yourself, then you would be taken here."

Siany stared out the window in amazement, seeing the enormous castle for the first time. What a magnificent wonder this place was. Her breath caught when she saw another royal carriage. Who else was here? Were they leaving someone to stay at the castle? Is that why her grandmothers were with her? Were they going to be left behind? Was her sister banishing them because they were frail?

"What Ebbalee says is true," Karis continued. "There were rules with the magic. Family members could visit, but if you stayed too long, then you couldn't leave. You could only visit a certain number of times before the magic started to take effect. Exposure to that type of preservation magic would have the opposite reaction outside the barriers. It sped up the aging process."

Ebbalee fitted her purple shawl around her shoulders. It paired nicely with her pale green dress, trimmed with purple satin. "Yes. Yes. Some, who didn't want to be there, yet their families forced them to be, tried to escape, but because they had been exposed so long and were too old, they just burst into dust right outside the gate." Siany felt sick, knowing they had just rolled over that very spot. "Karis. Siany. You two may want to bundle up. I don't know if they would have gotten the fires going yet or not."

"They?" Siany scrunched her nose.

"Yes, you don't think we would walk into an ancient castle that sealed in old people without protection, do you?" Ebbalee huffed again. "Honestly, my girl. I'm worried about this big plan."

"Plan?" Siany stiffened.

"Hush, Ebbalee. It's not for us to tell."

The driver opened the door and helped the royals out. Siany stood in wonder. The castle looked to be three times the size of the Avondelle palace and was made of large grey stones. Towers were scattered all around without any order. Some of them were pointed with enclosed, green clay shingles—the Elysian clay of Blissendelle. Others had open decks with four to five sides, overlooking the vast lands. The large, wood doors burst open with a cheerful welcome from a familiar face.

"Well, if it isn't my grandson Char! I wasn't expecting you to be here," Ebbalee's face lit up.

"You know I couldn't miss this," he kissed Ebbalee's and Karis's hands. "My my, I have to speak this now; you two are the fairest grands in all the kingdoms." They blushed and giggled.

Siany rolled her eyes. "Char, what are you doing here? It's obvious that Sealyn sent you."

"You tell me since you're so smart."

"Oh, no darling, this one's not smart," Ebbalee added. "We found that out in the carriage ride."

Char laughed. "On that lovely and insightful note, why don't you three come inside? Don't worry, Siany, I checked for ghosts. There are only a few left." He laughed again and escorted the older ladies indoors.

A wide, centered staircase met them in the large entryway. The entryway wrapped around the corner, extending beyond Siany's gaze. The floors were white marble and shined. Siany looked up at the sparkling chandelier and saw more staircases. She could get lost here. White marble columns were spaced evenly, with emerald water fountains strategically placed to catch the sunlight from the tall windows.

"Right this way," Char led the group past the staircase to a pair of doors, which opened to the biggest eating area Siany had ever seen. Three long tables sat parallel to each other. The center one was filled with a glorious breakfast. She noticed the royal guard stationed around the room, and her father and Madam Bip were already seated at the table.

"Father?"

King Father Ryker stood, "Welcome, Siany. I hope the ride over was pleasant."

"Yes, of course, father, but why am I here? Why are you all here?"

"Let's sit down and have some delicious breakfast first."

They sat down, and the smells of cinnamon, bacon, and eggs filled the air. Siany's stomach growled. She dove into the food, allowing the sustenance to quench her hunger and fear of the castle.

Madam Bip broke the sounds of munching, "Princess Siany, we're all here today 'ta show you Queen Sealyn's vision." Siany tensed. So, this was a ploy. "As you know, our world now has magic wildly flowing 'tanks to Queen Sealyn unlocking it, but 'dis comes wit' consequences."

Siany tried to listen to the crackling fireplaces to stay calm, but it wasn't working. They all tricked her. She didn't want to hear Sealyn's plan. If Sealyn had caused consequences, then she should deal with them.

"The consequences are 'dat each human has 'de power to possess magic and wield it. Do you remember 'de 'tree types of Luxe magic?"

Siany remembered Madam Bip and her mother sitting in her room discussing all the types. She guessed that land magic must be called Luxe because everyone called Sealyn and Madilina "Luxens," and Madam Bip had referred to herself as a Luxen when she told her the types. She steadied her mind. Madam Bip said there were three types of Luxens: Tethered, which is what Bip was; Transference—which was what Madilina was; and Cognition—the most powerful. Siany quickly spat out, "Tethered, Transference, and Cognition."

"Correct," Bip clapped.

Ebbalee smacked the table. "Well, call me a rabbit's fanny. The girl does have some smarts."

Char choked on his juice, sending liquid out his nose. Siany smacked his arm.

"Mother…" Ryker scolded.

Madam Bip laughed her deep belly laugh, then continued. "Now, 'dat Siany has regurgitated de types of Luxens, let's move on. 'Dese powers can stay dormant for years or a lifetime. A person must accept 'de new magic, or else the process will never happen. We have already had several others show signs of being Tethereds and Transferences, and 'dey're scared, 'specially 'de children."

"Children?" Siany panicked.

Another door opened at the opposite end of where Siany had entered, and then Sealyn glided through the doorway. "Yes, the children. This is why I brought you here."

"You mean tricked."

"I prefer 'a guise with supervision from the chronologically-gifted,'" Sealyn winked at her grandparents.

"See, I told you she'd say something smart," Ebbalee crunched on her crispy bacon.

"Here's the big plan, Siany. I want you to run a school for Luxens. They're scared and need guidance."

"What could I possibly teach them? I'm not a Luxen."

"…Yet. You're not a Luxen yet. You have power within you, waiting for your acceptance. I believe it will happen sooner than later for you. In the meantime, you have the wisdom of books to guide our new generation of Luxens, including the adults. We will all need training and guidance. I have complete faith in you to take on this challenge."

"Wait, what are you saying?"

"I'm saying… you are the new and first Headmistress of the Luxen magic school. We can come up with a name for it later."

Siany didn't know what to say. Her sister believed in her and valued her. Sealyn saw greatness in her abilities. How could she have been so blind? How could she have been so petty? Siany burst into tears. Sobbing, she said, "I don't deserve this. Not after how I've treated you."

Sealyn walked over to Siany's gold chair. "We're sisters, and we have the same tenacity. Repentance is how we move forward. I apologize for letting my temper beat me, too. I should not have spoken to you the way I did, either. Are you ready to accept the task?"

Siany quickly stood, knocking the table and spilling juice onto Char's pants. "I am. I really am."

"Excellent. Madam Bip has all the books to start with. I believe Lady Adalina has a little spell to mass-produce books. Her news pamphlets are quite…"

"Be nice, Sealyn," Char teased, still patting dry his pants.

"Something. They're something. I really must be off. I wish I could stay longer, but I must prepare for the diplomats' arrival," Sealyn winked at Siany. Siany blushed. "I will see you all at dinner." She kissed her family's cheeks goodbye, then turned back before closing the door. "Oh, Siany, I believe the rose garden by the lion statue would be most romantic. Don't you agree?" She smirked and left.

Siany's cheeks were red. Novaly must have told her, but she could barely think about her date. She was now the Headmistress of a massive school for magic! Her spine went cold. She thought about the living graves lingering about. "What about the preservation spell?"

"Oh, 'dat. It broke after 'de Second Chance. The land magic was cursed, so you can't have infected magic keep its properties. I 'spec there may be some poor souls still a-wanderin' because Abyss magic is incredibly powerful, but I've scanned 'de place and didn't find any'ting."

Siany did *not* feel reassured. She had to learn how to teach controlling magic to magic wielders with possible spirits, or humans, or really old humans wandering around. But she smiled to herself. She had found her purpose.

CHAPTER 7
KISSED HIM BACK

Another painful blister formed as Doebromir scrubbed the splintering ship deck. He promised himself that he would never walk onto another ship *if* they survived. His bald head blistered welts from sunburn, and he was agonizingly dehydrated, but this was an easy torture compared to what they thought would happen to them. He looked across his shoulder and saw Sune still mending the nets. The two Elysian men had to switch days of net mending because of their blisters. Doebromir would rather scrub than mend nets.

Sune's curly red hair had grown along with his beard, but he still had his stunning looks and broad shoulders. The captivity was wearing on him, so he daydreamed about the possibility of courtship with Sorcha. He needed to think positively because all his other thoughts were of him tearing the Stoltlanders limb from limb. He dreamed about summer swims in Turtle Lake, autumn festivals and games, dancing with her at the legendary Trundatta ball, and finding peace among the spring flowers. He liked solitude and promised that one day he would give that back to himself. But first, he wanted to take Sorcha to his favorite pub and have their first private meal.

A scruffy Stoltlander walked by Sune, kicking a bucket of water over. The ratty sailor growled. "Why'd you do that, Pretty Boy? You know the penalty for prisoners being wasteful, don't you?"

"No, please. Sir, please don't," Sune begged.

"Sir? Address me as Lord, you Elysian scum."

Sune nodded frantically, "Yes, my lord or king. Whatever you prefer."

"Ha! King? Do you want my head to roll? I would never have someone address me as king—that's treason. Was that a sneaky ploy? Wanting me to die for treason? I think it was!"

"No. No. I just meant I'll call you whatever name you want, just please—please don't…"

The pirate turned and yelled to the back of the ship. "Bring her out! Time to teach a lesson."

Below deck in the kitchen, soldiers grabbed Sorcha. She kicked and screamed. She knew what was happening. Her mind couldn't take anymore. They brought her above deck, where she saw soldiers holding Sune and Doebromir; then she saw the net. Her stomach dropped, and she felt her body go hot, then cold. She felt faint. Sounds were muffled, except she could hear the waves, those terrifying waves.

She saw Sune yelling, but her mind was drifting. She must let it; otherwise, her mind wouldn't survive this voyage. The soldiers threw her into the net, and then instantaneously, she was hoisted up, and the beam swung around until she was dangling over the deep waters. She wanted to scream, but she didn't want to give them satisfaction. They had laughed at her for showing she was afraid before, so instead, she crawled inward, shoving down her fears and anxiety. She forced her thoughts to focus on the individual threads of the net.

Sorcha could barely decipher the words "I didn't do anything, Sorcha" from Sune. She closed her eyes and thought about Avondelle: skipping in the market, eating Chocolate Jabbles, twirling at the royal balls, and Sakul. Tears slid down her ebony cheeks. She missed him so much that her body hurt. She needed her home. She needed her friends. She needed her family. Where was Sealyn? Where was their rescue?

The ship's warning bell rang loudly, and the sailor in the crow's nest screamed and pointed in front of them. They all turned and saw the horrific sight of two gigantic squid-like creatures attacking the lead Stoltland ship--*Archetydons. Their tentacles were breaking banisters and grabbing Stoltlanders. The soldiers stabbed and chopped at the tentacles while archers shot arrows at the creatures' heads.

Sune yelled, "Bring her back on board. We're sitting ducks like this."

The captain nodded to the scruffy soldier, and Sorcha was dropped back on board. She fell with a hard thud. She clawed at the net's restraints and brushed off the entanglement like she was covered in spiders. Sune broke free of his captor and helped Sorcha to her feet, holding her close.

"Take them down to the gully and lock them in, then return. We must find out how far off course we are."

"Off course?" Doebromir asked.

"Yes! Off course," the captain stomped to the edge of the ship and pointed for emphasis. "You see those monsters? Those don't exist in the Margyger Seas, which means either we're off course or those fishy Mer Clans allowed the creatures to come in their waters. Queen Corentine won't forgive that."

"Captain," a gruff, scared voice sounded. "That storm last night blew us off course, but not by much. We will have to fight the currents and, apparently, the creatures in front of us. A few miles past them, and we're back on course for Hostile Channel."

Doebromir remembered all the battles that took place and continued to take place in the Hostile Channel. These were the waters that separated Elysium from Korpam. That channel had never been friendly between the two kingdoms. He was sure Korpam would protect the Stoltland ships, but first, they would have to make it through the gigantic squid monsters.

"You can't be thinking of sailing through them?" Doebromir questioned. "Look what they did to your lead ship!"

The new captain had panic in his eyes. It was obvious he shouldn't be in charge. He was now desperate, which makes for a very selfish captain. He walked frantically to a bell and sounded the code for their right-side ship to sail ahead.

"What are you doing?" Sune protested. "You're sending the people aboard that ship to their deaths." Sune was shocked that he even cared, but this surely wasn't the way.

"They will be our decoys, and we will go around to the left. He rang the bell again to instruct the other three ships what to do; then, he ordered the oars to drop and the men to row. They saw the terrifying waves made by the creatures moving toward the decoy ship while the other ship was left in fragments.

Sorcha felt faint. She couldn't swim. If those creatures came for them, no matter what, she was dead. Sune wrapped his arms tighter around Sorcha.

He whispered. "I'm sorry this keeps happening to you. You're stronger than our chains, Sorcha. Fight through the madness."

The captain yelled, "Fire!" The archers released their arrows, aiming for the creatures' tentacles. The Elysians watched in horror as the Stoltlanders sent a wave of arrows at the decoy ship, killing several of the crew but hitting the creatures. They heard the monsters' loud groans. The arrows enraged them. The captain yelled for the ship to move faster.

The creatures' wrath left the decoy in pieces. Broken wood planks, bodies, and barrels floated past the ship, and the water turned a deep crimson. Surviving Stoltlanders swam for their lives, but tentacles and hungry mouths found them.

The main ship was almost out of harm's way—almost. One of the large squids turned its gaze of fury toward them. Their hearts sank when they saw the creature coming in their direction. The captain barked at the rowers to push themselves faster.

They needed to make it into Hostile Channel. The entrance offered refuge from sea monsters because it had long, strong sea kelp that would latch on to anything with a heartbeat and strangle it to death. This meant easy passing for ships.

The enormous squid was gaining on them. They were mere minutes away from being smashed alive. The sailors screamed for their rowers to hurry while running to the front of the ship, hoping to avoid a collision.

Doebromir saw the entrance to Hostile Channel, but he felt it in his bones that the monster would reach them before they escaped. He waited for impact. The wind felt like it was beating his face, and the saltwater sprayed his cheeks. He longed for home. He felt Sorcha's hand grab his wrist. It was all she could do with her chains.

Sune's heart panicked when he heard from the Crow's Nest, "Brace, yer selves!" This couldn't be it. He saw Hostile Channel's entrance. They were right here. Surely, they couldn't die this close to safety. Sune looked down at Sorcha and finally allowed all the feelings he had held back for so long to overtake him. With his hands in chains, he pulled Sorcha's chin up and pressed his lips to hers.

He could taste the salt water on her chapped lips and savored each second. Maybe it was the fear of death. Maybe it was the longing for the comfort of a lover's arms, but Sorcha kissed him back. Their lips were hungry for each other. After all, they had been through so much: surviving the Arkootha bear attack, Rivers' death, the catacombs of graves, and now prisoners. How could they not give in to the desperate need for comfort?

A loud crack sounded, and they were all flung forward. Everyone hit the wooden deck hard and waited for the worst, but it did not come. They stood and saw the giant squid entangled with the kelp. It fought for its life, but the kelp was too much. The creature joined the other carcasses at the bottom of the sea who thought they, too, could outbest the sea kelp.

Cheers rang out across the ships that made it through. Though relieved they weren't food for the sea creature, the Elysians were still prisoners.

One of the sailors reported that a tentacle had hit the back of the ship, cracking it. Water was pouring in. They would have to abandon ship and join the others. The two ships quickly anchored near the sinking one, and as the sailors scurried back and forth like ants, saving food and water, all Sorcha could think about was that kiss—that delicious, unforgivable kiss.

Elysian News

The Latest News and Gossip

Issue #8

Painted above: Queen Sealyn left and King Jace right

Declare War or Declared Weak?

Our queen still deciding.

Greetings, my fellow Elysians. It's me again with all the juicy details about our beloved kingdom. Today's most considerable debate is whether Queen Sealyn will declare war against Stoltland or walk away from her responsibilities.

Now, I know what some of you may think: "That was harsh, Lina." But hear me out. What kingdom was responsible for the Battle of the Betrayals? STOLTLAND! What kingdom was responsible for encouraging Lady Pyry's betrayal? STOLTLAND! What kingdom was responsible for eradicating an entire generation of Nichts with dragon fire? STOLTLAND!

So I ask again, my friends, should we officially declare war against Stoltland? If your answer is anything but yes, then I dare question your reasons. Perhaps your reason is that you share the same sympathy as our dear king?

Is King Jace the only reason Queen Sealyn won't declare war? Is he asking her not to? Is he the reason fellow Elysians can't receive justice for their loss?
~Lady Adalina (Lina)

Princess Siany Spotlight	Lady Pyry says goodbye	Baker Nicht's Secret
The juiciest gossip	*A friend tells all*	*Prepare your kitchens*
Which diplomat will Princess Siany choose?	Lady Pyry bids farewell to her father and sails for Reformation Rock.	Baker Nicht finally reveals her secret ingredient for her Puffin Pies.
Please visit your local tavern to place bets.	Lady Pyry's father's body has been burned.	Full recipe included along with instructions.
Page 3	Page 4	Page 6

CHAPTER 8
ASSASSINATION ATTEMPT

Sun rays glistened across Jadelyn's golden dress as she glided across the stone floor of Sealyn's glass-encased natatorium. This was her first time inside, and it was every bit as breathtaking as everyone said it would be. The blue pool looked inviting. She longed to sink into one of the velvet green couches with one of the hundreds of books lining the stone bookshelves and listen to the singing plants. No wonder this was Sealyn's favorite place to get away.

"Admiring the singing plants?"

Jadelyn jumped at the sound of Sealyn's voice. "Yes, Your Majesty. I understand why you love coming here."

Sealyn smiled. "It's where I can find peace and solitude," she motioned for Jadelyn to sit on one of the green couches. "Please make yourself comfortable." Jadelyn sat fidgeting with her sleeves. This did not go unnoticed by

Sealyn. "Jadelyn, I've asked you here because, as you know, we're setting sail soon for Shunal, your home kingdom, and I need to know what we're truly up against."

Jadelyn's cheeks flushed. "We're a peaceful kingdom, majesty. We pride ourselves in trade. Our kingdom is an island that connects all kingdoms." She bit her lip, hoping that would appease Sealyn's curiosity—it did not.

"Excellently rehearsed, and I believe the exact same wording as your sister's speech before she quit this position," Sealyn's eyes narrowed. "Jadelyn, if you want to remain here and help save your kingdom, you will have to do better than that."

Jadelyn nervously twirled the ends of her dazzling blonde hair. She was scared. Shunal had many dark secrets. If she revealed them, she risked being a traitor. Could she trust Sealyn? Could Elysium truly be the answer she's been quietly begging for?

"Jadelyn, I mean you no harm. You will have my protection." Sealyn could see the anxiety welling up in Jadelyn's yellow eyes. Perhaps she needed to use a different tactic. "How about I tell you my plans?" Sealyn waived for Maekel to bring them tea. "The summary is to rescue the captives, free any slaves we encounter, and claim Shunal's source of power. Once we do this, the curse will be broken, and I will need an ambassador for me." Sealyn paused as Maekel finished organizing the tea and treats, then fluttered with her pink wings to the tables on the far side to finish reading her book.

Sealyn eyed Jadelyn as she sipped her tea. "I would like that person to be you, just like Lady Zuri is the ambassador for Len Nove. She's stationed there at the palace and keeps us informed."

Jadelyn felt a wave of relief but still wasn't sure if Elysium could break the curse. If they failed, then she would be left in the hands of *them*. They were too powerful. There's no way the Elysians could overthrow the longest-reigning royals Shunal had ever had. Their bloodline was ruthless and would kill anything or anyone trying to steal their power. She set her teacup down, shaking.

Sealyn reached out and squeezed Jadelyn's hand. "I'm trying here, Jadelyn. I need you to let me in past the surface."

Jadelyn sighed. If there was anyone in all seven kingdoms who stood a chance to break the torment of her land, it would have to be Sealyn. "The surface is all it takes, Queen Sealyn."

Sealyn's brow furrowed in confusion. "What do you mean?"

A single tear slipped from Jadelyn's golden eye. She untied the ribbons securing her sleeve, then rolled back the golden fabric, revealing Shunal's curse.

Sealyn gasped and clasped her hand over her mouth. "Oh, Jadelyn. What? What is the meaning of this?"

Jadelyn sniffed. "Shunal's curse is greed. Greed takes over your mind on what to value," she said as she rubbed the precious stones embedded in her skin. "It starts when you're born. Our parents carve a place on our right arm and implant the first precious stone, then that's all you live for—earning your next stone and the next. The more stones you have on your body, the more valuable you are."

Sealyn stood abruptly. "This is insane. Shunalians are cutting out pieces of their skin and inserting gems, then letting the skin heal around the stone?!"

"Yes," Jadelyn said with a whimper. "I did this to myself as well. I wanted to be seen as wealthy. You show your wealth by displaying your stones."

"Wait. Jadelyn, how much of your body is covered in gems?"

More tears slid down Jadelyn's porcelain skin. With a sagging posture, Jadelyn began to motion over her limbs. "Both arms are covered to my wrists and three rows over my chest," she coughed uncomfortably. "They form the outline of the top of my breast line."

Sealyn blushed. "That explains why you don't wear plunging necklines like others in my kingdom."

"Please, Queen Sealyn, you won't tell the others, will you?"

Sealyn paced and put her hands on her hips. She couldn't fathom what would possess someone to inflict such pain on themselves just to show the world their wealth. This meant, though, that once they stepped past the ports of Shunal, her people would see the secret. She could not keep this from those traveling on the quest.

"I wish I could, but those attending this quest will need to be prepped," Jadelyn dropped her head. Her body felt nauseous. "But I can offer to keep this from Elysium." Jadelyn's head snapped up. "Only those traveling will have the knowledge of the gemmed skin. Outside of them, it will be your choice who knows."

"Will you give me a list of who will know?"

"Absolutely," Sealyn took the seat next to the sad Shunalian. "However, I need you to hear my voice and trust it when I tell you this: your value does not come from gems. You are worth so much more than all the precious stones this world offers."

Jadelyn's nose turned pink, and tears poured from her golden eyes. She threw her arms around Sealyn. What kind of friendship was this? No one had ever spoken to her as Sealyn had. She actually felt—special. Special! She let out a tiny laugh, which prompted both women to giggle.

"Now, Elysium will need your help. From what my scouts tell me, your rulers are completely infected with the curse and have no reason to form an alliance with us. Is there anyone you can think of who could help us? Perhaps a group or diplomat?"

Trying to hide another secret, Jadelyn shook her head slowly, then paused, acting like she wasn't already thinking this. She didn't want to seem too eager, or else that would give away her connections. "Wait, yes. There's a group who call themselves the Trica Rebels. They've been trying for years to bring down the reigning monarchs but so far have failed. They've become quite a nuisance, living up to their name."

"Rebels. Hmm. Rebels might be a key to winning all seven kingdoms. They most likely need backing to take over. Do you know a way to contact their leader?"

"Their leader? No, he stays very hidden and protected, but I have heard of another. I believe he may even be his second in command, but again, this is all hearsay."

"Well, let's reach out and see what we see."

"I don't know if he will be the greatest help, though."

"Why's that?"

A cheeky grin formed across Jadelyn's face. "Just from the rumors, he's almost exactly like Lord Char, except multiply the crazy by 10,000."

"You have *got* to be kidding me? What's his name?"

"Herbmando."

Music filled the green and gold ballroom, and colorful dresses twirled across the green grass dance floor. Sparkling amber ale and Sealyn's infusion wines filled golden goblets on the spring-flower-decorated drink tables. Banners from the six Elysian territories unfurled from the perimeter balconies, welcoming the diplomats and their families.

Lord Commander Tilmond shifted uncomfortably in his dress clothes. He was the tallest person in the room and kept his chocolate hair trimmed short and groomed to perfection. He preferred his military leathers, though. Tilmond watched as his wife danced with his three children. It made his heart happy to see them, and right now, he needed to feel happy. His anxiety was in overdrive since they had received several threatening reports.

Lord Max, leader of the archers, stood close to Commander Tilmond and whispered, "My treetop archers reported no movements at any of the other kingdom Tors. They will remain all night, nevertheless."

"Someone will make a play for Sealyn's life tonight," Tilmond quietly spoke.

"How do you know?"

"There were over fifty threats just this week. My issue is the increasing number of Elysian threats."

"What? You didn't say that in our meeting," Max tugged on the sleeves of his coat. His face was still young and handsome, but his green eyes now held pain and age from the Len Novian quest.

"I know. I didn't want to cause panic."

A waiter walked by with a tray of goblets filled with purple PurFizz. Max snatched one of the goblets, looked inside, then downed its contents.

Tilmond looked puzzled. "Why do you always look inside your drinks before drinking?"

"That's off-topic and doesn't matter. Commander, we need to know who else to look for. Were the diplomats' convoys checked upon entering the local Tors?"

"Of course," Tilmond huffed. "But one can never be too trusting. The kingdom is restless since Sealyn has made no declaration of war against Stoltland, and those shameful newspapers Lady Adalina keeps writing aren't helping the royal family win any favors."

His light brown hair glowed from the white fireflowers, and his gaze fell over his beautiful wife, Lady Madilina; then Lord Max took another sip of his PurFizz. "Not to worry. I will inform Lord Favien to alert his Groundlers."

"No. This could be good training for our new squad—King Jace's Shadow Walkers."

"You think Lord Ashur is ready to lead?"

"If one is never given the chance, then we'll never know."

"At your command, my lord," Max nodded and left to find Lord Ashur, the uncommonly handsome soldier from Elysium's Port Rowin. Max was not surprised to find Ashur surrounded by ten ladies, all ogling his ebony skin and sculpted muscles.

Max cleared his throat, "Lord Ashur." Max's ivory face was charming, but he sometimes did wish he could turn heads like Ashur.

"Yes, Lord Max?"

"I need to speak with you in private. Ladies, will you please excuse Lord Ashur?"

Max could hear the disappointing groans. Ashur looked relieved. He smiled and patted Max on the shoulder. "Thanks, Max. You saved me from deciding who I should dance with next."

"Well, as glad as I am to rescue you from hungry ladies, Commander Tilmond has a much bigger rescue mission in mind. We need you to ready the Shadow Walkers."

"What? Here? Now?" Ashur leaned in close. "Why? What's going on?"

"Tilmond believes there will be an assassination attempt on Queen Sealyn's life tonight. Too many reports align with this prediction."

Ashur's green eyes widened, and he rubbed his short-cut black hair. He loved this kingdom and the royal family, especially Jace. With everything they all went through in Len Nove, he felt like they were his family now. When King Jace asked for him to be the leader of his new squad, he felt such excitement and pride. He was itching for his first assignment. "I'm ready."

"Good. Have your Nicht alert the squad members, and Ashur, stick to the shadows," Max winked.

Ashur smiled his wide smile and immediately vanished.

Sealyn had already made her introduction speech, danced five dances, and held at least three diplomatic conversations that made her want to scratch their eyes out since the ball started. She was exhausted, but something felt off. All night she felt like she was being watched and not like her security watched, but like an enemy watching her. It was time for her to slip away. She quietly stepped into the garden library, and with a quick unhooking of the gold leaf clasp at her waist, her emerald ballgown skirt fell away from her sparkling top. Sealyn always had her battle leathers on under her gowns. She never wanted to be caught off guard.

Sealyn quickly tossed the skirt behind one of the couches, then walked to the bookshelf beside the door. She pushed the book *A Phoenix's Tale of a Tail* until she heard the click, then slid open the smallest section of the bookshelf. It was a tiny, narrow walkway—big enough only for one person to pass through at a time, hence why she had to remove her puffy skirt. This walkway was Sealyn's little secret; no one knew about it.

The path led around the entire perimeter of the ballroom. The walls provided many cracks for her to hear and see around the room. Sealyn used this as a child to uncover many plots against her kingdom and family. No one ever understood how she knew the information.

She walked soundlessly, taking note of what she heard and saw.

There was the diplomat from Hill Chimes, Lord Saemeon, whispering to his father. They exchanged head nods, and then Saemeon walked across the room to the drink table and stood, eyeing Princess Siany dancing with Lord Edvard from the Blissendelle territory. Clearly, there was a rivalry between those two men.

She caught movement in the corner of the ballroom. The corner was in complete darkness, but she definitely saw movement. Shadow walkers. Why would the Shadow Walkers be activated? There must be a clear threat for Tilmond to issue such a command.

Sealyn crept further down the walkway, mere inches from the Clarien representatives. Something was off. They seemed too tense. Back and forth whispers. She saw their gazes locked with Lord Saemeon. He nodded back. What was happening?

The music ended, and Saemeon called to Siany. Sealyn saw how much Siany's face lit up when she was with Saemeon, but she also saw something special between her and Edvard. The way Saemeon and the Clarien representatives were acting made Sealyn less trust them.

Walking further, she overheard different gossip: Lady "so and so" wants Lord Jem. Lady "so and so" doesn't like Lady "so and so." Lord "who cares" kissed Lady "thinks she's perfect." Sealyn resisted the need to grumble. She knew those details would probably be the highlight of Lady Adalina's gossip column.

A flash of gold caught Sealyn's emerald eyes. Saemeon was handing Siany a goblet. Surely, Siany wouldn't accept. Royals do not accept drinks handed to them except by their trusted attendants. Sealyn's heart sank. She watched as her sister accepted the goblet and drank! She rounded the corner of the walkway to get a better look at the Clarien representatives, who were all making their way toward her parents, and a slight gasp escaped her lips. "Jace."

No. No. No. Sealyn sent her panic down her connected line to Dun, the fierce giant Green Phoenix. Sealyn slipped her shoes off so she could run back down the hallway without being heard.

Her head jerked when she heard the crowd gasping. She saw her sister, in the arms of Lord Saemeon, passed out. That vicious pig poisoned her sister! Sealyn prayed to Creator that she was still alive. Madam Bip rushed to Siany's side.

Tilmond scooped Siany into his arms from Saemeon and left for the royal hospital wing.

Sealyn looked back at her parents and Jace. The Clarions were slowly saying their goodbyes. Why? This couldn't be right. Her sister was just rushed to the hospital. Diplomats don't leave after something like that.

Shadow Walkers on high alert. Clarien and Hill Chimes' territories seem to be working toward something. Siany is possibly poisoned. Was Siany a distraction? And if so, from what?

A scream sounded. Sealyn looked up and saw at least ten black hooded figures jump from the ballroom balconies. How did they get in? What happened to the archers stationed at the top? Where was her guard? All these questions needed to be answered, but later. She had to protect her family.

Sealyn slid the door back fast, only to find Lord Char passed out on one of the couches.

"Char! Are you hurt?"

Char snored once, and then his eyes opened. "Sealyn! Why are you scaring me?"

"You're drunk?! Right now?"

"Of course, now. It's a party, isn't it? Are you barefoot? Now, who's drunk? And where is your skirt? Have you lost your mind?"

"Char, get up. There's an assassination attempt happening. We must protect our family."

Char let out a frustrated yell. "I'm sick of this sh…"

"We don't have time for your complaints. Let's go." Sealyn's eyes glowed green, and strands of her hair turned blue by her face. She felt her Elysian powers but also her mammoth strength. She flung the door open and saw complete pandemonium.

"So much for a quiet night," Char drew his sword. His military training on Pax Island boiled in his blood. He was a warrior, hoping to go unnoticed. "Where's your weapon, Sealyn?"

"I am my weapon."

Sealyn's palms grew hot, and a green-flamed sword formed in her hands. She saw her father and Jace fighting off two attackers. The clanging of swords, cracking of bones, and the echoes of screams resonated in the ballroom. The Shadow Walkers were fending off more of the assailants. Sealyn turned to Char, "Protect my sister. They took her to the hospital wing. Saemeon drugged her. Protect her, Char. Blood for blood." Char dashed away, eager for blood.

A tall assassin jumped in front of Sealyn. She ducked under his sword, feeling the wind on her face. Sealyn blocked out the screams of her guests and focused her attention on the dagger in the assassin's other hand. She broke the dagger with her Luxen sword and readied herself for a painful blow, only to watch the hooded figure fall lifeless to the floor. Blood pooling from underneath the enemy.

She looked up from the dead body and saw red eyes staring back. "Perfect timing, Lord Jem."

"Anything for you, majesty. I need to get you to safety."

"Not until my family is safe."

"Majesty…"

"Don't argue, Jem. You can have my back in battle, but I'm not leaving."

"As you command, majesty." His Havasian red eyes sparkled every time he saw her.

Sealyn shouted down the bond to Dun that he needed to stop the Clarions from leaving. They were a part of this infection. Ashur dove before two hooded figures, tripping their advances on the royal family. Favien jumped on top of one of the fallen attackers and slid his arm around his neck, quickly forcing the man to pass out. Ashur smashed the other one's head against the flooring; crimson stained the grass floor, and he reveled in his unconsciousness.

Jace's sword collided with another hooded assassin's sword with a loud clash. The grey-eyed king blocked strike after strike, kicked his attacker's feet out from under him and watched the traitor fall backward. Jace's sword hung over the heavy-breathing man's chest, and he froze. He remembered Adalina's article: was he a murderer? Did Drystan surrender? Did he not possess mercy because of his Stoltland blood?

The treacherous villain took advantage of Jace's hesitation and lunged for him, but King Father Ryker blocked the killing blow with his sword. Jace snapped out of his trance and stabbed the assassin through the heart. Jace yanked his bloody sword from the hooded figure and watched as he dropped to his knees, coughing blood.

"Thank you," Jace said breathlessly.

"Next time, don't hesitate. Stay out of your head, son."

Sealyn's green-flamed sword sliced through an attacker, burning a hole through the abdomen. Swiftly, she kicked another with her mammoth strength, sending him flying across the room and landing in front of Max. Max's eyes widened at the sight of Sealyn's strength. He wasted no time and stabbed the attacker in the throat. The room went silent when King Father Ryker yelled in pain as a sword stabbed his arm.

Sealyn screamed, "No! You came for me, not him."

Sealyn's words caught the attention of the hooded woman just enough for the traitor to turn her back on her mother, who always had a dagger. Queen Mother Graelynd stabbed the attacker in the upper back, and then Ryker delivered the killing jab to her side.

They took a moment to pause. The screams were now coming from outside the walls of their guests, and twelve black-clothed individuals were dead on the bloody ballroom floor. The royal guard stood over their bodies, trying to identify them.

"Father, how bad is the wound?" Sealyn asked frantically.

"I'll live. It's just a flesh mark. Where is Siany?"

Tilmond emerged from the main entrance, running. "Majesties, is everyone safe?"

"Yes, yes. How's my daughter?" Ryker questioned.

"She's safe. Sleeping off whatever was put in her drink. Madam Bip says she can counter it with a potion. She'll awaken within the hour." The royals let out a sigh of relief.

Dun's loud screech echoed into the ballroom, metallic stench in the air. The Clarions walked in, slowly etching backward, never taking their eyes off Dun. He towered several feet over them with his large golden beak close to their faces. He stomped his golden claws for emphasis.

Sealyn was thankful they redid the ballroom doors so Dun's size could fit through. He was so intimidating, and she loved it.

The Shadow Walkers made fast work of pulling the dead bodies together in a row, blood streaks trailing. Lord Ashur ensured each body was inspected twice to confirm what they found.

"Queen Sealyn, these assassins wore black to pin the assassination attempt on Stoltland, but clearly, they're hired from Clarien and Hill Chimes." He handed her their territory patches they had ripped off their clothes, hidden underneath the black cloaks.

The Clarions dropped their heads. Sealyn stepped in front of her family, staring at the Clarions. "Why?" is all she asked.

The grumpy old father of Clarion's diplomat spit. "Because you refuse to declare war against Stoltland!" Jace's jaw tightened. He figured Sealyn had refrained because of him. "Stoltland has killed so many, too many, of our people, yet our queen remains in perfect harmony with them."

Sealyn's hands started glowing. Her anger was beginning to overtake her. She had not mastered her rage versus her power. "Why would a lion consult with a field mouse over his decisions?"

"Are you calling me a mouse?"

"What would you have me do?"

"Declare war!"

"Then what?" Sealyn folded her arms to keep from strangling the idiot in front of her.

"What?"

"What happens after I declare war?"

"You. You. You go fight them."

"Excellent, and would you sentence the captives to die while you're at it?"

"No, of course not."

"Then you want our quest to fail?"

The father huffed. "No. I didn't say that."

Lines of confusion formed on Jace's brow. Where was Sealyn going with this conversation? He knew everything was his fault. Sealyn was probably stalling to protect him, like she always did.

"But you see, small one," Sealyn tilted her head. "You did. With your reckless declaration of war, you would condemn our mission to free our captives and, in turn, the possibility of freeing Shunal. Shunal's policy for entering its kingdom is 'No kingdom is allowed to step foot on its land if at war with another kingdom.'"

The old man blinked. "I. I didn't know that, majesty."

Sealyn's eyes glared. "See… mouse."

"Please, Queen Sealyn, please forgive me and my household."

"Tell the truth. The assassination attempt wasn't on my life, was it?"

The room froze. "No, majesty."

"It was for King Jace?"

"Yes. We thought you held your hand because he was from Stoltland, and well, it was his mother, after all, who ordered all the killings."

Sealyn needed to show strength. Part of her did wait for a more secure reason not to declare war because of Jace, which is why she had so many attendants researching Shunal for an extended period of time. Once Quinley and Revalyn found the port policy, she was relieved.

"So, you figured if you eliminated the love of my life, then I would be distraction-free. The trouble is, you've committed treason and attempted murder, so it's the dungeons for you all until your trial date, of which I can already guess the outcome."

With several guards, Lord Edvard and Lord Char walked in with swords drawn to Lord Saemeon's and his father's throats.

Sealyn nodded. "Nice work. They'll join the Clarions in the dungeons."

Char punched Saemeon and grinned. "Killer party, Sealyn."

CHAPTER 9
MOON AND STARS

Weeks had gone by, and finally, Jadelyn heard back from Herbmando. His response ignited the start of preparations for the journey to Shunal. While everyone was busy packing, Lady Pinx sat at her new classroom desk admiring the craftsmanship. Pinx's long black hair was halfway pulled up with pink ribbons.

She volunteered to teach the new course, Phytocology. Pinx adored her classroom and the castle. Several Earth Nichts fluttered above her top shelves, dusting and organizing her subject's books. Most had dazzling blue and green wings. During her wedding, Pinx discovered more about who she was. After they returned from Len Nove, she and Favien immediately married. They wanted to waste no time. She pondered the memory of her brother, Captain Graegory, walking her down the aisle with her father.

It was the happiest day of her life, but as she stood facing Favien with butterflies in her stomach, she couldn't help but wish she had more flowers around them. The wedding was so fast that they didn't have time to prepare.

She felt a sense of longing but not of inadequacy. It was more like something was missing from her life—like a part of her had been missing, yet only in this moment did she feel it. Although she was supposed to be focused on being a bride, she allowed her emotions and body to explore this longing and embraced what it would tell her. Floating green sparks began forming around Pinx. Favien jumped back, not knowing what was happening.

Madam Bip was so excited. She stepped out from her chair and handed Pinx a flower; then, in a flash, flowers began blooming in the trees, on the chairs, on ladies' dresses, in the grass, and in the lake behind them. Pinx laughed at the memory. It was like being kissed for the first time.

Since then, she had been studying with Madam Bip and was quickly learning how to control her Tethered Luxen magic. This magic had so much depth, so she began journaling every discovery. She and Madam Bip made the first book for the school, *The Study of Phytocology*. She was so excited when Sealyn and Siany asked her to teach at the new school. What a gift teaching is.

Her class will correlate with Madam Bip's class, Phytotherapy. Bip is the master of potions, so that was an easy choice. Pinx's class will focus on the spreading and profusion of florae, the results of ecological dynamics upon the profusion of plants, and the communications between florae and florae and also between plants and other creatures.

She doodled another drawing of the olosaegan weed, said to have magical properties of allowing one to see in the dark if ingested properly—if ingested improperly, said person could go blind.

"Working hard, I see," Sealyn said.

Pinx dropped her feathered quill. "Oh, Sealyn. You scared me."

"My apologies…professor."

"I like the sound of that!"

"I knew you would. How is everything coming along?"

Pinx smiled. "Excellent. We're receiving more books daily, which has been amazing to review. I'm stunned at how much information has already been logged and filed in these books. Can you imagine what a hundred years from now will be like?"

Sealyn chuckled. "No. I really can't, but if we continue what we're doing, then the world will be a much better place."

The emotion of Favien leaving soon hit Pinx. "Sealyn," Pinx choked. "Promise me you'll look after Favien?"

"I will do what I can. This is the part I loathe about being queen--dangerous quests that take family members away from each other."

"I meant to ask sooner, but how has your family been doing since the memorial of Ezen?"

"Everyone is doing the best they can be. It's so painful to lose someone so young. His parents, as well as his sister, are struggling. The Shunal quest announcement hit them with another wave of grief." A flash of green glowed in Sealyn's eyes.

"Sealyn? Are you well?"

"I'm fine," she bit back. The Earth Nichts startled and flew out of the classroom. "Sorry, there's just a lot of pressure and grief just—well, I'm tired of grief. I'm tired of my people suffering it, and Stoltland remains untouched."

Pinx pressed her hand to her chest. "Sea, stop. Take a breath. You must be careful with these thoughts. Comparing your life to the people of Stoltland isn't healthy. It would be best not to compare yourself to anyone truly. Be careful with that road. It can easily lead to…well, you know."

"Envy? Can a person be envious of another over grief?"

"Why not?" Pinx rose from behind her desk, walked to the front, and took Sealyn's hands. "Jealousy doesn't always come in the form of materials; it can be circumstantial."

"Interesting theory. I appreciate your words of wisdom," Sealyn hugged Pinx. "I must be off now. I have more preparation to do, but I stopped by to make sure the school would still open soon. I hate we will miss the start day, but I'm sure it will be terrific."

Pinx fiddled with the secret scroll inside her dress pocket. She and Norella had discovered the scroll before the Len Novian mission and swore they wouldn't show Sealyn until the time was right, but she was tired of holding onto the secret. Pinx's green, almond-shaped eyes watered. "Sealyn, I have something to show you."

"Can you make it quick?"

Pinx dropped her head; her black, flowy locks came forward. "I. I. Do you remember the prophecy about Stoltland and Elysium?"

"Prophecy? What's this about, Pinx?"

"Norella and I discovered a very ancient scroll in the martyr's coffin. We didn't know when to tell you because so many awful things kept happening," Pinx sighed. "I'm sorry, Sealyn." Pinx handed the scroll to her queen with a shaky hand.

Sealyn reluctantly took the scroll. She read the parchment twice, then a third time. She shifted her weight and began to read for a fourth time when tears formed in her eyes. She looked at her best friend, and with only a whisper, she asked, "Is this true?" She sucked in a breath.

Tears slid down Pinx's cheeks. "It follows the same pattern as the original prophecy and is signed by the same author and seal. I see no reason for it not to be true. Again, Sealyn, I'm so sorry."

Sealyn slammed the parchment on the desk, wishing away its existence. "You knew. All this time, you knew, and you said nothing. How can either of you call yourselves my friend? A friend wouldn't keep something like this hidden. I don't know how to trust you right now or ever."

"What?! No, please don't say that. I would never do anything to harm you intentionally."

"And yet you kept the biggest secret of my life from me. Actually, it's the kingdom's biggest secret. You withheld sensitive kingdom information for months—months, Pinx.

Don't you think the entire royal family should have this information?"

Pinx's crying intensified. "Sealyn, please. I swear I didn't mean to do anything wrong. I just couldn't bear what this would do to you. You see, it's already hurting you."

"No, you hurt me. Do you think me so fragile that I couldn't handle this?" Sealyn picked up the parchment and shook it. "This rotten poison. This thief of happiness. This…" Sealyn's voice cracked. "This prevention of joy." Sealyn fell to her knees, sobbing. Pinx latched onto Sealyn, rocking her into calmness.

The two sat in tears for what seemed like hours. Sealyn finally leaned back, and Pinx wiped the tears from her queen's face. "I'm so sorry, Pinx. I should not have taken it out on you. You didn't deserve that. I'm not mad at you. I'm mad that I'm no longer ignorant of this information."

"All is forgiven. I understand. What are you going to do?"

Sealyn wiped her nose and leaned her head against the desk. "I can't keep this from Jace. The moment a married couple stops communicating, especially about the hard subjects, is when the covenant ends."

Jace approached the swan pool with tension. The night sky twinkled with stars and orange *Lenettes danced in the moon's glow, but they did nothing to subdue his nervousness. Sealyn did not usually summon him for a late-night meeting in the gardens, but that's precisely what he was walking toward. He saw his stunning wife sitting beside the pool with her long, brown hair loose around her face. She looked sad.

"My love," Jace said softly. "Is everything all right?"

Sealyn sighed and shook her head gently, trying to find the words needed for such a moment. She held out the scroll to Jace. He lightly grabbed it and read its contents. Jace looked up from the parchment and glued his grey eyes to Sealyn's.

"What's the meaning of this?" he snarled.

Sealyn shook her head. She prayed for strength to get through this conversation. "Jace, you know the prophecy your mother spoke of when she was in the garden library?"

"I remember her speaking lies."

"Jace, some of what she said was her trying to rip us apart, but there's more to that prophecy."

"I refuse to believe this ancient piece of parchment has any hold over our lives."

"Jace…"

"No, Sea. This isn't true," Jace looked at the scroll and began to read aloud.

"Seven curses bind together. Seven curses remain, for only three clean bloodlines can lift one curse. Use the third for all--the bond is strong.

Cursed more are the beginners of Pride and Envy, who cannot grow light, so the joining of a Stoltlander and Elysian will not produce life."

Sealyn listened to the crickets. She needed a distraction. Lenettes glowed in the distance, and their beautiful orange wings danced in the trees.

"Sealyn, tell me this doesn't mean what I think it means."

"And what do you think it means, love?"

"Don't do that. Don't make me say it," Jace said as he sat next to his bride and grabbed her hands. "Tell me it doesn't mean we…," his voice broke, and Sealyn began to cry. Jace tried again, "That we can't have children?"

Sealyn looked into the stormy silver eyes that captured her heart long ago. "Yes, my love."

"No! Oh, Creator, no! Then I've…I've ruined your life, our life. I've ruined everything."

"Stop that, Jace. You've ruined nothing. We are in this together. We both decided to be together. It's not one person's fault."

Jace dropped his head into his hands. "This is not happening. This is not happening."

"Jace, please look at me."

He lifted his head, barely making eye contact. "Sea, if you knew this information before we met, would you still want to be with me?"

"That's not fair to play hypotheticals, but honestly, yes."

"Don't lie to me."

"How dare you accuse me of such. I'm being open and honest with you. Jace, no one has cared about me the way you have. You make sure I wake up to peonies on my pillow. You make sure I clear my schedule for my grandparents at the same time every day because you know how important they are to me. You ensure I have extra blankets on every journey we take because you remember how cold I get. You bring me silly finds from every military excursion you go on, from a weird rock to that funny singing tree branch you found the other day."

"C'mon, Sea. Those are ridiculous things."

"Not to me. Those things tell me that you think about me throughout your day, that you genuinely want me to participate in your life, and that you listen to my needs. What more could a queen desire?"

"But I can't give you life. I can only ever give you nothing."

Sealyn desperately looked around, needing to convince Jace that he was all she needed. How could she show him that he was her world? She looked over at the pool, with the night sky reflecting in still waters. Sealyn shifted to face Jace. She cupped her hands. "Jace, fill my hands with the water."

Jace looked at her incredulously and sighed. He lifted himself and filled his hands with water, then poured the water into her hands.

Sealyn angled her hands as best as she could, allowing the water to still. "You say you can give me nothing, but Jace…"

"It's true, Sealyn. You're queen, the queen. You deserve the entire universe, and I'm…"

Sealyn giggled. "You're doing exactly that."

Jace's brow furrowed. "What?"

"Look at the water in my hands. You, Just Jace, gave me the moon and stars."

Jace looked at the reflection in Sealyn's hands. He saw the bright moon and glistening stars. His face softened. How did he deserve a woman, a wife, a queen like this?

"Jace, my identity and worth are not wrapped in my ability to have children. My entire existence and purpose is not just to be a mother. We don't know exactly what this prophecy means, but please, believe me when I say I have enough joy in you to last me my entire life."

Jace lunged forward, wrapping Sealyn in a hug, only to gain a squeak from her. "Jace! You made me spill water all over me." They both laughed and sat in their wet embrace with tears of joy and sadness, haunted by those ancient words.

Elysian News

The Latest News and Gossip

Issue #10

Golden Goddess or Golden Snake?

Lady Jadelyn has a secret.

Greetings, my fellow Elysians. Your Lina here, ready to spill all my frustrations for today's cover.

Rumor has it that Queen Sealyn is protecting a dark secret of Lady Jadelyn Haerrinaro, Council of Lands for Shunal.

This secret has been apparently only shared with those attending the Shunalian Quest. I don't believe this is fair! We have a right to know.

Painted above: Lady Jadelyn Haerrinaro

I heard that this secret holds evidence of Shunal's curse: greed. If a foreigner wants to be a citizen of our kingdom and work on a council for our queen, shouldn't the people be privy to the dark secrets? Do we have a say in who should enter our uncursed land?

You may be wondering why I'm being so harsh toward a lady who is also my friend, but that's just it: I'm her friend, and she refuses to tell me. That is what makes me not trust her. If you can't share a secret with a friend, it must be horrible.

I will always ask the uncomfortable questions. ~Lady Adalina Roedellen

Princess Siany Spotlight	**Assassination Attempt**	**Luxen School Updates**
The juiciest gossip	*Target: King Jace*	*Weekly Reports*
Is she brokenhearted over Diplomat Saemeon?	King Father Ryker injured during the fight. Queen Mother Graelynd hero?	New classes available with Lady Norella's Luxen Laws.
Who will she choose for marriage now?	Lord Jem saved Queen Sealyn.	Parents are encouraged to follow progress.
Page 2	Page 4	Page 7

CHAPTER 10
BUT NOT IMPOSSIBLE

Flowing pink hair cascaded down Jashun's chest. He grazed the perfect ivory-skinned arm that wrapped around him. He leaned in for a kiss, only to be abruptly awoken by Lord Favien and Lord Finn.

Favien shook Jashun's shoulders again. "Jashun, get up. What are you doing in here?"

Jashun blinked, realizing it had been a dream. He took in his surroundings. He had fallen asleep in the military lounge hall.

"You missed early training, but there's a makeup session in three hours. Looks like you could use some coffee and breakfast," Finn said.

Jashun sat up, massaging his sniff neck. He shifted the brown pillows back to their normal place on the green couch and grabbed his sword, which was lying on the dark wood coffee table. The previous evening, Jashun had been planning how to get an invitation to the Mer Clan palace. He was still lost.

Favien, Finn, and Jashun joined their comrades at the mess hall, which smelled of savory sausage and sweaty soldiers. The military was starting to shift. Some soldiers had found their Luxen powers, and others had not. Cliques were forming. Everyone was nervous that a jealousy plague would soon spread, so Queen Sealyn ensured that Faith Commissioners Herb and Jesh were present during all feedings in the mess hall.

Jashun sipped his savory coffee and listened to his comrades talking.

"I still don't see why our naval ships couldn't have just blasted those Stoltlanders out of the sea and rescued the prisoners," a young recruit, whose name Jashun didn't know, said.

"Shut your trap, boy," Favien ordered. "You know nothing of military exploits or how to rescue people."

"Oh yeah? Then why? Tell me if you're so smart. Why hasn't Queen Sealyn sent a rescue mission with our ships?"

The burly, blonde-headed Brehan huffed. He had arrived in Avondelle from Fort Kippen days earlier. He and Ajorn asked Sealyn if they could join the efforts to rescue the prisoners. Their close friend and comrade, Sune, was one of the captives. "Because it has everything to do with protecting lives rather than killing Stoltlanders." He glared at the young recruit, who choked slightly on his food.

"Exactly," Favien interjected. "Which you probably don't know because all you read is this garbage in the newspaper." Favien threw Lady Adalina's latest edition before the young soldier, splattering part of his eggs. "Lady Sorcha can't swim, so any rescue mission threatens her life."

"Wouldn't the Mer Clans just save her as the princess did for Lord Jashun?"

Jashun blushed. He didn't realize his story was public knowledge. He looked to Ashur for help. Ashur smiled, then spoke, "Well, that would be a nice thought, but we don't know their swimming patterns, and trying to broker a deal with the Mer Clans to fight in a battle against Stoltland is proving to be more complicated than our queen expected."

"So, we're seriously stuck with them docking at Shunal and working with the most notorious pirates?" Two Nichts sped by their heads, carrying scrolls.

Jashun had had enough. "It appears so, but if you and your little weasel brain want to discuss your unhappiness, then why don't you tell Queen Sealyn or, better yet, her 'ten foot something,' giant green phoenix!"

The young boy's eyes bulged, and he jumped up from his seat and ran to the trunk room.

Favien stared at the uneaten food on the plate left by the scared recruit. He felt tears prick his eyes. "Doebromir would be the first to eat his food." Favien's brown beard had thickened, and he kept his hair trimmed with shaved sides. His emotions were starting to eat at him. He wanted his friends back.

Finn patted Favien's shoulder. "We miss him too, Favien. Don't worry. We'll get him back." Finn was a gentle soul to the group. They were glad he stayed in Elysium, not returning to his home kingdom of Len Nove. He had light brown hair with blue eyes, was short with a muscular frame, and was a fierce companion.

Lord Commander Tilmond walked up to the table. The men had to bend their necks to see his face; he towered so high. "I just received orders. We are to be packed and ready to head out after lunch."

Commotion sounded. They looked to the military Luxens. No issues were coming from them, just their usual growing plants and practicing potions. One had figured out how to channel his dog's night vision, so his eyes had a strange glow all the time now.

They heard the yells again, and this time, they most definitely heard the word "Dragon!" Everyone stood from the wooden benches, drawing swords and knocking over drinks and plates.

"Get back here, you stupid beast!"

Favien looked to Finn. "Was that Max's voice?"

"Don't hurt him, Max! He didn't mean anything by it!"

Favien nodded. "Definitely Max's voice because that was his wife, Lady Madilina."

The wooden doors to the mess hall burst open, and a small white dragon flew inside, with Max and Madilina trailing behind. The creature landed on the table in front of Favien and his friends. It leaned its head back and looked like it was preparing to spit fire.

The men readied their swords. Madilina screamed out, "No! Don't harm him!"

With hesitation, everyone dropped under the table for cover. When nothing happened, Finn opened his azure eyes first and saw a tiny bubble, then another, and another floating down beside him. "Uh, Favien," Finn said. "I think this may just be the *bubble dragon."

They all rose to see a room full of bubbles and relaxed. Max quickly grabbed the small dragon and put a harness around it. "Sorry about that, fellas. This one is super smart at getting out of his harness, and then the little jerk spit bubbles into my face, and well, here we are."

The baby dragon stuck its long green tongue out at Max, then curled into Madilina's arms. Madilina stroked its head and nuzzled her nose to its nose. It let out a squeak of happiness.

"My apologies," Madilina said. "He likes to play pranks on people. He's very friendly but sometimes takes his mischief too far."

Captain Graegory, brother to Pinx, stood at the far end of the table with his arms folded. He hated dragons. None of them standing near the baby dragon had experienced the horror its mother had done on Avondelle. "And where is its sibling?" he growled.

Madilina looked at Graegory with concern. "She's guarded all hours of the day and night. Her training is going well. She's even taken to some of the younger Transference Luxens."

Graegory glared and nervously brushed back his raven-black hair. "A dragon will always be a dragon. Never forget that."

The tiny white dragon coughed a bubble and licked Madilina's cheek. "Well, there's certainly no need to fear this little one. I'll take him back now. Max, will you escort me?"

Graegory's green, almond-shaped eyes watched the couple exit. He couldn't believe Queen Sealyn allowed the baby dragons to live. He grabbed his gear. He was ready for everyone to leave for the journey to Shunal. Vengeance flooded his veins. Stoltland needed to pay.

As tradition before setting off on a big quest, Elysians celebrate with a grand festival the night before. The royal family, the queen's guard, the Elysian army, and hundreds of guests arrived in Port Saevus of the Clarien territory. The large port city was decorated with yellow fireflower vines, green and gold flags, food tables everywhere, and lots of ale.

Music played from every corner of the city with dancing and laughter. Elysium took extra precautions with security, considering last year's was the epic poisoning and kidnapping, so it was no wonder hundreds of guards swarmed a small, unidentified boat that docked near the queen's ship.

The guards grabbed the two occupants and dragged them toward Sealyn and Jace. Lady Jadelyn ran over to Queen Sealyn, waving her hands. "Wait! Wait! That's him. That's him, majesty."

Jace tilted his head. "That's who, Sealyn?"

Sealyn motioned her hands, signaling the guards to release the two men. Sealyn took one look at the skinny, old man who was obviously just a paid boat paddler. Motioning for him to leave, he scurried off to join the party; then, she watched the golden eyes of the dark-headed figure standing in front of her with a cheeky grin. He was average height with a round face, and one could slightly tell he didn't miss a meal. His V-neck shirt revealed gemmed skin across his chest. Those standing around her were baffled by the jewels carved into his skin.

His face read troublemaker, yet there was something in the gold flecks of his eyes that Sealyn felt she could trust. He bowed and smiled.

"This is Herbmando, second in command to the rebels of Shunal," Sealyn stood and shook his hand.

"Ah, so everyone thinks I'm second."

Jace narrowed his eyes. "You're not?"

"One cannot be too careful with his secrets, majesty. We must keep the enemies guessing, do we not?" He let out a contagious laugh. "I hear there's a party tonight. Who feels like celebrating?"

Jadelyn laughed. "I did warn you, majesty."

"You warned the queen about me? In what way?"

"She believed that you are quite similar to my cousin, Char, in certain ways."

"Did I hear my name?"

Sealyn groaned. "Yes, Char. This is Herbmando of the Trica Rebels."

"Char Araelien? You're the one who helped save Len Nove from its curse?" Sealyn's mouth dropped, and Char stood a little taller and nodded. "You also won against Malum at Pax Island."

"I didn't know I had such a reputation."

"Ah, man. This is great because it means you organized an ale tasting all over Elysium."

Char laughed. "Now, we're getting somewhere."

"It is my pleasure, my lord, to meet you. Care to show me how Elysians party?"

"No, no, no," Sealyn said. "Char, Herbmando has to be fit to lead us in strategy meetings on our ship early tomorrow."

Char propped his arm over Sealyn's shoulder. "She worries too much. I'm sure a rebel from Shunal knows how to handle his ale."

"And more," Herbmando's smile grew wide. His sparkling yellow eyes looked like they held a thousand secrets.

"Hurry. Let's go before Her Majesty starts filling your head with nonsense about how she was the one to save Len Nove."

Ale after ale, a shot of port after port, Char, Herbmando, Sakul, Favien, and Finn enjoyed the festival like there was no tomorrow. Laughing and dancing, they all forgot about their responsibilities for the next day. Char was happy he wasn't going on this quest. He was worried about his family and friends, but somehow, he felt calm about it; maybe it was the port.

Jashun and Jem joined the merry crew. Herbmando took a double glance at Jem and blinked slowly. "Uh, man. You must be super drunk or very potioned to have such red eyes."

Char laughed and smacked Herbmando's arm. "No, you crazy rebel. He's from Havas."

"Ohhhh, the land of foxy ladies," Herbmando wiggled his eyebrows. Jem rolled his eyes and looked toward Queen Sealyn, who was dancing with Jace. Herbmando nudged Char and nodded at who Jem was staring at.

"Yeah, he's not subtle," Char tried to whisper drunkenly. "Ever the wishful."

Lady Pinx walked over arm in arm with Lady Norella, who was giggling. Pinx saw the state her new husband was in and was angered. "Favien! How could you let yourself get this far gone the night before?"

"I feel like I'm seeing four women," Herbmando said.

"Double the vision, double the fun—that's where we're at," Char said. "But which one is brave enough to taste Port Saevus's famous mixed drink? It's called *To Sea We Go*. We just received five drinks."

The deep blue, sparkling drink looked mysterious and intriguing. Stepping up to the crowd she didn't know, Quinley spoke, "I'll do it!" Her golden hair glowed from the fireflowers.

Lady Quinley and Lady Revalyn were invited by Queen Sealyn to work for the palace after their excellent research skills they showed at Fort Kippen. Quinley took the small crystal glass and downed its contents. The drink tasted sweet but not too sweet and tingled to her toes, prompting her to want to dance. "Who's coming to dance with me?"

Herbmando chugged another drink. "Your wish is my duty, my lady." Herbmando took Quinley's hand and escorted her to where others were dancing. Quinley's friend, Revalyn, was left standing with the crew, again not knowing any of them.

Char grabbed one of the drinks and gently shook it side to side, eyeing Norella. "What do you say, Norella? Shall we give it a go?" He wiggled his eyebrows.

"You do realize Brehan could snap you in half."

"Brehan? What, are you guys a thing now?"

"Not officially, but…"

"Well, let's unofficially dance, or can you not keep up?" He downed his drink, followed quickly by Norella. She didn't take challenges lightly.

"Favien, don't you dare touch that drink. All you're doing is going to bed right now!" Favien stumbled out of his chair and around the small fire. The two left the festival while Lady Revalyn grabbed the last drink, feeling she needed extra encouragement to join the dance floor. She raced to the others.

"Are you gents joining?" asked Jem.

Sakul shook his head. "No, dancing makes me miss Sorcha too much. I think I'm going to call it a night. If they ask, I went to my chambers."

"I agree," said Finn. "I mean, not about the Sorcha part. Although I'm sorry for you there, my friend, but I do need rest, too. Us archers must be stationed incredibly early for the sendoff."

Jem looked at Sealyn and Jace, who were holding hands and leaving the festival. "I think I will turn in as well. I want to be up early to do extra security searches."

While those three left the festival, the others remained dancing and singing to the music. Jadelyn twirled her golden dress and clapped her hands. She grabbed Char's hand, and he spun her around. Norella giggled and shimmied forward and back with Quinley. Being dipped by a dashing tall man, Revalyn blushed and laughed, then spun around. Novaly's red braids bounced as she jumped to the music.

Nichts flying above dropped gold sparkles and white petals. Everyone held their hands up, trying to grab the gold sparkles. Herbmando glided across the floor, showing off one of Shunal's famous dance steps. Jadelyn joined him, trying to teach others the steps, then the music again demanded jumping from each dancing participant.

While jumping, Herbmando opened a small, folded package from his pocket. He breathed in the aroma of sweet chocolate with a hint of mischief. He broke the chocolate in half and handed it to Char.

"What is this?"

"Oh, my friend, have you never heard of potioned chocolate?"

"Not potioned. We have Chocolate Jabbles and Moon Roons."

"Not a Roon Roon," he drunkenly spoke. "The potion chocolate will change your life. Trust me."

"Trust me" was all Char remembered after he ate the other half of the foreign chocolate.

With an odd headache, Char opened his eyes and winced. He didn't want to wake up yet. He wanted to stay in his seaside view inn and reminisce on the fun he had last night. However, he felt like the bed was swaying. Was his hangover this bad? Why couldn't he feel his right arm? And why did the room smell like hay?

Reality started settling in. He felt the scratchy feeling against his face, the familiar rocking back and forth. The smell of the fresh sea was close, too close. He forced his eyes open and felt nauseous at the blurry site of the gully in front of him. With a giant moan, he sat up, pressing on the mound of hay he was lying on. His hair was filled with pieces of hay and twigs.

What had happened to him? Was this last year repeating itself? Was he alone? Then he heard a sound across the room. There on another hay mound was Herbmando, snuggling a Rana frog. Char tried to replay the night's events but could barely recall what happened after the dancing. How had they ended up on a ship? Who's ship? Were they still docked?

Sealyn would kill him if he didn't get Herbmando to the strategy meetings. Char stood, stumbling, and made his way over to Herbmando, bracing himself on the wooden columns along the painful journey. He kicked Herbmando's dirty boot, disturbing the Rana frog, who frantically woke up, which was not good because once a Rana frog is scared, its pores leech a yellow, gooey substance. The goo oozed onto Herbmando, and the giant frog scurried away.

Herbmando rolled, trying to ignore Char's efforts to wake him, but Char kicked his foot again. Once Herbmando sat up, Char laughed, seeing the hay stuck to the goo. They both felt like death.

"Herbmando, I have no idea how we got here, but you must get to the meetings."

Scrambling to his feet and covered in gooey hay, Herbmando stood and motioned for Char to follow. They both took a few steps of running, then vomited. The Rana frog returned to them, grateful for breakfast.

"Oh, hello, old friend," Herbmando spoke to the frog. "Char, running might not be the best idea."

"I have no clue how we're going to manage today." Char winced after he spoke. Even speaking was making him nauseous.

Herbmando grabbed Char's shoulder and steadied himself. "Ah, my friend, today might be difficult," he said, lifting his finger for emphasis. "But not impossible."

And so, the two began the long climb of the staircases to the upper deck. Their legs ached and burned as they reached the top. Once he walked through the hatch, Char felt the wind and saw nothing but water. This could not be happening. Were they sailing? He walked fast to the ship's railing, which validated his fears. They were sailing in Hostile Channel. He noticed the flags and ship's name; they were on Sealyn's royal ship. His heart sank.

He looked to the other side of the ship and saw a frightful sight. It was one of the largest ships he had ever seen. The ship had several more decks than a normal warship, but he saw the flag—the Pirate Captain's flag.

They were minutes away from being next to the most terrifying pirate his generation knew. Char's stomach dipped and turned. This only meant one thing. He, once again, was on one of Sealyn's outrageous quests.

Elysian News

The Latest News and Gossip

Issue #11

Breaker of Hearts

Lord Jashun, the womanizer

Painted above: Lord Jashun Kafur

Greetings, my fellow Elysians. It's your favorite Lina to explore all the dirty details about someone I once considered a hero, but now? He's merely Elysium's zero.

Lord Jashun was set to marry Lady Brenna, but he got himself captured by the Stoltlanders. On purpose? Well, it sure is convenient that he would have an excuse for being a prisoner rather than fulfilling his duty to Lady Brenna.

Rumor also is that he had dalliances with Princess Kailani! If this man is willing to do this to such a sweet person as Lady Brenna, what hope is there for us other ladies?

Unconfirmed rumors: Did Lord Jashun betray Lord Sakul? Did he seduce Lady Sorcha while they were imprisoned together? I'm not accusing Lady Sorcha of being unfaithful to Lord Sakul, but I am willing to bet that Lord Jashun would take advantage of an emotional woman. Ask yourself the tricky question: is this a man we can trust?

Further news: Lady Brenna has fled with her daughter to the Southeast part of Seanove territory and has resigned from the Vinurs of the Court to Queen Sealyn. ~Lady Adalina Roedellen (Lina)

Princess Siany Spotlight	**Love is in the Air**	**Luxen School Updates**
The juiciest gossip	*Lady Norella*	*Weekly Reports*
First Headmistress of the Luxen School of Magic	Lord Brehan writes romantic letters to Lady Norella	Lady Madilina has accepted a professor position.
When will she achieve powers?	Will he propose soon?	Parents are encouraged to follow progress.
Page 2	Page 4	Page 6

CHAPTER 11
DIRTY LITTLE SPY

Sealyn and Jace stood on the upper royal platform, which was located at the back of the ship. The wind tasted of the sea, and the sun smiled down on them. Jace tried not to let his boyish notions get the better of him. Since he was a small child, he loved hearing tales of pirates and their adventures. He would dream of escapades on the open waters with sea creatures and fighting against the cruel rulers of the kingdoms. He felt his childhood dreams coming to life, but as king, he had to remain calm and on guard.

This was no dream, and this pirate was no hero. He could feel Sealyn's nerves and watched her fidget with her hands. He grabbed one and kissed her fingers. "We'll be fine, love. We have an army ready for battle."

Sealyn gave him her casual smile, the one she hoped would mask her worry and instill confidence. "Of course," was all she could say. Her heart fluttered when she watched the first rope from the pirate ship land on hers. The three green phoenixes at the front upper deck stomped their feet and flapped their wings almost in protest, but it was merely anticipation. Everyone was on edge.

Out of the corner of her eye, Sealyn caught the dreadful and pitiful view of Char and Herbmando. She threw her green cape's warmth behind her. It flapped angrily as she marched down the stairs. She fitted her hands on her hips and frowned at Char. "Care to explain?"

"I'm just as confused as you are, Sealyn."

"Sealyn?" the Elysian queen folded her arms. "No, today you will address me properly. We have too much riding on this, Lord Char."

"Yes, Your Majesty," Char bowed and ultimately agreed with his cousin. He felt terrible.

"And you," Sealyn turned her anger to Herbmando. "You're disgusting, smell, and you missed the meetings to discuss our morning tactics."

"Freedom never felt so good," Herbmando said with a raspy voice, swaying.

Sealyn was furious. How could this creature really be their way of breaking Shunal's curse? She would have to find a backup plan immediately. "Go below to clean up. Your chambers are on deck two. You will have to join us later."

Char and Herbmando bowed and left for the second deck. The rest gathered on the main deck, waiting to board the Pirate Captain's ship, *Justice*. Sealyn had to give credit to the pirate—she liked his dark sense of humor, but she was curious about what secrets it held.

Both ships were anchored with ropes secured, and once the final plank was laid across the banisters, the Elysians stepped across and boarded the *Justice*. The Swordsmen and Groundlers went first, and then the royal guard accompanied Sealyn, Jace, and her companions. Archers readied themselves just in case.

Only one word could best describe the main deck on this pirate ship: chaos. Sailors were scattered doing odd jobs and random sword fighting; several were passed out, and then there was the extremely loud yelling coming from below deck. This was different from what they were expecting, but what should they expect. These were pirates, after all. There was no order to them.

The below deck hatch flew open and out stomped the Pirate Captain himself, wearing his famous tiger helmet, but he was not alone. A young man with dirty blonde hair followed him with a heated red face from yelling. He had a small frame but was tall and seemed oddly familiar.

Trailing close behind the yelling tall blonde was another young lad, who was also arguing about something with a very thick book in his hand. He looked only a few years younger than the first but had light brown hair.

The Pirate Captain threw his hands up and yelled, "That's enough! I don't have time for this. We must prepare for the Elysian arrival."

"Unbelievable! I tried to discuss this for weeks, but you were too busy then as well," said the blonde. Sealyn then noticed he was wearing a cooking apron over his warrior clothes. She was confused. A chef was a chef, not allowed to participate in battles, but obviously, this young man was a trained swordsman, as evidenced by his sword sticking out from his apron.

The other lad quickly responded, "Before we have any confabulations with the Elysians, we must have them sign the contracts I drafted. Did you review them?" The three were so locked into their conversation that they didn't even notice the Elysian presence.

"Confabulations? What a word when spoken!" the chef-soldier said. "We need first to decide why we're even trusting the green eyes."

The Elysians folded their arms and quietly chuckled to themselves. They weren't expecting a show, and this was highly entertaining.

"Confabulation is a professional way of stating discussions and agreements between two parties. Would you like me to use the less-smart way of stating? Perhaps the word 'chat' is better for you," the younger one jeered.

Sealyn thought they were about to duel, but the older one spoke instead. "I'll deal with you later. Right now, we must decide if we can actually rely on a kingdom that has never had peace with Korpam." His orange eyes blazed with storybook memories of past battles between Elysium and Korpam.

"I hate to agree with my brother, but I would like to know why we suddenly believe we can trust Elysians. You haven't said why we're doing this."

The Pirate Captain threw his dagger into the mast in frustration, which made his crew all turn to watch. "I don't care about contracts, and I don't care about your opinions. What I do care about is…"

"My darling," panted a beautiful blonde lady. "The Elysians," she gasped for air. She had been running after the men from below. "Have arrived." She pointed toward the crowd of green eyes, staring back at them.

Sealyn was almost happy they caught the legendary pirate off guard. Now, she would get the opportunity to see how the jungle cat would react when he felt off balance.

The air stilled. A coldness crept over everyone's skin. They now had the full attention of the Pirate Captain. He approached slowly. He nodded at his crew, who immediately drew their swords. The Elysians did the same, except for Sealyn and Jace. He eyed Sealyn, continuing forward. His walk reeked of confidence, too confident. When he was only a couple of feet from the Elysian king and queen, he stopped and removed his tiger helmet.

Sealyn remembered her cousin's words, reminding her that she would know why he told her to trust the pirate—it would be in his face. She froze. She was having another mind battle.

Her recurring nightmare took over: She stood atop a hill overlooking a massive battleground. Dead bodies everywhere. Fires streaked across the ground. She feels pain. Some physical, but the main agony is emotional, spiritual--that she's lost someone, but she doesn't know who; then she looks up into the flaming eyes of a man, a stranger with a blurred face.

A seagull squawked, snapping her out of her mind's trap. She adjusted her focus on the Pirate Captain's face. How could her cousin tell her this was the face of a man she could trust? His orange eyes held disgust for her people. She had no idea if she could rely on this man.

He bowed slightly. "Majesties, welcome aboard *Justice*." His voice was thick, full of secrets and threats.

Sealyn hesitated, then Jace stepped from behind her and extended his hand. "Greetings, I'm King Jace. It's an honor to come aboard." Jace was thrilled to meet a pirate. He often snuck pirate novels from Stoltland's palace library to escape into a life on the high seas. Jace would fantasize about fighting sea monsters and rescuing mermaids, so this moment for him was like meeting a lifelong hero.

The pirate paled at the sight of Jace, and Sealyn saw only for a split second a different emotion displayed across the hardened face. This was a pirate, a scoundrel, a criminal, a killer, so why did she see fear in his orange eyes? Why would the Pirate Captain be afraid of Jace?

The cornered pirate composed himself quickly and, similarly, extended his hand to Jace. As the two stood in unison, Sealyn realized what Will, her cousin, meant. She watched the similar gestures, the shape of the jawlines, and the identical stances. She commanded with her eyes for the pirate to look at her. When they locked gazes, she tilted her head, slightly smirked, and nodded, allowing the pirate to know she knew. The air felt like it crackled. The fierce pirate glared at Sealyn, jaw tightening. She could tell this knowledge could cost him something, but what? The sea breeze blew, relieving the heat between them. From then on, she and the tiger pirate shared a secret.

The lovely blonde lady, the wife of the pirate, stepped forward. "Would you care to come this way? We've prepared a lovely brunch in the captain's lounge."

Sealyn stepped forward, not glancing at the pirate, and took his wife's hand. "Thank you. That would be wonderful. And your name is?"

"Liva, your majesty."

"Pleasure to meet you, Lady Liva."

"And these are my sons," she pulled the one wearing the apron close. "This is my eldest, Laisren, and…" she then pulled the other to her other side. "This is my youngest, Taeg." Liva smiled with pride over her sons. Sealyn could tell she was trustworthy—the verdict about her husband had not been settled yet.

The sea breeze blew softly through Jashun's black locks as he stared across the open Emerald Lagoon at Port Rowin. Small waves flooded over his tan toes, and the stones crunched beneath his movement. He was nervous. Kailani was meeting him, and he would start his first undercover mission. He wrestled with telling her what Sealyn wanted, but that would be breaking his vow to his queen. He needed to prove himself trustworthy.

Several yards away, he saw her head rise above the water. Even from a distance, her beauty overwhelmed him. She motioned for him to join her in the emerald water. Normally, Jashun would have wavered, but with Kailani, he wasted no time.

He waded through the water and then swam out to meet the girl who met him in his dreams each night. This time, Kailani stayed in her Mer form. Her hair was still pink but also purple, with several streaks of blue blended in. The crown on her head was made of silver coral with stones Jashun had never seen before. He didn't even know there was such a thing as silver coral, but it sparkled in the sunlight, enchanting him even more.

Her skin had a bluish tint compared to her human form. A pattern of tiny scales slid up her neck on either side, forming a V shape below her chin. Jashun blinked several times. Seeing a mermaid was so mesmerizing.

"Good morning, Lord Jashun," Kailani cooed.

"Good morning, Princess Kailani." Jashun treaded water, hoping the conversation could eventually lead to land.

"Well, you sent word for me to meet you, and here I am."

"Yes, of course, I'm sure you're very busy, so I don't want to keep you away from your duties, but I, um, well…"

Kailani giggled her intoxicating laugh. "Jashun, let's pretend we know each other. Just tell me what you want."

"I'm sorry, Kailani. You're just so amazing, so I, well, finding words is hard around you."

"I understand, but if you don't mind, I have a banquet to attend, so I need this to be short."

Jashun pictured a group of Mer-clans swarming a reef, eating fish—scales and all. He shivered. "I was wondering if we could get to know each other better?" Kailani grinned. "I mean, I know I'm not good enough for you, but maybe friends?"

Kailani wasn't naïve. Mer-people were all highly intelligent. Jashun was sent to spy on her, but she could feel the sincerity in his voice. He wanted a friendship—and more.

She needed him for information just as much as he needed her.

"I would be honored to be your *friend*, Jashun," the word "friend" dripped with flirtation.

"Really?"

"Yes, of course. Actually, why don't you join me at this banquet? You can be my guest of honor."

Jashun thought about circling the reef again. "I don't know if I can handle that."

Kailani laughed. "I have a feeling you don't know much about our clans. I promise you can handle it. Do you trust me?"

Jashun wanted to say no, but he had to push himself if he was to get any information for Sealyn. "Sure."

Instantly, Jashun felt Kailani grab his hands, and he was pulled under, water rushing over his body. He watched as she mouthed words over sea kelp, then pressed it over his lips and blew. A large bubble opened around him, encasing his entire head. He could breathe! He vaguely remembered something similar when she rescued him.

The journey deep below was long and tiring. Kailani had to keep stopping to refill the air bubble and allow his ears and blood to adjust. He liked when they stopped for air adjustments, not only because she pressed her lips against his, but he liked watching her crown. Above the surface, the coral lay almost flat, but underwater, it floated almost a foot above her head. She looked incredibly powerful, like a true royal.

Finally, when Jashun felt like his body could handle no more, he saw blurry images of lights below and then noticed the bottom of the ocean, the seafloor. They slowly descended to the bottom, his air bubble shrinking.

In front of him was a massive glistening wall that looked like it was swaying slightly. His feet touched the sand, and he glanced around, seeing giant, bright coral reefs everywhere. How was this possible? Electric-colored fish from tiny to large swam past. He felt relieved at the peaceful sight and to have a moment to catch his breath.

Kailani motioned for him to step forward, his feet dragging in the sand. The wall looked like it had a doorway but no doorknob. How was he to get through? He felt Kailani push him. He smacked into the wall that felt like thick jelly and slime. Hands pulled him through the thick jelly. Once he was through, he smacked his lips. They tasted salty. He felt his body and had none of the wall substance on him. What just happened?

He was confused. He looked around the medium-sized room that was made of black sea rock. In the middle, a giant orange Gorgonian Sea fan stood six feet tall with a blue, glowing root that spider-webbed its way through the fan, illuminating the room. To his left sat a small grey stone bench with brown boots beside it. Boots? Why were boots beside a bench? Then he realized he was alone. Alone! Where was Kailani, and whose hands had pulled him through?

He jerked his head to the right and saw a stone armoire with opened sea fan doors, exposing the clothes hanging. He blinked, then realized the air bubble was gone, and he was breathing normally. He grabbed his spinning head. He was in a room with air, not water. How was this possible, and why?

A door clicked, then he heard a man's voice. "My lord, is there anything I can assist you with?"

"Uh, I'm not sure. Can you explain all this?"

"My apologies, my lord. You have entered Keawev, the capital of Mer Clan Kaiana. I am Cinwell, here to serve you. If you look to your right, you will find clothes suitable to your size and boots that should fit as well to your left. Once you have changed, I will be outside. I'm leaving a tray with refreshments to help you adjust from the swim."

Thousands of questions swarmed Jashun's mind. He changed into white clothes and ate the biscuit and oranges, then downed the lemon water. Surprisingly, his dizzy head felt better. He stepped outside, and his mouth dropped in wonder.

A dazzling sea city sparkled before him. Cinwell bowed and motioned for him to follow. The two walked side by side while Cinwell informed Jashun about the waterless city. Jashun looked up and saw the jelly-like dome above his head. Sea creatures swam outside. This was not what he expected, and again, where was Kailani?

"This walkway extends around the perimeter of the border wall. It forms a circle with the palace at its center. Only five bridges allow you to enter the city from the border walkway."

Jashun felt the sand stir beneath his shoes but saw that it did not stick to his boots or Cinwell's bare feet. Cinwell was tall with broad shoulders. His hair was blue, and his eyes matched. He had cocoa-colored skin and spoke with poise and dignity. He didn't seem like a servant to Jashun.

They started over an entry bridge made of seashells, coral, and gems. It was beautiful. Jashun looked below and saw dark water filled with creatures he had never seen before. They bared their teeth, and he almost lost his balance, but Cinwell steadied him.

"Careful, my lord. Those creatures are our protection," Cinwell pointed forward. "As you can see, each entry has several shops with trinkets, mostly oddities of what Mers have found from shipwrecks."

"Wait. Are you a mermaid?"

Cinwell snorted. "No, my lord. I am a merman from Clan Kahakoe. We are of the fourth class here."

"My apologies. Please forgive my ignorance. What does fourth class mean?"

"We operate under a five-class system. Royals and government officials are first, then the military second. Scholars, gatherers, and merchants are third. We, the helpers, are fourth, and last is the Maelama Clan, the preservers."

Jashun didn't want to offend Cinwell, but he was curious. "Does it bother you?"

"Bother me?"

"Yes, to be ranked?"

"No, my lord. We are not seen as ranked but as where we are suited best. Our talents are valued and put to proper use. I understand that on land, this is not so."

Jashun didn't know if that was a question or an accusation. As they walked through the city, Jashun made mental notes of how it looked in case Sealyn would want to know. Tall buildings that looked like miniature castles were everywhere. Rows and rows of these miniatures, then water with bridges. Luckily, these pools were filled with colorful fish and fountain statues, not creepy creatures.

Once they reached the castle, servants ran outside to greet them with more lemon water. They bowed and scurried back inside.

"Enjoying the enchanted lemon water?" Cinwell asked.

"Enchanted?"

"Yes, how else do you think your body can breathe easily in our bubble of salt?"

Jashun choked. "Salt bubble? I'm breathing salt?"

"Yes and no. You see, for us Merpeople to breathe air, we must have salt. It's part of our molecular structure. Our magic is powerful, and I won't go into all the enchanting details, but a short version is that we grind sea salt extremely fine for us to breathe, but when a guest from land comes, we make this potion to filter the salt from your lungs."

Jashun swallowed the lemon drink, and an eerie feeling fell over him. Without the Merpeople providing him with this potion, his lungs would eventually burn and fill with salt; then, he would die. Also, even if he left right now and tried to swim home, he wouldn't be able to make it back alive without Kailani's help. He was completely at their mercy.

Kailani opened the castle doors, now as a stunning human, wearing a form-fitted, glistening silver gown that swirled with multiple colors. Above the knee, the bottom flared into what looked like multicolored scales. She placed her hands on her hips and glided down the seashell steps.

Jashun's heart pounded at her elegance. He tried not to stare at the deep V-shaped top, so he focused on her bright pink eyes. He thought he saw anger there, so he quickly bowed.

"Hello again, Your Majesty. Thank you for having me here."

"I'm glad you're enjoying yourself," she stepped closer. Jashun could smell her scent of the ocean and some flower he couldn't remember the name of. She stood so close their lips almost touched. He wanted those luscious, pink lips. His body began to crave her. Everything about her. He didn't just want her body. Oh, how he wished for that body, but he actually wanted her heart, too. He wanted her to desire him back. Could there be a chance for him and Kailani to become more than friends?

He remembered their feverish kisses in the ocean and tried to form words. "I am, princess. Cinwell has been most helpful."

Kailani leaned in, her chest against his, and whispered in his ear, "Good. Now, let's discuss how you're a dirty little spy."

CHAPTER 12
DON'T LOSE HOPE

Tap. Tap. Tap

The same blue bird was at the window again. This was the fifth time this bird had shown up, and Siany was now agitated. She was trying to focus on the hundreds of books in front of her. Overwhelmed felt like an understatement. The school's grand opening was days away, and she felt immensely underprepared.

Tap. Tap. Tap. Tap.

She glared at the bird through the glass window. A pain fell over her. Siany had hoped her Luxen powers would present themselves to her by now, but sadly, nothing had happened. How was she to lead a school and not have any powers of her own? She desperately wanted to help her kingdom, especially the children who were scared.

Tap. Tap. Tap. Tap. Tap.

"You insistent bird! Will you leave me in peace?!"

The bird looked at her, moving its head back and forth. Siany wondered if she should let it in, so she walked to the window, opened one side, and expected the bird to fly in, but it stayed on the windowsill.

She felt something strange come over her, like tasting sugar for the first time, and then her fingers tingled with green sparks at the end. She looked at the bird, whose expression was amused. Amused? Could birds be amused? She reached out to touch the sapphire-colored bird, then her vision changed. She was looking back at herself.

She stumbled backward and fell to the stone floor, startling the bird, who took flight. Siany felt sick as she watched in horror. She was heading straight for the ground, yet she could still feel the coolness of the stone floor. She watched as she saw herself, falling to her death. A loud scream escaped her mouth, but right as she was about to hit the grass, she swooped into the nearest tree branch. Tree branch? This couldn't be right. Was she not getting enough sleep?

She watched as Lady Madilina trained the dragon, then she was in flight again. What was happening? She was flying around the outside of the school castle. She could see everything—the treetops, the grass meadow, the castle walls, yet she still felt her fingers on the floor in her classroom. She landed on top of a statue at the front of the school and watched as Madam Bip exited a carriage. She heard Bip thank the driver and hugged Lady Pinx. They began discussing potion theories as they walked inside. How did no one notice her flying around? Unless…

The bird flew back through Siany's window. She saw herself, again. Sitting on the floor, she held out her hands, and the blue bird landed in them. The bird chirped, and the channeling was over. Now, she was seeing the blue-feathered creature with its long tail.

"Wait. Did you just give me your sight and hearing?"

Chirp.

"Can you understand me?"

Chirp. Chirp.

Off the bird flew. Siany had no idea if that was yes or no or merely a bird being a bird. What she did know is that she was finally a Luxen, a Transference Luxen! She was excited. Channeling creatures was a dream come true. They had gathered enough intel to know that once a person could channel an animal, the animal must also be willing to be channeled. It would decide what to give of itself.

This bird had decided to allow Siany to channel it, and it had given her its ability to see and hear wherever it flew. That kind of power could be very useful in the future.

She heard footsteps running. She could hear someone yelling her name. What was happening? Guards filed into her room along with an out-of-breath Lady Norella.

"Princess Siany!"

Siany stood from the floor in shock, wiping her hands. "Yes? What's the meaning of this?"

"I heard you scream. Are you hurt?"

Siany snickered happily. "Oh, that, well, no. I'm not. I'm now a Luxen."

Norella gasped. "Majesty! That's so wonderful. Which type?"

"Transference."

With twinkling blue wings, Miola flew into the room, panting as well. "Majesty?"

"Everything is fine, Miola. Go back to your speech lessons," Siany said.

From Sealyn's encounter with the Earth Nichts on her way to Len Nove, Ivy, the beautiful, cinnamon-colored Nicht with yellow-tinted wings, had agreed to come to teach speech classes to all Nichts who wanted to learn how not to overpluralize words. Miola and Maekel were the first Nichts to sign up. Both, along with hundreds more, were doing well.

"Yes, Majesty," Miola spoke slowly to show off her new speech. "I will return to class if you are safe."

Siany clapped. "Well done, Miola. You're making excellent progress."

Miola's wings fluttered, and her cheeks blushed.

"You're not the only one having successes, Miola. Your princess is a Transference Luxen," Norella praised.

Miola squeaked and flew to Siany to give a tiny, Nicht-sized hug. "I'm so happys for you. I mean, happy for you."

"Thank you, but sounds like you need to return to your classes." Miola chuckled and was almost out the door when Siany said, "Miola, how is Maekel?"

The room quieted. Everyone remembered the saddest day in Elysium's history, and Maekel's loss was a part of it. Corentine's dragon burned a field of baby Nichts, and one of those innocent teeny babies was Maekel's.

Miola's face saddened. "She's as well as can be expected. Queen Sealyn leaving was very hard for her."

"Understood. Thank you. Now, go be the star pupil in Ivy's class."

Norella waited till Miola was out of earshot. "Princess Siany, I heard that Lord Edvard is coming to the school's opening."

"Is there a question in there somewhere?"

"Yes," Norella laughed. "Are you going to start courting him officially?"

Siany's freckled face blushed at the thought. "I'm not sure, but I won't make that sort of announcement at the opening if that was your underlying question. The opening needs to be focused solely on the school. We need parents and children comfortable."

"Understood. I think more professors have arrived. Madam Bip and Pinx have set up a welcome dinner in the great mess hall. Will you be joining us?"

"Of course. I'm looking forward to it," Siany paused. She didn't usually engage in small talk outside of Novaly, but she wanted to get to know her colleagues better. "I read that article Lady Adalina published." Norella dropped her head and folded her arms over his mint green dress. "How are you doing?"

Norella sank into one of the wooden chairs. "I don't understand why she's doing this. I thought we were friends. It's one thing to write about the royals, but it's another thing to go after someone like me or Brehan."

"Why?"

"Royalty equals spotlight, but I'm just a lady. My life should be kept private."

"And our lives should be put on display?"

Norella caught the irritated tone in Siany's voice. "My apologies. Honestly, no, it shouldn't be like that either. I'm just hurt she would try to use rumors about Brehan and me to sell her stupid newspapers."

"So, the rumors aren't true?"

"No. We've just been writing letters to each other. I only saw him at the send-off party. We wanted to take things slow. Three years ago, his late wife died of a sickness, then his daughter shortly followed, so he's paranoid to fall in love again."

"Oh, how sad, and you?"

"Well, the last interest I had turned out to be a scummy traitor, and then there was the cheating guy who lived in Hill Chimes. Sure, other lords have shown affection toward me, but none have created a spark in me like Brehan."

"I wish you good luck then. I'll see you at the dinner."

Norella curtseyed and left. That was the longest conversation Siany had had with someone outside of her Vinurs. It was uncomfortable, but she did it. She felt proud. She could do this. She could be the leader of this great school.

The Golden Lake lived up to its name, Sorcha thought as they sailed further to Shunal. The bottom was covered in gold coins, gold jewels, and gold rocks. The water was deep, but the water was so clear that the gold looked like she could reach just below the surface and grab a handful of coins.

The Golden Lake surrounded Shunal and was cursed for Shunalians, though. The lungs of any Shunalian who dared venture below would solidify to gold. Sorcha shivered at the thought, especially knowing among the gold staring back at her were probably layers of hundreds of human lungs.

Sorcha tensed as the wooden steps creaked, leading her to her cage. She could barely breathe like her lungs were already filled with gold. The iron bar door slammed closed, echoing the sound of captivity, and with the click of the key locking, tears slid down her sharp, ebony cheeks. She sunk to the straw floor, hugging her knees to her chest, she started to lose hope. Where was Sealyn? Why had they not sent a rescue team? Was Sealyn even alive? Were any of her friends?

Sune and Doebromir crawled to her and embraced their friend. They needed each other, and their hearts were at their breaking points.

"What did you see?" Doebromir whispered.

"We've arrived at Golden Lake, and it's every bit as the books describe."

Doebromir scratched his reddish beard. "We will be arriving at Shunal's port within the next day or two at the max."

Sorcha sniffed and wiped her nose. "Max," she chuckled. "You remember when Max didn't know Char put a frog in his ale, and then…" Sorcha started laughing, which prompted Doebromir to start laughing. "He. He drank it and then spit that frog right down Adalina's top. She started jumping around."

"Max was puking while this was happening, don't forget." Doebromir chuckled.

"Oh yes. That's right. Char kept clapping for Adalina, telling her she was better at jumping than the frog."

"Ever since then, Max has looked into his cup before drinking," Doebromir added.

The laughs continued, then slowly stopped. Sorcha looked into Doebromir's green eyes, tears forming. "I want to go home, Doebromir. I don't know how much more of this I can take." She burst into tears and fell into his brotherly embrace.

They huddled together in the cage, longing for freedom. Sune began to sing one of Elysium's old songs that was meant to warm a person's heart. He had a great singing voice. He hoped it would help soothe Sorcha.

They heard footsteps, and then the hatch flung open. Several guards stormed down the steps. The Elysians had no idea why they were here—this was off-schedule for them. The guards forcefully hauled them to the main deck. The wind hit their faces, and they drank in the fresh air.

The gruff captain told them to kneel, and they reluctantly obeyed.

"Excellent," the Stoltlander said. "My lady, would you be so kind as to join me?" Sorcha looked at him wearily but stood beside him, facing Doebromir and Sune on their knees.

The captain drew his sword. "Since we had to ration food, you will decide who lives and who dies."

"What? No!"

"You dare to defy me?" He slapped her. Sune tried to stand, but he was held down by a guard.

Holding her throbbing cheek, Sorcha pleaded, "I. I. I can't make such a decision. I will share my food. Please, don't make me do this."

"Sorry, gorgeous, but rules are rules upon entering Shunal's port. Everything is about perception. If any member on your boat looks like a slave or prisoner, then you can't enter. We need you all to look well-fed and like you want to be with us."

"That's the stupidest thing I've ever heard," Doebromir said, and the guard behind him immediately smacked him.

"Sounds like you need to be the one to die."

"What I'm saying is that no one at Shunal's port will buy that the Elysians want to be on a Stoltland ship."

"We have a story for that. Don't you worry, your pretty, bald self," he pointed his sword back and forth. "Now, choose who dies."

Sorcha could barely process. She needed to think of something fast. Her stomach growled, begging for attention. She blocked her desire for feasting and focused her wit on outsmarting the dense Stoltlander. Could she be brave enough to sacrifice herself for them? Or was there a way to convince him that they were all worth more alive than dead?

"You're one lucky Stoltlander, you know that," She squeaked out.

The captain paused. "Why?"

"You just so happened to have the three most valuable prisoners."

"Really? Do explain."

She needed to lie but have truths around the lies so that Doebromir and Sune could play along. "Well, as you call him, Baldy was Queen Sealyn's second in command. It was rumored that she was going to name him her overall commander, but her cousin became angry, so she gave the position to Tilmond. Baldy knows all of Elysium's military tactics."

Doebromir gasped. "How dare you tell him that!"

"Pretty Boy, as you named him, is Queen Sealyn's childhood friend from her time in military training. He knows her strengths and weaknesses."

Sune glared. "You wicked traitor! I can't believe I fell for you."

The captain grinned an evil smile. "And you, my lady…who are you to Queen Sealyn?"

"Me? I'm her best friend. She would do anything, pay anything to have me back with her."

"Excellent," the captain showed his yellow teeth. With two swift moves, he sliced through two sailors passing by. "Toss their bodies to the gold. Now, we have more than enough food for such valuable guests."

After they were locked in their cages, along with their magnificent meals, they stared at each other closely.

"I think we're alone," Sune said.

"Great job, Sorcha! That was some quick thinking!" Doebromir praised.

Sorcha exhaled in relief. "I was so hoping you guys were on the same page."

Sune smiled and took a big bite of his meat. "One truth and two lies."

"A fun little game," Sorcha remarked with a mouth full of potatoes.

"You passed a good lie about Tilmond not being the first choice when he always was, and I surely don't know any classified information," Doebromir sipped the fresh water with delight.

"Exactly, and I wasn't in the same training camp as Sealyn. That was Ajorn. I only saw her during meals and parties."

Sorcha's brow furrowed. "I didn't know that, Sune. I thought that was the truth, so if that was a lie, what do you think was my truth?"

Sune looked up from his meal and tilted his head as if the answer was the most obvious thing in all the lands. "Sealyn will do anything to get you back, and she will pay anything for you," He snickered. "But her 'pay' isn't what everyone always thinks. It most likely will be 'pay*back*.'"

Sorcha's eyes stung and threatened tears. "Do you really think they're coming?"

Doebromir laughed a confident laugh. "Honestly, Sorcha, it wouldn't surprise me if they were on their way with an army right now."

Elysian News

The Latest News and Gossip

Issue #12

Special Edition: A Tribute to Lady Sorcha Berwin

Greetings, my fellow Elysians. Today will be a wonderful dedication to our friend, Lady Sorcha. Lady Sorcha volunteered at the local hospital, saving lives, helping others, and spending time with the injured.

She's a selfless lady, always putting others first. There's magic in her, and we can only hope and pray that the magic will find her. I ask that we live our days trying to be more like Lady Sorcha and give back to others in need.

Painted above: Lady Sorcha Berwin

Lady Sorcha is a fantastic dancer, has an infectious laugh, is willing to play pranks, and has a beautiful singing voice.
One of her most brilliant accomplishments was creating an elixir that counteracts a *Needlebob's poison.

She also played a crucial role in securing the Heart of Elysium's whereabouts, which are still secured. Before the Len Novian quest, she trained as a warrior and soon became one of the training program's top Civilian Warriors.

Lady Sorcha once mentioned that she has family she doesn't know, so I beg you, if you're Lady Sorcha's family, please come forward.
~ Lady Adalina Roedellen (Lina)

Princess Siany Spotlight	Pub Tour Cancelled	Luxen School Updates
The juiciest gossip	*Rumors confirmed*	*Weekly Reports*
Finally, she's a Transference	Lord Char is gone! Where is he?	Time to pick up your schoolbooks.
		Available at *Market Library*
What does this mean as Headmistress?	The palace refuses to comment	Parents are encouraged to follow progress.
Page 2	Page 3	Page 6

CHAPTER 13
TAKE ONE FOR THE TEAM

Coming to an accord with the Pirate Captain was not easy. His demands were long, but they were probably a few days behind the Stoltlanders and needed to catch up. Sealyn leaned on the railing at the ship's bow, ready to see the golden waters as they sailed down Hostile Channel.

The Pirate Captain leaned on the banister next to her. She felt like she could feel darkness around him, or perhaps anger; after all, he was from Korpam. Neither looked at each other. They kept their eyes on the ever-changing waters.

He cleared his throat. "So, you know."

"So, I know."

"Will you keep my secret?"

"For now."

"'Till when?"

"Until I no longer deem it necessary, *pirate*."

He chuckled. "Fire. I expect nothing less from a phoenix queen."

Sealyn smiled to herself. She would almost like him if it wasn't for his murderous reputation. "Let's get some things clear now that we're alone," She turned and faced him. "Your secret is a distraction, and I can't have any distractions for this mission." The pirate nodded. "Next, I could care less about all your silly demands. I know you want something, so you might as well come clean with your hidden agenda." She folded her arms, waiting.

He smiled and shook his finger at Sealyn. "You know, I think I might just like you," He crossed his arms and adjusted his stance. "I'll give you my name in exchange for a request. You can toss the other demands."

"Ah, so I don't need to heat your food to a certain temperature when you dine with us?"

He laughed. "My son, Laisren, likes to play jokes. He wanted to see how far he could push our limits for demands."

"Good to know. Why would I care about your name?"

He propped his back against the banister, leaning against his elbows, and stared up at the sails. "Since my request is to have Elysium's army backing me in my claim for Korpam's throne..."

"What?! Why would I ever do such a thing?"

"Well, that's because my name is Tyrdon Steig."

Sealyn gasped. "You're supposed to be dead."

"Sorry to disappoint, majesty."

"So, you faked your death?"

Tyrdon shrugged. "After the uprising, I simply disappeared. I met Liva several years later on one of my many raids of Korpam. We built a fleet ten ships deep and kept to a small island that Korpam doesn't inhabit. It's not even on a map."

"Why are you telling me all this?"

He stood, gripping the railing with one hand. "Because my family is the rightful heirs of that throne. It's my kingdom," he growled. "I want it back."

"And you expect my army to do that for you?"

"I expect that as payment. I will help you break Shunal's curse. Let's not pretend your sole mission is to free those prisoners."

"Why not bring this up in front of the others?"

He laughed. "I haven't made it this far without being paranoid about who to trust."

"And you...*the Pirate Captain*... trust me?"

"I wasn't sure initially, but you broke Len Nove's curse and won the mammoth's respect. Plus, Lord Prince William is a trustworthy man, and he said I could trust you."

Sealyn paused, thinking about the mention of her cousin. She trusted him will all her heart, so maybe—just maybe, this mission could work. "All right. Let's say we trust each other. Instead of your ships being lookouts at the ports, I propose another mission for a select elite of your pirates."

Tyrdon tilted his head. "I'm intrigued."

"With the time it will take us to find the rebels and hunt down the underground market, I won't have time to hunt for the power source of Shunal."

"Easy enough."

"I'm not done," she stepped closer. "If we're captured, I want your vow that you and your crew will do whatever it takes to rescue us."

His eyes flashed orange and glared. "My secret already assures that."

Shunal's ports were impressive. The entire kingdom was one massive island with hundreds of docks encircling the border. The Shunalian navy governed the Golden Lake with barrier checkpoints, making sure no ships passed through to other kingdoms. They marked the Golden Lake only for trade routes, which is another reason why Shunal was the richest kingdom. If one wanted the fastest option for traveling to another kingdom, then the only way was through one of Shunal's traveling trade ships.

The Stoltlanders kept one ship anchored in the bay of Golden Lake, and the other docked at the Liquid Market port sector. Their ships still had the barrels of ice from Len Nove for Stoltland's water needs, but they would need to trade a few barrels for passage to their kingdom. Shunal didn't care to acknowledge the Nicht slave trade, so they merely acted like Nichts didn't exist to preserve the barrels of ice.

Sune thought his heart was going to beat out of his chest when he looked at Shunal for the first time. He hated that the Stoltland captain made a smart move and kept Sorcha on the anchored ship. This way, they had to play along with whatever story the Stoltlanders had in mind.

He and Doebromir stepped on the dock--their first time on sturdy ground in months. His knees buckled, then steadied. The boards creaked under their scuffed boots as they made their way to the market. Sune took one final glance back at the anchored ship, then stepped on Shunalian soil.

He breathed in the smell of wine and fresh bread. They both glanced around in amazement. They had never seen such busy streets. Each tent or stone establishment was painted in its kingdom's yellow colors, parading the finest drinks. Scattered throughout the many liquid sellers were small tents selling food to pair with the drinks.

Sune's mouth watered, and he looked at Doebromir. "Should we?"

"We must keep our wits about us. Grab bottles of ale, but only rinse your mouth with the taste, then spit either back in the bottle or behind a bush," Doebromir whispered.

Once their group was cleared to walk in the marketplace by the Shunalian patrol, the Elysians grabbed the first bottles they could get. They wanted to make the Stoltlanders think they were stupid enough to impair their minds. Hopefully, the black-clad sailors would let their guards down.

"Aye, what 'ya 'tink yer doin'?" shouted one of the Stoltlander sailors. Clearly, he was the brains of the group.

"Just trying to show Shunal how glad we are to be here with you wonderful escorts," Doebromir said happily.

The black eyes of the sailors flared. "Fine, but no more 'dan 'dat."

The crew walked into the first tavern they saw. It was painted gold, representing Shunal. Gold-cushioned nooks with windows were on each wall. Gold-painted tables and chairs scattered the large room, and the round bar was at the center. The ceiling was covered in sparkling canary yellow fabrics with random strips dangling to the floor, providing room separations.

Their crew, consisting of six Stoltlanders and two Elysians, sat at a large table toward a back corner. The yellow haze of Shunal's curse dazzled in the sunlight. The crew did not want to draw attention. A heavy-set woman with raven black hair and caramel skin came to their table carrying two trays of golden ale. Doebromir tried his best not to stare, but he couldn't help it. Not only was her enormous bust about to spill out of her corset, but she also had gold coins embedded in her skin, covering her chest and neck.

She noticed him staring. "See somethin' ya like, honey?"

Doebromir opened and closed his mouth, unable to find words. All he managed was a quick head shake.

"That's a shame. Welcome to the *Golden Goblet.* What'll it be, gents?"

The group leader spoke quickly, "We'll just have the tavern special for each."

"Right away, sir."

Doebromir watched as the leader examined the room and nodded to another figure in the opposite corner. He couldn't see the figure's whole face due to the hanging fabric, but he didn't like knowing more Stoltlanders were here. Scanning the tavern, he saw no signs of other Elysians. He longed to see fellow green eyes beside Sune's. He felt alone, noticing all the yellow eyes in the room. A wave of nausea swept over him, seeing all the gemmed skin covering the faces, arms, and legs of the Shunalians.

The leader lowered his head to his crew. "Stay here. I'll be back." He left the table for the other corner.

The barmaid returned with plates of bread, cheeses, fish, and nuts. She hesitated before leaving, looking too long into Sune's eyes. "Say, I don't see green eyes much in here," She propped the empty tray on her waist and twirled her black hair. "Actually, we never see green eyes here."

"What's your point?" grumbled a black-eyed sailor.

"My point is, our yellow eyes are to watch for suspicious activity in our kingdom, and this is the epitome of suspicion."

"Back off, woman. You're an ignorant tramp who knows nothing."

Her yellow eyes teared. "I know more than you think!"

"Is that so? Then, why don't you be a good girl and bring back more ale and shut your mouth."

"There's no need to be cruel to her," Sune said.

"Exactly," Doebromir stood. "Apologies, my lady, for their rudeness. They mean no disrespect. We're just all exhausted from sailing."

She glared. "Only because these Elysians know how to treat a woman, I won't report you all to my boss. You best eat up and get out quick."

The sailor looked around the tavern and noticed a staircase at the far corner where his leader was still in conversation. "Is this place also an inn?"

"Doesn't matter for you," the barmaid snapped.

"Why not?"

"Because you're not welcome to purchase a room."

Doebromir didn't want to return to the docked ship and sleep in a cage. "Please, madam. I beg your forgiveness. Is there any way we could make it up to you so we could secure rooms?"

Her eyes twitched, and then she walked closer to Doebromir and turned her gaze to the rude sailor. "I tell 'ya what. You give me a couple of hours with this lad for free, and I'll reserve your crew a few of our finest rooms."

Doebromir's eyes bulged, and he threw up his hands. "Wait, madam. I hope I didn't give you the wrong impression."

"Deal!" the Stoltland sailor said, reaching his calloused hand across the table, laughing.

"What? Wait!" Doebromir protested.

She grinned. "I'll just go put my apron behind the bar."

Doebromir looked to Sune for help. "Sune, what am I supposed to do?"

Sune laughed. "Honestly, I don't know whether to advise you to take one for the crew or to enjoy yourself or…"

"Or?"

"Maybe ask for some passionate conversation?"

"I can't believe this is happening," Doebromir looked at the barmaid, whispering to the bartender, who nodded. "I don't know what to do. She's coming back."

Sune patted Doebromir's shoulder. "Good luck, my friend. May Creator be on your side."

Flirtatiously swaying side to side, she motioned for Doebromir to follow her. Doebromir downed his ale and then trailed the Shunalian, while she fidgeted with her corset strings up the stairs.

Once in a private room, she slammed the door and began connecting yellow petals in front of the door. She grabbed another hand full of yellow petals and began speaking a language Doebromir could not understand. He noticed the petals ran along the perimeter of the room. What was she doing? Was she about to poison him?

"Look, madam."

"Hush. I'm almost done," she continued the foreign language. When she finished, Doebromir felt a change in air pressure in his ears.

"What was that?" he asked.

"A spell."

"Are you a Luxen?"

"Yes, a Tethered Luxen," she pointed to the petals around the room. "I've experimented with boundary spells. The one I just cast is made with the evening primrose flower. The flower can hear approaching bees in its natural state, so it sweetens its nectar, enticing the bees for pollination."

"That's a great plant lesson, but what does that have to do with bartering me for a few hours?"

She giggled, cleavage bouncing. "Because I used this flower with my spell, the room is now sealed from our words leaving these walls." Doebromir swallowed. He did not like where this woman's words were heading. "And because I'm me, I added a few extra herbs to the spell so that when people do walk by, all they hear is—well, um, passionate sounds."

"I'm so confused."

"I needed our conversation private. No one can hear it."

Doebromir blinked. He must have heard her wrong. "Conversation? You mean, we're not...I don't have to..."

She laughed, stoking the fire, then poured tea. "No, silly. Although that would be fun," she winked. "I have another agenda at play."

"Which would be?"

"I'm no fool, Elysian, and I'm no typical barmaid. I can tell you're not here by choice." She sat at the small table and gestured for him to join her. "My name is Vaelinthia, and I'm part of the Shunalian revolution known as the Trica Rebels, *and* I believe we can help each other."

CHAPTER 14
LUXEN CLASSES

Siany's heart skipped a beat as Lord Edvard's hand grazed hers as she toured a group down the new school halls. She tried not to be distracted by his intoxicating scent of evergreen because she had a full day's worth of tasks in front of her. She walked into Lady Pinx's classroom, full of tables scattered with herbs and potted plants. Lining the walls were several bookshelves stocked with fresh, new books for the students.

"As you can see, Professor Gunnolf, or as most know her, Lady Pinx, has her classroom ready for tomorrow's launch. She will be teaching *Phytocology*. We feel that her class will evolve into several levels, so just like our *Enchanted Potions* subject will have three levels: Potions First Term, Potions Second Term, and Potions Third Term, we predict her class will do the same."

"And just for clarity," Lord Edvard said. "A term is one full year of study, correct?"

"Very good. Someone has been paying attention." The group giggled at Siany's flirtations.

Princess Siany slid her fingers down the spine of one of the many green books that said "Phytocology" in white lettering. She hoped she was doing a good job. Everyone seemed to be enjoying themselves. Her group consisted of several diplomats, a few pairs of parents, and two members of the Council of Wisdom.

Lord Stev was among the Council of Wisdom. He was an older gentleman with thinning white hair and a face that always had a red tint to it. Stev cleared his throat, "Princess, you mentioned earlier that students staying at the castle would be divided into their Luxen abilities: Tethered and Transference. Only those two since none have shown Cognition abilities."

"Yes, correct."

"Are you or any of the professors worried this will cause division amongst the students?" he asked.

Siany steadied herself. The professors and herself had already had this same debate but reached a firm conclusion. "No, Lord Stev. We think it's best, at least for the first two terms, that students should get to know others with similar talents, struggles, and needs. Since we are all walking in unknown territory, we recognize that this may need to change and are open to it if it does. We've discussed blending third terms or perhaps waiting until later," she laid her hand on his shoulder. "I want to assure you. After they complete their second term, we will properly evaluate each student and make well-researched decisions."

"Excellent," Stev smiled and grabbed a book to thumb through. He squinted his eyes to read; age was catching up with him.

They heard Novaly yell, "No, don't do that! Don't! You'll…" A huge explosion sounded, and a gush of sparkling red and gold dust blew past Professor Gunnolf's classroom doorway. It smelled of burnt apples and old cheese. They raced past the red and gold-dusted walls and entered Lady Novaly's classroom.

"Professor Draemamoor! What happened?" Siany demanded. She hated having a harsh tone with her best friend.

Novaly blinked through the red dust caked on her face and pointed, "It was his fault. I told Professor Rendell not to add the red phoenix feather to the mixture."

Hueweyn, also covered in red dust, panicked when he saw the tour group. He hated crowds but was somehow calm to teach children. He volunteered to teach *Magical Creature*

Studies when his Transference powers were showcased. Now, he wished he had never stepped foot in Novaly's classroom. He only wanted to wish her good luck for tomorrow. "I'm ever so sorry, majesty. It slipped, and I…"

"No need to worry, Professor Rendell. I'm sure with you and Professor Draemamoor, this mess will be cleaned up in no time," Siany glowered, hoping her point was made. She could not have professors blowing up potions in front of students. Novaly and Hueweyn nodded and quickly headed for the broom closet. Several Nichts flew in to assist with the cleanup.

Siany walked down the hallway, trying to steal back the tour's focus. "Shall we continue this way? Have no fear with Professor Hueweyn Rendell. He's marvelous with children, and in fact, he will not only be teaching *Magical Creatures Studies* but *Channeling Creatures: First Term,* too."

Lord Edvard chuckled. "What will the charming Professor Draemamoor be instructing?"

"Oh, Novaly? I mean, Professor Draemamoor. She will be teaching *Enchanted Potions: First Term,* hopefully with less enthusiasm from the cauldrons."

Once the last tour guest left the castle, Siany breathed a deep sigh of relief. She sank into her chair and leaned back, chuckling about how silly Novaly had looked covered in red dust. Several Nichts adjusted a few final books on her shelves, then flew to the next room for final inspections. The Nichts were all very excited about the new school and had been a huge help in preparing the castle. Siany sat up when she heard a knock at her door.

King Father Ryker walked in. "Mind if an old man graces your presence?"

"Old? You mean ancient?" Siany teased and gestured for him to sit.

"How did today go?"

"It was perfect if you don't count a red-feathered potion explosion."

"A what?"

"Never mind. Take my mind off the day. How are things with you leading the kingdom again?"

Ryker folded his arms. "Well, let's see. Len Nove is making excellent progress. The great mammoth king, King Nawrooshall, even granted me access to channel communication with him since Sealyn is…off saving the world."

"That's wonderful news."

"Lady Zuri is taking nicely to her position as ambassador, but we've had to send some troops from Fort Kippen to help defend against several Stoltland raids on Len Nove's western coast. They use Shunal's travel routes to sneak past Len Nove's patrols."

Siany shook her head. "Always Stoltland. Do you think they will ever stop?"

"Honestly," Ryker sighed. "As long as Corentine breathes, Stoltland will continue to hurt the innocent."

"I would have to agree with you." She leaned on her desk, covered with books and papers. "I heard Korpam attacked along our western border again."

"That's true, but it seems to be organized attacks instead of their usual random ones," Ryker stood, pacing. "I can't quite put my finger on it, but they made a scene, almost wanting us to see their attack."

"Normally, they hide in the darkness and use surprise."

"Precisely. This time, they attacked in broad daylight."

Siany's brow furrowed. "Like they wanted to cause a distraction?"

Ryker stopped pacing, and his expression read that he was on the verge of a great discovery. "That's it! I need to investigate if anything was stolen." He walked to the window, gazing at the sky.

"Stolen?"

"Yes. I believe there's a connection between the raids. A few weeks ago, a library in Port Rowin complained that some children had broken in and stolen some books."

"Which ones?"

"Books on Korpam's history. This is all making sense now," he clapped his hands once. "They are stealing our books on their history. They're searching for something that they haven't found yet. I need to order all history books on Korpam to be brought here, to the capital, for protection."

"I'm glad I could help," Siany winked.

Ryker walked to his daughter and kissed her head. "You always do. Now, I must go, and you have a grand opening to prepare for. You make me so proud."

"Thank you, Father."

Ryker quickly walked down the stone hallways with his new mission in mind. Why would Korpam suddenly be so interested in their history? What in their past would their monarchy be willing to die for or willing to kill for?

Elysian News

Issue #15

The Latest News and Gossip

<u>Trouble in Paradise?</u>
The golden couple struggles

Greetings, Elysians. I'm here with some exciting and possibly distressful news.

We all love Lord Max and Lady Madilina, especially the heroic stories about their bravery in fighting against the evil Commander Malum; where Max fought for his freedom with several stabs and a fever, then Madilina saved his life by channeling a flying horse, who gave her its wings.

But, with all that said, I sadly report that the couple was seen arguing before Lord Max left for the special quest. Witnesses say they heard Max telling Madilina he wants her to stop training the fire-breathing dragon. He believes it should be killed. Madilina, apparently, loudly disagreed. The last report was that Max stormed off yelling, "And I won't be writing to you until the beast is dead."

Madilina continues to train both dragons. Yes, we know how many of you complain about the bubble dragon sneaking around and blowing bubbles to scare people. Madilina assures me that he's harmless but loves trickery.

What do you think? Can the couple survive? ~Lady Adalina Roedellen, Lina

Princess Siany Spotlight	**New Fashions Available**	**Luxen School Updates**
The juiciest gossip	*Just in time for Autumn*	*Weekly Reports*
Does she have feelings for Lord Edvard?	Lady Princess Anadelvia showcases new line	Grand Opening! Get tour tickets now!
Lord Edvard to attend grand opening	Available at *Look Twice*	Available at the *Market's Library*
Page 2	Page 4	Page 6

CHAPTER 15
THAT'LL DO

"You're insane!" Tilmond yelled. "My apologies, Queen Sealyn, but I think this time, you've crossed the line of insanity."

"Why? Just because it's never been attempted from this far?"

"No, because it's literally our cousin's theory. Will even said he had only tested this method twice. Once was a complete disaster."

"But…" Sealyn interrupted. "The other was a success with some minor changes needed, which he fixed and added to the small boats on this ship for this *very* reason."

Tilmond turned and faced Jace. "King Jace, can you speak some sense to your wife?"

"Have you just met your cousin?" Jace smiled seductively toward Sealyn. "She's illogically logical with this plan."

"Do explain," Tilmond huffed.

Jace stood pointing to the map displayed on the oval-shaped table in the royal meeting room of the ship. The room had dark wooden walls with maps hung like tapestries.

"Our ship docking would draw too much attention, but the pirate ship would just be a normal ship docking for supplies and trade," Jace said, sliding the small boat representing the pirate ship to the drawn Shunalian port.

"Then why can't we just have Queen Sealyn's crew hidden on the pirate ship?" Max asked. Tilmond threw his hands up, showing his support for Max's question.

Jace shook his head. "You're forgetting Shunal's checkpoints and their patrols. The small boat would be docked among twenty other small boats. These aren't watched as the pirates already said."

"Trusting the word of pirates now, are we?" Favien questioned. Favien wanted to make sure everyone knew his opinion was not to trust them. Something about the Pirate Captain's face seemed odd. It was familiar yet not, so because of this confusion, Favien promised himself never to trust the pirates.

"Who else has personally been to Shunal's ports?" Jace asked.

No one raised their hand.

"See, there's my point," Jace continued. "I agree with Queen Sealyn. The pirate ship docks, our ship stays anchored in the Golden Lake and Hostile Channel border, and the small boat takes a group of pirates with the Elysians underneath."

"Don't forget to add the trusty rebel Shunalian to your group," Herbmando chuckled.

"What about the curse potentially pulling you to a golden death?" Tilmond asked.

"Fair point," Herbmando said. "I must go with the large pirate ship, so I don't possibly have an unfortunate episode aboard the small boat." He pointed to Finn. "Ol' blue eyes will be fine riding in the small boat. No one will question his eyes. Besides, Elysians should be safe from turning to gold. That is our Shunalian curse."

"Should? *Should*?!" Max said incredulously.

"Enough!" Sealyn slammed her fist on the table, cracking the wood. Her eyes flamed blue. "I'm done with the excuses, and I'm done with fear. For those who do *not* want to risk their lives for the sake of Doebromir, Sune, and Sorcha," her voice wavered over Sorcha's name. "Then stay on the ship. It's time to execute the plan we've been talking about. I leave tonight with those who wish to rescue them and break another curse for the sake of peace for all kingdoms."

The crew was ready to launch their mission as the day turned to night. They watched as the pirate ship sailed with speed toward the dock. They had attached a long rope from the ship to the small boat, so the force of the large ship would help make the small boat's journey faster. Once it was close enough to the dock, they were instructed to cut the rope so their speed would not look suspicious.

The small boat held ten pirates plus Finn, and if their plan was successful, they would return to the Elysian ship in three days for more Elysians. Of course, Char pointed out that none of their plans had ever worked, but Sealyn quickly silenced him.

Under the small boat was a carved-out hull that would allow people to breathe underwater, but only briefly. Lord Prince William installed bamboo shoots securely to the outside of the boat, wrapped underneath so the people in the air pocket could breathe fresh air when needed. He ensured the bamboo shoots' diameter was the perfect size to not interfere with the paddles or be noticeable.

Everyone was concerned about holding onto the handles in the hull. As the mission began, the large ship's current pulled on the Elysians' joints. Their fingers ached, and water splashed into their eyes, burning them. These would be long hours crossing the Golden Lake.

Char let out a groan. "This is exactly why I didn't want to come."

"Hush, Char and focus," Tilmond snapped. Grunts and groans echoed in the chamber.

Ashur felt his grip loosening. "My fingers. They're slipping!" Wrinkles of straining exploded across his ebony face.

"Hold on, Ashur!" Favien commanded.

"I can't. My fingers," Ashur felt his grip, leaving the handle. Only the tips of his fingers were on it. He would drown if he let go. It would be hours and hours of swimming in the dark to their Elysian ship, and with his arms exhausted, he wouldn't make it.

Ajorn joined the encouraging, "Stay strong, brother. Focus on a tight grip." He tried to speak without panic. Ajorn looked at Ashur like a little brother. He had always wanted a younger brother. Panic flooded him when he saw his comrades' efforts failing.

Max, beside Ashur, tried to wrap his legs around him, but the waves made it impossible for him to connect both legs. The water level reached their chests and felt like giant hands pulling them down. Max saw the fear in Ashur's eyes and noticed he only had the tip of two fingers on the handle. "Hang on, Ashur. I'm trying..."

Ashur's fingers slipped. Max let go of one handle and tried to grab him, but he missed; water slapped him in the face. Ashur's other hand began slipping. From behind him, Brehan tried to wrap his legs around him, but the force of the water wouldn't allow him to lift his legs. They were all powerless, except one.

Ashur yelled out as his remaining grip released the handle, and he knew he was going to drown. He felt like he should feel death's embrace, but what he felt was tingling around his wrists. He felt himself being pulled back to his handles, and he saw green and blue swirls of hands holding him. His eyes followed the trail of sparkling green and blue light to Sealyn's eyes.

"Grab the handles, soldier."

Ashur blinked in shock.

"That's an order!" Sealyn yelled with strain in her voice as blood dripped from her nose over her lips.

Ashur quickly grabbed the handles and adjusted his grip for a better hold. Once he was secure, the green and blue swirls dissipated. Ashur and Sealyn breathed hard, hearts pounding. There was a long pause before anyone spoke.

"Thank you, Your Majesty," Ashur let out, sounding exasperated.

Jace saw the concerned look in Sealyn's eyes and the blood dripping down her chin. No one could find out what they all had witnessed. He was scared for her, now more than ever. They already knew she was a Luxen, but no one could figure out what type. Her saving Ashur exposed one of her darkest secrets: her power was Cognition.

Jace cleared his throat, and in the chaos of the waves, he spoke. "It goes without saying, but I'm asking for everyone here to swear to secrecy over what was just witnessed." Sealyn looked at Jace with gratefulness.

The crew said in unison, "Understood, King Jace."

Finally, they felt the wake's force lessen, which meant the rope connecting them to the pirate ship had been cut. They were almost there. Their breathing through the bamboo shoots was rapid, and their muscles throbbed. They heard the clash of the paddles in the water; the pirates and Finn were rowing. Ajorn took the role of encourager upon himself. He kept repeating for them to breathe, how great they were doing, and how brave they were. Ajorn was always the motivating presence everywhere he went. Sealyn appreciated him so much since her strength was dwindling from the magic and the waves.

Pounding was heard above them, the signal to stay quiet. The small boat approached the dock. Their hands ached. Muffled sounds were all they heard. Sealyn's heart pounded. She replayed all the conversations she had with the pirate. Had he betrayed her in any of his words? Would an army be waiting to capture them? Did her impulsive decisions cost the lives of her people?

Vaelinthia felt the cool breeze from the night air on her face as she opened her bedroom window. It overlooked the main port, entering Shunal's liquid sector. It had been two days since she revealed herself to the Elysian. So far, they had managed a few notes slid under goblets throughout the days.

She was grateful that the owner allowed the Stoltlanders to stay extra nights, but she hadn't heard anything from the rebels. She feared that they had moved their camp, and messages would take longer if that were so.

Her dark hair spilled past her shoulders, and she dreamed into the moonlight, hoping for a better future. She watched the night's lights dance in the water and noticed the newly docked pirate ship. She shivered at the flag flying. Then, motion caught her sight.

She saw the golden cattails splitting into a pathway. The cattails were tall, so she couldn't tell if it was humans walking through. It could just be a *magna constrictor. Those yellow and orange snakes were thick as grown pigs, yet short. Thankfully, they were as friendly as pet dogs.

Vaelinthia decided to be brave and investigate. Her room had a secret exit from the tavern. It was a tight squeeze for her size, descending the winding stone steps, but she made it and dashed across the streets, hiding between tents and shops until she made her way in front of the cattails.

She heard the swooshing of water and the harmonies of crickets. Cattails snapped, making her jump. The movement was no snake. Several hooded, wet figures were making their way through the golden cattails. She was about to report them when moonlight reflected off the lead person's eyes. Green. She gasped. These were Elysians!

Tilmond pulled apart the golden cattails like a curtain, leading the sopping-wet group. They tried to make little movements to avoid sound. Ajorn tapped Tilmond's right shoulder, signaling him to stop. They paused, listening for footsteps. All they could hear were frogs croaking and crickets chirping.

As they moved slowly through the thick vegetation, they kept the royals in the middle of their line, with Brehan last. One false move and all the seven kingdoms' hope could be lost. Tilmond began moving again. He took two more steps and found the bank. He was about to jump on land when golden eyes met his. He fell back in shock, stumbling into Ajorn. Everyone drew their daggers.

Vaelinthia smiled and slipped into the water and golden plants with the Elysians. "Now, we're talkin'." She ogled Ajorn. "You won't be needing those daggers with me. I have no time to explain, but you must come with me now."

Sealyn stepped forward. "Give me one reason why we should."

Nothing ever really surprised Vaelinthia. She had seen so much from being a rebel and a tavern girl, but seeing the Queen of Elysium in front of her—she was in awe. Even dripping wet, Sealyn had a commanding presence.

"You must be Queen Sealyn of Elysium. Doebromir told me about you."

Sealyn nodded once. "That'll do. Let's go."

They followed Vaelinthia through the gold-dusted streets and tents, back up the narrow winding staircase into her bedroom. The group piled into the tiny room and watched Vaelinthia perform the same magic she had done before to seal the room's sounds. They gave each other accusatory glances, understanding that she was a Luxen.

"Let me introduce myself." Vaelinthia started stoking the fire, motioning for them to dry themselves. "I am Vaelinthia. I'm one of the Trica Rebels."

Sealyn folded her arms, and water dripped from her elbows. "If you're a rebel, let me speak to Herbmando."

A cheeky grin spread across Vaelinthia's face. "Ah, well, that would be difficult because he hasn't been seen in quite some time now, but you would already know that since he's with you."

"Why would you say that when only green eyes are here?"

She walked from the fire, and Vaelinthia sat at her small table, chair creaking. "Because you named him. Cruz, our leader, is the only name people know, but those trusted by someone in our ranks know our names."

"Well, that's confusing," said Max.

"Perhaps to you, sweet phoenix, but here in Shunal, the name of Cruz gives hope to the people. He's the only name the public knows. This is why I know Herbmando must either be with you or has guided you here. We never give out personal names unless you already have an in with the head of the rebel alliance."

Sealyn thought of Jadelyn. She knew there had to be more to Jadelyn, and now she had proof. "If that's so, why trust a foreigner?"

"Ah, but you're not just any foreigner, are you? You are green-eyes and the queen who broke not just one curse but two."

Char stepped around the men, warming themselves by the fire. "She did have help. I want to point that out and have it on record."

Vaelinthia chuckled. "I must say, majesty, you brought a handsome spread of men to my door." She froze as Jace pulled his hood off and turned to face her. Vaelinthia sucked in a breath. "Silver eyes. So, it's true then?"

Jace folded his arms and shifted uncomfortably. Vaelinthia stood, making slow steps toward Jace. Sealyn stepped in front of Jace and scowled.

"I, too, want something on the record. King Jace is our king and will be treated as such. Anyone with an issue with that will face his lioness," Sealyn's eyes flared blue, ready to use the mammoth strength given to her by King Nawrooshall.

"I like you, Queen Sealyn. You have fire."

"We are the phoenixes."

"Speaking of, where is your almighty green phoenix?"

Sealyn took a step closer. "Exactly where he should be, rebel. Now, stop asking questions and start giving us answers."

"What would you like to know?"

"Doebromir. Where is he?"

CHAPTER 16
HIS LIONESS

The light burned Jashun's eyes as he was dragged through Keawev's palace hallways. His eyes were having a hard time adjusting after being held in Kailani's prison, which was total darkness. He hated being in another cage, and he was glad he could finally see colors again, even if he was still a prisoner.

The Mer-guards shoved Jashun into a silver chair at the end of a long, flat, white coral table. He gazed around the tall, rectangular room. The walls were made from a translucent stone that glowed blue from luminescent roots along the room's bottom perimeter. Paintings of underwater creatures hung on the walls. Jashun felt like the glowing walls made the room feel like you were floating.

Jashun's toes played with the sand floor. He hadn't had time to put his boots on before being dragged away. He felt happy for just a moment until the doors at the opposite end flew open, and an angry Kailani and her court came marching in.

He hated how much he loved seeing her, but he knew this would be bad. Confused, he watched her court take seats at the empty silver chairs. Mer helpers swarmed the table, serving wine and seafood. The silver plate piled with food before him made his mouth water, and the fresh shrimp's steam made his stomach growl.

"Lord Jashun, please do eat. I'm sure you must be famished," Kailani cooed.

Jashun's eyes narrowed. What game was she playing? Locking him in a dark room for two days, maybe three, with only water, then showering him with delicious food and wine? How did any of this make sense? He observed her carefully as he took his first bite. It tasted so good. Jashun lost himself in his food and completely forgot all his troubles. He downed the wine and then filled another glass.

Kailani sat back in her chair, holding her silver goblet, watching Jashun intently. "Surely, Jashun, now that you've satisfied your hunger and quenched your thirst, you would like to delineate us with true reasons for your being here."

Jashun felt lightheaded but was delighted to answer the gorgeous princess. "It would be an honor, princess."

Everyone at the table chuckled. "Queen Sealyn sent me here to find out what you would demand from her to strike a deal for Abyss magic, specifically, the magic spell used to keep the old shack at Port Rowin protected."

He suddenly felt confused and upset. Telling the truth was right and fun, so why did he feel bad about it?

Kailani curved forward, setting her elbows on the table, swaying her goblet back and forth. "Ah, that's what the little bird is up to." She set her glass down and propped her chin on her hands. "Tell me, my handsome lord, what secret did you tell Sealyn after I left the room?"

Jashun's hands started sweating. What was happening to him? "That secret is of my betrayal to our king, princess. If I told you, then you may think less of me."

"I could never," she flirted.

"Of course, how could I think that of you." His mouth went dry, so he drank more wine, which immediately made him feel better about sharing his secret with Kailani. Telling the mermaid would be pleasurable! "Well, princess, before I was captured by Stoltland scum, we had an encounter with the Pirate Captain."

The room gasped.

"Oh, yes. I know. He's quite scary," Jashun said. He loved how involved the table was with his story. He liked their attention. "So, there I was face-to-face with the orange-eyed demon," he growled the word "demon" for dramatic effect. "He was ready to kill us because Doebromir and Sune didn't provide him with information that he thought was useful, so I bravely saved my comrades by telling him about King Jace." He raised his silver goblet, toasting himself.

Kailani tilted her head. "What specifically did you tell him about Jace? That he's a fierce sword fighter and killed a traitor? Or maybe that he has in-depth knowledge about Stoltland's spy forces?"

Jashun laughed. This silly girl. He needed to correct her ignorance. "No, princess. That he is Corentine's son. He then asked if he was the grey-eyed child, which I said yes to." Feeling relieved, Jashun munched on steamed shrimp and sipped more of the addicting wine.

"Now, why would the most fearsome pirate of the realm care about that?"

Jashun shrugged and smiled dreamily. "I honestly do not know."

Kailani looked at the Mer helper and nodded. He sat water before Jashun, which he guzzled down like he had been in the desert for weeks. His mind began to clear, and then the gloom of what he had just done washed over him. He had betrayed his kingdom once again! But how? Why? His heart did not want to do that, so why did he willingly give in?

Jashun smacked his hand on the coral table. "What? What did you do to me?"

Kailani stood along with the rest of her court. "Veritas potion." She turned and walked out with her court trailing behind.

Truth serum. She had used truth serum on him. Jashun peered inside the silver goblet. No wonder the drink tasted so different from normal wine. He yelled at the now-distant group. "You made me a traitor! Elysium will hang me for this!"

Vaelinthia rose early to hang sheer curtains around the corner table by the staircase. The Elysians wanted proof of her story, so she would hide their green eyes behind the canary-yellow, iridescent fabric and allow them to see Doebromir and Sune with the Stoltlanders.

The Elysians were sore from sleeping on the hard floor of Vaelinthia's room and the pounding of the waves on their joints, but they didn't care. They were moments away from seeing their captive friends. Trying to fit all ten of them at the table would seem too suspicious, so Sealyn, Jace, Char, and Tilmond stayed in Vaelinthia's room, waiting for confirmation.

Since Finn had blue eyes, he sat freely at the bar, not drawing attention, and Ajorn, Favien, Ashur, Max, and Brehan gathered around the corner table. Everything was ready. Their hearts pounded in silence. All that was left was to verify that their comrades were, in fact, alive and within grabbing distance.

Sunshine illuminated the tavern, bouncing rays off the yellow haze of the city. The air sparkled and smelled of old wood and sizzling bacon. The pub was bustling with breakfast-hungry sailors and tradesmen. Finn enjoyed the fresh juice and eggs, reminding him of the many times Doebromir would finish everyone's breakfast plates before morning trainings. He was ready to have his friend back. He could only hope being a prisoner hadn't changed him.

Vaelinthia parted the curtain and brought more sausage and juice to the table. "The only guests who haven't come down yet are the Stoltlanders and your Elysians."

"You better be right about this, Vael," Ajorn whispered.

"You already have a pet name for me? I love it, and stop worrying. I keep my word to green eyes, especially Queen Sealyn. That's not a force I want to mess with." Vaelinthia left them to their breakfast.

Max leaned in. "Why did she refer to Sealyn as a force?"

"Come on, Max. Don't read into it," Favien said. "You do this all the time."

"No, I don't. I mean, are we really not going to talk about what happened under that boat?" Max looked at each soldier at the table, hoping someone would speak.

Ashur's shoulder hit Max. "No, we're not. You know why? Because she saved my life, and King Jace asked us not to. Whether people want to call her a force or a weapon or whatever, I'm calling her my savior because that's literally what she did for me. She saved Len Nove too, Max."

"I know that, but we know what the legends say about Cognitions…" Max was always one for conspiracy theories. He loved debating and always needed more answers, and Sealyn's powers opened a treasure trove of questions.

Finn asked for another juice, which was the signal that he saw black, Stoltland eyes coming down the stairs. The Elysians stopped talking and watched intensely. They could almost feel each other's heartbeats. They counted but then stopped when they saw Doebromir's bald head, followed by Sune's bright red curly hair.

Ajorn's ebony hand grabbed Brehan's forearm. His eyes watered at the site of his brother-in-arms. He had to force himself to stay seated. Brehan lightly cleared his throat and whispered, "Do we all verify?" The group nodded.

Doebromir felt exhausted. He looked across the room at Vaelinthia wiping a table. He locked eyes with her, and as he was passing the bar, he saw her head slightly nod toward it. Was this a signal? Just in case she was sending him a message, he looked to his right and almost stumbled. Finn! Finn was sitting at the bar eating eggs. Was he really seeing this? Was he hallucinating?

Finn pushed his unfinished eggs aside, nauseous anxiety creeping in. Doebromir took advantage of the moment. He clapped his hand on the back of Finn's shoulder.

"Pardon me, traveler. Are you done eating those eggs?"

Finn froze, forcing words out. "Uh, yes. Yes, I am."

"Excellent. I'm famished. Do you mind if I finish them?"

Doebromir saw the slight uptick in the corner of Finn's lips as he slid the plate to him. They both nodded, understanding everything was about to change.

Favien hurried up the stairs to inform the royal line. He could barely form sentences he was so happy. "It's them, Sealyn. It's really them."

"And Sorcha? She's not with them like Vaelinthia said?"

"I'm sorry, but no. She's not with them. She must be on the ship like Vael told us."

Sealyn put her hand on her head and walked around the room in frustration. "How are we supposed to get her and them?"

"Easy, Sea," Jace said. "We need to stick to the plan."

"I agree," Tilmond added.

Sealyn huffed. "Really? You agree to do nothing?"

"Sealyn, we're in a strange kingdom with no allies except a rebel force that we haven't even made contact with."

"Tilmond is right," Jace grabbed Sealyn's shoulders. "We must play this one smart. We can't overreact."

Sealyn pulled away. "The problem is—we're not thinking like Stoltlanders."

"Explain that," Tilmond spat. The last thing he wanted was to turn into a Stoltlander. Tilmond always made sure to follow the moral and ethical codes, and going down a path toward Stoltland's ways seemed too far for him to go.

"I will, cousin," Sealyn snapped. "It's obvious! They're here for a reason. They've been here longer than we have, so their plans may be over soon. You heard Vael. They've been talking with several other Stoltlanders who are known to move people illegally. What if today is that day, and we do nothing? Then we're too late!"

Tilmond folded his arms and shook his head. "If you cause a scene, then our cover is blown, and we're screwed." There. He said it. Sealyn had to listen to reason. Their lives were at stake. Plus, Sealyn truly needed to focus on breaking the curses.

"They're right down there," Sealyn pointed. "We must act now."

Char sighed deeply. "I reeeeally hate to agree with my psychotic cousin, but I think Sealyn's right."

"Oh, good. I was hoping we'd hear solid advice from the pub touring, not in the military Char," Tilmond said incredulously.

"Excellent jolt, Commander," Char laughed. "But think about it. If we have this one chance and don't do anything, and they smuggle them out tonight, how will you ever live with yourself?"

"Guilt? Now, who's throwing low blows," Tilmond barked back.

"Enough!" Sealyn said. "I want to see for myself. I need to see them, and if there's even a hint that something bad is about to happen to them, then I'll act; otherwise, I won't." Sealyn wasn't sure if she could hold herself accountable to those words or not. She knew she could sometimes react before thinking, but she wouldn't sit idle, not while her people needed them.

Unable to argue with the queen, the Elysians quietly walked down the stairs and slid quickly behind the curtains.

"Anything odd to report?" Sealyn whispered.

"Nothing yet, majesty," Brehan said.

As freely as dogs and cats roamed Elysium's streets and pubs, snakes slithered through Shunal. Elysium didn't have many snakes in its kingdom, only harmless garden snakes and a small blue one that lived close to the Len Novian border. Most Elysians were either afraid or uncomfortable around snakes because of this. Unfortunately, a snake was the one creature that Ashur feared the most.

"Jace," Ashur said. "Did you just touch my leg?"

"No, stop being weird. I can't hear. Shhh."

"Quit playing with my leg then. This is serious."

"I know that, which is why I'm not messing with you."

"Then what is…" Ashur leaned back to look under the table, only to be met with two beady golden eyes looking back at him. He jumped up, swallowing his scream. His chair pushed Jace outside the curtain. Before Jace could duck behind the fabric, the Stoltlanders saw him.

"Aye, you there!"

Jace froze, not sure what to do. He didn't turn around.

"You look somewhat familiar. What's ya eyes, kid?"

Jace saw Sealyn's head shaking slowly.

"Aye, I'm talkin' to you. Turn around and show us your eyes."

Doebromir and Sune swallowed hard. Vaelinthia's breathing sped up, and Finn grabbed his dagger, ready for anything. Jace gradually turned, cursing his birth. He didn't want his eyes to be yet another reason for anyone getting hurt. He prayed they wouldn't recognize him.

"Well. Well. Look 'a there. Grey eyes. We got ourselves a mixed breed, folks." The Stoltlanders laughed. Doebromir's fist tightened, and Sealyn could feel the rage boiling inside. She discretely readied her bow just in case.

"Come here, boy," the scared face Stoltlander said. Jace walked closer, very steady, hand on his sword. "Well, dragon's scales! Lucky you got some looks," he laughed. "You know most of your kind are born deformed and defective. I heard some can't even speak. You know how to talk?"

Jace glared. He wanted to unleash his wrath on these fools, but he couldn't cause a scene, so he shook his head, hoping the Stoltlander's ignorance would save him.

"Aw, poor monster. He can't even talk. I bet he can't read either," he spat toward Jace. "You aren't fit to even exist, much less breathe the same air as us. You know most of your kind is killed at birth. You're lucky, but you disgust me. Get out, you scum."

Char jerked his head toward Sealyn. He saw the intensity and watched in horror as she confidently stood with her bow pulled back. The arrow released and cut swiftly through the curtain, landing in the throat of the ignorant Stoltlander, knocking him out of his chair. He lay lifeless on the stone floor, blood pooling around his head.

"His lioness," Vaelinthia whispered, then ran to take cover.

The Stoltlanders scrambled to their feet, and the Elysians poured out from behind the curtains with their swords drawn. Sealyn released her second arrow, dropping another Stoltlander with an arrow to the neck. Jace threw his sword to Doebromir, who caught it with all the familiarity of a warrior. He raised the sword, clashing against one of his captor's swords.

Finn jumped on the bar and fired his arrows. He shot his weapons through a Stoltlander's thigh and then chest; blood pooled around his chair. Max jumped on the bar with Finn, launching arrow after arrow. Swords collided, blood splattered the curtains and tables, screams rang, customers ran from the tavern, and prisoners were freed.

The Elysians stood over the Stoltlanders' dead bodies, then looked at Doebromir and Sune. They all ran into a huddle, embracing.

"Is this real?" Sune asked. He was almost frightened to ask.

"Afraid so," said Ajorn. "You're stuck with us again."

Doebromir laughed a painful laugh. Tears threatened his eyes. "Well, if we have no choice."

Vaelinthia walked to the group. "You weren't kidding about being his lioness, Queen Sealyn."

Sealyn smirked at her comment, walked to a Stoltlander, pulled a bloody arrow from the body, and placed it back in her quiver.

Vaelinthia chuckled. "On that cheerful note, we all need to leave immediately."

"How soon until the patrol is here?" Jace asked.

"Any minute. Hurry back to my room. We'll exit the way you came in."

"You're coming with us?" Ajorn questioned.

"Yes, you Elysians blew my cover for sure. Now, hurry."

Elysian News

The Latest News and Gossip

Issue #17

Votes are in!
Who's least likely to succeed?

Greetings to Elysium. In last week's issue, #16, I asked which professor would be the least likely to succeed. Well, I have the results! You guessed it—Professor Draemamoor or, as most know her, Lady Novaly. The following are quotes from fellow Elysians:

Sir Clive: "I've heard that each day, there's an explosion in Professor Draemamoor's classroom. How are parents supposed to feel comfortable with that happening?"

Madam Daenaren: "She's the youngest among all the professors, which begs me to question her maturity to handle such a grand responsibility."

Painted above: Professor Novaly Draemamoor

Lady Sortash: "The girl is strange. I can't see that type of personality doing well in a classroom environment."

While Professor Draemamoor did receive the majority votes, others spoke highly of her:

Sir Nijeel: "Lady Novaly is perfect for the job. She loves children, and I've seen her at my café, working tirelessly on her Tethered notes. Mark my words, she will do great things."

Please see the top ten rankings for professors continued on page 2. ~Lady Adalina Roedellen, Lina

Princess Siany Spotlight	**No News is Good News**	**Luxen School Updates**
The juiciest gossip	*from King Father Ryker*	*Weekly Reports*
New idea for this year's Feydom: students play the game.	No news from the Shunalian quest	Welcome Tushar Jokul, first student from Len Nove
Has she lost her mind?	King Ryker gives interview	Blue-eyed boy's first day recounted
Page 3	Page 5	Page 7

CHAPTER 17
BEING A PHOENIX

Boom!

An explosion of blue and green sludge rained over the students in Professor Draemamoor's classroom. A doe-eyed, small boy scooped globs out of his green eyes, praying he wouldn't be in trouble. Novaly stood in front of the table in shock and shook her arms, sending goo to the floor. Not another one.

"Einar! Didn't I tell you not to add dragon mucus to this potion?" He nodded frantically, sludge still dripping down his face and shoulders. Novaly wiped her face. "It was supposed to be white glue, borax, two pixie tears, and one vial of unicorn breath."

"Oh, I mixed up the unicorn breath with dragon mucus," the young Einar said. The class snickered.

Novaly threw her hands up. "Well, I don't think we're getting much else done today with goo everywhere. Why don't you all head to your dormitories to clean up before lunch?"

The students shook their books and bags, trying to leave as much slime behind as possible. They filed out the door, laughing at what had just happened. Novaly followed them and leaned against the doorway. She eyed the trash bin with the crumpled news article about her. Were they right? Was she the worst professor here? How was she supposed to get through teaching these classes if she couldn't make it through one day without an explosion happening?

The cleanup Nichts flew into her classroom without hesitation. They knew to be ready for her class. Pinx walked by Novaly's students, who were covered in goo, and saw Novaly leaning against her doorframe.

"Professor Draemamoor? Is everything all right?"

Novaly sighed. "Another day. Another slimy eruption."

"Sounds about right. Anything I can help with?" Pinx tried to hide the copy of Lady Adalina's newspaper tucked under her arm.

"Thank you, Professor Gunnolf, but I think this will be a long learning curve for both the students and me,"

Novaly said, pitifully smiling at Pinx. "How are your classes?"

Pinx almost felt sorry to answer, but she was quite proud of her students. "Excellent. We're slowly bridging botany and channeling plants, and the students are learning so fast. I'm really proud of them. One little girl grew a small lemon tree from seed to fruit within three minutes. It was marvelous to watch."

"Three minutes. Really? Impressive," Novaly felt a tinge of insecurity.

"Yes, but that's not as impressive as the Luxen twins, Pinny and Paevoly."

"What about them?"

"Well, as you know, Pinny has been channeling silkworms, and Paevoly can wield cotton. The two combined their skills in making clothes. They asked Princess Siany if they could design a school uniform for everyone."

Novaly felt speechless for a moment. "That's incredible. Who knew that was possible?"

"Exactly! This school has opened so many possibilities for these children. Their futures are going to be amazing."

"That's if Queen Sealyn can break all the curses," Novaly carelessly blurted. She immediately regretted her poor choice of words.

Pinx dropped her head. Her heart ached for her husband, Favien. She sent a silent prayer to Creator to keep him safe.

"Oh, Pinx. I'm so sorry. I didn't mean to…"

"It's fine, Novaly. I miss my husband and all our friends. It's terrifying to think what they might be facing."

Pinx felt a tiny tapping on her arm. She turned around and saw a small, blonde-haired boy whose face was covered in freckles.

"Hi, Wullen. What can I help you with?"

"Professor Gunnolf, I found this old book volume set hidden in the rafters of one of the attics." He handed her three faded, old green books held together by several chains.

"Wullen! What have we told you about snooping in the attics?"

"I know. I can't help myself," he dropped his head. "These seemed important, though. I looked for the key that fits the lock but couldn't find it."

Pinx smiled at the boy. "Thank you, Wullen. I'll take it from here. You better hurry to the food hall. Lunch is about to be served."

Wullen skipped away, pleased he didn't get in trouble. The professors stared at the books. Pinx spread apart the chains, exposing the cover, and gasped. She looked into Novaly's frightened eyes.

"What does this mean?"

"I don't know, but nothing good."

The patrol was catching up. Char felt his lungs burning. He didn't know how many more steps he could take. The group skirted to a halt and pressed themselves against a yellowish-stone shop. Tilmond peeked around the corner, breathing hard.

Quickly, he snapped his head from view. "There're five patrol guards mere feet from us. Where should we go now, Vaelinthia?"

"For starters, you Elysians have on dark green clothes, which gives you away, so I say, I go in this shop right here," she patted the stone wall behind her. "And buy you all some Shunalian clothes."

Sealyn grumbled to herself. She hated wearing another kingdom's colors. She remembered the way Commander Malum made her wear the blue ball gown to see if her people would think she had betrayed them. Deep in her heart, though, she knew this had to be done, and she was the reason why. They were supposed to be moving only during the night, but her reaction to the Stoltlander's insults made that impossible.

"Fine," Sealyn said, handing a small sack to Vaelinthia. "But only day cloaks because we'll need to move fast. I'm not wasting time on proper fittings."

Vaelinthia nodded and pulled her hair around her face, then untied her apron that she still had on and patted the sweat on her brow. She handed it to Ajorn and winked. She let an old-looking magna constrictor slither by, then walked around the corner and into the shop, not drawing the patrol's attention.

The shop had rows of fabric designs overlapping each other on almost every wall. Dresses and tunics were displayed on cotton mannequins. In the middle of the shop was a glass display case filled with gems for adding to clothes. Vaelinthia longed to one day come into a luxury shop like this, be fitted for a high-class gown, and wear it to a palace ball, but she was far away from that particular day.

She remembered her mission, went straight to the desk, and declared, "I'd like to buy thirteen golden day cloaks, please. Two female sizes and eleven men sizes."

The old man was wearing a bright yellow vest that displayed his arms, both covered in an array of yellow, white, and blue gems, along with his neck and cheekbones. He had a receding hairline of black hair and yellow eyes that matched his vest, and a white and yellow snake wrapped diagonally across his chest. "And just how would the likes of you pay for so many cloaks?"

"Depends. How much?"

He pointed to his sign of pricing. Her eyes widened. She couldn't dream of spending that on a cloak. Then she opened the bag Sealyn had given her, and her heart stopped.

"Excuse me, girl. Are you just in here wasting my valuable time?"

Vaelinthia struggled with her words, sweat dripping down her back. "I see you don't have any emeralds in your gem case."

"Of course not. Those Elysians don't trade their emeralds. They're selfish like that, which makes the emerald the most valuable gem on the market today."

"Well, today is your lucky day then," she said, pulling out an emerald the size of her thumbnail, placing it on the wooden counter, and keeping her finger on it. "How about *the likes of you* go get me those cloaks now?"

Sealyn stared up at the open, yellow-laced parasols strung over the alley. What a clever decorative idea, she thought. She felt Jace's hand interlock with hers. She looked into his silver eyes and wished he wasn't her weakness, but time had proven that he was. She longed to run away with him and not have this burden on her shoulders. He gently kissed her lips, and she laid her head on his shoulder. She thought about the prophecy. Sealyn's heart didn't care if they couldn't have children—Jace was all she would ever want, or so she thought.

Their moment was interrupted by Vaelinthia rounding the corner with a mound of cloaks. "Hurry, we don't have much time. I think the shop owner suspected foul play, and the patrols saw me. We need to put these on and go back the way we came. There's a river we need to cross to lose them."

They could hear the patrol's voices coming closer. Wasting no time, they took off down the alley while clasping their golden cloaks.

"Hey! You there! Stop!"

"Run!" cried Favien.

They slipped and sprinted around corners, choking on the yellow air. Their mouths desperately needed water. Vaelinthia kept giving directions to Tilmond, but the patrol was nearing them. Her mind was dizzy from running. She wasn't even sure if they were going the right way.

Patrol voices sounded from all around them. Tilmond took another turn, then realized too late that it was a dead end—only another stone wall. "We have to go back," he said.

Max gasped for air. "We can't," he said, taking another deep breath. They're coming from all angles. We're surrounded."

"Halt right there!"

The group stiffened. What were they supposed to do? They couldn't kill these Shunalians—that would lead to war. The patrol marched closer as the Elysians backed up. The wall was too tall to jump. They were trapped.

Sealyn stepped in front, keeping her hood over her eyes.

"Sea, what are you doing?" Jace whispered.

"Being a phoenix, my love."

Sealyn clapped her hands, sending a burst of white and green light into the patrol. They grabbed their eyes, screaming. Sealyn ordered her men to knock the patrol unconscious and tie them together. She then made a green light staircase for them to climb over the wall, with another staircase on the other side.

Her people stood in amazement. Sealyn's powers continued to baffle them. They zipped over the stairs—their shoes clicked like the magic was made of marble. They feared the patrol would wake up any second. Once they were safely on the opposite side of the wall, Sealyn collapsed.

"Sealyn!" Jace held her in his arms. "Wake up, Sea. Wake up."

Char flashed back to the memory of Sealyn after she used all her power to break Len Nove's curse. He thought she was dead. He could see the magic trying to take from Sealyn again. "She needs nourishment."

"I agree with Char," Favien said, breathing hard. "We're all beat, and Sealyn keeps having to use her magic to save us, and we haven't had a solid meal. She missed breakfast, remember?"

A shadow crept across the group, and then a familiar voice spoke, "Well now, I will have to say, when I heard a group decided to kill a bunch of Stoltlanders this morning, I knew it was my Elysian brothers and sister who did the fantastic deed."

"Herbmando!" Char cheered.

Sealyn coughed. "For the record, I'm actually glad to see you."

"The honor is all mine, phoenix queen. Allow me." He pulled out oranges and Puffin Pies from his bag. The pirates with him also handed out yellow apples and dried meat. The team was grateful and finally started to feel better. Now, their challenge was to find Cruz, the rebel leader.

CHAPTER 18
BLACK PHOENIX

Keawev Palace was breathtaking, and this tour was no different. For days, Kailani had Jashun brought to different palace areas to talk. Today, he sat on broken rock steps leading to a lagoon. All around him were ancient ruins of what once was a magnificent castle, but only the perimeter walls and several columns were left. It reminded him of the Avondelle market.

Green sea moss grew on the tops of ruins and around the grove. Illuminating purple Alveopora corals draped from the columns, always connecting to the roots of the ground floor. In the distance, Jashun saw sparkling waterfalls and high mountain formations. The beauty of this place brought tears to his eyes.

He watched air bubbles rise from the lagoon along with Kailani in her mermaid form. He couldn't take his eyes off her. He both hated her and longed to touch her skin. She laid on her back on a smooth, slanted sand patch near the lagoon's edge, waiting for Jashun to break the silence.

Jashun tried not to ogle her body, but every second became harder. Jashun exhaled. "Enough, Kailani. I'm so tired of these games."

"Whatever do you mean?"

"This," Jashun waved his arms around him. "Bringing me out to see lush beauty, then sending me back to a dark prison cell. You ask me silly questions about my childhood, and then you're done with me. Just send me back, Kailani."

Kailani's pink eyes flared. "You dare to give me a command?"

"At this point, I don't care. I was a prisoner on that ship, and you know that yet you still throw me in a cell each night. You pretend to be a friend during the day, even though you've caused me to be a traitor and not by choice."

"Jashun…"

"No. I'm not finished. I might have come here with the mission of finding out information for Queen Sealyn, but it wasn't to harm your people. It was information to help bind our kingdoms together to form a partnership. I'm literally a breathing dead man. If I leave your bubble, I die. If I return to Avondelle and tell them what happened, I die. I refuse to be a prisoner for another day, so release me, or so help me, I'll jump in that water and inhale till I'm free of this world."

She clapped. "There's the spark I wanted--the man I knew you were."

"What?"

"I've been waiting for you to stand up for yourself. For you to finally have a commanding presence over your own life. That's the kind of man I want."

"Seriously, Kailani. What crazy fish-bish are you talking about?"

Kailani laughed. "Fish-bish? I definitely want to keep you now," she laughed again.

"Keep?"

"Jashun, you and I have something—*epic chemistry.* I want to follow that and see where it goes."

"Kailani, you realize I despise you right now, don't you?"

"Despise or desire?" She lifted her eyebrow seductively and bit her bottom lip. "Not a day goes by that I don't think about that day in the water."

Jashun stood. "That's it. This is just cruel, Kailani. I'm a *person* with feelings, and mocking what I consider the best day of my life is not okay."

"I'm not mocking you. I'm agreeing with you," Kailani flipped on her stomach, propping herself up on her elbows, tail swishing. "My treatment has been wrong, but in my defense, I had to know what Sealyn was up to. My father made me swear I would use the truth serum immediately, or else he would kill you."

"Kill me?"

"Yes, he didn't know if he could trust you, but I knew I could because you protected our secret in front of Sealyn."

"So. So you protected me by making me a traitor?"

"In a twisted way, yes. And believe me, Jashun, I want you."

"But you're royalty. You must run a kingdom."

Kailani giggled. "You're so silly. I'm fifth in line for the throne. I have six siblings. Three older brothers, one older sister, and two younger sisters."

"What are you saying?" His head was starting to ache. He was tired of games and all this yapping. Kailani needed to say the truth and be done.

"I'm *saying* we can make this work. We can be together."

"So, no more dungeon?" Jashun's heart leapt.

"No more dungeon. You'll have a royal guest room, and then we can visit your kingdom and give them the good news that we want to work with Elysium."

"This doesn't seem real."

Kailani sat up and dove into the water. Suddenly, her body sparkled with variegated colors and then cleared, showcasing her human form. Jashun could see her ivory legs in the clear water, along with the rest of her body.

"Join me, Jashun. We have some making up to do."

With a loud clang, Siany dropped the chained book volume on the war room table in front of her father. The vast room resounded the books' warning. King Father Ryker stood and examined the books. Dun, the giant Green Phoenix, walked to the table, his yellow eyes narrowed.

Ryker held the books to Dun's beak, who snapped the chains like dried twigs. The king traced the drawing on the cover with his finger. Dun's eyes dilated. There, in the center, was a picture of a black phoenix. Dun clapped his beak and stomped his golden foot.

Ryker looked at Dun. "You know about this?"

The Green Phoenix nodded.

The king opened the book and read the first line,

"The history of the black phoenix begins with the rise of the green phoenix and the explosion of fire."

He snapped the book shut and closed his eyes, "Dun, does this mean there's an evil you out there?"

Dun stomped his feet and squawked.

Ryker shook his head. "I don't know what that means," he turned and faced the table. "It's regrettable that he only communicates with Queen Sealyn." He swallowed. His throat was dry, and he was filled with annoyance. "I want all scholars, investigators, and anyone else with high intelligence to pour over these books. We must know if there's about to be an invasion of black phoenixes."

"It makes sense, though," Captain Graegory said.

"What makes sense?" Prince Adomin asked.

"The balance of nature. Light and dark." He saw their blank faces and continued. "Take that awful mother *Noxhorn dragon. She gave birth to an evil dragon and also a dragon with no evil. I dare say a dragon of light, but that bubble dragon keeps popping up out of nowhere, spraying bubbles."

"Easy, captain. Let's stay focused," Ryker said.

"Apologies, my king."

"Captain Graegory makes a good point. We still don't know all the history behind the legendary creatures. They're entangled with the curses." Ryker paced the room, staring at the books. "We know that the Hill Chimes Forest is the breeding ground for the green phoenixes. We still don't know why. I'm guessing the music of the trees helps, but now, we need to focus all our efforts on uncovering the dark secrets of the black phoenix."

"Let's be logical," Prince Royce said. "If we believe these books are true, then that means the black phoenix is already here? Or perhaps its anchor is here, but there's a missing element since we haven't witnessed it?"

"Explosion of fire," whispered Graegory. "Has anyone inspected the burned grounds near Stoltland's Tor?"

"Of course. The ash forest is constantly under watch," Ryker said. The king felt uneasy. There was something he was missing. "Bring in Lady Quinley and Lady Revalyn. They were the ones who found the information needed to help break Len Nove's curse. Have them start reading these books immediately."

Elysian News

Issue #19

The Latest News and Gossip

Special Edition: A Tribute to Dun, the Legendary Green Phoenix

Greetings, my fellow Elysians. This is long overdue.

Dun has bravely protected our kingdom from so many evils that we should sing his praises loudly.

He protected Queen Sealyn from Corentine's black magic spear with his wings.

He saved Lady Sorcha's life when the Stoltland soldier cut her neck.

He saved Lady Zuri's life when traitors poisoned her.

He fought against dragons entering our Tor and sustained wounds, including a dragon claw lodged in his leg.

He killed several dragons and Stoltlanders on The Saddest Day in Elysium's History.

Elysium is genuinely grateful for Dun's sacrifices and his leadership.

~ Lady Adalina Roedellen (Lina)

Princess Siany Spotlight

The juiciest gossip
Several letters to
Lord Edvard

Will she choose him?

Page 2

New Shop Opening in the Market

Potters Hands
Goblets, bowls, décor
and more!

Get all your kitchen
and household needs
Page 3

Luxen School Updates

Weekly Reports
New school uniforms
will be issued based off
classifications.

Parents are encouraged
to follow progress.
Page 4

CHAPTER 19
THE NAME'S SKARPIN

Sealyn crouched low in the brushes. A purple and yellow fuzzy snake smiled at Sealyn as it glided over her boot. Well, that was, perhaps, the friendliest snake she had ever encountered. She fixed her ears to her surroundings. Sealyn could hear the running stream in front of them and the bustling of the market behind them. Being undetected was key to their survival. They needed to cross under the bridge to find the rebel leader.

Favien rose, ready to take the first step, but quickly dove back down. "Do you hear that?" Everyone tried to quiet their breathing and lock their ears onto what Favien asked about.

"I don't hear anything," Jace said.

"Me either," agreed Max.

Sealyn's eyes squinted toward under the bridge. "Wait. I hear something. It sounds like whimpering." She rose from her hiding place. Her heart pounded. She had to be careful, or else they could all be dead. She took a step forward from the shadows.

"Stop, Sealyn," Jace pleaded.

"Stay here. I have a feeling."

Char shook his head. "I never like those."

Sealyn stepped lightly and quickly across the sandy road, threw herself against the lemon-colored stone bridge base, and slowly stepped closer to look under the bridge. She could hear the sound growing louder. It sounded like someone was in pain. Was she stumbling upon a gang torturing someone? Her people couldn't be seen, but she had to know if innocent people were hurt.

She inched her way forward, glancing back at her people one last time before looking around the wall. She saw the beautiful stream full of gold coins, and there in the pebbles leading up to the water was a small boy crying-- bleeding and crying.

Sealyn couldn't explain what she felt at that moment, but all she could do was walk toward the boy. She felt a pull, a calling.

"What is this crazy woman doing?" Char exclaimed.

"No idea, but it seems like everything is safe. Let's go—one by one," instructed Favien.

Stones crunched beneath Sealyn's boots as she approached the small child. She stopped a few feet from him and knelt.

"Hello" was the first word that echoed between them, changing their course of history forever.

The timid boy sniffled and shifted backward, huddled low. "Who…who are you?"

"How about I start with, I'm a friend." Sealyn saw his arm bleeding and the dull knife in his tiny fingers. "What about you? Are you a friend?"

"No one wants to be friends with the likes of me."

Jace and Favien ran across the road, followed by Doebromir, Vaelinthia, and Max, with dust kicking up behind them.

"That doesn't seem right. Why do you say that?"

"'Tis true, ma'am. I ain't got no parents. No gems, so no value. No one wants to be friends with no-value, street scum like me."

Sealyn's heart broke into a thousand pieces. She cleared her throat, trying to escape the tears that so desperately wanted to flow. "Well, I'd like to be your friend. Would that be okay with you?"

The small child's big golden eyes grew wide. "Really? But you're pretty. Aren't the pretty ones high society or something?" He paused and squinted through his tears. "Hey, wait, your eyes are green—emerald green."

"Why yes, they are. Isn't it fun to see something different rather the same ol' same?"

The dark-haired child laughed. A sound that Sealyn desperately wanted to hear again and maybe forever. The boy inched forward, still hesitant, and replied, "I guess so. Green fits you."

"And gold fits you."

"I wish I had actual gold," He looked down at his bloodied arm, aching for someone just once to love him, for someone to wrap caring arms around him and tell him it was all going to be okay, but no one ever did. No one ever hugged him. People walked by him every day, tossing their trash at him. Deep down, more than gold or gems, he wanted a family, a bond that would claim and value him.

"So, dear friend, may I ask if I can hold that knife?"

The boy stiffened and clutched the handle tighter. "But I haven't finished. I need it."

Herbmando, Tilmond, and Ashur made the dash across the road, then listened to Sealyn and the boy's encounter.

"Will you tell me why you're not finished?"

Tears fell from his golden eyes. "Because I can't swim deep enough to get the gold coins in the river, so I'm tryin' to put these here pebbles in my arms to maybe, I don't know, trick people into thinkin' I'm worth something."

Again, a lump formed in Sealyn's throat. How many more times could this boy break her heart? Sealyn looked back and saw Jace. Her mind trailed again to the prophecy, then she looked deep into the child's yellow eyes. "Can I share a secret with you?"

"I'm excellent at keepin' secrets, ma'am."

Finn, Sune, and Ajorn dashed forward, avoiding being seen. Brehan and Char were about to go when they saw a group of babbling young Shunalian girls. They shivered at the sight of their jeweled faces. Why would they do such a thing? Could they even have expressions? Once the girls had passed out of sight, they sprinted hard for the bridge.

Sealyn continued her conversation with the boy, covered in rags. "I figured you were an excellent secret keeper, but the payment of the secret is that knife."

He let out a soft sigh and handed Sealyn the bloody knife. She saw the cut out of his skin where a tiny white pebble was embedded in his arm. The skin was swollen red, and dried blood formed around it.

"Thank you, my young friend," Sealyn moved closer and knelt in front of him, taking his bloody hands. He couldn't be more than five years old. "The truth is none of these gems or gold coins matter; only you do." The boy's brow furrowed. "Your value doesn't come from wealth, my darling boy. It comes from you just breathing air into your lungs. Your heart beating means you have a purpose. You blinking those golden eyes means you matter to this entire world." His lip began to quiver. "I see your worth in you just being sweet, innocent *you*."

Through gulps of tears, the boy said, "No one's ever been that nice to me. No one's ever cared. Do you truly think those things about me?"

Sealyn nodded her head as fast as she could and smiled. "Absolutely. There's no doubt in my mind, but I want you to believe them, too."

"I can try, ma'am, but it's not easy out here on the streets."

"You have no family? No one claims you?"

"None. My mother died givin' birth to me, then my father killed himself because of it. My aunt said that's love." Sealyn winced at the lack of understanding love. The child continued, "My aunt took me in and raised me 'till I was five, then she caught the gold sickness. I'm guessin' you green-eyes know nothin' about that, but it's when you get the itch to dive for the gold in the Golden Lake. No one ever comes back. So, I've been on my own since then."

"Since you were five?"

"Yes, ma'am."

Sealyn glanced back at Jace. She felt something, something she didn't think was possible for them.

"Oh, Jace," Char said. "Brace yourself. That's the look I was worried about."

Jace looked at Sealyn's teary eyes. He knew what she wanted. He nodded.

Sealyn turned and cupped the small boy's dirty, tear-streaked cheeks. "How would you like to go on the adventure of a lifetime?"

"Me? You mean it? Does it involve food?"

Sealyn chuckled and reached into her bag. She pulled out a wrapped Puffin Pie and handed it to the boy.

He bit into the delicious food, crumbs covered his tiny lips. "Oh, Creator. What is this? This is the best food I've ever tasted!"

Sealyn motioned for her group to come closer. "Well, dear friend, that food is very common in my kingdom."

He looked up intently, licking his lips. "Your kingdom?"

"Yes. Now, here's the secret. I'm Queen Sealyn Araelien of Elysium, and I'm here to break your kingdom's curse. Would you like to join us?"

The little boy swore in amazement. "I can't believe this. I get to go on an adventure with you? And them? And eat delicious food?"

The group laughed. "And what shall we call you?" Sealyn asked.

"The name's Skarpin."

"It's a pleasure to meet you, Skarpin," Sealyn shook his tiny hand. "Now, we need to meet a very important leader at a hidden place." Herbmando stepped into view.

"Holy roasted unicorns! You're Herbmando! Second to Cruz!"

"Did this kid just say something about roasting unicorns?" Char asked.

Herbmando laughed. "Uh, kid, we don't roast unicorns; we dance with them." Char high-fived Herbmando. Since the kid knew his name, Herbmando knew Skarpin had probably spied or ran errands for the rebels. At the moment, they were in a zone of the city that he didn't know well, but Skarpin… "Say, kid, do you know a faster route to Lay Merid Fountain?"

Skarpin's eyes sparked with mischief. "Of course! I can take you where no one will see us! Follow me." He took off in a flash with the group on his heels.

Jace grabbed Sealyn's hand. "Wait a moment, Sealyn. Did we just…"

Sealyn smiled. "One step at a time, love, and maybe—just maybe—we did."

"Be warned. Keep out. Sickness here," Favien read from the ratty sign painted in red. "Obviously, the boy has led us into a bad spot."

"Have not!" Skarpin squeaked.

"No? What do you call a darkened corner of the city with barricades and signs warning of sickness?" Favien asked with a bitter tone. He startled himself, realizing he was arguing with a five-year-old.

Herbmando put his hand on the boy's black, shaggy head. "Skarpin is correct, my friend. We took advantage of the big sickness that happened last year." Herbmando walked to the sign and patted the post. "It's fake, and no patrol wants to risk finding out if it's not." He motioned with his hand. "Come."

The group walked past the broken fences and long, worn linens that blocked anyone's view beyond. To their right was a small dried-up fountain cracked down the middle, and etched in stone were the words "Lay Merid Fountain." Favien rolled his eyes at the words. Once they emerged past the facade, they saw beautiful bridges and stone buildings with large, yellow-leafed trees growing beside them. Butter-colored moss grew on the sides of the trees and buildings. This area seemed wild and untamed, yet full of hopes and dreams.

Even the golden haze was barely noticeable in this section. Sealyn realized what that meant. Those who inhabited this part were resisting Shunal's curse. These people said no to it. They were brave and walked away from the pressures of the darkness. Who were they? Only one name came to Sealyn's mind: rebels.

"Wait here," Herbmando instructed.

The group was happy to rest finally and enjoyed sitting on the stone steps leading to a deep river with a short width. As dusk settled in, yellow fireflowers illuminated the arches and pathways.

"So, I've wanted to do this for a while now," Sealyn said. She stood and embraced Doebromir and pulled Sune to her, too. The rest of the group followed Sealyn's lead. Tears stung their eyes as they laughed and patted the rescued prisoners' heads.

"What's going on?" Skarpin asked.

Sealyn drew back to address Skarpin. "Well, to be forward, Stoltland captured these two," she pointed to Doebromir and Sune. "And we rescued them."

"That's wild! I wish I could have seen that!" exclaimed Skarpin.

"Thank you, your majesties, and to all of you," Sune said. "We know our rescue came with sacrifices, but now, can we discuss Lady Sorcha?"

Sealyn softened. "Yes, from what Vaelinthia told us, she's on the ship in the harbor?"

"Correct, so what's the plan to free her?" Sune asked. He realized this had been the longest he'd gone without seeing Sorcha since meeting her. His mind went back to their kiss. Sune knew he was hopelessly in love with her.

"We need to secure passage back to the docks and then get back on our ship," Tilmond said. "Once we have Doebromir and Sune safely on the ship, we will send a rescue team for Lady Sorcha."

Sune crossed his arms. "Then we need to leave now. I'm sure someone has informed the Stoltland ship about what happened in the tavern. They might have killed her already!" Tears threatened his eyes, and he choked on his words.

Sealyn's head tilted, catching what he wasn't saying. There was more than fear for a companion in his tone. His eyes showed fear for someone he loved. Sealyn's heart sank, knowing Sakul was onboard her ship, waiting for the moment he could hold Sorcha again. Sealyn caught Char's expression, who obviously was thinking the same thing she was. Regardless of a potential love triangle, she wanted her friend back and would do whatever it took to achieve that.

"Elysians, welcome," a dashing, wavy black-haired man said. "Welcome to our paradise of Shunal."

"Cruz!" Skarpin yelled.

Sealyn stepped in front of the rebel leader. "You must be Cruz."

"And you have to be the emerald queen."

Jace didn't like the flirtation in Cruz's words. "I'm her husband, King Jace." He extended his hand.

Cruz snorted and shook his hand. "Of course, Majesty. A pleasure to meet the famous, grey-eyed Elysian king. Please come this way. We can eat some delicious food and discuss why you're here."

Sealyn looked at Sune, then at the darkening sky. "No."

"No?"

"No. We don't have time. We can eat on the run, but we need the cover of darkness, and I'm afraid our other friend is running out of time being Stoltland's prisoner."

Herbmando whispered in Cruz's ear. Cruz whispered back, almost arguing. This went on for a few minutes. Cruz finally spoke, "Fine. We will help you, but you won't like the way we will have to travel."

Sealyn stepped closer. "I don't care."

Herbmando laughed. "Ah, beautiful queen. You might not, but I hear your boy over there might." He pointed at Ashur.

"Who me?"

"Yes, you, Ashur." Herbmando nodded to a rebel atop the bridge, who then blew a horn.

Ripples flowed down the dark blue stream. The group shifted their stances with unease. Something was coming.

"What's going on, Cruz?" Char asked.

"Our ride is coming."

"What ride?" Max questioned, voice shaking.

A rakish grin spread across Cruz's face. "Snakes."

"Snakes?!" screamed Ashur. "What do you mean snakes?"

"Jormungons, to be exact," Cruz replied.

Ashur shook his head. "And *what* is a jormungon?"

"See for yourself," Herbmando pointed to the deep river.

Ashur's mouth dropped when he saw the first jormungon pop its ginormous head from the water. It was green with yellow stripes and a large mouth with dull teeth. They looked like human teeth.

"That thing could fit five grown men inside it!" Ashur shouted at Cruz.

"Precisely, my friend. This is how we sneak around. Jormungons will conceal us through the waterways and into the harbor to your ship. What say you?"

Favien dropped his head. "I don't want to ask this, but how?"

"Simple. We walk into their mouths. While their jaws are closed, they swim underwater, and we're undetected." Cruz elbowed Doebromir's side.

Herbmando smiled. "So, which Elysian will be the first to walk into the mouth of a snake?"

CHAPTER 20
WINGED CREATURES

Jashun watched as Kailani hugged her father goodbye. He still felt some bitterness toward the man who wanted to kill him, but since he was going home with the promise of a treaty, he was ready to let go of any hatred. His nerves were still unsettled about his treachery because of truth serum, but Kailani assured him that they did not need to inform Elysium of this since they were willing to sign the treaty. He turned and faced the giant clam that looked worn from years below the sea. He shivered, knowing what was going to come next.

He felt Kailani's fingers clasp his. He sucked in a breath.

"Are you ready, my love?" she whispered.

"To travel through a magical Tor that hopefully delivers us to my capital? Yes, of course. Sure, no hesitations here."

Kailani smiled and spoke a strange language, and then the clam opened, exposing swirling colors of green and silver. The couple looked at each other, then bravely stepped into the clam and were pulled through a colorful vortex. Wind, or at least Jashun thought it was wind, beat against his face. He could barely open his eyes. His stomach lurched as they dipped and jerked, and then he felt the abrupt stop.

He opened his eyes to a blurry wall. He reached out and touched it. It felt gooey, similar to Keawev's wall, so he pressed his hand further, feeling the air on the other side. Once he stepped fully through, he felt relieved to be on solid, and then he vomited on the soft, green grass.

Kailani felt bad for Jashun and rubbed his back. "That always happens on someone's first time." She gazed around. "I see our Tor is still the beautiful willow tree by Turtle Lake."

Jashun took in his surroundings. They were inside the long, flowy branches of the giant willow. The tree's trunk had the same green and silver swirls dancing across it as the clam had. Sunshine crisscrossed through the willow branches. He got an odd feeling, though. Where were the guards? Someone should have greeted them by now.

"Kailani, something isn't right."

"What do you mean?"

"All Tors are supposed to be heavily guarded. We need to be cautious."

They slowly peeled back the long, green branches that smelled like home for Jashun. Kailani gasped and dropped the foliage, stepping back like she had seen a ghost. Jashun's eyes burned with anger. Those couldn't be dragons. Dragons could not return. Their barriers were too fortified, and the phoenixes patrolled all borders and Tors.

He stared hard, trying to get a better look, but the creatures were far across the large lake, and the sunshine was bouncing off the water. Something shiny flickered nearby, and Jashun looked at the horrifying scene beside the blood-splattered turtle statue. There were the bodies of the soldiers who were supposed to be guarding the Tor. They were torn apart. Heads were missing, blood soaked the ground into the lake's water. Like a beacon for help, their helmets echoed the sun's light, but it was obvious no help came.

Jashun swallowed down a cry of hate and grief for his brothers and sisters in arms. He saw near the leader's severed hand the horn that should have been sounded for help. It was shattered. He let the branches fall closed.

Kailani cupped her hands around Jashun's face while hot tears flowed down his tan cheeks. "My love? My love, what is it? What did you see?"

"It's not safe out there. Those beasts slaughtered all the guards."

"They're dead? Jashun, should we go back?"

"No, this treaty is too important, and we must warn Avondelle about these creatures. The horn for help is broken, though."

"So, what are we to do?

Jashun tried to think of a plan, but his mind was cluttered with the sight of soldiers' limbs missing and large gashes across their chests and entrails hanging from their bellies. There was so much blood.

Kailani could see he was struggling. She grabbed his hands and squeezed. "Think, Jashun. If those creatures see us, then we're doomed. We need a way to conceal ourselves."

The word *conceal* triggered the memory of Sealyn concealing the Heart of Elysium with *Mirron hair. Mirrons! That was it.

"Yes. Lucky for us, Lord Finn always has his Mirron herd graze in the pastures nearby."

"Mirrons? Those are the horses with hair like mirrors, so everything is reflective, right?"

"Correct. We can't ride them because we would still be exposed, but if we got them to walk beside us, then we would be hidden."

"Only one problem, Jashun. How are we supposed to find invisible horses?"

Jashun shook his head, remembering one of their fun nights after one too many ales with Char, Sakul, Doebromir, and Favien. Before Sealyn was queen, and they were much younger than now, they had had a grand night of feasting and dancing at *Liquid Courage*, then ended up at Turtle Lake. Char had wagered Doebromir he couldn't ride a Mirron, and, of course, Doebromir couldn't turn down a challenge. They all ended up at what once were Lord Barkley's fields, which were later given to Lord Finn after Barkely's passing.

Sakul and Favien stood atop the only boulder in the thick green pasture, toasting each failed attempt by Doebromir. Doebromir kept pouncing in midair only to flop on the ground, which drew hearty laughs from his friends. Char and Jashun sat on the grass at the base of the boulder, leaning against the cool stone, and it was there that Princess Sealyn joined them.

Char went to fetch more ale from the wagon, and then Sealyn revealed the secret of seeing the invisible horses. After that, he could always see them.

"Jashun!" Kailani whispered harshly.

Jashun snapped back to his reality quickly. "It's ok, love. I can find the Mirrons. My friend and queen, although she was a princess at the time, taught me how."

They crawled out of the willow tree, heading toward the Mirron field. They stayed on their stomachs, using their elbows and knees to inch their way forward. They smelled the sweet, earthy scents and overheard bees buzzing above. Tall blades of grass kissed their faces, staining their clothes green. Suddenly, they heard a strange screech and paused. Jashun felt his pulse beating faster, sweat pouring down his face. If those creatures saw them, then they were dead.

He could hear wings flapping and felt their stomps vibrating the ground. Something must have spooked them. They couldn't remain there any longer. They had to move. Jashun tapped Kailani's hand, and he began slowly crawling again.

After slithering through the thick grass for what seemed like years, they made it to the Mirron field. They climbed cautiously over the worn wooden fence, then ran behind a boulder. Jashun felt a sting of pain from his memories of his friends. How long had it been since they all had a night with no cares, no burdens, no grief? He ached for the agony this world kept throwing at them to dissipate.

He leaned back on the cool stone, catching his breath, then saw Kailani's gorgeous gown ripped and stained with dirt and grass.

"Oh, Kailani, I'm so sorry about your gown."

"Trust me, Jashun, my gown is the last thing on my mind." She peered out onto the rolling hills of the pasture that looked as picturesque as a museum painting. "Do you see the Mirrons?"

Jashun squinted his eyes, praying the horses were out there. He didn't see them. He began to panic. Those Mirrons were their only hope; otherwise, they would be cooked alive. He took a deep breath, concentrated on Sealyn's words, closed his eyes, and visited the memory again.

"Have you had enough, Doebromir?" Favien slurred.

Doebromir popped his head up, coughing grass and dirt out of his mouth. "Neva! This future commander will find the invisible beasts and ride into the moonlight!"

The group laughed.

Sealyn took another bite of her strawberry Jam Pie and swallowed. "Wow. He really is super intoxicated."

Jashun chuckled. "Yes. Barm had some new northern wine he was testing out. Doebromir had a few too many."

Sealyn tossed a grape in the air and caught it with her mouth. "Want to know the secret to find Mirrons?"

Jashun sat up straighter. "You know it?"

"Jashun, I would shock you with how many secrets I know." Sealyn leaned her head against the boulder. "But you can't tell Char. I love hanging it over him that he doesn't know."

"Ha! I promise I won't tell."

She stood and helped Jashun to his feet. She led him, walking past the boulder, and pointed. "Watch out there. Do you see how the scenery you see looks like it's following us?"

"I do!"

"Those are the Mirrons."

"But Doebromir is way over there."

Sealyn giggled. "Exactly. We have hours more of watching '*the future commander*,'" she said in her most Doebromir voice. "Miss his target."

Jashun let out his breath, opened his eyes, and moved his head back and forth, then spotted the scenery that followed his movement. "There!" He pointed excitedly.

They hunched low in the tall, thick grass, trying to move faster than their crawling. Jashun felt such relief once they arrived. He was also thankful that Mirrons were not easily startled. These were fascinating creatures, and Jashun realized how much he truly loved the mystery and magic of his Elysium. He wanted to protect his kingdom and all the magic it held.

Unexpectedly, Jashun's fingers started flickering green sparks. He felt his hands growing hot, and an energy surged through him as if he had drunk an entire bowl of Madam Bip's PurFizz drink. What was happening? He felt a pull from the closest Mirron to touch it, and when he did, his eyes dilated, and the world seemed to be still. His fingers grazed over the Mirron fur, feeling slender scales of glass that tinkled at his touch.

He heard a panicked, muffled voice. It kept repeating, "Where are you?" He pulled his hand away from the Mirron and looked down at his legs, chest, and arms. What happened? He was covered in Mirron fur.

Kailani whispered again, "Jashun, please, where are you?"

Jashun finally answered. "I'm right here. Can't you see me?"

Kailani jumped at the sound of the invisible voice. "Jashun? How? What? You're invisible! How? How is this possible?"

"I don't know. I felt something odd, then touched the Mirron, and next thing I know, you're telling me I'm invisible. I can also see that I'm covered in Mirron fur."

Kailani gasped. "Jashun! You unlocked your Luxen powers! You're a Transference! This is amazing."

They heard the terrible screeches again, which jolted them back to their dangerous reality. Jashun looked frantically around and, in the distance, saw the road they needed to take to the capital. He pointed, which was in vain considering Kailani couldn't see him, then said, "Hurry. We need to get to that road to our right. We'll still take a few Mirrons to keep you covered, and because I don't know how long I will stay invisible." An eerie feeling crept over him. Is this permanent? Would he remain invisible? Who decides when the power will wear off? The Mirron? Himself?

Too many questions circled in his head. He decided to deal with those later and focused on the current threat. They had to warn the palace. Dragons were back.

Elysian News

The Latest News and Gossip

Issue #21

Mimby's Morsels voted #1
Your taste buds matter

I asked, and you answered! Here are your top ten places to eat in Avondelle.

1. ***Mimby's Morsels:*** Mimby's dishes are famous for pairing foods that don't often go together and making them taste magical.
2. ***Baker Nichts:*** The bakery is a local favorite. From Chocolate Jabbles to Puffin Pies, this is the perfect place to feed your sweet tooth.
3. ***Nijeel's Choice:*** Although Nijeel only serves tea cakes, his teas and coffee kept receiving votes, so I thought to include his café. It's the perfect pairing with the bakery. Be sure to stop by for his seasonal teas!
4. ***Magical Munchies***: Although relatively

Painted above: Mimby, owner of Mimby's Morsels

new to the market, this one is becoming a fast favorite! This is a quick grab-and-go spot for those in a hurry. Delicious premade and packed baskets of sandwiches, fruits, and nuts are ready for you.

5. ***Nice Ice:*** This is the new nightlife place to be! It opens as soon as the sun goes down. On the inside, everything is ice: the walls, ceiling, chairs, tables, and even cups and plates. Ice Nichts provide blankets for seats and serve cocktails with small bites. Everyone who's looking to mingle should be there!

6. ***Araelien Dynasty:*** Get ready to spend some coins! This restaurant is only open on the weekend during dinner hours. It's the most delicious food you've ever tasted, and decorated to look like the palace's dining room. Continued on page 2 ~ Lady Adalina Roedellen (Lina)

Princess Siany Spotlight	**Perdonair on the horizon**	**Luxen School Updates**
The juiciest gossip	*Get Ready!*	*Weekly Reports*
Another love interest from Port Rowin?	How to decorate your home	Rumor: Children from the school will participate in Feydom
How is Lord Edvard coping?	Lady Princess Anadelvia advises	Parents are encouraged to follow progress.
Page 3	Page 4	Page 6

CHAPTER 21
IN THE SNAKE'S MOUTH

Crunch. Crunch. Crunch.

King Ryker munched on salted cashews as he read another page in the black phoenix book. He made several copies for the Council of Wisdom and others with Madam Bip's magical ink. He sat at one of the tables in Sealyn's Butterfly Natatorium; the soft green velvet cushions of the chairs made hours of reading easier. Yellow butterflies twirled around the stone bookshelves, wishing for a story to be read aloud.

He kept finding himself coming more and more to this space. Maybe it was the vibrations of the singing plants that made him think better, or maybe it was the never-ending rows of stone bookshelves and dancing yellow butterflies that helped him feel peace, or maybe it was his longing to feel the presence of his youngest daughter. He missed Sealyn greatly and worried about her night and day.

Tears weld up in his Elysian green eyes. He still had no news from Sealyn's quest. He feared the worst. He reread the same words on the page over and over, yet his mind did not process them. He heard shoes clicking on the stone floor and looked up to see Lady Quinley.

She bowed before the king and Prince Adomin. "Pardon me, majesty, but I think I may have found something."

Adomin pushed up his spectacles and folded his arms, "Well, let's hear it then."

"I skimmed past the histories of the black phoenix. You know, all the jibber jabber in book one about who created them and so on, but it's in book two that we start to figure out what that first sentence means, '*The history of the black phoenix begins with the rise of the green phoenix and the explosion of fire.*'"

King Ryker closed book one, trying not to fixate on his worry about Sealyn, which was making him lose focus on their current situation. He motioned for Quinley to continue.

She tucked her blonde locks behind her ear and took in a deep breath, preparing to unload dark information. "Of course, majesty. In chapters two through four, the author tells of different scenarios of when the black phoenix did not emerge."

"Stop. Stop. Stop. Why are you telling us that?" Adomin interrupted.

"Silence, brother," Prince Royce said, pants rolled up as he dripped water from his knees down. He had been reading with his feet in the natatorium pool, but hearing this conversation piqued his interest, so he joined them at the tables. "Let the poor girl speak." He nodded at Quinley.

She eyed Adomin slightly, then continued. "Like I was saying, the author talks about times when wildfires happened, dragons burning forests, and Fire Nichts accidentally setting kitchens on fire, but none of these spots caused the black phoenixes to rise, but the first line of chapter five says this," she held up her copy of the book and read aloud. "'*You must now be beginning to doubt why I wrote: the history of the black phoenix begins with the rise of the green phoenix and the explosion of fire. Here is the truth as I know it, as we all have come to fear it—purity is at risk. Only spilled blood that is so pure mixed with fire will the beast of the night rise from the ashes.*'"

Ryker shook his head. "But we've watched the forest that the dragons burned. There are no signs of any creature, and plenty of Elysian blood was spilled on that ground."

"Could this author have it wrong?" Adomin questioned.

"Yes, maybe these creatures don't exist, or perhaps Dun killed them long ago?" Royce suggested.

Quinley cleared her throat, palms sweating. "Forgive me, but the blood spilled on that horrible day in the forest was that of adult soldiers."

"Your point?" growled Adomin.

"No one is perfect, my prince, not even a great Elysian soldier. We have all made mistakes in our lives, so if adult blood is not pure, then whose blood is?"

The doors of the natatorium burst open with Queen Mother Graelynd, Jashun, Kailani, and Captain Graegory.

"My queen," Ryker said. He was angered. The interruption robbed his mind of figuring out the answer to Quinley's question. It was on the tip of his tongue. "What is this interruption?" He paused, realizing who was with her. "Jashun? Princess Kailani? You two look terrible."

"Thank you, majesty," Jashun said with exhaustion. He was happy that the Mirron power wore off right when they stepped on the palace grounds. "We bring grave news."

"Speak."

"Dragons. They're back!"

"Where?" roared Ryker.

"We arrived at Kailani's kingdom's Tor of the great willow tree at Turtle Lake, and when we looked across the lake, we saw black dragons. They had brutally murdered all the soldiers. I saw them against the turtle statue, bodies dismantled and slashed across their chests and stomachs. They were all dead. There was nothing we could do. We used Mirrons to keep us hidden until we arrived at the palace."

"We must sound the alarm," yelled Adomin.

Royce nodded. "I agree. We can't waste any time."

Graelynd stepped forward and placed her hand on Ryker's shoulder, who was leaning on the table. "My love, listen to Jashun's words. Replay them."

Ryker was confused and looked at his wife. What was she trying to tell him? He replayed the words Jashun said. *The willow tree Tor. Black dragons across the lake. Bodies dismantled with slashes.* Wait. Slashes? Dismantled?

Ryker looked at Jashun and Kailani. "Can you confirm that what you saw were actually dragons?"

"Majesty?" Jashun questioned.

"Just answer the question. Do you know without any doubt that what you saw was dragons?"

"Well, no, my king. The sun's rays were bouncing harshly off the water."

"And you said that the bodies were dismantled with slashes?"

"Correct, majesty."

"This is not the way of dragons. Did you see any scorches of the earth?"

"No, majesty, but I heard their wings and screeches."

"Screeches?" Graegory questioned. "Dragons don't screech; they roar."

Jashun swallowed. What had they seen? He looked at Kailani, hoping she would validate his story.

"King Ryker," Kailani spoke. "We cannot confirm that these black-winged creatures were dragons, but if they're not, then what are they?"

The room stilled as if they all understood in unison. Ryker's head dropped. All the answers hit him at once. He knew what this meant. "The land across the lake from the willow tree." He paused, fighting back tears. "That is the field of the Emangaton flowers, where the last dragon burned the NexGen Nichts."

Pure innocence died that day, the purest of bloods gone. This realization sent the royals into a scurry. Without saying a word, they raced to the palace. They knew they were too late. The black phoenixes had already emerged undetected, and if Jashun and Kailani had mistaken them for dragons, then they were fully grown. What damage could a fully-grown black phoenix inflict?

The foul stench of the snake's mouth made Ashur vomit again. The team lifted their feet, allowing the snake's unusually large tongue to swallow the puke. A Jormungon was a unique snake, with teeth like a human, but it had an extra bottom row of teeth, which the rebels used as seats while the snake swam the watery channels of Shunal.

They swayed back and forth with the snake's movements. Jace tried to keep himself calm and focused. He had no idea what they would face once they exited the snake's mouth. They each had a wreath of yellow fireflowers around their necks to help see in the darkness. He glanced across and caught Cruz staring at Sealyn. Sealyn was looking down, eyes closed, holding onto the child.

Why was Cruz staring? Did this rebel not understand she was off limits? That was his wife! He decided to interrupt Cruz's ogling. Jace cleared his throat. "Forgive me, Cruz, but you seem awfully young to be a rebellion leader."

Cruz smiled a cunning smile. "You don't have to be old to be wise, King Jace. Just look at your beautiful bride. Is she not wise beyond her years and leading a great crusade?"

Something boiled deep inside Jace. "I'm not interested in hearing you flirt your way to overthrow your kingdom."

"Jace," Sealyn remarked. "What is this?"

Jace leaned in and whispered in her ear, "I saw him watching you, and not in a 'sizing up if he can trust you' watching, but a yearning watching."

"Oh, Jace. I'm sure you misread that. Cruz knows I'm married, and besides, I have no interest in any other man than you."

Herbmando shifted uncomfortably on his tooth. "Well, do you Elysians have any good stories to share?"

Char perked up as if on cue. "Absolutely! Would you like to hear about the time Sealyn walked into a tree while mouthing off to someone? Or maybe about the time I scarred her foot for life, literally? No, wait, my favorite. When our wagon got stuck in the mud, and Sealyn…"

"Char! Say another word, and you'll be this snake's dinner."

The group softly chuckled.

"Sounds like you two had a memorable childhood?" Herbmando observed.

Char and Sealyn looked at each other and laughed. Char nodded. "You can say that."

The snake came to an abrupt stop. The team fell forward.

"Brace yourselves. This is the dangerous part," Cruz yelled.

"Being in the mouth of a giant snake was not the dangerous part?" Ashur incredulously asked.

"No," Cruz said. "When the snake opens its mouth, water will come rushing in. Don't get swept away, or else you will be digested."

Ashur gulped.

They all tried to find grooves on the teeth to hold their positions, then came the rush of water. The giant wave of force hit them, knocking them off balance. Most remained grounded, but Skarpin slipped, and his grip faltered, washing him away with the current.

Sealyn screamed before water knocked into her face. Jace quickly adjusted his position on the tooth, then reached his arm out and caught hold of Skarpin's foot. The current was pulling them toward the belly of the beast. Sealyn looked underwater and saw Jace's grip slipping. She let the current take her to Jace's tooth, and right as she landed, Jace's hand slipped and was in the current.

Sealyn grabbed Jace's arm, feeling her shoulder joint jerk. She channeled King Nawrooshall and all the mammoth strength her body would allow. Indigo blue swirls swarmed beside Sealyn, and her eyes glowed an electric blue. The tooth began to crack; then they were floating. The water pressure inside matched the outside.

They swam as fast as they could from the snake's mouth and into the warm water of the Golden Lake. Coughing and gasping for air, the team managed to survive, even little Skarpin.

Sealyn could still feel the mammoth strength. She was glad Nawrooshall was allowing her to channel him still because they would need all the power they could get for this next part. They floated in the water, mesmerized by the Stoltland ship in front of them. The snake had released them right where Sorcha was being held captive.

Sealyn started to swim toward the ship, but Tilmond spoke. "Wait, Sealyn. We need a plan of attack."

"I have one: attack. There will be no mercy for anyone on this ship."

"Sealyn!" Tilmond whispered harshly. "Don't do this. Don't lose yourself. Think before you react."

"I have been thinking. I've been thinking about this for a while." She paused and looked at Skarpin, who looked tired. Her eyes caught him staring at the gold below. He needed to get out of this water before he succumbed to the curse. "I do think a small group should return to my ship, though." She nodded her head in the direction of her massive ship. They could see the twinkling lights on the deck.

"Who goes?" asked Tilmond.

"Well, if Cruz and Herbmando think they can resist the curse, then they can stay." She looked at the two Shunalians, who nodded back. "Excellent. Then the ones to go are Skarpin, Vaelinthia, Doebromir, and Ashur."

"My queen," Doebromir said. "Why am I going, and why is Sune staying?"

"I should never have to explain myself, but I'll say it fast. D, you need peace, and I trust you will get Skarpin to safety. The battle we will face is not for Vael. Ashur has been vomiting since we began—he's too weak for this. And Sune? Even if I ordered him to leave, he wouldn't." Sealyn peered into Sune's green eyes, telling him she knew about his feelings for Sorcha.

"I would like to point out," Herbmando began. "That some of us are a little more out of shape than others, so it would be nice to stop treading water and get on solid ground."

"Let's go," Sealyn said, then grabbed Skarpin one last time and kissed his forehead. "I'll see you soon."

With tears in his big golden eyes, he asked, "Promise?"

"For you? Yes, I promise."

The two groups split, and it was finally time to bring vengeance on the Stoltlanders. The rebels and Elysians swam quietly to the ship. They noticed two ladders folded against the side, but they were out of reach.

"Max. Finn. My archers," Sealyn said. "I need you two to shoot those ladders free."

"Sea," Max said. "I can't shoot like this, being in the water."

Sealyn could magically form platforms, but she needed to reserve her strength for the Stoltlanders, so this plan would have to be with pure human strength and willpower. "Tilmond, Jace, and Ajorn, you three will go under Finn and raise him up enough to hit the first ladder's ties. Favien, Brehan, and Char will hold up Max, who will do the same for the second. Hurry, now. We are wasting time."

Deep inhaling, the divers went below their archers and began hoisting Finn and Max. Rising out of the water, the archers grabbed their soaking wet bows and arrows. They could feel the weight of their quivers filled with water, which threw them off balance, not to mention the movement of the water and shaky arms of the men below. Finn fired his first arrow, and it missed. Max fired his, also missing.

Sealyn, Cruz, and Herbmando encouraged them to keep going. Her men didn't have long with air. Finn fired again, missing. Max fired and hit the target, but it didn't come loose all the way. Finn fired his third shot and hit the target, releasing the ladder. Finn was super surprised at how steady his comrades were holding him, or at least one of them was. He would have to think about that later.

Max fired again but missed. He felt the pressure and could feel his friends giving out. He fired his last arrow, sinking the target and liberating the ladder.

The divers came up, gasping for air.

Sealyn narrowed her eyes. "Let's climb."

CHAPTER 22
YOU'RE MY PULSE

Tilmond and Favien reached the top first, scanning the deck. With their fingers, they showed how many guards were on duty and on which sides. Their first priority was to find more arrows for the archers and silently take out as many guards as they could before the entire ship knew they were there. The two nodded to each other and jumped over the railing, quickly hiding in the shadows of barrels, sending a family of rats scampering away.

A Stoltland guard came down the steps of the upper deck and turned to walk past Tilmond and Favien. Tilmond stuck out his leg, tripping the guard. Favien spun on his back, holding up his dagger, allowing the guard to fall onto it, not making a sound. Tilmond pulled the guard off Favien and laid him in the shadows.

"Well, that's one down," said Favien.

Brehan and Ajorn were next to jump the railing. Brehan held a foothold for Ajorn, who, like a stealthy cheetah, jumped up and over the upper deck. Favien quickly turned around and used Brehan's foothold to follow Ajorn. Ajorn swiftly threw two daggers, landing in the throats of two Stoltlanders.

Ajorn whispered, "Grab their weapons. Look, there's five quivers full of arrows in that corner."

Back at the railing, Finn and Max jumped over and huddled beside Tilmond and Brehan. Favien looked below and motioned for the archers to come to the upper deck. Before they could jump over, two Stoltlanders walked by and drew swords. Brehan and Tilmond tackled them while Finn and Max stabbed them with their daggers. They dragged the bodies and stacked them on top of the other one. Blood started flowing around them.

"It's getting a bit cramped back here," Tilmond said. "Finn. Max. Hurry and secure the upper deck. We need archers to have our backs moving across the deck."

Sealyn and Jace jumped the banister and joined Tilmond and Brehan. Jace sweetly kissed his queen. They needed to celebrate the little wins, but Jace had a bad feeling. Sealyn felt off like something dark was following her. For the first time, he sensed her essence was monstrous.

They heard the bird call, signaling the front of the ship's deck was secure. Sune and Char jumped onto the ship, followed by Cruz and Herbmando, who struggled to climb the railing.

"We will need more archers on the top deck," Sealyn said. "So, I will join Finn and Max. We need two more men on the other side of the ship to even the sides out." Cruz and Herbmando raised their hands. "Excellent. Let's go."

Brehan hoisted up Sealyn, Cruz, and Herbmando to the upper deck. They were ready. It was time to get their friend back. Sealyn nodded to Finn. He rang the bell next to him. They wanted the Stoltland rats to come up on the main deck.

Exactly as they planned, Stoltland soldiers poured out from below deck like ants. Elysian arrows flew, taking out the enemies one by one. Sune could stand it no longer; he wanted Stoltland's blood. He raced forward, his sword colliding with another Stoltlander's sword. He swung for another blow, jabbing into the soldier's side, ripping out the soldier's life. The rest of the Elysians and rebels joined in the fight.

More Stoltlanders came from below decks. The Elysians were completely outnumbered. The archers tried to take out as many as they could, but they did not anticipate how many soldiers were still on board and not in Shunal.

Sealyn's heart sank. She watched in horror as a black blade went into Ajorn's upper right shoulder. He went down in agony, holding his shoulder with blood dripping in between his fingers.

Sune and Brehan screamed in anger for their comrade. A black arrow shot Tilmond in the leg. He fell to his knees, still swinging his sword. Jace sliced through another Stoltlander, blood splattering his face and looked to Sealyn. He saw something dark and sinister forming around her feet. Was that the dark mist? No! Was his mother on this ship? She couldn't be. No, the mist was huddled around Sealyn.

What was happening? Jace cried out to Sealyn. She looked down at him just in time to see a Stoltlander sliced across Jace's chest. His ripped clothes showed the massive gash. Blood poured down his pecks and abs. Jace fell, writhing in pain. Sealyn screamed, and a forceful pulse sent a wave across the deck, knocking everyone down.

The captain and a crew of fifty men came from below with Sorcha in chains. Sorcha cried out, seeing her friends bloody and beaten. She saw Sune covered in blood. Was it his or their enemies'?

"Spare them. Kill me instead. My life for theirs," Sorcha pleaded, but her innocent words fell on deaf ears because once the captain saw the emerald queen, he could think of torturing no one else.

"Isn't this the pitiful creature you came for?" The rotten-teethed captain held up Sorcha's chains. "I'm glad I waited until now to kill her. Her death would have been spoiled if I did not have this grand audience."

"Touch her, and you die slowly. Free her, and your death will be quick."

The captain cackled waspishly like he had gargled with shards of glass. "My dear little bird, you have lost this battle. Your small crew is no match for my numbers. We will be merciful and kill your crew, but you and the grey-eyed traitor over there will be our new captives. Besides, the outcast's mommy misses him. But if he dies today, no one will care. I will be glad to watch him die. He's a mixed breed, a worthless nobody."

Char inhaled. "Oh crap, this won't be good."

Sealyn tilted her head. "You have no idea what army I come with, and let me make this perfectly clear: King Jace is my *everything!*" She roared the last word. Her eyes glowed green, and green flames burst all around her. The flames on her back looked like flaming phoenix wings. She started walking down the steps and held her arms to the side, glowing palms up. Large wind gusts of green and blue swirls of light and flames formed animal-like beings behind her. A phoenix flew above, a mammoth to her left, and a lioness to her right.

She sent the creatures forward, plowing through and killing the hundreds of Stoltland soldiers. She had no idea this was the kind of power she could wield, and she liked it. Sealyn swung her sword with the speed of the legendary phoenix and the strength of the mighty mammoth. Her sword was covered with the Stoltlanders' blood, and she felt good taking their lives for imprisoning Sorcha, Doebromir, and Sune.

The power was becoming too much. She could see the creatures dissipating. Only a handful of soldiers were left, but they dropped their swords. Black flames started creeping into the green flames surrounding Sealyn. She hated the man holding Sorcha's chains. She didn't care that these men were surrendering. They were cowards and had made their decisions beforehand. They could have released Sorcha, but they chose to keep her bound and tortured.

Sealyn swung her sword, chopping off the first head of the surrendered soldiers. "There will be no mercy!" She saw the captain panic and raise a knife to Sorcha's heart. Sealyn threw her blade without hesitation. The sword cut through the air, going straight through the captain's neck.

Sorcha fell backward with the captain and watched as Sealyn sliced through each remaining Stoltlander. Blood splattered Sealyn's face and clothes. She was lost in rage and couldn't stop. Sorcha begged Sealyn to halt, but a force kept her from hearing her friend.

Char scrambled to Jace, helping him to his feet. His sliced shirt hung in tatters. While looking for Sealyn, Jace took the remnants of his shirt off, exposing the huge bleeding gash, his muscles bulging with black veins popping. Something was not right with this wound. Jace froze at the sight of Sealyn slashing the Stoltland bodies.

"Jace, I know you're in agony, but you've got to do something. Sealyn's gone mad," Char pointed.

Injured and in excruciating pain, Jace ran to his wife, jumping over bodies and crates until he was in front of her. More blood and puss oozed from his gash with his movements. He didn't care. Sealyn needed him. He ducked one of her swings, then enveloped her with his arms. He winced as his wound collided with her body.

"Sealyn, my sweet Sealyn. Come back to me, my love. Remember who you are," Jace whispered in her ear. Her eyes were bloodshot and bluish-black. Her nose and ears were bleeding. "Let me be your lighthouse, love. I'm here. Lean on me."

He heard her sword drop, and the flames settled, yet Jace was not burned. He was sweating from the heat, fear, and injury.

Sealyn could barely speak. "Jace?"

"Yes, love. Talk to me. I'm here."

"Is Sorcha safe?"

"Yes. We have her. She's going to be fine. We all are."

Sealyn blinked, and her eyes turned back to their emerald, green color. Then she passed out. Jace shook Sealyn, gently patting her blood-splattered cheeks, praying for a miracle. "Please, love. Please come back to me. Don't do this. Don't do this. You're my heartbeat."

Jace held her limp body in his bloodied arms and quietly sobbed into her neck. "I need you. This world is not worth living in without you. You're my pulse, Sealyn."

Sealyn deeply inhaled, and her chest rose violently. Ever so slowly, she opened her eyes. Aided by the moonlight, Jace gasped. "Sealyn, your eyes are gold."

Elysian News

The Latest News and Gossip

Issue #23

Princess Siany: Headmistress or Quackmistress?
Parents talk

Greetings, my fellow Elysians. Today's topic will be tough, but asking the tough questions is what I do.

Parents are concerned for their children's safety. Princess Siany has officially announced that children from the school, not professional athletes, will play Feydom this year.

Painted above: Princess Siany Araelien

Luckily, the rules changed, and weapons will no longer be allowed, but did our princess come up with that idea, or did someone else? Shouldn't the headmistress be concerned first about safety and, last about new ideas that will elevate her popularity?

Other parents are eager for their children to play in Feydom. They think it brings something new to the kingdom, especially during our uncertain times. We know for sure that the kids attending the school are incredibly excited.

We can only hope that the results are safe and worth it—for Princess Siany's sake and the children's. What do you think? Send me your letters!
~ Lady Adalina Roedellen (Lina)

Princess Siany Spotlight	**Perdonair Recipes**	**Luxen School Updates**
The juiciest gossip	*Mimby's secrets*	*Weekly Reports*
Who will she choose for her Vinurs of the Court?	Most served meal on Perdonair	Sign-ups for Feydom are open!
See the list of ladies	How to make the perfect holiday meal	Parents are encouraged to follow progress.
Page 2	Page 3	Page 5

CHAPTER 23
ATTACK OF THE BLACK PHOENIXES

Siany wrote her final note of the day, placing her green feathered quill back in the ink jar. Today had been a good day. She was excited for the season. They were weeks away from Perdonair, the fall holiday celebrating King Perdon. Her favorite part was the game Feydom. This year, they were changing how the game would go.

Only children of certain ages attending the new school would participate and only play the Clod portion of the game. Each team would have three days to capture fourteen flags. Whichever team collected the most at the end of the three days would win, and whoever had the fewest flags on day one was ejected sand excused from the game; the same was true for day two.

Siany leaned back in her chair and almost fell when her father and his entire royal guard burst into her classroom.

"Father? You scared me. What's this about?"

"I'm sorry to startle you, darling. We need to know, and I hate to ask this, but are there any students who show promise of magical abilities that could help our military?"

"What?!"

"Siany, please listen."

"No, I will hear nothing of this. Children are just that. Children! They have no place in war."

"In all other circumstances, I would agree with you, but right now, we're in a unique situation, and I'm asking not as your father but as your *king*."

Siany's mouth fell open. In all her years, her father had never used those words before. "What is going on, Father?"

Ryker put his hands on his hips and sighed. "Brace yourself because this isn't easy to share." Ryker explained every detail about the black phoenixes, Jashun's discovery, and the Emangaton flower field. He saw his daughter's disturbed expression and remembered her kneeling at the burning field on the saddest day in Elysium's history.

"So, they're here and have already killed soldiers but haven't attacked the capital. What are they waiting for?"

"That's something we don't know and makes me very uneasy." Ryker folded his arms. "We were caught off guard by this, and honestly, Siany, if your student hadn't found those books in the attics, we wouldn't have the information we do right now."

"I'm just so speechless."

"We got lucky with Jashun and Kailani, too. If they hadn't seen those phoenixes across the lake, then we would still be just researching, which is why I'm here desperately asking you this question."

"Wait. Kailani. Father, that's it. Kailani is here."

"Yes. She's here with Jashun."

"But Jashun went to find out what it would take to form an alliance with Elysium and her Mer Clan. If she's here, then doesn't that mean they want the alliance?"

"Actually, yes. They did manage to tell me that before I left to come here."

"Sign the documents now. If you do, then Kailani's people will be allowed to practice Abyss Magic on Elysian soil. I know that was one thing Sealyn shared with me. She needs that to happen for some reason, but right now, this alliance could save our people."

Ryker paused. "Abyss Magic was banned long ago, and for many reasons. I'm not sure if we can trust the Mer Clans. But just for curiosity's sake, are there any students demonstrating anything that could protect us?"

Siany did not want to lie to her father, her king, but she also wanted to protect certain students. Who came first? She had a moral responsibility as headmistress but a loyal responsibility to her king. "No, father. Nothing of value yet."

Ryker's eyes twitched, and then he repeated, "Yet. Well, I need to have more conversations with the fish apparently. I wish Sealyn would have shared these sneaky plans with me before she left." Ryker stepped closer to his daughter. "We've already sent the distance Nichts out to call the Phoenixes back from the borders, and apparently, Lord Edvard is coming back with Dun through their Tor."

Siany's cheeks went red at the mention of Lord Edvard's name. "I'll prepare the school for lockdown and have the protection spells doubled around the borders and castle."

"Excellent. I will send two Phoenixes to guard as well." He hugged his daughter. "We will get through this." He kissed the top of her head and left with his guards, leaving Siany's mind swirling with thoughts of the evil black phoenixes and how she was going to protect a castle full of innocent children.

The quill etched Kailani's signature in green ink. Her eyes glowed pink as soon as she returned the green feathered quill to the jar. She could feel the freedom of power itching to be released. Her heart pounded like war drums, ready to help protect the Elysian people.

"We need to get you to your Tor to bring back reinforcements," Ryker said, shaking her hand.

"I agree. We're ready to do battle against this evil with you."

A terrible ear-piercing screech sounded through the walls, alarming everyone to the horrifying realization that the black phoenixes were there and Elysium's Green Phoenixes hadn't arrived yet. Panic radiated from each person's eyes and bones.

Ryker wasted no time in handing out commands. "Captain Graegory, ready the troops. Tell the archers to fire at will." Graegory ran from the room, ordering his speed Nichts to send the messages to all divisions. Ryker grabbed Queen Mother Graelynd's hand. "You already know what to do, my love."

"Think no more about us. I will get our family to the secret chambers, but what about Siany?"

Ryker hated the thought of not being near his daughter to protect her. "We will trust that Madam Bip's protection spells will hold. Besides, I think someone is there who can help protect them."

"Who?"

"Let's not forget Lady Madilina's powers and who she's been training." Ryker wondered if that was who Siany had been unwilling to disclose, but his heart told him there was a student she was protecting.

Graelynd remembered Sealyn's recount of Madilina channeling the Caelidon, the flying horse. Could she potentially channel a dragon?

They felt the castle vibrate and heard the screams of the soldiers outside. Everyone raced to their positions. Jashun pulled open the front doors to the palace and gasped as he saw six massive black phoenixes flying and diving, attacking his people.

He turned to Kailani. "Can't you do some kind of epic Abyss Magic now?"

"I need water, Jashun."

"There's water everywhere: in the plants, in the ground…"

"It doesn't work that way. You must understand why we were banned from using this magic on your land. I could siphon all the water from the soil and plants, but then it would destroy that land—never to grow back. I could also accidentally pull water from you humans since your bodies are mainly water."

"What are you saying?"

"I could kill you without even touching you, Jashun. I could kill you without breaking a sweat. We are the monsters your ancestors wanted to protect your land from."

"But you're not a monster. Kailani, we need you."

Jashun looked out and saw two phoenixes dive and snatch three soldiers, then break them in half, letting their broken bodies fall from the sky. The next sight frightened him even more. He wasn't prepared for the lava. Liquid fire flowed effortlessly from the dark creatures' mouths. This was how the evil phoenixes would ensure their survival. They could breathe liquid flames over pure blood and live forever.

Ryker stood with Jashun, looking out at the madness before him. He watched the faces of the phoenixes. They looked like they were searching for something. Something that clearly wasn't here.

Lord Jdru, Char's brother, fired a large arrow from the top tower, just like he had during the dragon battle. The arrow collided with one of the phoenixes' hearts, exploding in flame and black smoke. The military cheered, but the other phoenixes screamed with anger.

The beasts forced their attention on Jdru's tower, and, exactly like before, they ran for their lives down the winding steps, feeling the hot liquid behind them. Jdru looked back just to make sure everyone was safe, but steam and ash engulfed him. They singed his reddish-blonde beard and burned his eyes. He toppled down the rest of the stairs, screaming in pain, grabbing his eyes.

The leader, black phoenix, clapped his beak and squawked, which signaled two phoenixes to leave. The leader and two others remained, attacking Elysian soldiers. Jdru's men carried him inside the palace. His screams caught Ryker's attention.

"What happened?" Ryker demanded.

"Majesty, the steam and ash of the lava burned his eyes," one of the soldiers said.

A lump formed in Ryker's throat. This was his nephew. His blood. "Take him to the hospital immediately. I think Madam Bip has a remedy for this, but I can't be certain."

Ryker turned back to the chaos, unsure of what to do next. "Kailani, I overheard you say that you need water."

"Yes, majesty."

"I think those horrid creatures are looking for innocent lives to kill."

"Majesty?" Kailani questioned.

"They're hunting children," Ryker growled. "There's a lake at the new school of magic. I need you and Jashun to get there as fast as possible. The Mirrons are in the stables. They're faster than normal horses."

"Right away, my king," Jashun said. They turned to leave, but Ryker grabbed Kailani's arm.

"I'm trusting you with the future generations of Elysium. Honor the pact and wash away your ancestors' mistakes." Ryker's eyes glowed green.

Kailani nodded, understanding the insinuation, and ran to the stables with Jashun. Luckily, the cushioned saddles were already secured to the Mirrons. They quickly slid the bridles on and climbed on top. They looked at each other, nodded, then kicked their horses and flew like the wind toward the castle filled with children.

Two black phoenixes flew toward the school castle, confirming King Ryker's fears. The beasts wanted pure blood.

CHAPTER 24
NIGHTLIGHT & GORM

Lava spilled over the protection dome around the castle grounds' borders. Siany channeled the bird that kept coming back to her. Her heart sank when she couldn't see any help coming. Where were the Green Phoenixes? Her view shifted when she saw movement in the tree line. Jashun and Kailani riding on air? No, they were riding Mirrons.

She watched as the two cut through the border spell since Madam Bip secured it with an intention clause: intent to harm, no entry—intent to help, allow entry. She released the bird and raced down to the grounds. Siany had already changed into her battle leathers; this would be a fight to the death.

Jashun and Kailani jumped off the Mirrons in front of Lady Madilina. They all looked up as the dome kept taking hit after hit. The phoenixes were clawing and stabbing at the wall of magic. They were getting desperate to enter.

"Hi, Madilina," Jashun said. "It's been a while."

"It has, and I hate we're seeing each other again under these circumstances." Four white *Caelidons stood beside Madilina with her juvenile Noxhorn behind them.

"Is that a…"

"Yes, Jashun. She's a Noxhorn dragon, but she will fight for us."

"Well, if anyone can train a dragon to do that, it's you. I trust you," Jashun said. With that, the dragon walked forward, sniffing Jashun, and sat beside him.

"Looks like I'm not the only one she's willing to deal with. Jashun, are you a Transference?"

Jashun held up his hands. "It literally just happened, and I'm not sure how to control anything."

"That's ok. Let the creature teach you," she looked at her Caelidons. "I will channel the Caelidons, and Jashun, you will channel Nightlight."

"Nightlight? Seriously, Madilina? You named a Noxhorn…*Nightlight*?" Jashun questioned incredulously. Kailani snickered.

"What? She is my little night light."

"Wow. You are as sweet and innocent as your reputation," Kailani extended her hand to Madilina. "I'm Kailani. While you two channel your creatures, I'm going to use that lake over there."

Siany slowed her jog once she reached Madilina, Kailani, and Jashun. "Hi, how can I help?"

"Well, I'm…" Kailani started but was interrupted by screeches from three more phoenixes. More flames poured over the barrier. They saw a few spots in the spell starting to split open, with droplets of lava falling to the ground. They all looked at each other with fear in their eyes.

Siany readied her bow. "I'll fire arrows from inside the castle's protection spell. Everyone ready?"

Nightlight looked at Jashun and gave her best dragon grin. Jashun didn't know whether to be terrified or emboldened. One way or another, he was about to be the first Elysian to channel a Noxhorn. He held out his hand and laid it on top of her head.

His eyes dilated, and his body felt like it was on fire, but not too painful, more like a heatwave, then it settled. Suddenly, he felt weightless. He didn't realize he had closed his eyes; timidly, he opened them, and he was in the air being carried by his own set of Noxhorn wings, just like Nightlight's.

He looked at the small dragon, who roared her mightiest roar. Deep inside himself, Jashun felt a yearning. A need to release something burning in the pit of his stomach or lungs; he didn't know which. As he opened his mouth, blue flames shot across the air.

Madilina flew next to Jashun with her white feathered wings. "Impressive, Jashun. She even gave you her eyes. You look wicked crazy." Madilina readied her bow. "This won't be easy, but we must protect the school."

Siany yelled from the base of the school, "I can see the palace guard coming, but they won't get here before that first border breaks."

Jashun looked confused at Madilina. "Oh yes, that's right. You don't know," she said. "Princess Siany is also a Transference. Her little bird friend gives her his sight while he flies."

"I love Luxen power," Jashun marveled.

"Let's just hope your new pink-haired girlfriend can bring a new element to this because I highly doubt we can hold off these wild beasts by ourselves."

They heard sizzling above their heads, then dodged the burnt protection spell and the lava coming through. Madilina ordered her horses back to the stables along with

Nightlight, but Nightlight positioned herself next to Siany instead.

The first phoenix dove through the opening, straight for Madilina. She ducked, the spray of liquid fire barely missing. Jashun and Madilina both headed for the lake, hoping to draw the phoenix's attention.

Siany fired arrow after arrow, but it looked like the arrows weren't penetrating her target. She looked to Nightlight. "Got a light?" Nightlight glared at Siany's lame joke but obliged. Siany fired the blue flaming arrow. She saw that it at least cut the phoenix, but no solid damage. How were they supposed to harm these beasts?

The second phoenix entered along with the other three. They were now facing lava and claws from five black phoenixes. The creatures sped toward Madilina and Jashun. Jashun sent flames of his own at the impending death coming for them. They flipped, bypassing his fire, shooting their liquid fire back at him. Jashun felt the force of impact from the lava knock him back, but luckily, he wasn't burned. Nightlight must have given more than he expected.

Kailani emerged from the middle of the water in her mermaid form with glowing pink eyes. Her arms flailed around the water's surface, speaking a language Jashun didn't understand. With swirls of silver and pink, giant waterspouts formed. She threw her arms at the phoenixes, and water tornadoes hit the feathered creatures, knocking them down.

The phoenixes gathered their composures, scratching the ground and snapping their red beaks. Jashun sent more flames, Kailani sent more water, and Madilina and Siany fired more arrows. Ice Nichts flew from the school castle, joining the cause, sending beams of ice, trying to freeze the creatures into submission.

They could see the ice cracking. Jashun shouted for additional water and ice, but lava was seeping into the ground, melting the ice.

An odd squeak came across the grassy field. Jashun suddenly felt scared but didn't know why. He looked at Nightlight in case she was in danger, but he saw her looking at the tiny white dragon flying. Her brother, the bubble dragon, was coming from the direction of the palace. Nightlight roared at her brother.

He landed beside Siany. Nightlight huffed steam of anger. The ice around the phoenixes cracked more. The bubble dragon grabbed Siany's arrow with his tiny arms. Siany tried to pull it back, but Nightlight snapped her jaws at her. Siany dropped it quickly.

"Fine. Have it, Gorm, but you're not supposed to be here," Siany argued with the little dragon.

Gorm smirked, blew his bubbles onto the arrow's tip, and then handed it back to Siany.

Siany looked at the arrow, confused. "Gorm, now is not the time to play."

Gorm shook his head and looked toward the iced-over phoenixes. Siany couldn't figure out what this little dragon wanted, but her thoughts vanished when she watched the black phoenixes burst from the ice. Shards of ice and liquid flames spewed all around. Drops of lava scorched Madilina's arm. She yelled out in searing pain. Kailani threw water, extinguishing the lava's power. Kailani screamed, "The lake is running low. We can't keep this up much longer!"

Siany armed her bow and released the arrow with the bubble residue on the end. It sunk into one of the phoenixes. The phoenix screeched. Siany gasped. What just happened? Gorm looked at her and smiled. He flapped his wings, hovered above her quiver, and pulled out all the arrows so he could get to the points. With excitement, Gorm cast several waves of bubbles over the arrows, then flew toward the phoenixes.

Nightlight roared again. She took off after her brother. Siany fired arrow after arrow, causing more pain and wounds to the black phoenixes. Ice Nichts shot beams of ice, freezing together black feathers. Finally, the palace military arrived, spilling onto the burning grass of the castle grounds. The smell of smoke and burnt flowers filled the air. The phoenixes dove after the soldiers and charged for Siany.

Gorm swung past one of the phoenix's wings and poured bubbles onto its side. The black phoenix's feathers and skin melted away from the little white dragon's efforts. Nightlight then released her blue flames upon the exposed skin. She burned a hole right through its stomach. The beast screeched, then fell from the air, landing with a boom to the ground, sending up dirt, grass, and entrails.

Four more phoenixes remained, but they all realized there was much more to that bubble dragon. Gorm became their target. The four flanked him and Nightlight and, all together, whacked them with their fearsome claws. The two small dragons hit the ground hard, not moving.

Jashun fell from the sky, landing with a crack that sent pain up his leg. The channel between him and Nightlight had been broken, and so was his ankle. Siany was out of arrows that could penetrate the phoenixes. The lake was almost empty, and too many Ice Nichts had been killed by the liquid fire. What hope did they have left?

Like a silent prayer being answered, green flames sped through the skies from every direction the Elysians could see. The black phoenixes screeched with anger and fear. Their reckoning had just arrived.

Bursting from his green flames, Dun pinned the leader of the black phoenixes to the ground, pounding and clawing at the evil creature. The black phoenix tried to kick free, but Dun sunk his golden beak around the dark beast's neck and snapped his head off. Black blood dripped from Dun's beak.

The other Green Phoenixes attacked the remaining black phoenixes. The black creatures were no match to the green force. They ripped off black wings and tore open their stomachs with no mercy. Finally, the last breath of darkness was drawn, and the battle was over. Black and green feathers scattered the battlefield. Chunks of lava hardened, forming large boulders. Children peered out the windows, trembling, but they were safe.

Siany held Jdru's hand as it lay on the clean, white fabric of his hospital bed. Lord Quinten, Jdru's father—youngest brother to King Ryker, sat in a chair on the opposite side while his mother, Lady Tintalina, busied herself knitting a scarf for when he would wake up.

King Ryker and Jdru's crew members walked up to Jdru's bed. "How is he?" Ryker asked.

"Lord Prince Brandle said he thinks between him and Madam Bip, they can restore his sight. It's going to take quite a while, though," Quinten said.

"And he may need reading spectacles," added Tintalina.

Ryker folded his arms and swayed on his feet. "I just don't understand. How was Jdru the only one able to fire an arrow at a phoenix and kill it, but no other arrows penetrated them?"

"It was a pretty big arrow, majesty. Same as those arrows used to shoot the dragons," one of the soldiers said.

Ryker shook his head. "My gut is telling me there's something else to this."

"My arrows did," Siany added.

"Your arrows did what?" Ryker questioned.

"They penetrated the black phoenixes."

Lord Quinten leaned in. "How?"

"Gorm."

"*Gorm*. Gorm what?" Ryker said curiously.

"That's right. Gorm," Siany let go of Jdru's hand and stood next to her father. "Gorm blew his bubbles on the arrow tips, then the arrows broke the phoenix skin for some unknown reason."

"That still wouldn't answer the question as to how Jdru managed it."

Gruffly, Jdru said, "Oh yes, it would." Quinten and Tintalina rushed to his side, helping him sit up. He had white bandages wrapped around his eyes and bald head. "That little bubble dragon loved to harass me. I don't know why he always chose me to prank, but he was hiding with the dragon slayer weapons that morning. I entered the weapons room to prepare them for a possible attack once Captain Graegory's Nicht gave me the order. I had an arrow in my hand, and he popped out from behind a barrel, spraying me with those annoying bubbles!"

Siany snorted, imagining Gorm pranking Jdru. "Well, looks like that little dragon saved a lot of lives. Did you find out from Dun if Gorm and Nightlight will be ok?"

"I'm sure Lord Jdru will be happy to know that he will have many more days of being pranked by Gorm because both juvenile dragons will fully recover. I guess the lesson to be learned here is that even the smallest and meekest can make a huge difference—everyone has value."

Siany smiled. "Wise words from a wise king."

Elysian News

Issue #25

The Latest News and Gossip

Black Phoenix Invasion Report
Battle Details

Here are the latest updates:

32 soldiers dead
57 wounded
3 unaccounted

Crystal Palace Hospital supplies
needed: Blankets, pillows, bandages,
thread, needles, cauldrons, sponges,
soap.
Volunteers are still welcome.

Special recognition goes to Lord Jdru
Araelien for his gallant efforts in killing
the first black phoenix. Unfortunately, his
eyes were burned during the battle, but
doctors are reporting that he will fully recover with the aid of spectacles.

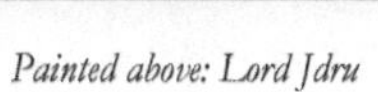

Painted above: Lord Jdru

Heroism Awards go to Nightlight and Gorm, the Noxhorn and Bubble
Dragons. These two saved the day with their sacrifices and extraordinary
magical powers, giving Elysians hope that dragons could be good.

Also, could someone please send me details on Lord Jashun's and Princess
Kailani's abilities? ~ Lady Adalina Roedellen (Lina)

Princess Siany Spotlight	**Heavy security seen at Clarion's ports**	**Luxen School Updates**
The juiciest gossip	*What could this mean?*	*Weekly Reports*
The warrior princess fought against the black phoenixes	A former soldier speculates several possibilities	No cancelation of Feydom so far
Her interview	Vote on what you think	Parents are encouraged to follow progress.
Page 2	Page 3	Page 5

CHAPTER 25
MY ANCHOR, MY UNDOING

Sealyn opened her eyes, seeing blurry images. She blinked, willing her eyesight to focus. Skarpin shifted next to her. He looked so peaceful curled up like that. She didn't want to wake him, even though her hand wanted to stroke his black curls.

She was back in the bed chambers of her ship, with no memory of how she got there. She looked around the white-paneled room and saw Jace sleeping on the chaise. He was shirtless and bound with white bandage wraps, slightly blood-stained. Her heart ached knowing he had suffered, that any of her people had suffered.

The main doors slid open, and Jadelyn walked in, pushing a cart full of food and medicine. She stopped by Jace first, checked his pulse, and then placed a bowl of broth and water on the small table beside him. Pushing the cart toward the royal bed, Jadelyn paused once she saw Sealyn was awake.

Sealyn put her finger to her lips and nodded to Skarpin and Jace. She did not want them disturbed. Jadelyn pulled the cart next to Sealyn's bed and sat next to her.

Jadelyn took Sealyn's hand and squeezed it. She whispered, "Queen Sealyn, I can't tell you how happy I am to have you alive and safe. I'm sure you're thirsty, so let's start with water and broth before you start peppering me with questions."

Sealyn smiled. It seemed her friend knew her well. Sealyn treasured the water and broth. It felt like life was coming back to her. Her throat had felt like ash, but now it was revitalized.

With a raspy voice, Sealyn began her saga of questions. "Let's start with: is everyone accounted for and safe? Any casualties?"

"I need you to eat these mashed potatoes while I talk," Jadelyn handed the bowl of rosemary mashed potatoes to Sealyn. "No casualties, majesty. Ajorn and Tilmond are nursing some pretty nasty wounds. Ajorn took a stab to the shoulder, and Tilmond--an arrow to the thigh." Jadelyn poured coffee from the royal teapot into a teacup, then stirred in milk and sugar. "Jace, as you know, also received severe wounds but is mending nicely. The others sustained cuts and bruises that were easily treated." Jadelyn sipped her coffee.

"Sorcha. How is Sorcha?"

Jadelyn dropped her head. "She's not in great shape. She's greatly malnourished and barely speaks, and when she does, it's only to Doebromir. Obviously, something happened between Sune and Sorcha. Sakul has been walking around the ship like a madman. He and Sune have almost come to blows twice now." She added more sugar to the cup.

"How long have I been out?"

"Three days. The team commandeered the Stoltland ship, which is now anchored next to us—that's how you all came aboard. Each day has been about rest, recovery, and nourishment. Everyone is gaining strength, but honestly, they're eager to return."

"Return?" questioned Sealyn.

"Of course, majesty. Don't you mean to return home now? You rescued Sorcha, Sune, and Doebromir. You also allied with the rebels, which I'm guessing means you'll fund their rebellion. I met our rebel leader, Cruz. He is way hot. I hope he's single."

Sealyn glared, remembering what the rebel, Vaelinthia, had said, *"Cruz, our leader, is the only name people know, but those trusted by someone in our ranks know our names."* Sealyn took another bite of her potatoes and swallowed. "Jadelyn, you knew Herbmando's name."

"Yes, why?"

"Only those trusted by the rebels would know any other name other than Cruz, so you want to tell me the real reason those rebels trust you?"

Jadelyn sipped her coffee, eyes darting around the room. "Well, I come from a wealthy family, and I witnessed something horrible being done to one of my friends when her family lost their fortune. I decided to find the rebels and fund them from my father's estate. I provided food and supplies each month, but once my sister returned from being on your council, I took advantage of the opportunity in hopes of forming an alliance with you on behalf of the Trica Rebels. I notified them of my new position once I received your letter. All I received back was a small piece of torn parchment that said 'Herbmando, my second. Burn this.'"

Sealyn shook her head and drank more water. "So, you lived up to your kingdom's creature—you're a snake!"

Skarpin stirred, and Jace opened his eyes, unknown to the others.

"No, majesty. I promise I didn't betray you. My kingdom needed your help."

"You embedded yourself into my kingdom, drinking our wine, eating our food, dancing at our festivals until your cause became more important."

"Please, no. Please don't see it that way. I beg you. I told you all the secrets I knew of our kingdom, even revealed the shame of my gemmed skin. I only wanted what was best for my kingdom."

"With deceit."

Jadelyn sobbed. "I'm sorry I didn't tell you everything, but honestly, I didn't think it would matter."

"You don't think it would have mattered for me, the queen of Elysium, to employ a Trica Rebel supporter?"

"Ok, that looks bad, but no one outside of the rebels knew, not even my eleven sisters."

"Good Creator, your poor mother."

Jace chuckled. Jadelyn and Sealyn both turned to look at Jace. "Sorry, ladies. I couldn't help but overhear."

"Jace, are you okay? How do you feel?" Sealyn asked, panicking.

"I'm fine, love. You can relax and rest," he smiled his charming smile, but his face was pale. "And, Jadelyn, don't worry about Sealyn being mad. If she were in your shoes, she would have done the exact same thing."

"Jace!" Sealyn scolded.

His mouth parted seductively. "Tell me I'm wrong."

"Fine. Yes, if I were you, I would probably do the same thing. Let's move on."

Jadelyn's lip curved up, and Jace leaned his head back on the chaise, feeling weak. Sealyn finished the potatoes and broth, then pulled the blanket over Skarpin's shoulders.

Jadelyn hesitated but decided she had to ask. "Majesty, are you sure your quest is not complete?"

Jace sat forward, wincing at the pain. "What?"

Sealyn sighed. "No, *Jadelyn*. No, *Jace*. My mission here is not done. Just because I'm allied with the rebels and our people have been rescued does not mean it's done. I'm here to break the curse, and the curse knows it."

"That's why your eyes were gold," Jace said.

"Jace, you knew this. I didn't hide my mission from you."

"I know. I just thought with Sorcha's condition, you may want to return home."

Sealyn nodded. "My ship will return home, but this is where the pirate alliance comes in. Jadelyn, you will go back with Sorcha. I want her surrounded with silk and feathers. Make sure those boys don't argue in front of her. She doesn't need that." Sealyn paused and looked at Jace. "The injured must return as well."

"Sealyn! Don't you dare."

"Seriously, Jace. Can you swim? Can you swing a sword or climb a wall?"

Jace let out a grunt of frustration, waking Skarpin.

"Queen Sealyn? You're awake?" Skarpin clung to her.

Sealyn smiled and cupped the child's face. "Yes, young one. How are you?"

"I'm great! I told them I wouldn't leave your side. I would protect you," Skarpin looked at Jadelyn with his big golden eyes. "Excuse me, but are those Puffin Pies I smell?"

Jadelyn chuckled. "Certainly, I brought a few for you in case you would wake up hungry."

Skarpin took the Puffin Pies, eating like he had never eaten before, spilling crumbs onto the green covers. Sealyn looked at Jace, who was still steaming with anger.

"Jadelyn, can you take Skarpin to the kitchens to get a proper meal, one that includes fruit and vegetables with meat?"

"Yes!" Skarpin bounced off the bed, running through the doors. Jadelyn pushed the cart after the boy and slid the doors closed.

Jace managed to stand and walked to the bed. He grabbed Sealyn's hand. "You can't ask me to leave you. I don't want to be separated from you again."

"I don't want you to leave, nor do I enjoy being separated, but Jace, when I saw that soldier slice open your chest, I lost part of myself. It's like you're my anchor and my undoing. You're my lighthouse in the storm, but you're also the match that would spark me to burn cities to the ground."

Jace's face dropped. "The prophecy…"

Lady Pinx recited another spell, trying to undo the massive vines one student created during the chaos. He had held onto one of the vines from a potted plant in the great hall, which grew into hundreds of large vines growing over the floors, tables, walls, and ceiling. Each vine needed to be told the same restoration spell, so her mouth was incredibly dry by the time she finished.

"Pinx," Lady Norella cooed. "Care for a drink?"

"Norella! The students."

"Relax. Princess Siany sent them all home for the next few days to be with their families."

Norella set down two gold goblets and one bottle of Sealyn's wine infusions. She poured the intoxicating liquid into the goblets, and the girls clicked their drinks together. They sipped in silence, still amazed at what they had just survived.

"Great job on getting rid of the vines. I know that was draining," Norella said. Norella was taller than most women and had long blonde hair with sun-kissed skin.

"Thank you. It was hard work, but nothing compared to what Novaly is probably still cleaning up." Pinx took another long sip. "I heard that one of your students made your history books fly."

Norella laughed. "Not just fly, but act like chomping piranhas, and the books started chasing me at one point. I had to beat those things with a broom. Once the child saw we were safe, all the books fell. Took me hours to sort the books back on their shelves."

Making books fly would need to be researched. How the child did this was still a mystery, but the image of Norella beating flying books with a broom made Pinx laugh. She couldn't wait to write Favien and tell him all the news. Even though Elysium suffered the loss of many soldiers, they were victorious over evil creatures again. It was worth celebrating.

Madam Bip walked into the great hall carrying a bottle of sparkling liquid. "Looks like you ladies had 'de same idea as me." She plopped down next to Pinx and poured her drink into her gold goblet. Bip was a heavy-set woman with ebony skin and black curly hair. She sighed deeply before taking a long sip of her blue drink. "Well, 'de second level's floor stopped fillin' wit' sand. Don't know why 'dat boy had sand in his pockets, but he did. We still have more sand ta shovel, but I 'tink we're goin' ta put it on 'de grounds for 'de kids ta play on."

"That's a great idea," Norella said. "I'm sure Lady Madilina can use it when she teaches students to ride the flying creatures, too."

"How are Hueweyn and Novaly handling their classrooms?" Pinx asked.

Bip shook her head, curls bouncing and drank another large gulp. "Poor Hueweyn. Finally, one of his students channeled a creature, but it was one of 'dose *surzees from Len Nove. 'De entire child turned into a child-sized surzee-- big ears and blue tail." Bip laughed a deep belly laugh, which prompted Norella and Pinx to join her.

"And Novaly?"

"Present and accounted for!" Novaly sang, walking next to Hueweyn. She was covered in green powder and orange goo.

Norella gasped. "Novaly! What happened to you?"

"Let's just say that when you have several different already mixed potions in a room full of scared children, who accidentally knock over those pre-made potions, then those potions mix with each other… well, it looks a lot like this." Her hands waved up and down her body, shaking her head.

Pinx snorted, feeling the effects of the wine. "I'm sorry. I don't mean to laugh at you, but can we just take a minute and realize everything we just went through—and survived? This was wild."

Hueweyn reached for one of the empty goblets on the table. He was very happy each table had several goblets just sitting on them. Drinking in the powerful liquid, he gained the confidence to ask the question he had been thinking about all day.

"Are they still going to go forward with Perdonair and Feydom?"

Madam Bip leaned on her elbows. "I heard Madilina ask 'de same question ta Princess Siany 'dis mornin'. She said yes. Give 'dey people somethin' ta celebrate."

The group smiled. After the shock of the black phoenixes, an autumn festival was exactly what everyone needed.

CHAPTER 26
TRUSTING REBELS & PIRATES

A hush fell over the upper deck of the royal Elysian ship when Sealyn and Jace stood on the platform. The entire ship's crew gathered to hear Sealyn's announcement.

"My brave comrades. I stand before you in awe of the bravery and courage you all have shown over the past several days. I'm incredibly lucky and proud to call you my comrades but also my friends. Now, though, we have tough decisions to make. My mission here is not complete."

Whispers and gasps were heard through the crowd of people on the deck. Cruz unfolded his arms, eager to hear her next words.

"Our first quest was to rescue those taken by Stoltland, and we have done so. Doebromir, Sune, and

Sorcha, you all have earned your right to return home. You will be leaving at first light."

Doebromir and Sune hugged and shook the hands of a few soldiers standing nearby.

Sealyn dropped her head and then looked at Jace. She did not want to utter the next part, but she had no choice. "Those injured will also be heading home tomorrow, including King Jace."

Jace held her hand tightly, never wanting to let go.

Sealyn swallowed the lump in her throat. "For the rest of you, I can't take everyone. Only a handful of people can make the next mission work. Jem, you have done an amazing job protecting the ship while we were on shore, but I need you to return home and protect the royal family. Something feels off. Brehan, I need you to lead this ship back home since Commander Tilmond and King Jace are injured." She paused because she felt a slight pull to look over the ship and gaze upon the dazzling treasure below. Her heart pounded. Why not slip below the surface and grab a few coins? What was happening? Why was she suddenly thinking these odd thoughts?

Jace pulled her hand to his lips and kissed it. Her mind snapped back to her people. How was she going to do this without Jace? She took a deep breath and spoke, "We will break Shunal's curse. The regular ship crew will have to sail my ship back, so we will draw names of those who will be coming with me."

"My name doesn't need to be drawn, Queen Sealyn," Favien said, stepping forward. "I will go with you."

"So will I," Max said, looping his bow over his chest."

Patting Max's shoulder, Finn joined with, "And me."

Sakul looked at Sorcha, who couldn't hold her head up. She was so distant from him. She would need time and space to heal properly. Her family and friends would look after her, and while she processed everything that had happened, he would be beside his queen, fighting for a free world—a better world for his Sorcha. "I would like to go too, majesty."

Sakul's proclamation stunned the crowd. Sealyn's eyes twitched. She looked at Sorcha, who finally looked at Sakul. Tears streamed down her cheeks.

Ashur wrapped his arm around Sakul's shoulder. "I'm with you. I volunteer, too."

Sealyn's eyes filled with tears. "I can't express how much this means to me. You're all risking your lives for a quest when I cannot guarantee a safe return. I hope that is understood." Sealyn never liked to leave anything unsaid. She wanted the expectations set. The heads of the volunteers all nodded.

Shunal was too important of a kingdom to claim. It was the mecca of all trade and travel, which meant easier passage to other kingdoms. Now, the question was, where did the Shunalian rulers hide their source of power?

Char stood and stretched his arms. "Well, this has been a wild ride, and since I didn't volunteer for this mission to begin with, I'll be sailing back home in the morning, so it's time for me to get some sleep."

"You would really miss out on the adventure of a lifetime?" Herbmando asked.

"Trust me, Herbmando. I've already been on plenty of those." Char glared playfully at Sealyn.

Sealyn knew she couldn't hold Char to any vow to come on the quest, but he was oddly good in a pickle and an excellent warrior. She would have to make an offer he couldn't refuse.

Her eyes twinkled with mischief. Char saw Sealyn's entire demeanor change.

"No. No. No. I know that look, and the answer is no!"

Sealyn's lip curled. "*Liquid Courage*."

"What about *Liquid Courage*?"

"Before we left, Barm sent notice that he would like to sell *Liquid Courage* to a good owner. He still wants to work there but needs extra funds to help care for his mother." She paused for dramatic effect. "I said I would look for the right fit."

"And you want me to buy the tavern?"

"No, I would buy it for you. You would own *Liquid Courage.*"

"You stop that teasing right now, Sealyn. It's not right to dangle a man's dream like that."

Sealyn chuckled. She knew she had him. "No tease. Only truth. You go on this quest, and when we return, I expect your first action as owner of *Liquid Courage* is to buy us all a round."

Char smacked Herbmando's back. "Holy roasted unicorns! Looks like I'm going on another curse-breaking quest, my friends!"

"Why am I surrounded by people who want to roast unicorns?" Herbmando said with a laugh.

The next morning, Sealyn watched her people sail away from the deck of the Stoltlander ship. She wrapped her arm around herself and covered her mouth with her hand, sobbing. Her decision was correct. Jace's wound had become infected from poison. It was a foreign poison, one that tricked the victim into thinking he was free and clear, then would take over. He would need constant care. Tilmond's leg needed surgery, too.

Her eyes had purple bags from crying and staying up through the night with Jace. She had held him and applied cool cloths, trying to keep the fever away. As she watched the ship sail out of sight, she found herself feeling utterly alone.

Cruz walked up beside Sealyn and gripped the banister. "You do realize the red-eyed devil has feelings for you."

Sealyn wiped her nose and face. "Who, Lord Jem?"

"Yes, the one from Havas."

"You're ridiculous."

"Am I? Is it ridiculous for a man to take pleasure in how beautiful his queen is?"

Sealyn scowled. "Careful, rebel. I wouldn't want to confuse you with a snake."

Cruz held up his hands. "Wouldn't want that, your majesty."

"Is everything ready?" Sealyn changed the subject. She didn't like the intent in his flirts.

"Of course. Ready when you are."

Sealyn stared off at the watery horizon one last time, sending a silent prayer. It was time to finally start the quest to break Shunal's curse; only this time, she would trust rebels and pirates.

Ashur shivered as he watched the Shunalians walk into the mouth of the massive snake. He was thankful that Sealyn arranged for the Elysians to take the extra small boats from her ship, so they didn't have to ride inside the snake again.

They watched as the Stoltland ship sailed toward the Shunalian port. They ensured the ship would crash land several docks down from the Pirate Captain's ship. Once it was the perfect distance away, Finn and Max shot several fire arrows onto the Stoltland boat.

They needed a large distraction, and a fiery Stoltland ship crashing into the port would do just that. Crowds of people ran to the burning vessel; meanwhile, the Elysians pulled up next to the pirate ship. The large snake released the rebels, and they climbed up the ladder dangling on the side.

The first crew, consisting of Ashur, Char, and Finn, steadied themselves against the side. Char and Finn scurried up the ladder first, and Ashur held onto the bottom of the ladder with one hand and pulled the sinking hatch with the other. The boat started filling with water rapidly. He pulled himself up, the boat descending below him.

They could not draw any extra attention, which meant the boats had to sink. Favien, Max, and Sakul were in the last boat with Sealyn. Favien climbed up the ladder first, then Max.

Sealyn felt an odd feeling come over her. A desire to look over the boat and gaze below the waters. She just needed to see the gold for only a second, maybe even hold a few pieces.

Sakul caught Sealyn's arm. "Sea, did you hear me?"

"No, sorry. Say again," Sealyn tried to shake off that intrusive feeling.

"I pull this lever to sink the boat, right?"

"Correct, but don't pull…"

Sealyn's instruction was interrupted by Sakul opening the latch, and water filled the boat quickly. Once the water touched her boots, Sealyn felt a pain in her chest. She bent over, bracing herself on the side of the boat. It felt hard to breathe. She tried to inhale deeply, but her gasps kept catching on something.

"Sakul! What did you do?" Max yelled. "You were supposed to wait until Sealyn was on the ladder! Get off the boat!"

Sakul grabbed Sealyn's shoulders. The water kept rising. Sealyn leaned her head back, trying to gain air, but she felt such a weight inside her. She pounded on her chest, desperate for a full gulp of air.

"Sealyn, we've got to go," Sakul grabbed Sealyn's face. He let out a slight yelp. "Your eyes. They're… they're gold! Sealyn, what's wrong?"

Sealyn tried to form words, and then she coughed. Globs of liquid gold splashed into the water. Sakul's eyes grew wide. It was the curse of the Golden Lake. Sealyn's lungs were filling with gold. He saw her face turning a pale color of purple. Was Sealyn suffocating right in front of him? Small waves rocked the boat, sending panic down his spine.

Sakul looked at Max. "Max! I need your help! Come back down." Max immediately followed Sakul's plea.

Sakul hoisted Sealyn in his arms. She felt heavier than before—it had to be the gold. Sealyn coughed up more yellow liquid, and it dripped down Sakul's wet, cream-colored shirt.

The boat swayed and rocked, causing Sakul to stumble right before he could get Sealyn to the ladder. She fell face-down, splashing into the water. The boat was halfway full.

Sakul's muscles grew tired, but he fought through his fears and fatigue. He flipped his queen over and patted her back. More liquid gold came from Sealyn. Sakul saw how desperate she was to get the gold out of her lungs. Her facial color started turning more blue than purple. He feared he would watch his best friend die before his eyes, then he thought of Sorcha. Sorcha would not survive the loss of Sealyn. He could not survive the loss of both.

He picked himself up and grabbed Sealyn by the waist and threw her toward the ladder. Max caught her arm. Sealyn coughed more gold onto Max's clothes. She looked like a wet rag doll. He held onto her and tried to climb but couldn't. She was coughing too fiercely, and the ladder was too unstable.

Like a pendulum, the Pirate Captain swung from an overhead mast, grabbing Sealyn, then swung back up to the top deck. Sealyn collapsed in a puddle of water, gasping for air. She coughed and coughed, fighting to get the gold out of her lungs. Char pounded on her back, with silent, tearful prayers. Her crew surrounded her, yelling for her to breathe, to fight through the agony.

The dark spots in her vision cleared, and finally, Sealyn felt the rush of fresh air spread through every inch of her airways. She fell on her back, laying on the deck, trying to compose herself.

She opened her eyes to the crew, looking over her. Char extended his arm. She grabbed it, and they helped her stand to her feet. She dripped with water and felt light-headed. Her mouth tasted like metal.

The Pirate Captain stepped forward. "Well, we're not even a minute into this quest, and I've already had to save your life, and you puked on my deck."

Sealyn looked at the pool of gold that had now solidified, then looked up into those flaming orange eyes and smirked. "Consider that a down payment, *pirate*."

Elysian News

The Latest News and Gossip

Issue #27

King Jace

The King has returned to Elysian shores!

Quest complete! Prisoners Lady Sorcha, Lord Doebromir, and Lord Sune rescued.

Rumors: 3 critically injured and Queen Sealyn did not return with them!

More details on page 2

Commander Tilmond

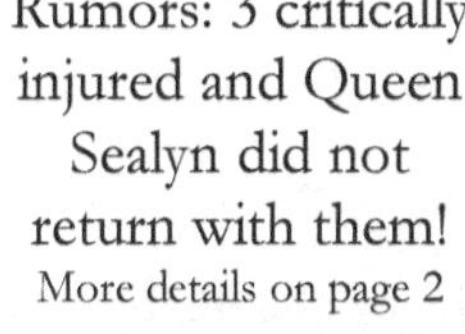

Lady Sorcha

Lord Doebromir

Lord Brehan

Lord Ajorn

Lord Sune

Princess Siany Spotlight	Headline continued…	Luxen School Updates
The juiciest gossip	*Who's in critical condition?*	*Weekly Reports*
How will the princess react to the king's return?	More names of who's returning and who's not	Tethered learns how to grow singing plants
A friend tells	What does Queen Sealyn's absence mean?	Parents are encouraged to follow progress.
Page 4	Page 2	Page 6

CHAPTER 27
COME ON, JACE! BREATHE!

Autumn colors kissed the face of Avondelle, bringing the healing it so desperately needed. The palace, market, and all surrounding villages were decorated for Perdonair, Elysium's annual fall festival. Colorful tents filled with trinkets and delicious treats were on every road and corner.

The highlight of the festival was the game Feydom. This year, the new rules were that the students at the school of magic were the players. They also decided not to have black as a team color since none of the students wanted to be on that team, so six other colored teams were set to face each other in the game.

Novaly sipped her tea, eyeing the Feydom arena from the towering royal enclosed seats. She and the other professors already had to undo several accidental spells the children had cast throughout the first two days. Now was the beginning of day three. Only the red, blue, green, and yellow teams remained in the game.

Siany walked into the room, startling Novaly. "Good morning, Novaly. I thought you left with everyone after Father announced the scores."

"I was going to, but it's kind of nice looking at the quiet arena."

"I understand," Siany agreed.

"Is it true that Queen Sealyn's ship docked yesterday?"

"Yes, but she's not on it. She remained in Shunal to finish her mission. King Jace, Commander Tilmond, and Ajorn are badly injured." Siany sat in one of the chairs, leaning on her elbows. She thought about how hard sending Jace home must have been for Sealyn. "No one has traveled injured through a Tor, so Dun left as soon as we received word. He will travel back with one injured person at a time."

"And all the former prisoners are safe, too?"

Siany leaned back, smiling. "Yes. I'm amazed at that news. Corentine must have been planning something for them if they kept them alive that long."

Novaly rolled her eyes at the mention of the Stoltland queen's name. "That red-haired witch! She gives us redheads a bad reputation."

Siany snickered. "Really? That's what you're worried about with Corentine?"

"I mean, it's at least one of the many," Novaly flicked one of her red braids behind her.

"Well, I'm heading back to the palace. I just needed to grab my scarf, which I left. The palace is preparing rooms for all those returning, and I want to ensure everything is perfect."

"I'm sure your mother has everything in order. Would you like company back to the palace?"

Before Siany could answer, Lord Edvard stuck his head in the room. "Princess Siany, did you find your scarf? If not, I heard there's a great little booth on the way to the palace selling the season's-colored scarves." He paused and stood up straight when he saw Novaly. "Oh, I'm sorry I didn't mean to interrupt."

Novaly bit back a squeal. "No interruption," she looked at Siany. "Well, I guess you don't need me to escort you after all." She winked.

The walk back to the palace brought Siany such happiness. Autumn flags draped from tree to tree and booth to booth. The festival events, which included comedy plays, fun games, and silly contests, happened throughout each day. Siany's favorite was the music. Elysium's melodies reverberated the streets with delightful tunes begging for her people to dance. Children ran and twirled with their faces painted with their favorite team's colors.

It was pure joy to see Avondelle celebrating. Yet, a shiver went up her spine when she heard a different type of running behind her. This running was with panic. She spun on her heels to find Lady Madilina sprinting toward her.

"Lady Madilina, what is it?"

Coming to a halt, Madilina gasped for air. "Princess, I was over by the Emangaton field observing the split in the ground where the black phoenixes arose from."

"Yes, and?"

Madilina gasped for air again. "It's festering."

"Festering? What do you mean?"

"It looks like the burnt earth is bubbling. I don't know what this means. Could more of those creatures rise?"

Siany blinked, unable to provide answers. Their city was vulnerable, and the children were exposed. She looked around at the smiling faces of the parents, watching their little ones dance and eat sweet treats. If more rose, it would be a blood bath of innocents.

Siany looked at Madilina. Her blonde hair blew in the gentle breeze. "We must get to the palace immediately with this information," Siany said.

Queen Mother Graelynd was stringing eucalyptus branches around Jace's bed when Siany, Madilina, and Edvard came barging in. The palace Nichts and servants yelped, dropping several items. King Father Ryker came from around the corner, carrying several books that he thought Jace would enjoy reading while recovering.

"What is the meaning of this outburst? Really, Siany. You scared your mother half to death!" Ryker said loudly.

"I'm sorry, but we have urgent news." Siany nodded to Madilina.

"Majesties, I saw the dragon's scar on the earth at the Emangaton flower field. It's festering and bubbling."

"What?" exclaimed Ryker. "What does this mean?"

Siany looked puzzled. "We were hoping you knew. Weren't you and the others reading those books? Surely, the answer was in them."

Ryker felt a wave of guilt wash over him. Once they had defeated the beasts, he had stopped reading and focused on celebrating. He should have kept reading. How could he have let that slide?

"I'm afraid I stopped reading once the battle was over, but perhaps one of the others kept reading. Trit!" Ryker yelled for his personal Nicht, Maekel's husband.

Trit flew into the room. His big brown eyes looked scared. "Yes, my king?"

"I need you to go to each person who was charged with reading those black phoenix books and find out if they read anything about the scorched earth. I need to know if it will continue to keep producing those vile creatures. And if the answer is yes, then find out if they know how to end it!"

"At once, Your Majesty." Trit flew out of the room, heading straight for Sealyn's natatorium.

"Someone, find me that bubble dragon immediately! I want him brought here to protect King Jace."

Madilina quickly left to find the tiny white dragon. She hoped she would find Jashun and Kailani with both dragons, but she feared they were off enjoying the festival.

They heard chaos down the hall. A servant shouted that Lord Ajorn just arrived in his room. Volunteer aids from the hospital went scurrying by Jace's room with a cluster of Nichts flying behind them. They heard Madam Bip and Lord Prince Brandle giving orders.

Graelynd quickly sped up her decorating and tidying of the room. She commanded everyone to get back to work until they had more information. She adored Jace and wanted everything to be perfect for him. The Nichts and servants arranged the potions and foods Madam Bip had ordered for Jace's injury along the side tables of the bed.

More shouts erupted from the opposite end of the hall. Commander Tilmond had arrived in his room. Ryker was relieved and shocked at how fast Dun was bringing the injured. Jace would be next. The king wanted to go to his nephew, Tilmond, but he needed to be here when Sealyn's husband arrived.

Ryker realized at that moment how much he wanted to be a father to Jace. He wanted to show Jace how much he was truly a part of their family, no matter what the world tried to tell him. Ryker vowed Jace would never feel alone or neglected.

The room gasped as the soldiers carried King Jace on a wooden stretcher into the room. Graelynd started crying at the sight of his infected wound. Madam Bip and Lord Prince Brandle entered, acting on instincts with potions and tonics.

With a gasp and a tisk, Madam Bip said, "I should've known. A poisoned blade did 'dis. We don't have much time."

"Everyone, please back away. Madam Bip and I need room to work," Brandle said.

Siany grabbed her mother's hand and guided her away. The two started praying hard. The kingdom could not lose King Jace. They needed stability, and even though he was a grey-eyed outcast, he brought a sense of togetherness that their people admired.

Jace moaned as Bip gently applied a smelly green paste to his wound. Nichts laid a cold cloth on his sweating brow. Brandle mixed a brew quickly, forcing Jace to drink it. Jace choked on the nasty-tasting liquid but managed to swallow it.

Time was ticking away. Jace's temperature kept rising. Ice Nichts came and created frosted blankets. The team worked in unison, trying to save the young king's life.

"Where is Dun?" Madam Bip yelled.

"He's bringing the last of them back. They thought it best for Lady Sorcha."

A servant yelled from Tilmond's room. "Bip! Come quick! His fever has spiked, and he's shaking."

Madam Bip ran from the room and paused at the doorway. "Make sure Lady Sorcha comes 'ta Jace's room. We will need Dun's magic 'ta do 'de rest."

"Madam Bip," Ryker said. "We heard that Sorcha is not herself. I don't think…"

"Forgive me, majesty, but 'dis is 'de exact place *she* needs 'ta be. Trust me." Bip took off down the hall to rescue Tilmond.

"Allow me, my king. I will go and deliver that message in person," Lord Edvard excused himself from the room, running to the main entrance.

Brandle began to shake Jace. He turned ashen white. "No. No. Jace! Stay with me, Jace. Jace!" He snapped his fingers for more cold water.

The Nichts threw a bowl of cold water on Jace's face, soaking the bed. Brandle shook him again. "Come on, Jace! Breathe!"

Graelynd and Siany wailed in fear. Were they about to lose Jace? How would they ever face Sealyn, and what would Queen Corentine's reaction be to her son's death?

CHAPTER 28
ROPE SNAKES

A sudden snap of a twig, accompanied by a piercing crow squawk, shattered the stillness. The quest group stopped, listening for footsteps. All they could hear were their own hearts pounding from running. They saw a dark forest ahead of them and the yellow fireflowers and nightlamps of the city, Scaleturn, behind them.

Cruz crouched in the brush, disturbing a nest of yellow dragonflies. "Okay, listen up. That," he pointed to the dark forest, "is No-Echo Forest. It lives up to its name."

"I'm guessing there are no echoes in there," Char amused himself.

"Exactly," Cruz said. "So, if you hear something—that means whatever made the noise is right beside you."

An ominous shiver went down their spines. What creatures could be lurking in that forest? They had encountered so many snakes thus far, so they all hoped no more were in there.

"We must move quickly. On the other side of this forest is Shunal's capital city, Orm," Herbmando informed. "There's a main road, but we obviously want to avoid being seen."

"There's one gate for the city that leads into the mountain, which is where the palace and entire bustling community of Orm resides," Cruz said.

Max switched his kneeling knee, trying to envision the mountain city. "You're telling us that the capital is a mining city."

"Correct, Lord Max," Cruz said.

"Oh, that's not good," Char grumbled and scratched his head. "I'm not good with enclosed spaces."

Herbmando chuckled. "Why not?"

"Well, let's just say that being trapped in an ice tunnel with no way out will do that to you," Char nudged Sealyn's shoulder. "Wouldn't you agree, Queen Sealyn?"

Sealyn glowered. "You want the tavern? Then you go into the mine."

"Blackmail is a good color on you, Sea."

Sealyn shrugged off her cousin's jokes, trying to steady her heart. This would be a test for all of them. Trusting pirates, rebels, and her traumatized group made her uneasy. She felt a tug at her heart. Something felt off, like a piece of her was slipping away. Jace? Was he dying? She tried to channel Dun, but her focus was foggy. She was trying to balance grief, idleness, and now greed.

"Still with us, Queen Sealyn?" the Pirate Captain asked with irritation.

"What? I mean, yes. Of course. I'm ready."

The Pirate Captain's eyes twitched. She was hiding something, but he couldn't call her on that—not yet. Their group was twenty-five deep. There's no way this many people would go unnoticed in this forest. The Pirate Captain whispered to his two sons, "No matter what, you two stay close to me." They nodded.

Part of being a ruthless pirate was being willing to sacrifice your crew for your agenda, but he was not willing to sacrifice his sons. The twelve other pirates would be on their own if trouble came for them. He also had no choice but to protect Queen Sealyn.

The darkness of the forest enveloped them like a thick blanket. They could barely see one another. With one hand on the person's shoulder in front of them, they stayed in single-file formation. The forest smelled like fresh rain and pine. Twigs and leaves lightly crunched under their feet. They slushed through shallow puddles, praying their boots would hold.

Cruz continually marked each tree as they passed. Oddly, this relieved Sealyn. She was glad that he was planning a way back from what battles lay ahead. A loud hiss sounded above them, which set off a series of hisses around them.

Ashur felt like snakes were crawling on him. The forest seemed to shift, closing its dark branches around his neck. He felt like he couldn't breathe. Needing a moment to rest and calm his nerves, Ashur reached out for a branch to steady himself.

The branch felt odd, almost squishy. He ran his fingers along it, feeling what seemed like scales instead of rough tree bark. Then he heard the hissing again. His heart plummeted.

"Uh, comrades. Are these trees filled with squishy, scaled branches?" he asked frantically.

Cruz turned his head back toward Ashur's voice. "What? No." Cruz whispered.

Ashur started shaking his head. "Then, what are these long things on the trees?"

Cruz and Herbmando paused and looked at each other. Cruz leaned in close. "You didn't take us through the right side of the forest, did you?"

"Slightly, yes, but almost no."

"What does that even mean?" Cruz whispered forcefully.

"It means that Ashur is holding onto a Rope Snake!"

Cruz faced the group and sighed. He couldn't make any hasty movements because once he did, it would be a race for survival. "Well, I hate to inform you, but what you're holding and need to let go of is, in fact, a *Rope Snake."

"What's a Rope Snake?" Sealyn asked.

"When I light this torch, you'll see, and may I also add, we need to **run**!" Cruz yelled the last word and lit his torch.

The orange light illuminated the dark forest, cascading a dancing glow high above the trees, showcasing long bodies of snakes that looked like golden ropes strung over hundreds of branches. The worst part was the several pairs of shining eyes, staring down with narrow mouths full of sharp teeth and moving toward them.

The group took off with complete disorder, some yelling, some running into trees. The Pirate Captain lit another torch, exposing more Rope Snakes approaching from their right at rapid speeds. He yelled for everyone to hurry and run with zigzag movements. He wanted to make the creatures tangle themselves.

A snake lunged its jaws at Char, but he darted forward, rolling to the ground. He looked back to see the snake's mouth wrapped around the neck of a pirate, then it started to swallow him. Char jumped up and ran onward, trying to keep up with Cruz's torch.

Swords sliced through several snake bellies, angering the beasts even more. Max saw a pirate wrapped in layers of a snake's body coiled around her. The snake squeezed so hard that he heard her bones crack. She was dead. There's no way she would survive. Max sprang forward, dodging a golden head of teeth, eager to be done with this forest of death.

Sealyn wanted to use her power, but with the darkness and chaos, it would be hard for her to focus her magic on the snakes. Her power would certainly draw attention, and they needed to be inside the mountain before that.

Two snakes descended on the Pirate Captain's sons, Laisren and Taeg. The captain thrust his sword but missed, only to have the tail of a snake smack his stomach. He sailed backward into a tree, which knocked the wind out of him. Laisren and Taeg tried fending off the snakes, but Taeg missed the coiled body from above as he focused on the head in front of him. Laisren tried to reach his brother, but the other snake kept striking.

Sealyn saw that Taeg was about to be crushed in layers of the snake. She dove and rolled, popping up underneath the snake, and slashed through the body. The coils sagged, and Taeg jumped out, gasping for air. Laisren juked another strike, slid under the other snake, and shoved his sword through the beast's head, hot blood dripped down his sword and arm.

The Pirate Captain joined his sons, limping and holding his stomach. "Everyone ok?"

Taeg adjusted his shoulder. "Yes, thanks to Queen Sealyn."

"Just repaying my debts," Sealyn tossed the torch to the Pirate Captain and smiled.

He caught the torch with irritation. Dodging tree branches and stumbling over roots, they ran toward the other flame, which was still in Cruz's hand. They were almost out of the forest. Their lungs burned from sprinting. Their shoulders could barely swing their swords. They needed food and rest. The echoes of screams and hissing hurt their ears.

Bursting from the thick forest, they smelled fresh water and grass. They tumbled to the ground and spread out in the tall, thick greenery. Some crawled to the water, sipping in between breaths. Cruz, Sealyn, and the Pirate Captain took inventory of their people.

Cruz was happy to see that Herbmando and Vaelinthia made it through with minimal scratches. Sealyn saw that her crew was alive, but there were several injuries. Ashur was limping. Finn's eye was swollen, and he had a bleeding lip. Sakul's arm had a huge gash, and both knees and palms had scratches. The rest had plenty of bruises and scrapes, but nothing to cause concern.

The pirates were less fortunate. They lost seven total. It was clear that land was not their forte. Everyone kept looking over their shoulders for the creatures, but Rope Snakes never ventured outside the forest.

They took the time needed to patch each other up. Sealyn used her magic to help stitch wounds, while Vaelinthia showed her skills, which came from mending those involved in tavern fights.

Sealyn stood at the water's edge with her arms folded. She could see jewels and gold at the bottom. She felt a pull, like a voice begging for her help from below the water. It would only take a few seconds for her to scoop up the gems. It would be harmless. Who would know? Why would it matter? She wanted those gems. They should be hers. Pebbles crunched beneath Cruz's feet as he stepped closer to the emerald queen.

He noticed her fixed gaze. "Careful, Elysian. These waters have even more terrifying creatures guarding the treasure beneath."

Sealyn jerked her head to Cruz. "I wasn't—"

He waved his finger. "That was your first lie. Let's make sure it's your last."

Sealyn didn't want to be honest with Cruz or anyone, but the truth was that she didn't know what she was doing. There was no guidebook on breaking all seven curses and the costs of the missions. She was losing herself and gaining new perspectives. She was a complete mess and didn't know how to handle all the changes she was experiencing.

"Let's hypothetically say I was struggling slightly with Shunal's curse. What would you advise?"

Cruz snickered--a sound that helped calm Sealyn's nerves. "Queen Sealyn, it's no secret that you are. I'm curious as to why an Elysian would have the same cursed struggles as a Shunalian, though."

Sealyn kicked a stone into the water, uncomfortable sharing information with the rebel, but what choice did she have? "Well, rebel," she smirked, winning a smile from Cruz. "What I've gathered is that the curses must be able to sense people's intentions, which should be obvious, but this is different."

"I agree. I don't see any other Elysian tempted like you are."

"It has to be because I'm the third-generation bloodline."

Cruz nodded. "Which means the curse knows you're different. You can break it, and because it can sense people's intentions, it allows you to be semi-cursed as well?"

Maybe this rebel had some smarts to him after all. Sealyn managed the courage to keep talking. "That's what I'm assuming. When I was in Len Nove, I felt such pressure to quit, just lay down and not do anything."

"Len Nove's curse is idleness, right? They fight against being lazy every day."

"Correct. It was like walking in deep mud to keep going."

"But you did. You broke Len Nove's curse, and now, you can do the same for us."

"I didn't do it alone. I had help, but also," she hesitated. She had already shared too much, but she needed an ally, and she still didn't truly trust that pirate. "Cruz, my power. It—it keeps growing and becoming more unpredictable, taking more and more of me every time I use it."

She could see Cruz trying to work out the details she just exposed. This was a weakness, and he now held her secret in his hands. Would he betray her and use this to his advantage? Would he fear her and leave them stranded? Or would he see her as a clear threat that should be terminated immediately?

"Sealyn, if I may address you so simply." She nodded. "You are aware of what this means? I'm no fool, and I gather you aren't either. I know the stories. I've heard the legends. With each curse you break, you become that curse. I've never seen anyone wield magic like you do, either. You're tethered to nothing nor channeling creatures."

"Get to the point, Cruz."

"You know where this leads to with you being a Cognition?"

Sealyn held her gaze with his. She wanted to make him say it. Maybe because she needed to hear it from someone else besides herself. "I do. I'm triple cursed, which means…"

"Death."

Elysian News

The Latest News and Gossip

Issue #29

Who is Skarpin?
Why does he matter?

Greetings, my fellow Elysians. Today, I bring you the juiciest gossip I could find, and it all centers around this small, yellow-eyed boy, Skarpin.

Skarpin is a 5-year-old boy from Shunal. From what I have gathered, he has no family. His parents died, along with the rest of his family.

Painted above: Skarpin

What makes this kid so unique? Well, apparently, he helped Queen Sealyn and King Jace on a top-secret mission that aided in freeing our imprisoned people!

Because of his bravery, he impressed our king and queen so much that they invited him to spend some time here in Elysium.

What could this mean for young Skarpin? For now, the palace is heavily protecting him. Their main concern is his malnutrition, and they want him to feel safe and loved. If you see him, please make sure to give him a warm welcome and thank him for his heroic efforts. ~ Lady Adalina Roedellen (Lina)

Princess Siany Spotlight	**Can the Black Phoenixes return?**	**Luxen School Updates**
The juiciest gossip	*And why?*	*Weekly Reports*
Princess Siany was seen arguing with Lord Edvard	What is the palace doing to protect us?	Professor Gunnolf urges students to study over holiday
What could this mean?	Should we be worried?	Parents are encouraged to follow progress.
Page 2	Page 3	Page 6

CHAPTER 29
SEAL THE GROUND

Once the injured were finally stable, King Ryker made his way to the scorched fields where the black phoenixes came from. The ground was, in fact, bubbling with a black substance. It smelled like burnt onions and looked like the ground was coughing. He feared that, at any moment, one of those horrible creatures would emerge from the dark pit.

Prince Royce stood beside Ryker and folded his arms. "After seeing this, what do you think?"

"It's hard to know what to think," Ryker pointed to the festering gash. "I don't even know what that black substance is. How are we to destroy something we know nothing about?"

"What about the bubble dragon? Couldn't his saliva be the answer?"

"Maybe, but he's too small. What are we supposed to do? Follow him around with a bucket and collect his drool?" Ryker snapped.

Royce threw up his hands. "Easy. I'm just trying to exhaust every avenue here."

Ryker sighed heavily. He hated not having the answers. He had confidently led this kingdom before the curse was broken, but now, everything was new—new magic, new creatures, new enemies.

"I'm sorry, Royce. I don't mean to come across as unkind. I appreciate you looking at every possible path."

More Elysians had gathered around the giant pit. Everyone speculated about what they should do, and even Lady Adalina walked around interviewing people. Ryker swallowed nervously. What if the kingdom revolted against the crown with an overthrow of no confidence in his family?

His thoughts were interrupted by the sight of the royal carriage approaching at high speed. The horses dug their hooves into the ground, stopping the carriage. Out jumped Captain Graegory, Lady Revalyn, and Lady Quinley. The two ladies had on almost matching light green dresses with panicked looks on their faces.

"My king," Graegory bowed. "We came as soon as these two ladies had information for you."

Ryker motioned for the ladies to spill the details.

"Majesty," Quinley curtseyed. "The final pages did not give exact instructions on how to destroy this pit. We discovered that the author died before he could finish writing the last book, but the royal family still decided to make his writing into books."

Revalyn cleared her throat, adjusted her glasses, and tucked her black hair behind her ears. "However, upon further inspection of the book, a hidden slip of parchment had been tucked into the back cover with the words 'seal the ground.'"

Ryker repeated the words. "Whatever does that mean?"

"We were hoping you might know," Revalyn said.

Royce shook his head. "How are we supposed to seal the ground?" He leaned over the festering earth and peered down. "I see no end to it. It's like the earth split open. It would take years to fill this hole."

Ryker looked at the Green Phoenixes standing guard. His kingdom was protected for now, and it would take more than a few minutes of standing around discussing matters to figure out how to seal the earth. His heart felt the tug of the palace. He needed to check on the injured. "Thank you for this information. Let us go back to the palace. We have the celebratory dinner with the yellow team tonight for winning Feydom, too. I hope to see you all there."

The great hall was adorned with autumn colors and green flags with painted yellow phoenixes. Long rows of tables with baskets and plates of scrumptious-smelling foods sat on top of beautifully decorated foliage. Musicians played the popular Perdonair holiday songs while everyone enjoyed the delicious food.

Doebromir laughed a deep belly laugh with Lord Jdru, who was almost fully healed from his eye injury. Jdru's vision was blurry, but between Madam Bip, Lord Prince Brandle, and Dun, he made progress each day.

Doebromir took another big gulp of ale and burped. "Ah, this is so much better than a prison cell."

"You think?" Jdru laughed.

"Without a doubt!" Doebromir took a bite out of a massive, roasted turkey leg.

"How is Lady Sorcha fairing?" Jdru asked.

With turkey still in his mouth, Doebromir answered, "Honestly, I can't tell. I heard that when they brought her to

King Jace's room, she freaked out for a few moments, but then ol' Bip calmed her down, and she just fell into the zone of medicine."

"I heard she unlocked her magic. Is that true?"

"I wasn't there, so I can't truly confirm, but Sune seemed to hint at that this morning when I had breakfast with him."

Jdru nodded his head. "Speaking of Lord Sune and Lady Sorcha, is it true that there's a love triangle between those two and Sakul?"

Doebromir stopped eating. "We went through some pretty horrible things as prisoners. Those tortures definitely bound us together, and I will say that I watched how much Sune cared for and protected Sorcha, so I can confidently speak to their connection. But I also know how much she spoke about wanting to get home to Sakul. I'm not sure what will happen. Sorcha is one of the strongest, bravest women I know. Whoever she chooses will be one lucky man."

"I feel bad for Sakul," Jdru said. "He was worried the entire time, and even volunteered to go find her, only to discover there's now another man vying for her attention. Just doesn't seem right."

Doebromir set his goblet down a little too hard. "Like I said, you don't understand what we went through. Sune is a good man, and so is Sakul. The focus needs to be on Sorcha's recovery."

"Absolutely. I'm sorry, Doebromir. I didn't mean to cause any trouble."

Doebromir saluted with his turkey leg and raised his goblet. "No worries, my friend." Doebromir stood, feeling the ale, and spoke loudly. "Let us drink to our great rescue, destroying dark creatures, and to the yellow phoenixes—the true champions of Elysium."

The great hall erupted in cheers and goblets banging. The children on the winning team yelled loudly, excited to be the center of attention.

Queen Mother Graelynd added more roasted potatoes to Skarpin's plate. Princess Siany giggled with Lord Edvard. Madam Bip filled her goblet a third time with Northern wine. Lady Novaly eyed Bip's choice and laughed.

"After 'de past few days, I need a big night of celebrating," Bip said.

"Completely agree," Novaly said.

Lady Quinley was seated next to Novaly and wore a dark green dress with tiny crystals around the V-neck. Her blonde hair was pulled into a loose bun with whisps around her round face. She leaned forward, head turned to Bip. "Madam Bip, do you mind pouring me a glass of that?"

"Of course," Bip said. "Did ya have a rough day, too?"

Quinley looked at the royal family sitting across from them, then back at Bip. "Kind of."

Bip handed her the filled goblet. "Oh, do tell, child."

"Well, Revalyn and I were charged with finding a solution to the scorched field, but all we managed to find was that the author died before discovering how to destroy the pit."

Novaly gasped. "That's awful. Is there no way to know if we can destroy it?"

Revalyn popped her head around Quinley. She wore a shimmering strapless emerald gown with a green ribbon choker. Revalyn had half her dark hair up in a braided bun and cherry-red lips. "Maybe, but we did find a hidden letter saying, 'seal the ground.'"

"Seal 'de ground?" Bip questioned.

The ladies nodded, all taking long sips of their Northern wine. Novaly felt the strong effects of the red liquid first. She felt light-headed but also like she knew every secret of the world. Her mind spun to the memories of the professors cleaning up the school from the reactions of their students.

She hiccupped. "Bip," she paused. "That's a fun name. Biiip. Bipppp."

"Oh my, child. I 'tink 'de wine has found its first victim," Bip chuckled.

"I was just thinking of the disasters we had to clean up! Too bad that student of yours wasn't sitting with his hands in his pockets at the pit."

Quinley squinched her face. "What is she talking about?"

Madam Bip tilted her head. "One of my students was so scared during 'de black phoenix battle 'dat he created mountains of sand. He can tether ya see. I didn't know he was holding on 'ta sand in his pockets." She froze mid-sentence, pondering the applications. She couldn't tell if it was the wine or the grand idea, but she felt tingling in her toes. "'Dat's it!'"

"What's it?" Quinley asked.

"How to seal the pit!" Madam Bip rose from her chair, stumbling slightly. She walked quickly to King Father Ryker. The other ladies trailed after her, wanting to know what Madam Bip meant.

"My king. My king!"

"Yes, Madam Bip. What is it?" Ryker asked.

"I know how to seal the ground!"

"How?"

She looked across the room at a young Feydom player. She pointed to her student, Wullen—the small, blonde-haired boy whose face was covered in freckles. The one who found the black phoenix books in the attics of the school, but also the one who could wield sand.

CHAPTER 30
YOU SHOULDN'T HAVE DONE THAT

The mountain of Orm City looked like glazed honey. It sparkled with the last of the sun's rays of the day. The golden gate locked its doors strictly at sunset. The group's plan was to sneak in with the last remaining stragglers since the guards were tired and barely checked anyone at the end of their shift.

They kept their yellow hoods over their heads and moved with the crowd of people. One bridge led over the waters surrounding the mountain. Once the sun was no longer, the large iron spiked gates at the beginning of the bridge closed. All those remaining on the bridge had minutes to get through the main gate of Orm City. No one wanted to risk spending the night on the bridge and possibly rolling into the water with the eels.

Sealyn's heart pounded. What was she thinking? Walking right through the front gate was insane. This would never work, but she kept walking. Her fingers tingled, begging her to dip them in the water and find the gold coins. She heard a buzzing sound, then ducked when something flew by her head.

"What was that?" she asked quietly.

"Careful. Those are the *Slitches," Cruz answered.

"They're what?" Char questioned.

"Slitches. You know, flying snakes," Herbmando said.

"What?!" Ashur squeaked.

"Hush! Don't draw attention to us," Cruz snapped. "Slitches are harmless. Bodies like short, skinny snakes. Wings like bats. Mouth like a snapping turtle yet can speak like a parrot. This is why they monitor the Orm bridge. Anything they see, they fly to the superiors and report."

"I hate snakes," Ashur grumbled.

"They don't even have teeth, my friend," Herbmando said.

Vaelinthia slipped her hand into Ashur's. "Let me keep you calm. Everything will be fine." Her eyes sparkled at Ashur. She had high hopes for him. What a romance they could have.

Yellow fireflowers that looked like daffodils illuminated their path on either side. The door to the mountain was triangular and large. Guards were only checking some of the entering people. Sealyn felt relief rush over her when they walked through the gate.

No one acknowledged them. They were now inside the capital of Shunal. It was exactly as described: a mining city. Bridges, archways, and staircases were as far up and down as their eyes could see. Homes and businesses were carved into the walls. It was impressive.

The Pirate Captain leaned close to Cruz and Sealyn. "Okay, now's the time to show your cards. Where are we supposed to start looking for the source of Shunal's power?"

"The library," Sealyn replied.

He laughed. "Really? Books? You think a book is just going to magically tell you exactly where to look, or you think the source is in the library?"

"Look, grumpy, I'm no expert in finding other kingdoms' powers. I just know that when I was in Len Nove, books were how I figured out where to look. The library will hold ancient texts and scrolls along with historic books. Those will help point us in the right direction."

The captain rolled his eyes. "How about this: you go hunt in the library while my crew and I go to that tavern over there?"

Sealyn was ready to argue, but out of the corner of her eye, she saw fast movement. A force of golden soldiers was headed straight for them, and above them was a swarm of Slitches, yelling "Intruders!" She felt nauseous. Did they prepare for a fight? How would they escape a fortified city?

"Halt!" yelled the commander of the Shunalian force.

Cruz whispered. "Don't look up. Let me do the talking."

The Shunalians surrounded the group and pointed spears at them. There was no escaping. They were trapped. The commander stepped forward and folded his arms.

"Good evening, Commander. What can I do for you?" Cruz spoke innocently.

"You can stop with the act. We know you have green eyes among you."

"Green? That would be news to me, Commander. We were just about to head to the tavern for refreshment. Would you care to join?"

The commander's face was covered in gems, yet he still managed to glare at Cruz. "Enough. Take off your hoods."

Sealyn swallowed. This would not be good. She was the queen that had not sent word ahead. Her ship was not in the harbor. She was clearly with pirates. Luckily, they had no clue that rebels were right in front of them. She started to remove her hood, but Char stepped in front.

Char threw his hood off. "Ok. Ok. Well, done," he clapped. "You caught me! I'm sure you recognize me. Yes, I'm *the* Lord Char Araelien of Elysium. The one and only who has the famous pub tour, and I heard that Orm's pubs are the most elaborate taverns in the entire seven kingdoms, so these folks behind me are just courageous, ale-obsessed lunatics like me, who wanted to see if your pubs are better than Elysium's. I hope you won't arrest us just for wanting to taste Shunalian ale?"

A girl screamed from behind the soldiers. "Is it really Lord Char Araelien?"

More girlish screams were heard. "It's Char! Char! Char, over here! We love you, Char!"

The commander looked confused. "Uh, my apologies, Lord Char. I wasn't aware of such happenings. I must question, though: you're with orange-eyed pirates. This doesn't look good for you."

Char squeezed Taeg's shoulder. "Oh, I'm sure you've guessed it. You seem smart. I had to hire these shmucks to get me in. You know pirates will do anything for coin."

At the word "coin," every Shunalian took a step forward. Char's eyes widened. He didn't realize how bad the curse was for them inside the capital.

The commander flinched. "Fine. Carry on with your pub tour, but next time, send word ahead."

Char beamed. The group relaxed and started moving toward the tavern. Sealyn was so happy she had convinced Char to come. What a relief.

A black-armored man stepped out from the shadows. Half of his face had burn scarring, but the non-burned side showed his black eye. He was a Stoltlander.

"Commander, wait. If I were you, I would check a little closer."

Sealyn started to sweat. It's like she could feel the evil coming off that man.

"Why?" the Shunalian questioned.

A sly smile crept across half his face. "Because according to the deceased Commander Malum, Queen Sealyn is always close by when it comes to Lord Char."

Char's face turned pale. Malum's name still haunted each of his dreams. He had tortured them for sport.

"Queen Sealyn? A crowned royal would not enter another kingdom without sending word ahead."

"Ah, then you don't know the little bird queen like I do," he spoke with a deep, dark voice.

Favien whispered, "Don't fall for it, Sea. Stay calm."

"Lord Char, your queen wouldn't happen to be among your companions, would she?"

"Of course not. I don't know who this bald Stoltlander thinks he is."

The large-framed Stoltlander approached. "Then, you wouldn't mind if we looked at each one of your—companions?"

"I think it's a waste of time, and I'd like to begin drinking as soon as possible."

"What's the harm? If your insignificant queen isn't among you, let us look." Sealyn tensed at his words.

"Easy with the insults, dragon lover. It's the principle of the matter. My word should be good enough. Why don't you go wrestle with a fire pit again; looks like you could use the practice."

The Stoltlander stepped closer to the group. Max made the first mistake. He stepped closer to Sealyn and grabbed the hilt of his sword.

The dark warrior noticed and smiled. "I'm sure the young queen isn't among you, but just in case she's not at home regretting her mistake of marrying a grey-eyed piece of…"

Sealyn threw back her hood and drew her bow and arrow. "Say another word, and this arrow will pierce your black heart."

Favien groaned. "You shouldn't have done that."

The Stoltlander laughed. "Oh, I knew it was you. Your boy-of-a-solider gave you away the moment he stepped in front of you. Rookie mistake. See, Commander. Now, I'm sure your high leaders will want to see all of them, and tell the king the *Hydrus Snake is the present I just dropped off. It will add some 'flare' if he plays his favorite game."

Elysian News

The Latest News and Gossip

Issue #31

Yellow Phoenixes win Feydom!
Congratulations

Huge congratulations to the Yellow Phoenixes on their victory! The Yellow Phoenixes triumphed by collecting 14 flags before the other teams.

Match results:
Day 1—Yellow 4, Red 2, Blue 3, Green 4, Orange 2, and Purple 0. Purple was excused after Day 1's results.
Day 2—Yellow 11, Red 8, Blue 9, Green 10, and Orange 7. Orange was excused.
Day 3—Yellow 14, Blue 10, Green 12, and Red 8.

Their captain, Coven Wilchard, steered the Yellow Phoenixes. Coven led the team not only in his leadership skills but also collected 8 flags, making him the top Roamer. Other Roamer points: Wullen 2, Jentree 2, Sheena 1, Graetamin 1. The Yellow Phoenixes' Tacklers also had superb defensive blocking. Well done, team!
~ Lady Adalina Roedellen (Lina)

Princess Siany Spotlight	**Avondelle misses Lord Char**	**Luxen School Updates**
The juiciest gossip	*Why didn't he return?*	*Weekly Reports*
Lord Edvard invited to spend the holiday with the royals	Top 5 theories and proof for each one.	Headmistress confirms mid-terms will happen after break.
Fact or fiction?	Lord Jdru gives statement.	Parents are encouraged to follow progress.
Page 2	Page 3	Page 5

CHAPTER 31
THIS WAS HER MOMENT

Sealyn could barely believe her eyes when they entered the throne room of Orm palace. Walls of massive yellow gems, gold floor, columns of pearl, and throne chairs of diamonds. This was the wealthiest room she had ever encountered, but she noticed it lacked feeling. It was cold and almost smelled of lost hope.

The king stood tall with his two sons on either side. They wore only gold vests that displayed all the jewels carved into their arms, chests, necks, and faces. Layers of necklaces hung around their necks, and golden silk capes draped over their shoulders. Sealyn felt sorry for their necks.

The queen and her court were in one corner, and the three princesses and their court occupied the other. Their golden eyes looked scared. Sealyn tried to figure out why they would be afraid.

"Kneel!" the commander yelled. All but Sealyn knelt, and the commander yelled the same order again.

Sealyn never looked at him. She only looked at the king. "I kneel for no one."

The king chuckled a deep laugh. "Your reputation proceeds you, Queen Sealyn. You would have been welcome here if only you asked."

"And now?" Sealyn questioned.

"Well, now I must ask myself why a queen would make such a foolish mistake?"

"I am no fool."

"Your marital choice would prove you wrong."

Sealyn stepped forward, but the commander stepped in front. Her nostrils flared from anger. "I'm not interested in your insults. Now, from one crown to another, let us go."

"But you arrived on such a special day."

"What day?"

The king wrapped his arm around one of his sons. "It's my eldest son's birthday."

Sealyn saw the queen cover her mouth. She was crying. Why would the queen cry over her son's birthday? None of this made sense. She looked to the other corner and noticed the daughters were all crying, too. What was happening, and weren't there supposed to be more princesses?

"As much as we would like to celebrate such an occasion, we must return."

"Why? Your precious Feydom is over."

Sealyn stopped her movements. How did he know so much about Avondelle's activities?

The king liked watching Sealyn squirm. "That's right, I know plenty about your kingdom. My spies also informed me that the Yellow Phoenixes won, not to mention the physical state of your grey-eyed king is critical."

Sealyn's eyes glowed green, then blue. She slammed her boot on the gold floor and cracked it. The Shunalians watched as the crack ran its way up the golden steps to the diamond chair.

"I said, let us go."

"You will regret that," the king growled. The Commander grabbed Char and held a dagger to his throat. "Here's how this will go. You will join us for the birthday celebrations, or Char will die."

Sealyn looked at Char, then back at the king. "Fine. Let's eat cake and be done with this."

"Cake?" the king questioned with a laugh. "Cake! You think that's how we royals celebrate? No, my dear young queen. A king must learn two things: first, how to obtain wealth, and second, how to kill for the first."

Sealyn folded her arms. "I must disagree with you."

"Really," he smiled an evil smile. "Look where I am, and look where you are. Are you really in a position to question my judgment?" Sealyn tightened her jaw. "We begin the celebrations with my son killing one of my daughters."

"What?!" Sealyn screeched. "What kind of sick game is this?"

"The kind that prepares my son to be the king and man this kingdom will need. If you want wealth, then you must take it. The fastest way to do that is by killing someone who has the wealth you want. Since birth, my daughters have been collecting riches beyond your comprehension. His joy in killing his sister will lie in collecting all she has obtained."

Sealyn's mouth dropped. Now, she knew why the queen and sisters were crying and why there were missing princesses; they were dead! Killed by this lunatic. This was wicked at its core. How could the king be this far gone? Had he given himself over to the dark mist? She would have to be extremely careful with her powers.

"And what do we have to do with this? You know your actions go against our Elysian culture."

"Of course, well, there's another game that we look forward to. Cast by magic gems, players must solve a series of puzzles to escape their deaths. This is where you all will come in."

"No! You can't do this. This is against all crowned royal protocols and protections," Sealyn hoped her protest would win over an ounce of logic in his lost heart.

Black mist formed around the king, and then he grabbed the rope at his hip. The rope extended and wrapped around Sealyn in layers of black coils. She couldn't budge. So, he was an Umbral, those who have given themselves fully to the dark. They allow the darkness to flow through them, doing the bidding of the dark mist. This also must mean that Umbrals had different types like Luxens. His grabbing the rope and wielding it meant he was a Tethered of the darkness.

"Do you see now, young queen? I can do whatever I want--however I want, whenever I want. You are nothing compared to me."

She needed to know what she was up against. "Understood, majesty. Forgive me. I didn't realize how mighty you were. This power you solely possess is remarkable." Favien about fainted at Sealyn's flattery. Why was she stalling? She could easily overtake a rope wielder.

"Ha! I knew you would be impressed. Yes, I am the only one who can wield such powers. My sons and daughters have yet to achieve such success."

Sealyn whispered to herself, "Good to know."

"Enough talking. It's time for the games to begin," he motioned to the soldiers. "Guards, take them to their positions. Explain the rules along the way. Come, my sons. It's time for the celebrations to begin."

The king released Sealyn, and she inhaled sharply. The soldiers led them down a winding staircase that led to a narrow tunnel. The walls were yellowish and smelled like mold. They finally came to a square room with only one exit—the way they entered. Once they were all in the sealed room, the leader spoke.

"Listen, because I'm only saying this once," he placed his hands on his hips. "Here's how the game goes. These tunnels are controlled by magic. We don't know how this magic survived the Second Chance, so don't ask. Once that wall opens, there's no going back. The magic ensures that. Each room has a different exit. You must find the door and figure out how to unlock it. Look for clues and perhaps, you might live. Many have died in these rooms, so you may see bones."

Vaelinthia gasped at those words. She was petrified. She wished she had never left the tavern. She wasn't ready for a quest of these high stakes. Her hand felt a warm embrace, and Ashur's hand was squeezing hers. She looked into his green eyes and smiled. Yes, she could do this. With Ashur by her side, she would survive and live a happy life far away from this kingdom.

"You have a set amount of time in each room: thirty minutes. Each chime you hear signals ten minutes have passed. Understand that these rooms are not easy. They're meant to test you. Some of you will even be broken along the way. If you find the door and unlock it in time, whoever makes it through before the door closes is who continues. Those who don't, die."

Taeg looked at his father with worried eyes. This was his first land adventure. He felt very unprepared. His brother nudged his shoulder. He couldn't believe Laisren was calm. Deep breaths. Deep breaths. He had to be brave and play the game wisely.

"The only good news for you is the last and final room—if you make it that far."

"Why is that room good news?" Max asked. He hoped it was a boat sailing back to Avondelle. He missed Madilina and hated that he left with them in a fight. He never wanted to argue with her again; he just wanted to hold her forever.

"The magic grants the person who completes the last challenge the desires of his or her heart."

Sealyn's head lifted, and her eyes darted to Cruz, then to the Pirate Captain. Could this really be true? Could they really get the source of Shunal's powers at the end of this? Surely, the king wouldn't let them play this game if that were at stake, but the king's arrogance kept him from seeing her purpose, so maybe he was completely blind to her quest.

A pirate rubbed his hands together excitedly. "That sounds amazing! I want ten ships filled with gold."

The Shunalians shook their heads. The leader spoke harshly. "You'll probably be the first to die. As a friendly warning—be careful what you let your heart desire. Years and years ago, a person who made it out alive wanted his house full of the most exquisite gems in all the lands, so when he returned home, it was empty at first, then once he sat in his chair, gems from the ceiling and floor came pouring in. Regrettably, he suffocated under all those gems."

The room tensed. How do you control your heart's desires? How could they request something pure after going through a torturous experience?

"And one last warning, the last room is the hardest. Especially this time."

"Why this time?" again, Max asked.

"Because this is the season that the *Naehass feeds."

Ashur shook his head. "I swear if you say that the Naehass is a snake…"

"A serpent."

Ashur threw his hands up. "Great! It's another snake."

"No, I said serpent."

"What's the difference," Max questioned.

"A snake is a snake, but a serpent is a legendary creature from the old magic, and the Naehass is like your Green Phoenix or Len Nove's mammoth."

Sealyn stepped closer to the Shunalian. "And how would you know any of this? You said the last person to escape this evil game was years ago, but the unleashing of these old magic creatures only occurred less than two years ago."

The soldiers looked at each other uncomfortably. The leader cleared his throat. "Because when our prince's birthday came after the creatures were unleashed, one survivor was sent out, but not how the game usually ends. The Naehass sent the boy out with a message of its return, but not without biting off his right leg.

"No. No. No. I can't do this! I don't want to do this!" Ashur yelled. Vaelinthia wrapped her arms around Ashur's waist, whispering sweet encouragements.

"I don't want to ask this," Max quivered in his voice. "But how big is this serpent?"

"You saw the size of the tunnels we came down." The group nodded. "Bigger. Good luck. We must go."

"Wait!" Ashur yelled. "That can't be it."

They heard footsteps coming down the tunnel, and then Char was thrown into their group.

Another soldier spoke up, "The king said there was no need to hold him hostage."

The leader nodded and motioned the troops into formation. They blocked the exit and held spears at the players. The wall vibrated, then a click. The wall rose. Cool, damp air from the dark opening flooded in. The soldiers jabbed their spears forward, urging them to hurry through.

Once they were all on the other side of the wall, it slammed shut. Torches around the perimeter of the ceiling lit at the same time. Sealyn felt her body go cold. This room was her Garden Library at the palace in Avondelle, only it looked like before the fire happened from the battle with Queen Corentine.

Thousands of books covered the walls of the dark wooden shelves, except for one wall that was filled with large glass windows. Even the maroon couches and soft blankets were the same. Large gray sitting pillows on top of thick rugs were near the fireplace. The dark wood fireplace had the lifelike carvings of a phoenix on one side and a horse on the other, too. Her family portrait was still on top of the mantel, with flowers in blue and white vases on each side.

She gazed up at the walkway running the perimeter of the bookshelves, then jerked her head to the black iron spiral staircase in the corner. Char leaned into Sealyn and whispered, "What is going on?"

"I'm, uh, I'm not sure, Char."

"Sealyn, this is the Garden Library. Everything is the same! Down to the stupid plants and this bowl full of lemons. Something isn't right."

"I agree with you."

They heard a loud boom. "What was that?" several people asked.

Sealyn kept shaking her head. She had to remember the room. She had so many secret passageways; perhaps one of those existed here. She ran to the bookshelf near the black iron staircase and saw the worn book that was the key to opening the passageway.

She pulled the book, but it fell into her hands instead of opening a secret door. "What the..." Sealyn stared at the book, then thumbed through the pages. They were blank. She looked at the group. "Check to see if the books have writing in them."

Sakul quickly grabbed a book and confirmed that it did, as did the rest of the group. Why would this one book be blank?

"Okay, so what did I miss from the instructions--give me the short version?" Char asked.

"Basically, there's hidden clues and gem keys around this room that will help us escape, and if we don't escape, then we all die," Taeg said.

Char nodded. "With that dazzling tale, I think we should all fan out and start looking."

Elysian music could be heard. They paused. Sealyn walked closer to the wall containing the door to the ballroom. She placed her ear against the wall. She gasped.

"I hear music and laughter. It sounds like one of our balls."

Suddenly, a younger version of Sealyn dressed in her coronation green ball gown burst through the door and settled on the couch. Sealyn screamed and pointed. "How? What is? I don't... Who is that?"

The younger Sealyn made no movements to indicate she could hear them. The group circled the young queen. Favien tried to tap her, but his hand went through her like smoke. He jumped back.

"Does someone have any explanation?" Max asked.

The ballroom door opened again, and in stumbled Jace, dressed in all black. The Sealyn in the ball gown jumped up from the couch and, with a muffled voice, said, "What is the meaning of this?"

Tears formed in Sealyn's eyes. This was the first time she and Jace had met. How was this possible? Why would the magic do this? The Pirate Captain took several steps toward Jace. He tried not to look interested but couldn't help himself.

Laisren and Taeg pushed on shelves, looked under rugs, and dug in the fireplace. Taeg finally had enough of everyone staring at what was obvious to him.

He snapped his fingers, "Hey, uh, you Elysians want to get back to work? Can't you see that this is obviously a memory sent to distract you from finding the keys?" Taeg shook his head. Obtuse Elysians. He couldn't understand how they were always so sidetracked.

"He's right, Sealyn. We need to focus," Favien said.

"Shhhh," Sealyn hushed. "Wait just one more minute."

They watched Jace trip over his words, and then he finally sighed and said, "I'm just Jace, Your Majesty."

Tears fell down Sealyn's cheek. This was her moment. This was when she fell in love with Jace. It might have taken her a little longer to realize it, but this was when he became Just Jace to her, which was everything she wanted.

She squeezed the necklace Jace had given her before they set off on their Len Novian adventure from Fort Kippen. Her heart ached for him. She felt sorrow and misery. She had to get back to him, and the only thing standing in her way was this psychotic game.

Her mind snapped back to their reality. "What reveals hidden ink?"

"What?" Cruz asked.

"What reveals hidden ink?"

"That would be lemon juice and heat," replied Taeg.

Sealyn looked at the torches on the walls. "Quick. Finn, climb on Favien's shoulders and get one of those torches. Laisren, grab one of those lemons beside you and slice it."

Finn scurried up Favien's shoulders and retrieved the torch. He handed it as fast as he could to Sealyn. She held the torch near the book and thumbed the pages again. She slid her finger on the sliced lemon and carefully moved her finger across the pages. The last page revealed the word "Vase."

Two seconds after Sealyn said the word, Laisren smashed one of the blue and white vases on the ground. Immediately, Sealyn's memory flashed back to Jace and Drystan fighting. The broken pieces of vase on the ground. Jace jabbing a piece into Drystan's neck.

Another crash, then a joyful yelp. She watched Laisren pick up a blue gem the size of his fist. Then they heard chimes.

"What was that noise?" Char asked.

"That means we only have 20 minutes left," replied Herbmando.

"Oh, good. I like hearing countdowns to my death," Char said incredulously.

CHAPTER 32
LAYERS OF SNAKES

Vaelinthia shouted, "Over here! I found something."

The trapped group gathered around the right side of the fireplace. Vaelinthia demonstrated how the tiles on the side of the fireplace could move. Each square tile had a different letter: A W O R C D.

Taeg glared at the letters. "Could be several small words or two words or maybe one word. I see the word 'word.'"

"Word?" Char said. "Does that mean anything?"

Sealyn shook her head. "Not to me." Sealyn felt herself becoming uncomfortable. She looked back at the couple sitting on the couch. How she wanted to go back in time and sit with Just Jace again. Then she paused and thought about what had just transpired.

The magic used the book that, in her reality, opened the spiral staircase. The magic also used a vase—the vase that was smashed in her memories. Could the memories lead to more clues? She flashed back to the battle and the fire in the library. Why was that side of the fireplace important? She tried to focus through the flames, through the smoke, and there, curled up next to the fireplace, was the king of Stoltland.

"Wait! I think I might have figured something out. During the Battle of the Betrayals, Corentine's husband, the king of Stoltland, hid next to this fireplace."

The Pirate Captain laughed. "Seriously? He huddled down like a scared little child. Ha! What a coward."

"Coward! Father, you're a genius," Taeg said. "Well, maybe not an on-purpose genius. You're like a 'I get lucky sometimes' smart person…"

"Taeg!" Laisren yelled. "Would you shut up and get to the point?"

"No need to be feisty," Taeg scolded while he slid the tiles in the proper order. Once he spelled "coward," a click sounded, and the head of the phoenix opened, revealing a purple gem. Sealyn's eyes sparkled gold.

"All right, Sealyn, what's next? What else happened in here?" Char asked.

She watched as the past Sealyn and Jace left the room. She felt a pull. She wanted to go with them. Char snapped his fingers, and Sealyn shook her head.

"Sorry. Um. During the fighting, I know they flipped over this couch. Did anyone check underneath?"

Chimes sounded.

"We only have 10 minutes left!" yelled a pirate.

Cruz flipped the couch quickly. They read aloud, "Tell me your fear." They all looked at each other.

"Who's supposed to tell the fear? All or just one or what?" Max asked.

"I'll go," said Sakul. "I'm afraid that when I get back, Sorcha will have chosen Sune, and they'll live a perfectly happy life while I'm all alone, wishing I had Sorcha."

Char patted his back. "Good news. If we don't make it out of here in eight minutes, then your fear is over."

"Nothing happened," Favien said. "Cruz, you flipped the couch. You tell your fear."

"No. This entire thing is orchestrated around Sealyn, so she should tell." Cruz didn't want to express what lurked below his emotions. Once said, he couldn't take it back.

Sealyn gave him an exasperated look. "Let's just see first if it's you. The couch could have sensory magic."

"Fine," Cruz shifted anxiously. "My biggest fear is that I'll never see Sealyn again. Happy?"

"Oh shi…" Char started.

A wooden hatch fell open under the couch, and out fell another purple gem. Sealyn had to ignore what Cruz had just shared. She walked to the spot where Dun had covered her with his wings. Four indentions of the exact size of the gems they had found appeared.

"There are four spots for gems. Looks like we need one more."

"We have maybe six minutes," Finn said. "What else was significant?"

Sealyn looked across the room at the window. She remembered Jace crawling to the windows opening them, gasping for air. "Check the windows."

Vaelinthia, Ashur, and Laisren raced to the windows.

"I don't see anything," said Ashur.

Vaelinthia breathed on the glass, creating fog. Ashur felt tingles watching Vael. He was definitely attracted to her, but he would deal with that after this game. A drawing of a tree with twisted roots appeared. Vaelinthia yelled out to the group what she saw. Sealyn immediately ran to the family painting above the mantel. She knew that was the symbol for family.

Behind the painting was a discolored brick. Sealyn pulled on the brick, and it slid into her palm. It was hallowed out, and inside was a large ruby.

"Hurry. Place the gems on the four spots over there."

Everyone sprinted to the location of the four indentions. They laid each stone down as they had collected them: blue, purple, purple, and red. Once finished, they stood back waiting, but nothing happened.

"Why isn't a door opening?" Cruz yelled.

A few torches fell from their positions. Carpets and books caught fire. They felt the heat instantly. Smoke started clouding the room. Everyone shuffled backward.

"Whoa! Why did that happen?" Max asked.

"Because this is how it ended," Sealyn said. "The library caught fire."

"Can't you just snuff out all the flames with your power?" Char proposed.

Sealyn was afraid to answer. She had already tried channeling her power, but it was blocked, or at least, it felt like a force was holding it back. How would her people look at her if she couldn't help when they needed it the most? Was this it? Would they die in flames, powerless?

"The magic is preventing me," she said. Another two torches fell, rolling to the couch. Blankets, pillows, and the couch caught fire.

"We've got to figure this out!" screamed Vaelinthia.

Taeg stepped back from the wall. "Queen Sealyn, does anything seem off? Can anyone see anything that would point to the order in which the gems should be placed?"

Another torch fell. The heat made them sweat. The smoke made them choke and cough.

"Well, I, for one, don't remember ever seeing a Havas tapestry nor any of the other Kingdoms for that matter," Char pointed to the wall.

"That's it! Havas is red. Put the red stone first. The next tapestry is Len Nove. They're blue, and the last two are both of Glantania—purple. Place the two purple stones last." Sealyn held her breath, trying not to breathe in the smoke.

Taeg followed the instructions, and with the final stone in place, a part of the floor slid open. Taeg jumped in first, sliding down. The rest of the group quickly followed. They had no idea how much time was left, and no one wanted to be on the wrong side of the door with the fire.

The last pirate was about to jump when the floor shut. He was trapped. Screams echoed down the stone tunnel. An eerie feeling swept over them. This game was no joke. It was life or death; there were no other options.

They landed in another room that immediately lit from what looked like a sunroof. They didn't know if this was the actual sun or if it was more magic trickery. The tunnel they came from closed, and they could see that three walls looked like cave walls, whereas one wall was smooth and was similar to glass.

"How do we know when to start?" Max asked.

"I'm assuming we can start anytime or maybe when the big boom happens like last time?" Taeg stated, unsure of himself.

Like clockwork, a boom sounded. "My brother, the brilliant," Laisren looked proudly at his brother. He was happy his brilliance was helping solve the puzzles.

"Be on your guard," Herbmando advised with nervous energy.

They heard what sounded like rocks scraping against each other; then holes opened from different areas of the cave walls. Snakes poured in, falling on the ground.

Along with the group, Ashur started screaming. The snakes slithered around, climbing people's legs. More snakes kept dropping to the floor, creating a thin layer of snakes.

Ashur could barely breathe. Being trapped in a sealed room with snakes, filling the space was his worst nightmare.

Finally, the holes closed, and no more snakes dropped in. Tears trailed down Vaelinthia's cheeks. Ashur was in a corner, kicking away as many snakes as possible. The Pirate Captain and Laisren kept slicing snakes with their swords. Others joined in with killing the snakes.

A bluish, white light glowed from behind the smooth glass wall. A dark, blurry figure appeared and looked to be walking toward them, growing larger with each step. Suddenly, glowing symbols around the cave walls appeared.

They looked like ancient paintings. Max reached out and grazed his finger across the symbol of the green phoenix. As soon as he touched it, the symbol created a hole, allowing more yellow snakes to pour in.

Ashur yelled. "Why did you do that?"

"I didn't mean to! All I did was touch it!"

"I don't understand what we're supposed to do?" Taeg panicked.

"Wait a minute. Look at the snakes," Favien said.

"I prefer not to," said Ashur.

"No, seriously. They're all yellow," Favien pointed out. Like a dagger to his heart, he heard the worst sound possible. Pinx, his wife, was screaming.

The group stilled, looking all around the room with snakes slithering around their feet. How could Pinx be here? She was supposed to be safe in Avondelle, teaching students. Did Shunal secretly capture her? They looked at the glowing wall and saw that the dark figure was now a blueish-black outline of Pinx.

She yelled and pounded on the wall. "Favien! Favien! Help me! Don't let them take me!"

Favien ran to the wall, smacking his hand against it. "Pinx, I'm here. Can you hear me? Pinx!"

Pinx continued to pound on the wall. "Favien! They're coming. Help me! Don't let them take me!"

Sealyn placed her hand on Favien's shoulder. "Favien, I don't think this is real."

"It is, though. This is my nightmare I kept having after Pinx was kidnapped by those Stoltlanders. It's all real for me."

Elysian News

The Latest News and Gossip

Issue #37

King Father & Queen Mother

A message to Elysians

From King Father Ryker:
To all our beloved Elysians, we ask that you not lose faith in our Queen Sealyn. Even though we have

not received word from her team, we remain positive and confident she will complete her quest and return home safely. We are continuing our efforts to create a safer Elysium by ensuring our borders and Tors are secure. Because of the increased number of Elysians joining our military, we have opened two more training classes. If you joined the military in the past three weeks, report to the barracks for training at sunrise. Please continue to send us your concerns. Your humble servant, King Father Ryker Araelien.

From Queen Mother Graelynd: My dear Elysians, we cannot express how much we truly love each one of you. We are forever grateful for your spirits and continued support. We ask only that you lift your queen in your prayers and thoughts. She is strong and will return home victorious. We do appreciate all the volunteers who have been such fantastic help at the Crystal Fort Hospital. Next month, we will hire four new paid positions, so if you're interested, please stop by the front table of the hospital lobby to sign up. Your humble servant, Queen Mother Graelynd Dovinus Araelien

Princess Siany Spotlight	**Lord Rielen returns!**	**Luxen School Updates**
The juiciest gossip	*An interview*	*Weekly Reports*
Who will Princess Siany ask to the Trundatta Ball?	"Len Nove wrecked me."	Winter Parents' Day is almost here!
I have the best guesses.	What retreat he attended and his status.	Parents are encouraged to follow progress.
Page 2	Page 4	Page 7

CHAPTER 33
SOLVE THE PUZZLE

Chimes sounded throughout the enclosed room. Twenty minutes was all they had, and they had yet to find one gem. Holes opened, and more yellow snakes dropped. The Pirate Captain and his team continued to kill the snakes. The smell of snake guts was becoming intolerable.

They had to focus, but Favien was glued to the wall, crying for Pinx. Vaelinthia sat behind him, trying to console him. The rest studied the cave walls covered in the paintings.

Taeg pointed, "Look. Each kingdom is represented by its own symbol and color. Taking what Favien said earlier when he pointed out that the snakes are all yellow, then we can possibly conclude that we need the symbol for Shunal, the yellow snake up there."

Finn wasted no time and jumped on Max's shoulders. He pressed the yellow snake symbol that glowed. A hole appeared with no snakes. Finn reached his hand inside and held a yellow jewel. He jumped down and raised the gem up, cheering.

A glowing yellow indention appeared on one of the cave walls. Finn ran to it and placed the jewel. More holes opened, and dark snakes with large teeth fell in. The fanged creatures attacked whoever was close to them. Sakul screamed in pain as one of the snakes sank its dagger-like teeth into his calf. Everyone drew their weapons, slicing the evil creatures. The holes closed, and they managed to kill the remaining beasts.

They rushed to Sakul and Herbmando, who were both bitten during the attack. They saw the wounds festering. Ashur knelt beside them and ripped strips of cloth from his clothes, then wrapped them tight above the bites.

"How did you know to do that?" Max asked.

"I hate snakes, so I couldn't help myself but be prepared for snake bites. This will help prevent venom from going through the body, or at least, I hope so. I'm no professional."

Sealyn stepped away from the group and noticed something odd. "Uh, comrades. Have you guys noticed that the only thing left from the dead snakes is their disgusting-smelling blood?"

They all peered around, and sure enough, the snakes' bodies had disappeared. Only the blood and rank smell lingered. The symbols glowed again on the walls in different locations.

"Oh, no. Did anyone see what color the snakes were?" Char asked.

"They were dark purple, right?" Cruz questioned. He wasn't sure but hoped someone else could confirm.

"No, they were black," Laisren said.

"Are you sure? They could have been dark blue, too," Finn added.

"Listen!" yelled out Sakul. His frustration came from his leg and fear of dying before seeing Sorcha again. "We don't have time to argue. Someone just press one of those symbols, and everyone be prepared to kill snakes if they come through."

"Don't go with my suggestion of purple," Cruz said. "I say we go with the pirate's choice."

Laisren stood with frustration. "Fine. I'll press the black dragon." Sealyn thought it was funny how the magic used a black dragon when the symbol for Stoltland had always been the horse, but since Corentine took over, the magic clearly sees them as the dragon kingdom. Fitting, she thought.

Laisren pressed the dragon, and everyone sucked in a breath. An empty hole appeared. Laisren did the same as Finn and reached inside, pulling out a large black diamond. He ran to the spot where the other jewel was placed and secured his gem beside it.

A large hole opened, and a thick Rope Snake entered the room. Its long body kept spilling onto the floor. It was so muscular and very good at dodging swords. Its coils wrapped around a skinny pirate. Bones cracking echoed throughout the chamber.

Cruz yelled, "The snake is blue! Press the mammoth!"

Max leaped over the snake's body and landed on the blue mammoth symbol, then scampered back when another long Rope Snake flowed out of the hole.

"Why didn't that work?!" Max screamed.

The Pirate Captain sliced the first snake's head off, then continued fighting the new snake. Its body pressed Favien, Ashur, Sakul, Herbmando, and Cruz against the glass wall. Sealyn and the Pirate Captain engaged with the strikes the snake kept attempting.

Vaelinthia cried out, "Look at the belly! It's green! Try the green phoenix."

With the help of pirates, Max jumped up and pressed the green phoenix. Chimes sounded. The hole opened without a snake. Max grabbed the large emerald. He tossed it to Finn, who placed it next to the black diamond.

The Rope Snake disappeared into dust, but Pinx continued, crying out to Favien. A round doorway opened from one of the cave walls with an illuminated tunnel of fireflowers. The group poured into the stone tunnel. Cruz and Vaelinthia helped Herbmando, and Finn and Ashur helped Sakul. Sealyn looked back and saw Favien still kneeling in front of the glass wall.

She ran to him and shook him. "Favien! It's not her! We must go!"

"I can't leave her."

"It's not her, though. She's safe. She's with her family in Avondelle. Pinx is safe and happy. She's waiting on you."

"You can't be sure."

"I am, and she made me promise to take care of you. I need you to get up and leave this place."

The walls started shaking. Rocks started falling. The Pirate Captain came back into the room. "What's going on?"

"He won't come! I can't leave him here," Sealyn cried.

The Pirate Captain grunted. He walked over to Favien, punched him in the face, and then chucked him over his shoulder.

"Why'd you punch him?!"

"You should know by now, queen. Sometimes us men need a good punch to the face to set us straight."

Sealyn smiled to herself as they walked through the tunnel. That moment validated her thoughts that there was much more to this captain than a cruel reputation—he had a humane heart, very similar to someone else she knew.

CHAPTER 34
WAKE UP, JACE

After a month and a half of practicing tethered wielding, Madam Bip thought Wullen was finally ready to complete the task of filling the bubbling pit. Guards had reported hearing screeches in the depths of the darkness, so whether he was fully ready or not didn't matter. This child had to complete this task.

Madam Bip stood beside Wullen, along with the other professors. The royal family and the royal guard were positioned behind them. Jashun, Kailani, and Madilina braced themselves for a battle. Wullen grabbed sand in his hand and began the steps Madam Bip had taught him. The ground coughed out black, rotten liquid, and sizzled.

The crowd heard the screeches from below. The sounds scared Wullen, which caused a large ball of sand to fall into the pit from his hands, but the heat and steam of the festering black substance melted the sand.

"I can't do it," Wullen whimpered.

Sweet Skarpin peered around the crowd, trying to see. He looked up at Elysium's mother queen. "Queen Graelynd, what's happening?"

"Wullen is struggling to create enough sand to pass through the heat."

"Probably because sand is too thin. Rocks are better." He tossed a rock in the air and watched it morph into two rocks, then three.

Graelynd noticed the magic Skarpin had just performed. "Skarpin, what did you just do?"

"Nothin,'" He folded his hands behind his back. He thought he was in trouble and didn't want to be sent back to Shunal.

"Skarpin, no lying. Is that tethered magic?"

"Maybe. I don't really know. Ever since I arrived here, I can make stones create stones. Sometimes, I can create big rocks, but nothing like a boulder. Boulders are pretty neat, don't you think?"

Graelynd was exhausted with this child's obsession with rocks, but he just might be on to something. "They are magnificent. Say, Skarpin, why don't you help Wullen?"

"Me?"

"Yes, you. I'm sure he's scared, and he could probably use a friend."

"You mean I can have friends?"

"Skarpin, of course, you can. I know you've been tucked away in Jace's room, but you're allowed to make friends too."

"I've never had a friend before. Is it hard to make a friend?"

Graelynd smiled at the innocence before her. "Sometimes, but today will be easy. You stand beside Wullen. Offer him some words of encouragement, then begin to fill the pit with as many rocks as you can—the bigger, the better."

"Will you come with me?"

Graelynd nodded and took Skarpin's hand. She led him next to Wullen, who was crying while his parents and Lady Pinx tried to console him.

Skarpin tapped Wullen on the shoulder. "Hi, I'm Skarpin. Want to be friends?" Wullen nodded and wiped his nose. "Wow. My first friend!" He beamed and looked at Graelynd with his big golden eyes. She nodded toward the bubbling pit. "Oh, yes. Hey, Friend Wullen, watch this."

Skarpin held a stone in his hand, and with his other, he threw a pebble that multiplied into hundreds and hundreds of rocks passing through the heat. "Neat, huh?" Wullen nodded and smiled. "Want to try together?"

Wullen nodded once and held tight to the sand in his hand and held out his other. The boys both wielded their magic, filling the pit with thousands of rocks and tons of sand. Choking sounds were heard below. The sound of hissing steam paraded through the air, with the stench of burnt onions and rotten bananas.

Graelynd clapped her hands, and the crowd joined in with cheers. The two boys laughed and continued the amazing feat of closing the black phoenix pit.

The crater was a few feet away from being complete when Skarpin yelled, "Wait!"

A hush fell over the crowd, and Wullen looked confused. Skarpin ran to the edge of the field and dug his little hands into the rich soil, then sprinted back to Wullen. Skarpin made Wullen drop the sand and placed the soil in his hands.

Graelynd placed her hand on Skarpin's curly black hair. "Skarpin, what are you doing?"

"This is the NexGen field, right? The Nichts will need the proper soil to grow their special flowers. I want Maekel to have a baby Nicht that I can befriend."

Graelynd couldn't hold her tears back any longer. The purity of children was so perfect. She stepped back and motioned for him to continue. Skarpin closed Wullen's hand.

"Ok, Friend Wullen, the last part is all you. Flowers don't need rocks to grow, just good, dark soil."

Wullen smiled and looked at the almost-complete pit. He filled the last remaining feet with the healthy dirt, then stood back, wiping his hands on his pants, admiring their work. They were both very tired from using that amount of energy but wanted to enjoy the celebrations.

Skarpin high-fived his new friend and enjoyed having everyone come up to them, hugging and shaking their hands. He looked at Graelynd and asked, "Queen Graelynd, can Wullen come to the palace? I'd like to introduce him to King Jace if that's ok?"

"Of course, my darling. I think that would be wonderful."

"Maybe King Jace will wake up with a hero like Wullen in the room."

"There will be two heroes in that room. You and Wullen, and I hope you're right. I wish Jace would wake up."

The white bubble dragon sat perched on the top of Jace's canopy bed. He kept spitting bubbles at Lady Sorcha, who was mixing the green paste for Jace's injury. She chuckled quietly to herself. She enjoyed the little dragon's antics.

Her mind often trailed back to her prison cells. She had been caged for too long. Sometimes, she felt like a wild animal that needed those cages, but she finally understood that was the enemy's goal through talking with Faith Commissioner Herb. They wanted to break her and remold her into something non-human. She would have to fight through the dark thoughts.

Sune brought her a single flower at noon every day. He apparently spent his mornings hiking the terrains and then came back with a unique flower for her.

Today, Sune left a White Fantalaya flower tied to the doorknob. The flower was beautiful. It had a white stem and tiny sugar crystals at the tips of the petals, making it look like the flower was covered in snow.

Sorcha brought the flower to Jace's room like all the others Sune had gifted her. Some were good for making teas, and others had aromas that helped Jace sleep better. The White Fantalaya was a favorite snack among unicorns. One potion book Sorcha had read contained scribbled notes on the side, which speculated that the White Fantalaya was the source of a unicorn's magic.

Sorcha felt herself wield magic for the first time weeks ago. Today was a day of experimenting. She took the Fantalaya flower and crushed the crystals into a fine powder. Then, holding half the powder in her hand, she tethered herself to the unicorn's magical source. She stirred in more and more of the powder with the green paste and caught a few dragon bubbles. Surely, those couldn't hurt; then, combined the powder and a few drops of lamb's blood in her hand. Tethering the ingredients, Sorcha gasped as gold blood collected in her other hand.

When she tipped its contents into the bowl, the concoction sizzled. Green smoke lifted from the bowl to Jace's nose. Sorcha saw the bowl now had a white and silver liquid with tiny gold specs in it. She quickly sat by Jace.

Jace inhaled the green smoke, and slowly, his eyes started opening. Sorcha held the bowl to his lips. "Jace, you must drink this now."

Jace slowly drank the white and silver swirling potion. Seconds ticked by as he swallowed the liquid, and his strength started returning. Sorcha was shocked at how fast the transformation was. Jace grabbed the bowl, slurping down the last of its contents. He wiped his lips with the back of his hand, breathing deeply.

"Sorcha?"

"Yes, King Jace. It's me. How do you feel?"

"Strange, but strong. I don't feel the cut on my chest anymore."

"Really? Would you like me to look at the dressing?"

Jace lifted the green shirt and showed the cloth laid over the wound, but it was evident there was no green paste underneath. Jace pealed the strips of cloth off his chest, revealing a perfectly healed purplish scar across his chiseled pecks and abs.

Sorcha tried not to focus on Jace's muscular physique, but she noted that she would make sure to tell Sealyn she was a lucky girl.

"How is this possible?" Jace asked.

Sorcha smiled. "Well, I think I've found my calling."

"You did this?"

"I gained my Luxen powers weeks ago. I've been studying how to use magic and medicine, and I think I've figured out a few tricks for poisons."

"Care to share?"

"It's complicated, but a quick summation is that I needed to logically gauge that the poison on the blade that cut you was like snake's venom and an illness. Not natural to the body, but with similar symptoms of sickness, so knowing lamb's blood cures snake bites and unicorns have healing abilities, I combined the two with a few additives and my magic."

"Sorcha, you're incredibly brilliant. I can't thank you enough, and you look happy. Is that because I'm awake or something else?"

She laughed—a real laugh. She couldn't remember the last time she laughed. "How about both? I'm happy you're healed and that I've found a passion."

They heard voices echoing down the hallway.

"Now, boys, you must keep your voices down. King Jace needs his rest," Graelynd instructed.

"No loud noises. Got it," Wullen said.

"But, I need to tell King Jace we defeated the pit! How else is he going to wake up? I know he will if me and Wullen tell him."

"You can tell him, but just don't get your hopes up."

Jace looked at Sorcha. He grinned and winked. She covered up his chest with a green, fuzzy blanket, and Jace pretended to be asleep. Graelynd and the boys walked in and greeted Sorcha. They were all instantaneously met with bubbles from Gorm.

"Any change?" Graelynd asked.

Sorcha smiled. "No change, but something feels different in the air." Graelynd's brow creased. "You never know, boys. Perhaps two heroes can share a tale with the king? I feel magic is present."

Wullen and Skarpin's eyes grew wide. Skarpin jumped on the bed. "King Jace! My new friend and I defeated the black phoenixes! We filled the pit with rocks and sand, and dirt. Everyone's safe. You can wake up now."

Graelynd's heart sank, and she fought back tears. She loved Jace so much and hated watching a child's hope dwindle. Sorcha looped her arm through Graelynd's. "Have faith, my queen. Miracles do happen."

Skarpin nudged Jace's leg. "King Jace?"

Suddenly, Jace sat up. The two boys yelped. "Skarpin, is that you?" Jace asked.

"It's me, King Jace! It's me! I knew it! I just knew it!"

"We did it, Skarpin! We woke the king up!"

The two boys started jumping on the bed. The little bubble dragon dropped on the bed, blowing bubbles, and jumped with the boys. Jace laughed and grabbed Skarpin, giving him the hug he'd always wanted. Skarpin latched his little arms around Jace and looked into the legendary silver eyes. For the first time, Skarpin felt like he had a father.

Elysian News

The Latest News and Gossip

Issue #45

A Gossip Collection
Shivers & All

Let this be a warning to those who want to take a stab at me—I am not afraid to air all the dirty secrets.

Rumors:
~Lady Sorcha created a potion that not only healed King Jace but also made his muscles even bigger and more defined. If Sorcha is this powerful, could she be related to Madam Bip? Perhaps the long-lost grandmother she's not allowed to talk to?

Painted above: Madam Bip

~Lord Sune continues to pine over Lady Sorcha by bringing her flowers every day. Has she forgotten about our friend Lord Sakul?

~Lady Norella was seen having dinner with Lord Jem at *Mimby's Morsels*, but the next night, she was having drinks with Lord Brehan at *Nice Ice*. Yet, Lord Jem has accepted another's invitation to the Trundatta Ball.

~Captain Graegory continues to receive letters from a secret admirer whose handwriting looks like Lady Novaly's.

~Lord Jashun and Princess Kailani returned from another trip to the Mer Clans, but this time, the couple did not look happy. Trouble in paradise?
~ Lady Adalina Roedellen (Lina)

Princess Siany Spotlight	**Trundatta Ball Details**	**Luxen School Updates**
The juiciest gossip	*An interesting theme*	*Weekly Reports*
Did Lord Edvard give Princess Siany an ultimatum?	Theme details, costume inspirations, and more!	Students return two weeks after the Trundatta Ball
Palace source	Best Dressed wins 100 gold coins!	Parents are encouraged to follow progress.
Page 2	Page 3	Page 7

CHAPTER 35
THE MAZE

The captives walked out on an open terrace overlooking a large outdoor garden. The room looked like it was nighttime, with a black sky and twinkling lights. Clouds rolled by, and crickets chirped. They breathed in the sweet, fresh aromas of grass and flowers. Looking over the terrace, they saw below a large maze.

A scroll sat on top of a white marble table. Cruz picked it up and read aloud, "Pick three to remain on top. They will be your eyes. The rest descend the stairs. You have one minute to decide."

"Obviously, I think Herbmando and I should remain up here. I don't think we would be much help with a maze," Sakul said. He looked at Favien, who was sitting on the ground with his head in his hands. "I don't know how everyone else feels, but perhaps Favien needs to stay with us, too."

Favien stood, not wanting to show weakness. "I'm ok. I can help."

"No, you're staying here, and you're going to man up and help us get out of here, or do I need to punch you in the face again?" The Pirate Captain had lost his patience. He hated being trapped and was ready to be on his ship. Underground was no place for a pirate.

Favien reluctantly nodded. They quickly hugged goodbye and descended the stairs. The boom sounded, and the tall staircase crumbled. Sealyn looked up at the terrace.

"How will they get down?" she asked.

"We'll worry about that when we have the way out," the Pirate Captain snapped.

"I agree," Laisren said.

Sealyn didn't like this. The pirates had no one up on the terrace, so what did it matter to them? She understood that they were tired of losing members of their orange-eyed crew, but that shouldn't mean leaving people behind.

"If we have a limited amount of time, and we have to get them off the terrace, then we better hurry," Char pointed out.

Cruz nodded. "Let's start with what everyone saw from above. I'll go first. Obviously, the entrance is over there." He pointed to a giant arch made of bushes with white flowers.

"I saw the exit for the maze on that side, in a corner with an actual door at the end," Max added.

Sakul cupped his hands around his mouth and shouted from above, "Let's go! Start moving through the maze, and we'll point you to the tables with the stones."

At the doorway, they were forced to choose right or left. They decided to split the group to gather stones faster. Sealyn led her group to the right, while the Pirate Captain and Cruz led their group left. There wasn't much light down the bush-wall pathways. A fog crept over the ground, like stream water. The only sounds came from their breaths.

Favien guided Sealyn's group from the terrace. Sakul had to guide the others because Herbmando had turned feverish. The snake bite was much worse than they thought.

Throughout the maze were several intriguing statues. The creatures looked incredibly lifelike. The fog had now covered the ground completely, hiding all the grass. The fog felt thick, and they noticed their steps were slower because of it.

Laisren patted and passed the tiger statue in an attack pose. He turned a corner and saw a red stone sitting on top of a white marble table. "There it is!"

Once Taeg picked it up, a ferocious growl sounded throughout the maze. The group stilled. Heads snapped back and forth, trying to locate the beast that made that sound. Cruz stuck his head around the corner, toppling backward to dodge the statue tiger.

The group yelled and started running. Sakul tried to tell them they were going the wrong way, but the group couldn't hear because of their screams and the tiger's roaring.

Sealyn's group could hear the commotion, but they had no clue what was happening. They had to stay focused, so she nodded for Ashur to pick up their first stone, a blue diamond. A loud pitch echoed. Sealyn, Char, and Finn knew that sound too well. It was an Arkootha bear--native to Len Nove. The same type of bear that killed their friend Rivers and attacked Sealyn, Char, and Sakul before Sealyn cracked the ground with her power in Len Nove.

Favien and Sakul looked at each other in horror. They hated watching their friends running from monsters. Sakul shook his head. "Favien, do you think that every time they gain a stone, one of those statues comes to life?"

"It looks that way, my friend. We must guide them out as fast as possible."

"Right now, we have to tell them where the beasts are."

"Good point," Favien looked at the bow and arrow strapped to Herbmando. "Do you think those creatures are made of stone or flesh?"

Sakul saw what Favien was looking at. "I don't know, but it's worth a shot. Are you good with a bow?"

"I'm not the greatest, but maybe I can at least provide some distraction."

Favien strapped the quiver to himself and readied the bow. He saw the bear stalking toward Sealyn's group. It was so close to Sealyn. If she came around the bush, then she was dead. Favien pulled back the bow and released the arrow.

Sealyn inched forward, ready to look around the wall of greenery. She heard something cutting through the air and barely had enough time to miss the arrow. It landed in the bush. She looked to Favien. He almost killed her. A curled claw came swiftly around the corner, swiping at Sealyn but only grazing her shoulder. Because Sealyn had just dodged the arrow, the claw didn't kill her. She promised to thank Favien later.

Sealyn quickly took the opportunity. She grabbed the arrow and jabbed it into the paw. Oddly, the body looked like stone, but the arrow sunk in like it was flesh. Grey blood spilled from the wound, and the bear roared in pain.

A pirate who knew nothing about Arkootha bears shrieked and charged forward with his sword. With his other paw, the bear stabbed the young pirate in the side and sank its teeth into his neck, soaking its stone teeth in blood.

Max and Finn wasted no time with the horrendous site that would surely haunt their nightmares forever. They fired arrow after arrow, and Ashur threw his sword through the bushes, stabbing the beast in the side. The bear moaned, took its final breath, and disappeared in the fog.

The group stood heavily breathing and silently, looked at one another, fear caked on their sweaty faces. Blood trickled from Sealyn's shoulder. They shook at the sounds of their comrades' screams. They had no idea what they were facing, but if it was anything like what they had just experienced, then they knew they were in trouble.

"Should we go help them?" Max asked as he looked at the lifeless pirate. The other female pirate closed his eyes with her trembling fingers as she cried.

"Honestly," Char started. "The best help is finding these stones and getting out of this torture."

Chimes sounded. They didn't know if the other group could hear over the yelling, but it prompted them to start moving. They saw Favien motioning directions, so they quickly followed his instructions.

The Pirate Captain, Cruz, Laisren, and Taeg surrounded the tiger. The other pirates stood in front of Vaelinthia, whose thigh was bleeding from clawed gashes. The captain nodded, and all four charged the tiger with their swords. The tiger bit down on Cruz's forearm but then released as the swords killed it, dissipating it into the fog.

Vaelinthia collapsed into the arms of the large pirate next to her. Cruz ripped part of his clothes and wrapped the cloth around his wounds, doing the same for Vael. Their group sustained several injuries and was now lost. The maze was silent and eerie.

"Did anyone hear the chimes?" Taeg asked.

Sakul yelled, "Can you hear me?"

"Yes, we hear you," Cruz answered.

"Good, now turn around and come this way. Take the next left."

"Keep walking straight," Favien instructed.

"I thought you said right?" Taeg yelled.

Sakul sighed, "No, that's Favien. Only listen to me."

They were tired, frustrated, hurting, and hungry. Every emotion was heightened. Every stumble on a rock or crunch of a leaf made them jump. Sealyn passed a statue made of several large foxes. She hoped that wasn't next.

Max and Finn led the queen's group, scouting ahead for more creatures. Max took a sharp left as instructed, then saw the orange stone sitting on the white table.

"We found it," Max called out to the group.

"Ok, now, since we're going with the theory that statues come alive when we touch a stone, set up a perimeter, and be ready," Sealyn ordered. They weren't sure which statues would be affected, so they guarded both entrances to the stone's entry. Sealyn nodded to Max.

Max grabbed the stone and put it in his pocket. He readied his bow and waited. He wished Madilina was there with them. He thought back to her with green feathered wings, flying above the arena. She was so magnificent. They sure could use her now.

A low rumble sounded. Again, Sealyn remembered that growl. "Uh, comrades. I believe that would be a mammoth."

"A mammoth!" exclaimed Ashur.

The ground shook. They felt and heard the heavy strides of the mammoth statue charging after them. Sealyn repeated the words, "That's not Nawrooshall. This is just a statue."

Finn and Max released their arrows, but the massive tusks blocked them. Ashur jumped over the first tusk, but the other slammed into his stomach. He caved over it, holding on. The mammoth shook his tusks, irritated at Ashur.

The blonde pirate Ortaega slid under the mammoth and jabbed her sword into its belly. The mammoth roared and stomped its foot, executing a crushing blow on Ortaega. "No!" Sealyn cried out. Finn and Max fired more arrows that finally landed on the mammoth.

Char took off toward the mammoth. He dodged the tusks and slid on his knees, slicing the heels of the creature. He stumbled but made it to the back legs and did the same, then rolled out from underneath. Sealyn and Ashur stabbed its side at the same time. The mammoth disappeared like it never existed.

Sealyn dropped beside Ortaega, brushing her hair. "She was so brave." Chimes blasted around the room. Sealyn jumped to her feet. "Did anyone happen to see how many stones it would take to open that door?"

Char wiped grey blood from his clothes. "I didn't. But we only have ten minutes left. Should we run to the door?"

They heard screams erupt. The other group had another stone. Sealyn prayed four stones would be all it would take. "Here's what I suggest. Finn and Max, you go help the others, and we will place the stones in the door. If it's five or more, then we'll go hunt for the remaining stones, but if it's only four, then we'll wait at the door. I'll climb on Char's shoulders and fire arrows from there."

Finn and Max took off toward the yelling, not knowing what they were about to face. Favien motioned for Sealyn, Char, and Ashur to run in the opposite direction. He guided them to the corner with the door. It was surprisingly easy to find.

Finn stumbled as he took a corner too fast. "Careful," said Max.

"I hear them. They're close by," said Finn.

They felt the heat first, then rounded the corner and saw one of the pirates on fire. They looked up and saw a dragon statue flying. It dove for Vaelinthia, who was hobbling away. Cruz and Taeg stepped in front, but the dragon knocked them both aside. Hitting their heads on a statue of a large bear, Taeg fell unconscious while Cruz lay motionless and dizzy. The dragon opened his mouth, ready to devour Vaelinthia.

She fell, turning over to see the creature's jaws opening. She threw her hands over her face and screamed. A large pirate jumped over her, sacrificing himself to the beast. The dragon flew above and tossed the lifeless body far away from the group. The Pirate Captain yelled in anger. He and Laisren gained their footing after the dragon's blow with its tail.

Finn and Max watched in terror as the dragon started its attack descent on father and son. They readied their bows and fired their arrows. They were excellent marksmen and hit their target. Cruz sat up, grabbed his head, and watched the beast shoot flames of pain in the air. Grey blood dripped on the group below.

The captain looked confused about where the arrows came from, but then he saw where the dragon was heading. Max and Finn continued to shoot their arrows, but this dragon was huge. The captain threw his sword, and it landed in the creature's belly.

They were now out of weapons. Laisren's sword was broken, one was melted, another flung over the maze, and now the captain's sword was in the dragon. Cruz tried to look around for his sword, but his vision was slightly blurry, and the fog was too thick. He panicked and patted the ground, trying to find anything to help. Finn went to grab another arrow, but his quiver was out.

"Max, I'm out," Finn yelled.

"Me too."

They saw the dragon coming. It was ready to dive, but another arrow flew with lightning speed, sliced through the creature's head, and the dragon disappeared.

"What just happened?" Max asked.

"We only need four stones," Sealyn yelled. "Hurry up and stop playing with dragons."

Finn and Max chuckled. Sakul and Finn gave instructions to the group. They made their way through the maze slowly. Finn and Max helped carry Vaelinthia, and the Pirate Captain carried Taeg. Laisren, Cruz, and the other pirate led the group with sore and beaten bodies.

They were greeted with hugs and laughter. They only had minutes left. Char had already secured their stones on the door. He took the other two from Laisren. Taeg finally woke from his head trauma and was glad he wasn't waking up to the dragon battle.

Before Char placed the last stone, Sealyn stopped his hand. "Remember, we still must go back for the others. We don't know what will happen once this door opens. A staircase could manifest underneath. The maze could disappear. No one knows, but we can't leave them behind."

The group nodded. Char placed the final stone. A click sounded, and the door swung open. A gust of violent wind sucked the group forward, then slammed the door closed. Sealyn stood quickly. She tried to wrap her mind around what had just happened.

"Is everyone here?" she asked. Everyone responded with their names. All had made it through except the three on the terrace. Sealyn replayed the rules. *You can't go back. Once you make it through the door, it's sealed.*

She felt nauseous. The rules were also clear. *Those left behind—died.* Her mind was dizzy. Did that mean…? She sucked in a breath. Were Favien, Sakul, and Herbmando dead? She remembered the screams from the first room they encountered of the pirate burning alive. Her promise broken to Pinx. They were gone. Her friends. Her chosen family that she'd known for years. They were dead.

CHAPTER 36
THE TRUNDATTA BALL

The Trundatta ball dazzled people's imaginations. Each year, the Avondelle Palace throws a winter ball with a unique theme. King Jace decided that Skarpin and Wullen should choose the theme. Skarpin said, "Puffin pies!" Wullen said, "Chocolate Jabbles." So, the grass-floor ballroom was decorated top to bottom with countless sweets and treats. Guests dressed in their best costumes, reflecting this year's theme, too.

A large chocolate fountain was in the center of the floor, and each column of the ballroom had edible chocolate garland with strawberries dipped in pink chocolate attached. Tables had tiered stands with cupcakes, Puffin pies, brownies, and Moon Roons. Also on display around the stands were delicious Jam Pies in all flavors.

Siany felt like a child again as she plucked a chocolate strawberry from the garland wrapped around a column. She loved the sweet, juicy taste. She leaned on one of the walkway banisters that guided the perimeter of the dance floor, watching her people sway with the music. She laughed at the kids spinning themselves around and around, no doubt from a sugar high. With a deep exhale, she found herself relaxing and giving in to fun. Elysium needed this.

She couldn't believe almost nine months had passed since she had been complaining about not knowing her purpose, and now, she was so overjoyed with her life's calling. Tonight, she would celebrate their victory and the return of the wounded.

When Jace walked down the white marble stairs from the golden doors, the room erupted in cheers and claps. The kingdom was overjoyed that their king survived. Jace couldn't believe the warm welcome. He knew if Sealyn were here, it would truly feel like home.

Standing on one of the slightly lower levels of the ballroom, Pinx and Norella joined Revalyn and Quinley, who were enjoying the steamy Moon Roons. The chocolate and cream desserts were so delightful.

"We heard you both were essential in solving the ending of the black phoenixes. Thank you ever so much," Pinx said.

Quinley blushed. "It was just reading books. The two boys really did the trick. By the way, I'm Lady Quinley, and this is Lady Revalyn. I know we haven't officially met."

"Wait, we saw you at the sendoff and at Fort Kippen right before we were about to leave for Len Nove, right?" Lady Norella asked.

"That's right!" Revalyn said excitedly. "We gave Queen Sealyn some information we had found."

Pinx held up her goblet. "Cheers to that because it helped save Len Nove."

"Are you ladies hoping for an invitation to Queen Sealyn's Vinurs of the Court?"

"Norella!" Pinx scolded.

"What? It's a simple question." Norella held up her hand, defending herself.

Quinley scrunched her face. "I wouldn't say that was our reason for helping. We helped because we wanted the kingdom to benefit, not just ourselves."

Revalyn nodded her head. "I agree with Quinley. I'm glad Queen Sealyn requested us…"

"Requested you?" Adalina interrupted Revalyn. "Now, why would Queen Sealyn specifically request you two?"

Pinx folded her arms. "Careful with what you say, ladies, or you might end up on the front page of the *Elysian News*."

"Wow. Why so icy, Pinx?" Adalina slightly slurred her words. She swayed after having one too many goblets of wine.

"I don't know. Maybe it's because you keep slandering the royal family, or maybe it's because you said awful things about Novaly, or…"

"Well, pardon me for questioning anything in life, little Mrs. Perfect."

"Perfect?!" Pinx squeaked.

Quinley and Revalyn looked at each other with wide eyes. They did not want to get in the middle of a lady fight. They tried to move slowly away, but Adalina stepped in their path.

"You must have heard about the two open positions, seeing as Lady Brenna fled to Port Rowin and I, myself, resigned to pursue my passion for exposing the truth."

Revalyn was scared to speak. She didn't want any spotlight, especially in the *Elysian News*. She stood uncomfortably, dressed in a red cupcake costume. Like the other ladies, she had a teased wig. Hers was white with red sparkles that looked like icing on top of a red velvet cupcake, her favorite. Her dress was red and covered in red gems, with a bell-shaped skirt that had vertical pinched fabric, looking like the base of a cupcake.

Blushing, Revalyn decided to speak. "Lady Adalina, we don't want to give the impression that our intent or presence will replace anyone. We're simply obeying orders."

Adalina wore a costume evoking a chocolate-covered strawberry. She wore a strapless, red, form-fitted gown with chocolate-colored ruffles across her chest that wrapped around her shoulders and back. She wore a teased brown wig with a chocolate-covered hat and bright green shoes. Her almond-shaped eyes glared at Revalyn. "So, it wouldn't interest any of you to know that Lady Lulana has also resigned?"

"What? Why?" Norella asked with interest. Lulana's leaving could potentially lead to her putting forth a nomination.

"Why indeed," Adalina mocked. "This is going to make for a great headline. I'll question--why more and more of Queen Sealyn's Vinurs keep leaving her service."

"Okay that's enough, you drunk strawberry!" Norella snapped. She had finally lost her patience. Pinx snorted, and wine dripped from her nose. "Lady Pyry, Lord Drystan, and Lord Tybalt were all traitors. Lady Brenna can't handle the fact that Jashun is madly in love with Princess Kailani, and seriously, who could blame him? I'm guessing Lulana wants to be near Brenna since they were inseparable, and you? Well, you want attention, but Sealyn doesn't have the time to give it to you because she's off trying to save the world."

Pinx lifted her finger. "Which, by the way, isn't the point of being a part of Sealyn's court. We're honored and duty-bound to serve her, and she's never abused our vows."

"Hasn't she though?"

"What could you possibly mean, Adalina?" Pinx was irritated and feeling heated.

Adalina pointed at Jace. "She made us all bow and serve a Stoltlander, and not just any Stoltlander, a grey-eyed one whose mother and kingdom continue to kill innocent Elysians, and we do nothing."

Norella gasped and covered her mouth. "You're speaking treason. Where is all this coming from?"

Adalina's jaw tightened. She tried not to think about the countless names of friends she read on the scrolls nailed around the city every time there was a battle, but when she thought about her best friend Rivers, a tear slid from her eye. She wiped away the tear with frustration and anger, and said, "Rivers," then stomped away, grabbing several Moon Roons as she walked by a table.

"Who's Rivers?" Revalyn asked.

Pinx looked down. "She was an amazing friend to us and a fierce warrior. She died during the Len Novian quest by an Arkootha bear attack."

"Oh my, I'm so sorry to hear that," Revalyn replied.

The ladies stood in awkward silence. They watched the dance floor filled with colorful costumes displaying candy, desserts, and treats. The tension broke as everyone erupted in laughter when Skarpin fell into the chocolate fountain.

Quinley seized the moment. "I really like your matching cotton candy costumes."

Pinx and Norella smiled and twirled. Pinx had whisps of pink and purple puffs as her dress and a fluffy pink wig, while Norella wore the same except for blue and purple puffs and a fluffy blue wig.

"And I love your costume," Pinx complimented. "I'm guessing you couldn't make up your mind and decided on all the candies?"

Quinley curtsied, "You guessed right! I love candy, so why not express it?" Quinley stepped closer to Pinx and Norella. She felt like she could trust these ladies and had a question she needed to ask. "I overheard a private conversation between Jashun and Kailani that has me questioning some things."

"Do tell," Norella said, couching low to hear better.

"They were talking about the treaty between Kailani's Mer Clan and Elysium. Jashun was shocked that Elysium was so willing to sign it because, as he said, 'I didn't know your magic could literally suck the lifeline of water out of us.'"

Pinx choked on her drink. "Wait, what? The Abyss magic can do that?"

Quinley shrugged. "Apparently," She leaned in closer and dropped her voice to a whisper. "Queen Sealyn asked us to research the old shack by the lighthouse in Port Rowin. She said it was made from Abyss and Luxen magic, but somehow, its magic remained intact after the Second Chance. Could the treaty and this research project be linked, and, if so, why?"

Norella pressed her finger to the side of her head, making round motions. "My head is spinning. Okay, so correct me if I'm wrong, but the Second Chance took away Luxen magic and was replaced by the curses, right?" The ladies nodded. "Then how did that one shack survive?"

"That's the million-coin question," Revalyn replied. "The Mer Clans weren't affected by Creator's punishment because they weren't in turmoil at the time. As a matter of fact, they were in year one hundred of their peace treaty."

As they contemplated, they took a sip of their goblets and watched Jace dance in circles with Skarpin on his shoulders as chocolate dripped around them. The royal family cheered and laughed; even the grandparents joined in the dancing.

Pinx tilted her head. "Can one channel both Abyss and Luxen magic?"

"Hmm," Quinley's brow wrinkled. "I haven't come across any text that has said that, but it doesn't mean that it's not possible."

"But, would it be a land or water magic-wielding person who could do such a feat?" Norella asked. She made mental notes to find books in the library on these subjects.

"Excellent question. Perhaps an offspring of one of the Mer people and an Elysian?" Revalyn suggested.

"I read that most 'inbred' children were killed," Quinley said.

"What? That's awful! Why would they do such a thing?" Pinx questioned.

"From what I read, the rulers were too scared to find out how powerful that type of being could be. Knowing children would be killed, land dwellers and Merpeople kept to themselves and avoided the risk," Quinley informed.

Pinx stood in awe at this information. If there's anything she's learned in the past year, it's that just because someone has mixed blood doesn't make him or her a freak. She looked at Jace and felt uneasy. Her question slipped out before she could stop herself: "Has a grey-eyed ever had magic?"

Quinley looked at Revalyn. She didn't want to say what she knew, then groaned. "The old texts confirmed that most grey-eyeds were killed as well. Others were taken as slaves and chained with magic spells preventing them from accepting their power's calling. Since the Second Chance, the tradition of killing grey-eyes didn't start again until that same horrible man claimed that Nichts should be wiped out." Quinley dropped her head. "Honestly, it's a miracle King Jace is alive. Most grey-eyes are either murdered or shipped to Havas for pleasure toys."

"That is the worst thing anyone could do," Pinx said loudly.

Norella whispered, "It was very evident that Jace had a horrible childhood. He was apparently the village toy.

Everyone tortured him, picked on him, abused him—I'm guessing it was much worse than he lets on. I wonder if that was a deal Corentine made, you know—let him live at his expense, their entertainment."

Pinx took another bite of her strawberry jam pie. She observed Jace. She felt an idea form like the answer to all their problems was right on the tip of her tongue. She thought about the Abyss magic, the Luxen magic, and the slaughtering of mixed-blood children. Silver-eyes had never been given the chance to channel magic. If that was true, then what could they expect from Jace?

Elysian News

The Latest News and Gossip

Issue #52

Lady Lulana Speaks Out
Queen Sealyn's Vinurs shrinking

Greetings, my fellow Elysians. Lina here with the latest juicy details of the inner circle of Queen Sealyn herself!

Queen Sealyn's Vinurs of the Court are dwindling. This started with Lady Pyry. Should we question Queen Sealyn's trusting nature? She obviously had a traitor among her chosen court.

Painted above: Lady Lulana

Lady Brenna has also resigned and left Avondelle. She would rather stay at Port Rowin than be a part of the most powerful court in all seven kingdoms. Why? Isn't being a part of Queen Sealyn's court what every lady dreams of?

Yes, indeed, I have also retired from Queen Sealyn's Vinurs, but I'm still welcomed at court—for now. I felt it was more my duty to the people to report what's not being said.

Now, Lady Lulana has had enough. She is officially retiring as well. From a personal interview: "There's too much stress on the Elysium court right now. I would have liked to be a part of the Luxen school, but I wasn't asked. I will move to Port Rowin and help volunteer where I'm most needed."

Officially, three spots are now open for Queen Sealyn's Vinurs of the Court. Who will be chosen once (if) she returns? I know two very eager ladies.
~ Lady Adalina Roedellen (Lina)

Princess Siany Spotlight	**Trundatta Ball Costume winner**	**Luxen School Updates**
The juiciest gossip	*Sweet Bliss*	*Weekly Reports*
Drawings of Princess Siany's costume. Who designed it?	Congratulations to Sir Clive, owner of *His Finest*	Students wanting extra credit should return immediately
Who did she dance with?	See drawings of costume	Parents are encouraged to follow progress.
Page 2	Page 4	Page 6

CHAPTER 37
CORENTINE'S VOICE

"No. No. No. No. *No!*" Sealyn fell to her knees and screamed. "Why is this happening?!" She looked up, tears flowing from her emerald eyes. "Do you not hear me? Why?!" She cried her heart out to Creator.

Char knelt in front of Sealyn. He didn't say a word because he feared he would never stop crying for his friends if he did. Sakul was his best friend. Sealyn looked at Char and fell into his embrace. She repeated muffled sobs, "I failed them. I failed them."

Lightning erupted in grey clouds, and thunder boomed. They looked around, trying to figure out where they were and what was about to happen.

A familiar voice resounded in the vast room. "Well done, little bird," the evil female voice said.

Sealyn stood fast and wiped her nose. She knew that voice too well. Her enemy's voice. Corentine, Queen of Stoltland. Sealyn looked around, trying to find her, but all she could see was darkness. She smelled moss and trees, but no light was shown after the lightning.

"Show yourself," Sealyn said, almost growling.

A loud cackle echoed. "You dare give me an order."

Sealyn whispered to herself, "This isn't real. That's not really Corentine."

Moonlight poured in through the breaking clouds. High rock formations surrounded them. Large river trees with giant roots were scattered around. Boulders and rocks split the running river. A tall waterfall was nearby, but it made no sound. Glittering gems were embedded in the rock walls. Across the river, a glowing figure that looked exactly like the Stoltland queen was walking toward them.

Her cherry red hair blew in the breeze, and she wore all black battle leathers, dragging a black sword. Her voice sounded unnatural. "I'm as real as you allow me to be. I'm as real as your guilt, as real as your fears, as real as your blame."

Sealyn tensed. She hated every word this vile creature said. Her fists tightened. She felt herself instinctively starting to grab her bow.

"You see, little bird. I know you wish you could blame me for everything, but the truth is—you only have yourself to blame. You are the reason for so much death."

"Stop it!" Sealyn hastily armed her bow.

Corentine's cackle sent ripples down the water. "I'm not here to fight you. I'm here because the magic chose me to represent it. You are unique because your heart's desire is not like anyone else who has come through these walls, nor any among you." Corentine stopped at the water's edge. "Normally, this would be the end. I would simply grant the victors' hearts' desires, and you all would be free, but because of yours, you have one more task ahead. You will be tested. What I cannot see is your intent. Do you seek power or peace? The test will tell." Corentine laughed once more, then burst into hundreds of black crows that flew into the sky, above the clouds.

"What does that mean?" Cruz asked. "What's your heart's desire?"

"What it's been this entire time: acquire and claim Shunal's source of power."

Vaelinthia stumbled to stand but finally made it upright with Ashur's help. "Wait, does that mean that if we pass this test, then you get Shunal's source, and since you're the third-generation bloodline, our curse is broken?" She grunted after her question, feeling the pain of her injury.

Sealyn placed her hands on her hips and walked in circles, then faced Vaelinthia. "I honestly don't know, but it does sound like it. For me--for us, it's hard to trust words coming from Corentine's mouth, but whatever is about to happen, we must make it count."

A boom sounded, and the ground shook. Their hearts started pounding. They had no idea what was coming for them. Sealyn's anger and grief burned. She tried not to think about telling Sorcha and Pinx about Sakul and Favien. She forced herself not to look at Cruz's saddened face. They could not let their deaths be in vain.

Pickaxes fell in front of Cruz and Vaelinthia. They looked at each other, confused. A yellow haze clouded the room. Cruz and Vaelinthia suddenly picked up the axes and started pounding against the wall. Sealyn was baffled. Why were they doing that?

"Cruz! Vael! Stop! What are you doing?" Sealyn shouted.

Cruz grunted with another swing. "Must," he slammed the ax in the rock. "Get," another strike. "The gems." Again, he slammed his ax into the wall.

Char leaned close to Sealyn's ear. "Was that yellow haze the curse?"

"I don't know, but Cruz and Vael both said they had been fighting against the curse. It barely affected them anymore since they turned rebel." Sealyn walked up to Vaelenthia. "Vael, you don't have to do this."

"I can't help it. I need the jewels. I'm nothing without them," Vaelinthia whacked the rock over and over.

Stunned, Sealyn stepped back. She turned to the group. "What are we supposed to do now?"

Before they could reply, an orange haze clouded the room, making the Pirate Captain, Laisren, Taeg, and the other pirate cough excessively. Once the fog settled, Taeg shoved Laisren. "I told you I should have stayed on the boat!"

Laisren shoved Taeg back. "This isn't my fault. Go ahead and cry about it!"

Their father yelled and scolded them, which led to a massive physical fight. Korpam's curse took over them. Wrath radiated through every punch and kick.

A blue haze appeared, and Finn slumped over and fell asleep. Max tried to wake him, but Finn simply slept. The Elysians looked at each other with fear. They were next.

"Be brave, my warriors. You can fight the curse. You know that!" Sealyn tried to encourage them, but she felt that no matter what, the curse would take over.

The green haze cascaded around them, and immediately, the boys started arguing over petty jealousies. Sealyn couldn't believe some of the things Char, Ashur, and Max were saying. It suddenly dawned on her that she wasn't affected. What was this game?

A voice sounded and sent emotional feelings to her core. It was her deceased grandfather, King Saven Dovinus. "My darling granddaughter, do you see? Do you see what will happen if you fail? The value of life will disappear. Father will fight son. Brother will fight brother, and relationships will crumble. You must keep going. You must deliver all seven kingdoms from these curses. I'm sorry the weight has fallen on your shoulders, but I know you can do it."

Sealyn sobbed; tears glided down her bloody, dirt-stained cheeks. "But how, Granddad? Please tell me how."

The evil laugh of Corentine echoed. She appeared again in front of the waterfall. "Keep crying, child. Time is wasting away, and this time, you will surely know the weight of what you want and what you will face."

A large boulder near the quiet waterfall rolled away, allowing Favien, Sakul, and Herbmando to slide onto a flat rock. Sealyn's heart leaped for joy. They were alive! They tried to walk off the rock, but a forcefield formed around them. It looked like a shimmering glass tube. They were trapped once again.

They watched in fear as a Hydrus Snake perched at the top of the waterfall. This was no true snake but a mixed breed of snake and dragon, gifted from Stoltland. It had the body of a thick snake, two legs with sharp claws, wings like a dragon, but a head like a snake with horns. Most importantly, this creature breathed water, not fire.

The beast started pouring water over the three captives. They screamed and pounded on the forcefield, but it didn't budge. Sealyn started running to them. She felt the ground shake and skidded to a stop.

"I'm sure how much time you have left is evident, but they are not your task. You see, each kingdom has its creature of old that must be mastered. Elysium—the Green Phoenix. Len Nove—the mammoth. Shunal's creature is the serpent. More specifically, the Naehass." The evil red-headed witch smacked a yellow butterfly, sending it spiraling to the ground.

Sealyn felt herself start to panic. She remembered the words of the guard, *"Because this is the season that the Naehass feeds."* Would she really have to fight a giant snake-like creature? What if she failed? Would everyone in here die?

With lighting cracking and thunder exploding, Corentine's voice said, "I call forth the Shunalian Naehass!"

Sealyn readied her bow. With nervous breaths, she looked side to side. The captives screamed as the water was at their ankles. They were soaked, spitting out water. Herbmando looked grey from the snake bite. Cruz and Vaelinthia had bloody, blistered hands. Taeg's eye was swollen, and Laisren's nose was bloody and broken. The Elysians started shoving each other. How could she think she was capable of breaking these curses? She created such chaos.

The water started moving faster, and Sealyn's heart pounded. She heard a tiny squeak below her. Looking down at her boot, she saw a tiny surzee, a Len Novian mouse. Its tiny hands motioned for her to come closer, and she crouched low to hear it.

"Solve the puzzle. Not everything she said is true," the blue-eyed mouse squeaked, then scurried away.

Sealyn repeated the mouse's words, "*Solve the puzzle. Not everything she said is true.*" What puzzle, and which words? Sealyn had no time to process the mouse's instructions nor that a mouse had actually given instructions.

She felt her stomach drop at the sight before her. From the dark cave in the corner, a massive two-headed serpent emerged.

CHAPTER 38
THE SERPENT EMERGES

Sealyn couldn't believe the size of this serpent. Its torso was the circumference of a large Angel Oak. The necks of the two heads were long and strong. Just the heads alone were roughly the height of a grown man and had teeth like a lion. She was scared. It was the same fear as watching Corentine's black spear speed toward her, only this time, she didn't have Dun to save her.

As soon as she thought of Dun, she felt the magic of the Green Phoenix flow through her veins. She also felt the mammoth strength pulse in her muscles. The spell was lifted. She could use her power. Now, this would be a fair fight.

Bright emerald, feathered wings with green flames on the tips formed on her back. Her eyes glowed blue, producing blue streaks through her hair, and she took her fighting stance. The serpent slithered toward her, preparing to strike. Sealyn released her first arrow at the Hydrus Snake, hoping that would solve her time issue, but the arrow went straight through like it was made of smoke. She turned her attention back to the Naehass. She fired her next arrow. It hit the creature, but one of its heads made a laughing sound.

The head with black eyes lunged for her. She tucked her wings and rolled away. Quickly, Sealyn formed her famous green flame bow and arrow. She fired quickly at the black-eyed snake's head. It dodged her arrow. Sealyn flew past the heads, ducking the strikes. She tried to dive into the top of the forcefield, but she face-planted into the shield.

She shook her head, perplexed. The top looked open, and water was clearly filling the tube from the dragon snake, so why couldn't she get in? It had to be the curse preventing her from killing the Hydrus Snake and not allowing her to rescue her friends.

"I'll find a way!" Sealyn yelled to them as they continued to pound the forcefield. She flew back at the serpent and launched another two arrows fast, but both heads dodged them. This continued: firing arrows, heads dodging. Heads striking. Sealyn flying from the attacks.

Catching her breath on one of the rock edges, Sealyn looked at the water level. It was to their chests. She was running out of time. She looked at Cruz and Vael, who were busy trying to use the tip of the axe to carve a place for the stones on their legs' skin. Sealyn winced and shot another green arrow at the golden-eyed snake head. It nicked it. Tiny yellow diamonds flowed out of the small wound.

Cruz and Vaelinthia's heads jerked in the direction of the diamonds falling to the rock ground. They felt the presence of potential wealth. Sealyn saw them start to move toward the hungry serpent. She screamed, "No!" They paid no attention to her. They only heard the call of the curse, hurrying with blood dripping down their legs.

Sealyn couldn't believe what she was about to do, but she felt like she had no choice. She dove toward them, wings taking her at Phoenix speeds. She tried to scoop both in her arms, but Vael jumped out of the way. Holding onto Cruz, who squirmed in her arms, she flew to the top of the tube. She prayed that the forcefield was only against her from going in and wouldn't prevent Cruz from entering. She tossed him, and he landed with a splash at the bottom.

She ignored Cruz's yelling and cursing. It was for his protection. Vaelinthia was inching closer to the small diamonds. The black-eyed head lunged for Vael, but Sealyn sent another green arrow at it. This time, it hit its target. Black diamonds spilled from the wound. The creature roared in pain.

Sealyn watched as the heads wailed back and forth. She took her opportunity and went for Vael, wind gusting through her green feathers. When she landed on the slippery rock, Sealyn felt pity as Vaelinthia scooped yellow diamonds into her blistery hands.

Vaelinthia sprinkled the diamonds in her hair and looked at Sealyn. "What do you think? Don't I look wealthy? I just know I'll be asking to a royal ball now."

"What I think is that there are two massive heads above us that we need to run from!"

Vael looked up and screamed like it was the first time she even saw the danger. She tried to run, but her injured leg slipped on the wet bedrock. She looked to Sealyn with true fear. "Sealyn, help! I don't want to die."

"Take my hand," Sealyn yelled and pulled Vaelinthia close. Her wings took flight, heading to the captives, but the black-eyed head swooped in front of her. Sealyn turned but collided with the golden-eyed head. The force of impact sent them to the ground hard. Sealyn coughed, trying to get air. She had landed to take the brunt of the force on her. Vaelinthia rolled off Sealyn, holding her wrist.

Sealyn coughed more and tried to wipe away sweat and dirt on her face. Blood trickled down her head. The emerald queen was desperate for this to be over. She wanted the peace and warmth of her bed with Jace's arms around her. She wanted to hear her family's laughs around the fireplace. This torture had to end.

The weight of using her powers for so long was taking its toll on her. Her nose and ears had crusted blood around them, and her vision was starting to blur. She didn't know how much more she could take. This creature was, after all, legendary.

The beast slithered toward them, crushing rocks under its weight. Sealyn saw the four captives treading water. They only had a few feet to go before there was no more air. She had to give everything she had.

Sealyn looked at Vaelinthia. "Vael, I'm commanding you to repeat these words, 'I am valued. I am loved. I am wanted. I don't need a fortune to matter.' You repeat them until you believe them. Is that understood?"

Vaelinthia choked out the words, "Yes, Queen Sealyn."

"Good, now you hide behind that boulder. I need to finish this." Vaelinthia shuffled behind the mossy boulder, peeking above it in awe of Sealyn walking straight for the two-headed animal, wings dragging behind her.

As Sealyn's boots clicked on the shiny, dark bedrock, she repeated the words, "*Solve the puzzle. Not everything she said is true.*"

The golden-eyed head struck. Sealyn dove to her right, scraping her knee as she fell. From her back, she fired another green flaming arrow but missed. Her muscles were tired. She thought back to the witch's words, "*Keep crying, child. Time is wasting away, and this time, you will surely know the weight of what you want and what you will face.*"

Sealyn's wings tried to fly her up, but the black-eyed head swung fast, slamming Sealyn against the rock wall. She felt one of its jagged edges pierce her side, crying out in pain. She tried to channel the creation of separate animals as she had done on the Stoltland ship, but she could feel the magic's resistance. She was limited in what she could do with her power in this place.

Her wings kept her in flight. They sped her past the long heads and over the stream to the mossy ground. Sealyn crumbled to her knees, holding her side. Blood dripped between her fingers, soaking her clothes. She tried to think of the words, but the pain was unbearable. She ripped up moss and stuffed it in her wound, hoping it would help stop the bleeding. She winced at the sting and gritted her teeth.

She repeated Corentine's other sentences: *"I'm sure how much time you have left is evident, but they are not your task. You see, each kingdom has its creature of old that must be mastered. Elysium—the Green Phoenix. Len Nove—the mammoth. Shunal's creature is the serpent, more specifically, the Naehass."* What wasn't true? Everything was true, except…her mind trailed to Dun. He wasn't hers to control. They were teammates. The mammoths weren't her slaves either. They were equals with an equal partnership.

The creatures of old weren't to be mastered. They were to be honored and treasured. At that realization, a flash caught her eye. Something that hadn't been visible before— a golden cuff with implanted yellow diamonds was clasped around each head. And then it clicked. Sealyn finally understood the puzzle.

With a loud cry, she slowly and painfully stood, aided by her wings. The two heads towered above, looking down at her like she would be a tasty meal. She took one final glance at the captives. Herbmando was struggling to stay afloat. They maybe had a foot left of air. Sealyn dropped her head praying, then focused her attention on the beast.

It was time. With all her might, she launched into the air. She barrel-rolled past the black-eyed head's attack and jerked to the right, then flew up high only to circle back down over the golden-eyed head. Sealyn fashioned an enchanted green rope around its head with barely any Elysian magic left and flew to the ground. She tied her rope to the boulder that was still hiding Vaelinthia.

The serpent thrashed against its binding, but the rope held. Sealyn saw the cuff's clasp and knew it would take all the mammoth strength she had to unlock it. Standing behind the flailing beast, she grabbed the cuff and began pulling. The black-eyed head crept from a low position, then raised up, catching Sealyn off guard. It moved to make its killing blow, but instead of its jaws wrapping around Sealyn, they met Vaelinthia, who had thrown herself in front of Sealyn.

Sealyn's eyes were wide, and she could not fully grasp what had just happened. She saw the serpent take Vaelinthia's body away, crimson raining from the serpent's jaws. Sealyn screamed so hard that her throat went raw. With the vision of Vaelinthia's sacrifice, Elysium's queen cried out, pulling open the golden cuff with the last of the mammoth strength she had.

Blood streamed from Sealyn's nose, ears, and eyes. She collapsed to the ground, gasping for air. The cuff landed with a loud clink on the rock. That was the first sound the room allowed besides her screams.

With the cuff's opening, the serpent released Vaelinthia's limp body. It fell lifeless. The water level dropped quickly in the forcefield. Once the captives' feet touched the ground, the forcefield and the Hydrus Snake disappeared. The Elysians and pirates stopped their fighting, and Finn woke up.

Cruz sprinted to Vaelinthia, cradling her bloodied body. Herbmando hobbled next to his fallen rebel comrade, tears pricking his yellow eyes. The rest ran to Sealyn. Char scooted under Sealyn and propped her head on his chest. She looked frail and drained of life, almost green. Her breaths were shallow, and she was wheezing.

Char frantically felt for her heartbeat. "Her heart is barely beating. C'mon, Sea. Fight! Don't leave us!"

They heard Cruz cry out. Ashur ran to his side. He saw there was nothing they could do for Vaelinthia. She sacrificed herself for her belief, her cause, and her queen. Ashur brushed her cheek with his fingers, agonizing over what could have been. She was so brave.

They felt uneasy as the serpent's heads lingered over them all. Cruz spat and yelled at the creature. The black-eyed head snapped at the rebel's leader, but the golden-eyed head growled and hissed at its twin head. It was now the leader. It was the ruler.

Sealyn slightly opened her eyelids and met the serpent's golden eyes. He spoke to Sealyn's mind. "Your last and final task. Are you sure you want this?" The golden cuff was in its mouth. It was clear that the cuff was the source of Shunal's power.

"Or," said the black-eyed head. "We could give you what you can't." His voice was deep, full of tricks and deceit, but when Sealyn heard a crying baby, she knew what that serpent meant.

She closed her eyes and recited the ancient scroll, *"Cursed more are the beginners, for Pride and Envy cannot grow light, and so because of this, the joining of a Stoltlander and Elysian will not produce life."* The snake was offering her a family with Jace, a bloodline to continue.

She heard a baby laughing with Jace's laughs, then the words, "Sea, come see what our son just did. Come, love. Come join us." Jace sounded so happy. This was torture. She now had to choose between hers and Jace's possible child or breaking the curses. How was this right for a person to face these obstacles? How could she decide this? Either way, she would lose. Either way, life would be lost. Could she really face Jace and tell him that she had the opportunity to give him a son, and she didn't take it?

Elysian News

The Latest News and Gossip

Issue #78

Painted above: The Pirate Captain from Korpam

Pirate: Friend or Foe?

Who is the Pirate Captain?

Greetings, my fellow Elysians. I hope everyone is enjoying the beautiful spring weather with the lovely Lenettes; they're my favorite.

I have been researching for months the mystery that is The Pirate Captain.

From speaking with Lord Jashun, Lord Doebromir, and Lord Ajorn, who have all had in-person encounters with this scandalous pirate, I have some interesting details. First, let me confirm that yes, he is indeed from Korpam, the kingdom known for rage fits. With that being said, the pirate cannot be trusted.

This pirate was also banned from his kingdom, so technically, he didn't choose a life of piracy; it was his only option. Imagine how much anger he has built up! He has a wife and two sons. According to Ajorn, he kept his word—whatever that means.

All in all, this man remains a mystery. Lord Jashun and Lord Doebromir are still holding grudges. I'm sure Lord Sune is, too, but he refused to comment. Most on the rescue quest refused to comment as well, and Lord Ajorn was extremely tight-lipped about the experience. What really happened over there?

~Lady Adalina Roedellen (Lina)

Princess Siany Spotlight	**Spring Festival is Approaching**	**Luxen School Updates**
The juiciest gossip	*When and Where*	*Weekly Reports*
New spring fashion for our princess	I have all the details about the Market Spring dances	A big welcome to Skarpin joining spring classes
What is the latest trend?	Who's performing on stage?	Parents are encouraged to follow progress.
Page 2	Page 4	Page 6

CHAPTER 39
MAUOR & KAZIMIR

Sealyn could feel herself slipping in and out of consciousness. She was in so much pain. Blood pooled around her injury. The serpent kept repeating for her to choose, but then she heard a small voice whispering nearby. She almost missed it. Sealyn opened her eyes to the surzee who had spoken to her before.

It smiled and handed her a gold-framed mirror. She took it and looked at the reflection, but instead of seeing herself, she saw Skarpin snuggled next to Jace, who looked sick. The images changed to Skarpin sitting on the foot of the bed, reading to Jace, who still looked unwell. She desperately wanted to help Jace. Changing again, the mirror showed Skarpin filling a pit with rocks along with another young boy. She saw her mother looking proud of him.

She didn't understand what she was seeing. Sealyn's heart leaped when she saw Skarpin and the young boy sitting on Jace's bed, who looked healthy. Then he sat up, startling the boys, and Skarpin jumped into Jace's arms. She saw that their embrace wasn't ordinary but that of a father and son.

Next, Jace was dancing with Skarpin on his shoulders at what looked like a candy-decorated Trundatta ball. She laughed and coughed when she saw Skarpin fall into the chocolate fountain. She watched as Jace ate lunch with Skarpin at the Luxen magic school. Her heart ached as she saw fuzzy, purple Ella, the *exiguum, curled up with Skarpin, who was in a deep sleep in his room. Jace kissed his head. Before he walked out the door, Jace leaned against the doorframe and watched Skarpin sleep.

Sealyn put down the mirror to thank the mouse, but the surzee was gone, as well as the mirror. Was that all a dream, or could it mean something more? After the mirror had shown all those lovely visions, Sealyn knew she didn't need to desire what she couldn't or didn't have. This was how one breaks the curse of greed—contentment.

She looked at the two-headed serpent and said with her mind, "I reject your offer, snake. I choose joy over misery. I choose contentment over greed. My heart's desire is to break all lands from these curses, and I'm willing to sacrifice my own life to do it."

The black-eyed head hissed with disappointment, and the golden-eyed head bowed in reverence. It laid the gold cuff beside Sealyn. With swirls of sparkling yellow dust, the cuff shrank to human-sized shackles.

Sealyn skidded her arm to the shackles, barely able to move it. Her fingers slid around the chain, igniting bright golden sparks. The ground rumbled, and across Shunal, the yellow haze split, resembling curtains being pulled apart, and evaporated like a memory lost in the wind.

"I am Mauor, keeper of the light," the golden-eyed head said with wisdom and kindness. "That is Kazimir, destroyer of peace." The black-eyed head gave an evil grin, showing his fangs. "Pay no attention to him. He's yours to control now. Tell your companions to open one of their canteens."

Sealyn's mind was fuzzy, and she felt blood still flowing from her wounds. "Water," was all she could say.

Char snapped his fingers at Max. They would eventually have to talk out everything they said to each other during the jealous rants. With shaking hands, Max untied his pack and handed the canteen to Sealyn.

Mauor lowered his head, slipping his fang into the canteen just enough so they could see the venom stream into the canister. Char drew his sword, along with the pirates.

Char yelled, "You really think she's going to drink your venom?"

Mauor blinked and continued his conversation that only he and Sealyn could hear. "I do not have venom. Your cousin is mistaken. I have potion that heals and revives. Kazimir is full of venom."

Kazimir flicked his black-forked tongue. "If you don't believe Mauor, then you're more than welcome to try my venom instead." His voice sounded sinister.

Sealyn coughed up blood. Char screamed her name. The group tightened their circle around her. She had minutes to decide. Setting the canteen on her bloody lips, she lifted it high and drank the smooth, sweet-tasting thick liquid. She felt burning inside her and yelled out, grasping her side. After a minute of excruciating pain, Sealyn felt relief, like laying in a meadow on a spring day with the wind tickling the tall grass and just the right amount of sunshine, dancing on her face.

She opened her eyes and saw the shocked expressions of her crew. She tilted her head. "Is everyone ok?"

"We thought you were dying. Why didn't the venom kill you? And why did you drink it!?" Char spat his words of anger and fear. Sometimes, his cousin could be so frustrating!

Sealyn was confused. "Didn't you hear Mauor? He said he possessed potion, healing potion—not venom."

"Mauor? What's a Mauor? And hear? You mean that monster spoke to you?" the Pirate Captain asked.

"Ah, yes, that makes sense. She does talk to the Green Phoenix and once-frozen mammoths, so talking to a hideous snake sounds about right," Char grinned at Sealyn, relieved she was already looking more like herself.

Kazimir snapped at Char, not liking the insults. The group helped Sealyn to her feet. Her clothes were blood-stained and dirty. She saw Cruz and Herbmando holding Vaelinthia. Herbmando looked worse than ever. He wouldn't make it much longer.

Sealyn looked up at the towering Mauor. "Can you save my friends with your potion?"

"My apologies, my queen, but the young lady is already gone. My potion is powerful, but it cannot bring life from death. I can, however, heal everyone else's wounds." He gently filled the canteen with this sparkling white potion.

Sealyn jogged to Herbmando and handed him the canteen.

Herbmando's eyes widened. "Snake venom?"

"Not venom. A potion. It will heal you."

Cruz tried to grab the canteen. "Give it to Vael!"

"I'm sorry, Cruz," Sealyn said. "She's already dead. She saved my life with her sacrifice.

"This is your fault, Elysian! If you hadn't put me in that forcefield, then I could have protected her."

"The curse had your body and mind. You were literally walking right into danger without knowing it."

"If that were true, then she wouldn't have saved you! She would have been focused on the gems. You're a liar!"

Both snake heads hissed. "Let me eat him, my queen. He reeks of sweat and annoyance anyways," Kazimir growled.

"What? No! Don't eat him. Don't eat anyone!"

Cruz scrunched his face. "What? I'm not going to eat anyone?"

"No, not you. Him," Sealyn pointed at Kazimir, who had drool dripping from his bloody mouth. "Listen, Cruz. I know you're angry right now, and that's valid. Just like you, the serpent was also under the curse's control. Look at your legs—you carved gems into them. I see that the gems fell out in the water, but the open gashes are proof."

"That still doesn't answer why Vaelinthia would save you if she were under the curse."

Herbmando raised his hand, "Uh, friends, I'm going to drink this now before I die." He lifted the canteen and felt burning pain run through the veins of his entire body.

"Because I gave her an order, and apparently, it worked."

"What?" Cruz bit. "You ordered a Shunalian to save you?"

Sealyn let out a grunt of frustration. "No, I told her: *'Vael, I'm commanding you to repeat these words, 'I am valued. I am loved. I am wanted. I don't need a fortune to matter.' You repeat them until you believe them.'* Her stepping in to save me is the only proof that, in her final moments, she truly believed she was loved and valued; otherwise, she would have stayed hidden, fighting the curse's calling."

Cruz fought back tears. His grief was overwhelming him. "Your green eyes still don't give you the right to order yellow eyes. You are not our queen!"

"That's it! I'm biting his head off," Kazimir hissed.

Sealyn held up her hand to Kazimir and looked at Cruz. "Vaelinthia called me her queen." Cruz folded his arms, not wanting to deal with this anymore. Sealyn continued,

"I'm not looking to rule Shunal, but I can't leave the current rulers in charge either."

Herbmando pushed himself up and stood next to Cruz. He patted him on the back and handed him the canteen. "Drink up, my friend. It's time to rejoice. We will celebrate Vaelinthia's life and sacrifice, but also, the curse is *broken*!"

The crew passed around the canteen, healing and rejuvenating each person. Mauor and Kazimir led them through its dark labyrinth tunnels, smelling of mildew and stale cheese. Char, Max, and Ashur talked through the vicious words they had said and forgave each other, and the pirates did the same. They all recounted their stories to Finn, who felt guilty and relieved for being asleep for most of the last test.

Char wrapped his arms around Sakul and Sealyn's shoulders. "You want to know what I'm looking forward to?" Before they could answer, Char led on, "The Trundatta Ball! I bet heroism will be the theme. Now, don't you all run off and dress like me. We need diversity amongst the costumes."

The group chuckled and shook their heads. They saw Mauor and Kazimir look at the group and then at each other. Something was off. Sealyn touched the legendary serpent's tail. "Wait. What's wrong? What aren't you telling us?"

Mauor looked back with a pitied expression. "I hate to be the one to tell you, but it's spring."

"Spring?" Sealyn questioned loudly.

"Spring, what?" asked Max.

Mauor sighed. "Yes, my queen. Time works differently in the magic tunnels. Autumn and winter are over, but as spring brings new life, you are bringing new change to Shunal." Kazimir rolled his black eyes at the gushy poetry.

As they stepped out of the cave, sunshine and the smell of daffodils welcomed them. The cave was on the left side of Echo Forest. Once they walked by the dark trees, the group trembled against the memories of the Rope Snakes, hidden in the shadows of the branches. A sickening feeling sank deep in their stomachs when they saw no one—no one crossing the bridge, no one guarding the main gate, no one. What happened to all the people?

CHAPTER 40
HERE TO INVADE

Herbmando gently laid Vaelinthia's body down. Cruz glowered at Kazimir. Sealyn's boots scraped against the rocks at the front gate. She stood with her hands on her hips, twisting and turning, trying to figure out where the people were.

The Pirate Captain stepped close to Sealyn. "This time, we need a plan, a much better plan."

"I think I have one, but you have to assure me of your ship as our return home vessel."

"As promised. Besides, my wife would not have left the port, but if she sensed danger, they would be anchored in the harbor."

Sealyn didn't want to split the group, but she had no choice. "Herbmando, do you have any connections to get word to more rebels?"

He looked at Cruz nervously. Cruz folded his arms and nodded his head. Herbmando cleared his throat. "Well, we've only been able to use this communication system twice, and both times seemed like pure luck, but it might be our only option with a barren city."

"And that would be?" Sealyn tilted her head, annoyed that they were still keeping secrets. Haven't they been through enough together?

"Peri Pixies."

Sealyn snorted. "Peri Pixies? Be serious."

"I am. I swear to it."

"He's telling the truth," Cruz said, now willing to spill their hidden truths. "I was there."

"But those creatures are just stories for children," Char chimed in, not wanting to believe that tiny creatures could be watching them.

"Oh, they're real. Their history is old, but real. They started as merely deformations of the original Nichts. Most died, but enough survived to create a new species. They can't perform strong magic like the Nichts, but they can make themselves look like anything they're standing next to, which is why seeing them is like a miracle," Herbmando said.

Max sighed with weariness and frustration. "Let me get this straight. You want us to contact childhood-fable Peri

Pixies that are essentially impossible to find because they're basically invisible."

Char chuckled. "I will admit. As a child, I loved the Peri Pixie stories. They liked sour treats and candies like I do, so I used to leave out Blurfuzzles at night…"

"Blurfuzzles?" Taeg questioned. "What's a Blurfuzzle?"

Char started digging in his pack. "They're these delicious treats that Baker Nicht created with lemon and lime juice, kumquat, kiwi, and sugar crystals." He pulled out a crumpled, folded wax paper, then carefully unfolded it to reveal three thick, cubed green treats with sugar crystals on top. They were smooshed by all the action of the quest. Char handed one to Taeg. "Here. Try one. I grabbed these from the ship before we left. These are the last."

Taeg bit into the treat, first met with sweet sugar, then a tangy bite made his jaws clench and his face wrinkle together.

"Stop! Don't move," Herbmando commanded. They froze, unsure of what danger Herbmando feared. A tiny, glowing figure stepped from behind a mushroom and flew to Char's shoulder.

"Easy, Char. This one's a young male," Herbmando whispered. The Peri Pixie looked curiously at the treats in

Char's hands. He looked like a tiny bald human, no bigger than Char's pinky finger. His legs had greenish-brown scales and small, webbed feet. With his wider-than-normal nose, he sniffed the sour temptation and smiled a child-like grin.

Char slowly lifted the Blurfuzzles to the pixie. His wings fluttered. He even had wings for ears that shook with delight, too. The creature snatched a small handful, gobbling the gooey treat with immense joy. Char noticed that his brown eyes were farther apart than a human's normal set of eyes, but he thought it made the pixie cuter.

The pixie's silver skin sparkled in the sunlight, and then Herbmando decided they couldn't waste any more time. "Excuse me, dear Peri Pixie. Can you understand me?"

The pixie smiled and nodded while licking his silver fingers.

"Good. Good. I need you to deliver a message. Can you do that?"

The creature's winged ears dropped, and his eyes grew wide. He was scared. Sealyn stepped closer and broke a small piece of Blurfuzzle off, and handed it to the pixie. His mood changed.

Sealyn laughed. "How about we make a deal, dear one? If you carry the message, you can have the rest of these treats. Do we have an agreement?"

The Peri Pixie glowed brighter and clapped his hands. Sealyn nodded, satisfied.

"I need you to deliver this message to Ivo. Since it's spring, he won't be that far from here. He should be at the old temple ruins in Scaleturn. Tell him, 'The phoenix has risen.'"

The pixie shimmered and then disappeared. Char blinked in amazement. "I thought you said it was a miracle to see these creatures?"

"He must not have sensed any danger since there's literally no people," Herbmando shrugged.

Char tilted his head and pointed to the excessively large serpent. "That doesn't strike a pixie as dangerous?"

"Hush, Char. We don't have time for this," Sealyn said. "Obviously, something is wrong. We don't know what has happened up here in the past months. Captain, I ask for your vow one last time. Stay and fight, but send your sons to your wife to ready the ship." The Pirate Captain nodded. The two sons hugged their father, then sprinted with the other pirate, happily avoiding Echo Forest. Sealyn looked to her Elysians. "Sakul, I need you to stay with Herbmando. We can't just leave Vaelinthia's body. The rest of you will accompany me to Orm's palace. We have a throne removal to attend."

"But…" Sakul started.

"This could turn very bloody, Sakul. I need trained warriors for this last battle."

Sakul dropped his head but understood. He made a vow to train in the art of sword skill if they made it back.

Sealyn pushed open the golden palace doors. Hundreds of twinkling yellow eyes stared back at her, so this was where all the people were. Each person was in chains. Why did the king do this? Was he really that scared of losing power? The people barely moved, only parting a path for her to the throne. Sealyn sent green smoke in front of her to cloud the vision of the king and his sons.

The king heard the crowd rustling, shackles clinking against each other. The king couldn't see anything through the smoke. Walking with royal confidence, Sealyn appeared in front of the green backdrop. The king tensed and looked at his sons.

"What is the meaning of this intrusion?" he yelled.

"My presence is not an intrusion. The word you're looking for is *invasion*." Sealyn's lip curled, taunting the Shunalian royals.

"Invasion?" the eldest son laughed. "You and what army?"

The Pirate Captain, Cruz, Max, Ashur, Finn, and Char glided through the smoke and evenly stood beside Sealyn. The royals laughed even harder. Sealyn didn't care. She wanted them to boil her blood. She would need to remember their wicked laughs when they begged for mercy.

"Why have you bound your people?" she asked.

"Be gone, little queen. The world has forgotten all about you," the king stood, becoming annoyed.

"No," Sealyn noticed the shaking princesses in the corner. They looked beaten and bruised. Only two remained. Their older brother must have killed one of them. She looked at the other corner. The queen was in shackles, very odd-looking cuffs. They looked like the shackles Mauor gave her.

"Guards! Kill them and be done with this insect!"

"Do it yourself, coward!"

"You green-eyed pigeon! How dare you speak to me like that! I'll have your head on a spike!" The king clasped the rope beside him and waved his other hand, expecting to wield it like all the times before. Yet, this time, the rope rejected him. He panicked.

Sealyn smiled. "Having some trouble, golden king?"

"Shut up, you piece of…"

"I'm guessing your magic isn't working properly anymore. You see, your Umbral magic works identically to Luxen magic under the curse, but…" She paused for dramatic effect. "Once that curse is broken, Umbral magic is weak and unpredictable. Only certain elements and beasts will participate with Umbrals, but to make matters worse for you, your family's bloodline no longer controls the source of Shunal's power." Sealyn reached into her side satchel and produced the gold shackles that glowed. "I possess Shunal's power now."

The king fell back into his chair, grabbing his chest. "What have you done!?"

Screams erupted from the smokey hallway. The curse-breaking crew knew what that meant.

Sealyn took a few steps forward, green smoke swirling around her boots. "Like I said before, I'm not here to intrude. I'm here to invade, and your throne is first on the list."

"Even without my powers, you seven are outnumbered by my guards."

"Seven?" Sealyn asked in a playful tone. She was toying with him. She looked back at her people. "Are there seven of us?" The group chuckled and played along with Sealyn's teasing. They pointed to each other, trying to count, pretending to lose track.

The king jumped to his feet, yelling obscenities. "Kill them now!"

Before the guards could move, Mauor and Kazimir slithered through the smoke and towered behind Sealyn. In a striking pose, the two heads lowered themselves on either side of Sealyn. Some guards fell to their knees in either fear or reverence. Others ran from the room. The rest remained, reluctant to hold their weapons, but feared what the royal family would do to them if they did not fight.

"Now, can I eat people?" Kazimir gruffly asked.

"Only the king's sons. I can feel they are too far gone for redemption, but I want the king to beg for mercy."

Mauor and Kazimir sprang forward. The sons didn't stand a chance. With the crunching of bones and blood splattering the gaudy steps, the two legendary heads devoured the male royal line in seconds. They licked their crimson lips with satisfaction.

Sealyn marched assertively up the throne's bloody steps and peered around the serpent's body. She stared at the evil king, who kept begging for mercy over and over.

"Mercy?" Sealyn questioned. "I will not be the one to kill you, nor will the serpent." Kazimir hissed. He would starve with her in charge. "Your death is not for me to decide." Sealyn looked up. "Guards, bring me your queen and princesses." The guards quickly brought the bound royals to Sealyn. "Unlock their chains." The echoes of their chains hitting the gold floor sent shock waves to the king.

Sealyn took the queen's bruised hands and pressed them to her forehead. Then, she slipped her dagger into the queen's distorted fingers. "His fate is for you to decide." Sealyn nodded to the dark-headed queen and her daughters.

Shunal's queen screamed and charged at her evil husband, stabbing him several times. Blood flowed like a river down the diamond steps. Sealyn dissipated the smoke, then sent streams of green and gold light to each person's shackles, breaking them. She had sensed the magic in the shackles when she walked by them. They were spelled to prevent the person enslaved from using magical powers—treacherous action done by a coward.

The Shunalians gathered shoulder to shoulder in the grand throne room with anticipation, smelling the metallic stench. Sealyn's group stood on the crimson throne steps. They saw fear, confusion, and wishfulness in their yellow eyes.

"My friends," Sealyn said. "I am Queen Sealyn Araelien of Elysium. Your curse is now broken. The chains that once bound you prevented you from using your powers. I'm guessing most of you don't know exactly what will happen, but I want to assure you that you do not need to be afraid of your enchanted gifts. We will create a Shunalian school of magic for everyone so your magic can thrive."

Cheers sounded throughout the room. Parents hugged their children, couples kissed, and the Shunalians finally felt free. Sealyn saw Sakul, Herbmando, and the rest of the Trica Rebels enter the already-packed, celebrating throne room.

"However, my first order of business is to appoint your new king. Your former queen and princesses have earned a quiet, peaceful retirement." The Shunalian royals looked relieved and grateful. "So, I would like to call General Cruz Platario to kneel and be anointed as King of Shunal."

Cruz's eyes widened. His hand went to his mouth. He looked at Sealyn and shook his head disbelievingly with a cheeky smile. The Trica rebels roared proudly. They chanted Cruz's name and watched as Sealyn laid the gold crown with large yellow diamonds on Cruz's thick, wavy black hair.

"Arise, King Cruz," Sealyn winked at the newly crowned king, then snapped her fingers, and golden fireworks exploded around the room.

Overcome with happiness, Cruz threw his arms around Sealyn and whispered, "Thank you for this, and forgive me for earlier."

Sealyn pulled back. "All is forgotten, your majesty."

Cruz leaned in close again. "Sealyn, you don't have to…"

"Let me stop you right there," Sealyn said. "Look around this room. Do you see the freedom your people have? One life is all it takes to *secure* that."

"Yes, but that *one* life is yours. Sealyn, please. Stay." He said the word stay with a prayer and a pledge.

Sealyn chuckled. "Do you not remember what happened on that ship? Those powers emerged because of my love for Jace, you know, my husband—the King of Elysium." Sealyn giggled again. "Cruz, you might be cute, but you're not that cute."

Cruz smiled. "Ok. Ok. If I must lose you to another man, then I'm glad it's him."

"Ha! You can't lose something you never had."

"Are you trying to hurt me on my special day? But seriously, Sealyn, promise me one thing."

"Maybe…"

"Promise me you will never stop fighting to find another way to end all these curses. Promise me you will take that other solution when you do find it. The world is a better place with you in it."

Sealyn stood silently, listening to the Shunalians' cheers and happy conversations. She wanted to give Cruz the answer he wanted, but she already knew what awaited her. "How about you never stop looking for another way? When you find it, get in touch with me right away."

Cruz sadly understood what she meant. He didn't want this to be his goodbye, but he had to let her go. She wasn't his, and she was greater than the Shunalian and Elysian courts. He clenched his jaw and withheld his tears of sorrow, for her destiny was a cruel fate.

Elysian News

The Latest News and Gossip

Issue #85

STOLTLAND INVADES HAVAS

Painted above: Queen Corentine
of Stoltland

My fellow Elysians, I bring you grave news. We have the official reports. Stoltland has invaded Havas by force.

The Havasians fought against the black army, but they were caught unaware of the power that plotted against them. Many lives were lost, and hundreds, maybe thousands, more were injured.

Stoltland has not taken control of Havas's capital yet, but it's only a matter of time. How could this happen without Elysium being aware? Could it be because the son of Stoltland's queen sits on our Elysian throne? Is he purposely blocking reports? Did he know? I think a full investigation with our expert, Caelimont, should be done immediately.

We also have reports that Stoltland has now entered into an alliance treaty with Korpam, our southern neighbor. What could this mean for Elysium?

In my humble opinion, we should finally declare war against Stoltland and anyone who stands with them. We should aid Havas and drive out all the evil Stoltlanders, and personally, I want Queen Corentine dead! Who's with me?

~ Lady Adalina Roedellen (Lina)

Princess Siany Spotlight	**Avondelle's Spring Festival**	**Luxen School Updates**
The juiciest gossip	*What to expect*	*Weekly Reports*
Princess Siany has received several bouquets of flowers	Games, performances, fireworks, food, and drinks	Plant Tethereds are seeing promising results for NexGen
But who are they from?	See the three-day schedule of events	Parents are encouraged to follow progress.
Page 3	Page 4	Page 7

CHAPTER 41
THE MAN OF HER NIGHTMARE

Jace crept around the stone floors and walls. He tried not to make a sound, stepping lightly. His presence would create absolute chaos. He was almost there, just a few more inches. Jace sucked in a breath and peered around the wooden doorframe. Luckily, everyone's backs were to him. He saw them sitting in orderly amphitheater rows facing a large black chalkboard that had a drawing of an orange *Metus dragon and, next to it, a small *Snapple Seef dragon.

Slipping past the door that read *Professor Hueweyn Rendell,* Jace pressed his back against the cold wall, folded his muscular arms, and watched Skarpin scribbling notes. From the moment they met Skarpin, they knew he was incredibly smart—highly intelligent for a boy his age. He was special.

Professor dusted the chalk from his hands after he finished writing another interesting fact about the Snapple Seef dragon on the chalkboard. "All life has balance. This is why when a Metus dragon gives birth, she gives birth to a new Metus and the tiny Snapple Seef dragon, too. The Metus breathes lightning, so to balance this type of power, the Snapple Seef is just a tiny dragon with teeth, possessing no fire or lightning. It does have exceptional strength, like that of an ant. These dragons tend to overindulge in sugary foods, making them stay largely overweight. However, the Metus sibling of the Snapple Seef will protect its sibling at all costs, even sacrificing its own life."

A little girl in pigtails raised her hand.

"Yes, Landy. What's your question?"

"Is that what happened with the Noxhorn dragon and the bubble dragon when they fought against the Black Phoenixes?"

Professor Rendell clapped. "Very good, Landy! Correct. Nightlight, the Noxhorn, will forever protect her brother Gorm, the Bellus dragon—or bubble dragon if you prefer."

"And what about the Novien Iceback dragon?" Jace loudly asked. All heads turned and gasped. "I've had reports that Len Nove has seen several blue eggs in their ice mountains."

"King Jace! King Jace!" the children exclaimed. Skarpin jumped from his seat, ran to Jace, and embraced him in a big hug. Jace lifted Skarpin to his hip.

"My apologies, Professor Rendell. I hate I have interrupted a thrilling class."

"Not at all, my king. Is there anything I can do for you?"

"I just need to take Skarpin for the rest of the day."

"As you wish, your majesty."

Jace whispered in Skarpin's ear, "Go get your books and notes. I have a secret to show you."

Skarpin obeyed quickly. They both hurried to the royal carriage waiting outside the massive school castle and raced to the palace. Once they arrived, Jace scooped Skarpin in his arms and sprinted up the stairs and into the Garden Library. When the doors opened, Skarpin squealed with excitement once he saw her.

The room was filled with all the royal family members, including Queen Sealyn. Sealyn knelt and held out her arms to Skarpin. He ran right to them, spilling tears of joy and asking a thousand questions.

She laughed. "We just returned. I knew we couldn't keep this secret too long from the public, so we wanted to make sure you found out this way instead of with everyone else."

"Did you break Shunal's curse?"

"We did and unlocked the Naehass."

"What?! The two-headed serpent! How'd you do that? Did you have to fight it? Was it really as tall as a tree? Is one head evil and one head good, like the stories say? Does it come out at night and eat children if we don't behave? That's what my aunt used to tell me."

Jace and Sealyn shook their heads, holding back laughs. "No, dear one. The serpent doesn't eat children at night."

"Oh, that's good to know. Does this mean I have to go back now?" His excited tone changed to meek and desperate. He didn't want to leave. He had finally found a place that felt safe, people who cared for him—a place he wanted to call home.

Sealyn looked at Jace, who winked and nodded. "Well, that's something we wanted to talk with you about. On behalf of the entire royal family, especially King Jace and myself, we would like to extend to you a permanent invite to stay and live with us. Would you like that?"

"Really?! You mean it? I can live with you, here in the palace, forever?"

"All you have to say is yes."

"Yes! Yes! Yes! Yes!" Jace and Sealyn hugged Skarpin. Sealyn remembered the vision Kazimir showed her, and a tiny part of her felt pain, but she took in the smell of Puffin Pies etched in Skarpin's hair, looked at Jace's teary grey eyes, and knew she had made the right decision.

"Actually, Skarpin. I want to be perfectly clear about what we're asking. Jace and I want to adopt you as our son."

Skarpin's golden eyes blinked. Huge tears filled them and ran down his cheeks. He sniffled. "No one's ever wanted me. You won't get tired of me and send me back?"

"We promise. We will be bound to you, and you bound to us."

Skarpin kept crying and nodding his head frantically. Char walked over to Skarpin. "Welcome to the family, buddy."

"Wow, thanks. Can I call you Uncle Char?"

"Sure, why not?" Char laughed. "How about I tell you all about our adventures, me being the hero—of course." Char grabbed Skarpin's hand and escorted him to the window's nook, giving Sealyn and Jace a private moment.

Still kneeling on the soft rug, Jace cupped Sealyn's face. "I missed you. Even in my feverish dreams, my heart still ached for you. Every fiber of my being burns with a deep desire just to be near you. You invade my every thought. You steal my breath with every touch of your lips. I am completely under your spell—mind, body, and heart. You have shown me how to love and what love truly is."

Sealyn felt her body tingle. "Jace, you can't say things like that in a room full of my family members."

He smiled devilishly. "Why, is it doing something to you?"

"Maybe," Sealyn blushed. She felt like a silly schoolgirl when it came to Jace's words. How could one person build her up with such confidence that she could fight the entire world but also speak romantic words that make her feel weak to her bones? Her love for Jace was a blessing and a sinister curse. She kissed Jace and melted.

She felt grounded and lost in the clouds. She needed him like birds needed wings to fly. Sealyn never wanted to leave this alarmingly handsome, chiseled masterpiece of a man. Before letting the kiss embarrass themselves and everyone in the room, they stood, and Sealyn tried to answer several questions.

King Father Ryker, Prince Adomin, and Prince Royce gathered around Jace and Sealyn. Ryker cleared his voice. "I don't suppose you had time to read the latest news reports?"

"I read them and the Elysian News on the way here," Sealyn said. "The agreement between Stoltland and Korpam won't last. Korpam's rulers are too unpredictable and too hotheaded. They'll end up breaking it, then either Stoltland will own them, or there will be war."

"What about Stoltland's attack on Havas?" Royce asked.

"Honestly, it makes sense. We claimed Len Nove, so she went for the neighboring kingdom to her like us, which is Korpam for them," Sealyn sighed. "We went after Shunal, so Corentine wanted to overtake another kingdom, too. Unfortunately for Havas, that kingdom is closer to Stoltland, so again—it makes sense."

Adomin crossed his arms and was reluctant to ask his next question. "Have you thought about the next move for us?"

"Yes. We could battle with Stoltland in Havas, but we risk vulnerability with Glantania in the north. We have no choice but to claim Glantania before Stoltland; then we'll have three allies to her two."

"I agree," Jace added.

"Glantania won't be easy. Do you think Shunal will fight with us?" Ryker asked.

Sealyn nodded. "Yes, King Cruz will be a strong ally, but I'm worried that he won't like his first move as king to be war, so I have a backup. I've had Cousin Will working on something big. I haven't had a chance to read his scroll yet, but I saw it on my message table. Uncle Royce, I'm sure your son has a great solution."

"I'm sure he does," Royce said proudly. "Well, I guess it's settled then. We start planning for the battle of Glantania."

Siany saw her sister drowning in talks of war, so she hurried over. "Please, gentlemen, may I have a moment with my sister?" The men nodded and walked to other family members chatting. "Sealyn, how are you—truly?"

Sealyn winced, thinking back to Vaelinthia's body in the serpent's mouth. She slightly shook her head and sighed. "Honestly, I haven't processed everything. When you're away on a mission like we were, you must suppress every emotion; otherwise, your thoughts will hold you captive. Now that I'm home, I'm one hundred percent certain everything will come crashing down on top of me."

"Well, promise me that you'll let me be there for you when it does. You can't do this life alone."

Sealyn smiled. "As you command, princess," she chuckled. "I would like a full recount of the school's pros and cons when you're available."

"Absolutely," Siany's words spilled with joy. "The children are remarkable. I think you'll be pleasantly surprised by the success. I'm ever so grateful to be part of this, Sealyn. Thank you."

"Don't thank me. You earned it. This was always meant for you. I'm very excited to see those Tethered skills, too," Sealyn cleared her throat and leaned in. "So, any news on the romance in your life?"

Siany blushed. "There has been some interesting turn of events. I look forward to discussing *those* pros and cons with you as well."

The two sisters fell into one of their sibling giggles but were stopped when Princess Kailani glided by Sealyn. She nodded and handed her a note. Kailani kept walking and exited the room with Jashun. Sealyn unfolded the note and read it.

"Queen Sealyn, we have much to deliberate. I will remain in the city. When you're ready to discuss the Abyss magic you so desperately want, send for me. Be warned--we know what power my people have, but you have no idea what power your king will possess. –Princess Kailani"

Sealyn winced. Did Kailani fear Jace? She turned, hunting for Jace, and caught sight of the pirate family in the corner. Her memory launched her into the flashback of her horrible nightmare. The nightmare where she's standing in a field scorched with burn marks, and bloody dead bodies are scattered everywhere. The smell of burnt flesh is overpowering. She gets the feeling that something or someone is lost, then sees the figure she's seen a hundred times that she's never been able to put a face to, until now.

The figure walks toward her, covered in blood. His face finally comes into focus. She lets out a tiny gasp. It was the same man standing in her Garden Library. The man of her nightmare was Tyrdon Steig, the banished king of Korpam—the Pirate Captain or, as she secretly knew him, Jace's father.

My dearest cousin,

I hope this letter finds you well and with another kingdom's curse broken. I'm writing from Hill Chimes' Pebbles Beach. I hope one day soon you will come to visit me. I have been working tirelessly on your secret request. It will take several £uxens and potions along with willing creatures, but I think I've unlocked the formula for an invisible, flying ship.

Contact me as soon as possible. Oh, and the Pirate Captain... was he who I thought? I can't wait to hear the details.

All my love,

£ord Prince William "Will" Dovinus

Tribute to the
Shunalians

LIBRARY OF CREATURES

- <u>RANA FROG</u>: First mentioned in Chapter 1. Rana frogs usually grow to the size of a large dog. They have jagged mouths and red eyes. Some have smooth skin, and others have warts covering their backs. Rana frogs love foul foods and, well, anything that smells horrible. Their colors range from midnight black to chocolate brown.

- <u>MER-MARA</u>: First mentioned in Chapter 1. Mer-Maras have the same tails as mermaids, but the torso and head look like a seahorse, with a snout shaped like a horn. Their snouts play enchanting music while they hunt with mermaids. They usually eat krill, but they like the occasional crab or lobster, too.

- <u>NICHT</u>: First mentioned in Chapter 2. Nichts are classified as non-human winged creatures. Nichts originate from the old magic and continue to thrive in population even after an

attempt to annihilate their species. Earth Nichts are the largest, growing to the size of human toddlers. Others are as small as a human's hand. They all have brown eyes but different hair colors that sometimes correlate to their wing colors. Their heads and eyes are much larger proportionally than compared to the rest of their bodies, and they have pointed ears. Nicht wings are crystalized and similar to butterfly wings. There are nine different types of Nichts, each with their own special powers. Nichts are known to make words plural when not necessary—yet some are now learning a new way to speak.

• <u>ARKOOTHA BEAR</u>: First mentioned in Chapter 2. These bears are larger than most bears and solid white with blue underbellies and blazing blue eyes. The outside of their front paws have long, sharp hooks that are curved like a mammoth's tusk. Arkootha bears have a high-pitched growl. They're also very fast, even in snow. They resemble polar bears but have heads more shaped like grizzly bears.

• <u>ARCHETYDON</u>: First mentioned in Chapter 7. Archetydons are extra-large squid-like creatures. They have multiple thick tentacles and massive heads with budging yellow eyes. Their mouths have rows and rows of razor-sharp teeth and are large enough to bite a whale in half. Archetydons are usually a dusty red color, but some less hostile ones are light blue.

- <u>LENETTE</u>: First mentioned in Chapter 9. A lenette is a creature from the old magic with black eyes that look too big for its tiny head. Smaller than a butterfly, they have bodies of golden caterpillars with two sets of wings: pink outer wings and orange inner wings. During the day, they soak in the sun's rays and then illuminate the darkness at night.

- <u>BUBBLE DRAGON OR BELLUS DRAGON</u>: First mentioned in Chapter 10. Bubble dragons are born from Noxhorn dragons. They remain small in size, growing the size of a small dog. They are white with yellow eyes and have green tongues. Bubble dragons spit innocent bubbles instead of fire. Their saliva and bubbles have special magical properties.

- <u>NEEDLEBOB</u>: First mentioned at the end of Chapter 12 in the Elysian News. They are in the spiny rodent classification. Most Needlebobs are shimmering gold, but those found in Stoltland have black tips. Needlebobs love thick forests and spend their days under ferns' shade, hunting beetles. Needlebobs may look cute, but beware—their needles contain powerful hallucinogenic poison. Once a needle pierces its victim's skin, the poison takes thirty seconds to release its effect. Hallucinations can last for hours and, in some worst cases, days. Needlebobs prefer to roll from one place to the next instead of walking. Their needles tuck and form around its body, allowing it to form a shell for easy rolling.

- <u>MAGNA CONSTRICTOR</u>: First mentioned in Chapter 15. Magna constrictors are yellow and orange snakes that are as thick as grown pigs yet short in length. They have a very friendly disposition. Most Shunalians have them as pets. They are vegetarians with dull teeth and like to lie in the sunshine during the day and swim in the lake at night.

- <u>NOXHORN DRAGON</u>: First mentioned in Chapter 18. Noxhorns breathe blue flames, the hottest of flames, for the longest period of time. They're also the smallest of the fire-breathing dragons. Their electric blue scales aren't as hard as other dragon scales, but they fight like nothing can kill them. They are blue with white bellies and blue eyes. These dragons are highly intelligent.

- <u>JORMUNGON</u>: First mentioned in Chapter 19. Jormungons have ginormous heads the size of an elephant's body and long tails. They are green with yellow stripes and mouths with dull teeth like humans. The bottom of the mouth has an extra row of teeth on the inside. Jormungons can swim fast, reaching speeds of sixty miles an hour, making them the fastest snakes in Shunal.

- <u>MIRRON</u>: First mentioned in Chapter 20. Mirrons have coarse hairs that have reflective properties like a mirror. They resemble horses but are larger and faster, yet very rough to ride. Due to their reflective hairs, Mirrons are often hard to see and can seem invisible.

- <u>CAELIDON</u>: First mentioned in Chapter 24. A Caelidon is a winged horse with its mane and tail composed of feathers. Fastest of the winged horses, they are very dangerous to ride. They are usually solid white with green eyes.

- <u>SURZEE</u>: First mentioned in Chapter 25. Surzees are like mice. They have giant ears, small round heads, and big blue eyes that glow. They have light blue tails that are skinny with fuzzy white tips. Their bones are light, making them almost weightless. They bounce from place to place like tiny mice. They have razor-sharp teeth that are strong like metal.

- <u>ROPE SNAKE:</u> First mentioned in Chapter 28. Rope snakes are extremely long snakes, sometimes stretching for hundreds of feet. They are found only in the Echo Forest of Shunal in the treetops. Their bodies are the diameter of the thick rope found on ships and are usually gold with yellow eyes. Rope snakes have mouths full of sharp teeth.

- <u>SLITCHES:</u> First mentioned in Chapter 30. Slitches are flying snakes, very small and short in length. They have bodies of skinny snakes, wings like bats, and mouths like snapping turtles, yet they can speak like parrots. The military uses them as scouts. They have excellent eyesight and hearing.

- <u>HYDRUS SNAKE:</u> First mentioned in Chapter 30. Hydrus snakes are a mixed breed of snake and dragon, native to Stoltland. It has the body of a thick snake, two legs with sharp claws, wings like a dragon, but a head like a snake with horns. The Hydrus snake spits water, not fire.

- <u>NAEHASS:</u> First mentioned in Chapter 31. Naehass is a legendary creature from the old magic. It is a giant two-headed serpent. One head is black with black eyes. The other head is gold with golden eyes. The rest of the body is a dull yellow color. The fangs of the golden head have a healing potion, but the fangs of the black head are full of deadly venom. The serpent's length reaches as tall as pine trees, and its body is as thick as an oak tree.

- <u>EXIGUUMS</u>: First mentioned in Chapter 39. Exiguums have a genetic code that prevents them from growing beyond the size of a newborn elephant. They still mature just like normal elephants but remain small for their whole lives. Exiguums are mainly purple and blue, but sometimes grey, and they are fuzzy instead of rough. Their eye colors vary from green to blue.

- <u>PERI PIXIE</u>: First mentioned in Chapter 40. Peri Pixies started as deformations of the original Nichts. Most died, but enough survived to create a new species. They have tiny bald heads with silver skin, and their total height is that of a person's pinky finger. They have green-tinted wings, and their ears look like another set of wings. Male Peri Pixies have legs with greenish-brown scales and small, webbed feet, while the females have pink-scaled legs. They have slightly wider-than-normal noses and have child-like faces with their eyes spaced farther apart than human eyes. They can't perform strong magic like the Nichts, but they can make themselves look like anything. Peri Pixies only appear when they sense no danger, and they love sour foods.

• <u>METUS DRAGON</u>: First mentioned in Chapter 41. Metus dragons are large orange dragons with two sets of horns on their heads. Metus dragons breathe lightning and have a roar that sounds like thunder. Their tails have sharp spikes and red claws.

• <u>SNAPPLE SEEF DRAGON</u>: First mentioned in Chapter 41. Snapple Seef dragons are small dragons with no ability to breathe fire or anything harmful. These tiny dragons are usually purple with yellow bellies and have incredible strength. They're able to lift and carry objects ten times their size.

• <u>NOVIEN ICE BACK DRAGON</u>: First mentioned in Chapter 41. Novien Ice Back dragons are native to Len Nove. These are white dragons with blue eyes, claws, and teeth. They are slow in flight but spit ice instead of flames.

ACKNOWLEDGMENTS

A third book completed? What? Stop it! Yes, I'm in shock. Why? Because it takes so much time, dedication, and sacrifice to complete a challenge like this. Burnout is real, and so many authors face this daily. I have such an extraordinary support team, so cheers to you all.

My incredible husband, Kyle Massie: thank you for giving me grace and time to write and read aloud. I appreciate all the encouragement and motivation you give every day. I love you as much as Sealyn loves Jace.

My supportive parents, Rhett and Gwen Salley: thank you for showing up. Just being there for book signings, events, and lunches is more than most can dream of, yet you continue to be there. Thank you for demonstrating dedication.

Mindy Salley, my sister: You rock! Thank you for the amazing family tree that helped you read the books! You're the best sister the Lord could have blessed me with.

Jess Tully Menges, author of *The Birch Cabins*, and C.A. Meadows, author of *Lost in a Nightmare, The Secret Inheritance, and Giovanna:* Thank you for connecting.

Authors need other authors to hold each other accountable and have *those* conversations that only authors understand. I'm glad I'm not alone in my writing.

To the LittleBatsLibraryClub: You ladies have been such an incredible support group. You have no idea how much I appreciate the likes, comments, shares, and encouragement. I'm truly grateful to have each one of you in my life.

To my friends: thank you for understanding my declines. It is not easy to say "no" to events or hangouts, but I needed to decline many times to finish writing. I'm very grateful for your understanding, patience, and participation.

To my Beta Readers: Michelle Blair, Jess Tully Menges, Cecilia Meadows, Gwen Williams, Kayla Falcone, Olivia Elswick, Theresa Tacopino-Shaw, and Jeanne Degatano. Thank you for taking the time to read each chapter in its raw state. Your feedback truly made a huge difference in editing and content for the book. I really appreciate you all so much.

My editor, Kristyn Winch: Thank you for the hard work, excellent corrections, and informative feedback. It means the world to me that you see the growth in my writing. Thank you again.

Miblart: Thank you for another excellent book cover. I also appreciate your patience in working with me and all the edits. I'm grateful to be working with your company with promos, as well.

YukKami Art, digital artist: thank you for the beautiful character and creature art you've done. Each piece is loved and adored. I appreciate your talent and time.

Above all, the entire credit and glory goes to the good Lord above. Thank you for giving me a creative mind and the many blessings you have given me. All praise to you.

ABOUT THE AUTHOR

MAEGWEN SALLEY-MASSIE is the author of *The Emerald Queen Rises, The Mammoth Awakens, and The Serpent Emerges.* She will be writing four other books to complete this series. She grew up in the Pee Dee Low Country of South Carolina with her loving parents and sister. Her childhood was spent mainly outdoors: building forts, riding horses, playing capture the flag, riding ATVs, and playing volleyball. She began writing *The Emerald Queen Rises* during the pandemic as therapy and since then fell in love with writing her high fantasy series. She is a woven polypropylene specialist by day, COO of 963 Film Group, and a fantasy fiction author by night. Her favorite food is sushi, and she loves to travel the world. Maegwen currently lives in Myrtle Beach, S.C., with her husband, Kyle, their cat, Khaleesi, and their new Australian Shepherd, Pogue.

Book 1 & 2
in
The Emerald Queen series

For more information about Maegwen and her books, please visit:

www.greenfernspublishinghouse.com

www.theemeraldqueenrisesbook.com

www.maegwensalleymassie.com

Or follow her on Instagram @MaegwenAuthor

Please consider leaving a review on Amazon, Barnes & Noble, and GoodReads.